THE CHAINMAN

By

BILL BAXTER

Disclaimer

The characters are entirely fictitious, and any resemblance to any person, living or dead, is entirely coincidental!

Table of Contents

Dedication

TO JAN WITH LOVE.

Acknowledgment

Eric Payne and his team!

About the Author

Willie was born in Ireland but lives in Scotland. He worked in the shipyards and then in the theatre. He has written three non-fiction books but prefers writing short stories and historical novels. Novels include 'MICK,' 'SHIABA,' 'RETURN TO SHIABA.', 'SHIABA NO MORE'

Chapter 1

The fourteenth of February, a Saint Valentine's dance in East Belfast; outside the hall, the laurel leaves droop in the frost and the gravel is rigid with ice. A sulphurous fog drifts across the glow of the single street light, smothering the sound of the city traffic. Everything shrinking in the intense cold. Tension in the air, as if, at any moment, the whole scene, silently resonating, could shatter like glass and cover the ground with splinters of ice.

As we step out of the hall, we carry with us the heat and the cigarette smoke. The doors swing shut behind us, muffling the din of thudding feet and the blare of the band. Dixieland jazz and jive. Swirling circular skirts and skin-tight sweaters, blazing horns and thumping drums, brothel creepers and Tony Curtis curls. We were seventeen.

A blind date. Spam had set it up, and I was always keen to please him. He had a date with a flame-headed nurse, and he expected me to keep Sarah, her friend, out of the way. When I saw her, I was delighted. A face from the Renaissance, a figure slender and shapely. A sharp, pointed nose and small, pinched mouth, shrew-like, but with an elegant jawline and brilliant blue eyes. I could not believe my good luck. Outside, against the wall, she kissed with polite restraint as if she yearned to be passionate but didn't dare to release the emotion. Yet she didn't object when I slid my hand down her thigh and slowly, with infinite care, rolled up the back of her skirt till I touched her skin. I remember how the fabric slipped sensuously over the nylon stockings.

'Get your finger outa there!'

I dropped the skirt hurriedly and looked around. Spam had emerged from the hall with his conquest.'Piss off!' I almost said but stopped in case it offended Sarah. 'Don't be disgusting,' she replied quietly on my behalf.

He laughed, satisfied that he had annoyed her.

His greatest pleasure, next to sex, was provoking people. Spam possessed an uncanny ability to detect the triggers and tweak them skilfully while disarming the victim with a mischievous grin. His crew cut, projecting like fine spines from his skull, gave him an expression of permanent surprise as if every moment was a discovery. His store of energy was prodigious, exploding in fights, in sprints from the police, in jive on the dance floor. The fights occurred when he misjudged his victim and the grin failed, usually at a dance when we would find a group of grim-faced youths waiting for us outside the hall. That night was no exception.

'We'll be in the car,' he shouted as he disappeared into the gloom. I returned to my task of trying to seduce Sarah.

'He's a wild man,' she said, 'I've heard all about him. Do you hang about with him all the time?'

'No, no. Just now and again.'

I pressed myself against her and tilted my head to kiss her, but she wanted to talk and put her finger on my lips. I restrained myself and smiled.

'Do you work with him?'

'No. He's a car salesman. His Da got him the job. I work in the yard.'

'The shipyard?'

She sounded surprised.

'You don't. You're kidding.'

'No. I do. Really.'

'What do you do?'

I hesitated. If I said I was an apprentice, she would know I was a Protestant, and she might be a Catholic. There were no Catholic apprentices in the yard. Her religion didn't matter to me. I had long since abandoned the creed of my family, but it might have mattered to her. Had her name been Bridget or Cathleen, I might have guessed but Sarah was indeterminate. Somehow, I felt that she was not a Catholic. Even then, we had developed a kind of intuitive ability to categorise, an invisible antenna, an instinct that led to the early detection of the other tribe. That radar was a mechanism that we absorbed unconsciously from infancy. It penetrated our system like a malignant organism, spreading irresistibly insidiously till we were completely contaminated. Spread from our elders in little toxic references, hints, nuances, glances, and expressions of contempt, it swarmed in our blood, claiming us for our race. Those who suddenly realised what was happening and, horrified by the infection, tried to expel it still carried its traces into their future, their minds pock-marked by the experience.

'I'm a spark. An apprentice electrician,' I confessed, watching carefully for her reaction.

'I work there too. In the tracing office.'

I relaxed. We were on the same side of the chasm. 'Maybe we could meet at lunchtime,' I offered.

'Yes. I'd like that.'

A signal to resume the embrace? I was just about to try again when the boys emerged from the hall. I could tell by their swagger and the way they strutted like midden cocks that they hoped to cause trouble.

'He came out here,' the leader snarled, 'I'm fuckin' sure he did. With that red-haired cow. I'm telling you. The bastard's out here.'

I could feel Sarah's grip around my waist tightening as I loosened my arms, ready for an attack.

'Is that him, Eddy?'

One of them pointed in our direction.

The leader looked round and padded towards me menacingly like a panther, his impression of feline power, however, spoiled by a slip on the ice. I had to suppress a grin as he skidded on his thick crepe soles, his arms flailing frantically in the air like a grotesque ballerina. Recovering his balance but not his dignity, he loped across the grass in our direction. I tightened the fist hidden by Sarah's skirt, turning around my new lion-head ring, which Spam had given me as a knuckle-duster.

'What are you laughin' at, you daft bastard?' he barked, prodding my chest with his finger. The long curl of carefully coiffed hair shook above his frown like an oiled spring.

'I wasn't laughing.'

'Better not be. I'll cut your balls off if I see you smile. You see a guy come out here? A guy with a young red-head?'

'I was too busy.'

'Too busy with this whore? I've seen better in a brothel.' I drew back my fist, but Sarah gripped my wrist sharply.

'I expect you have,' she said, 'It's the only way you'd get a girl.'

He glared at her angrily. For a moment, I thought he was going to slap her.

'Fuckin' hoity-toity,' he snarled and turned away, 'This isn't him, Eddy. Look round the back.'

He swaggered away, his thigh-length Edwardian jacket swinging, looking like some bizarre insect with his skinny legs and massive shoes. The gang moved away to search for Spam. 'I'll have to go,' I whispered to Sarah.

'You mean you want to go.'

'No, no. They're looking for Spam. They'll crucify him if they find him.'

'Can't he fight his own battles then? Just admit it, Billy, you're dying to go. Just go. I'll see you around.'

She broke away and started to walk back to the entrance. I caught her wrist.

'Listen. I really hate this kind of thing. He does it all the time, every dance. He provokes a fight and then gets me to jump in to help.'

'More fool you. You could say no.'

'He's my mate.'

'So you do everything he says. Like a puppet. He pulls the strings, and you jump?'

'It's not like that.'

'It's like that to me.'

A silence slipped between us. I felt myself squirming inside, torn between my loyalty to Spam and the prospect of losing her. She was drifting away. I could see it in her eyes, a hint of distaste, a shadow of contempt. She was seeing me as a thug. I did not want that. I wanted her to like me. Yet I had to help Spam. I had never been in that predicament before. I had spent more than a year trying to impress him, stealing cigarettes with him from the Italian ice cream shops, lifting bottles of beer from the back of delivery lorries or arming ourselves with stolen weapons. The excitement was addictive. It formed a bond between us, which I thought was impregnable. Not that I worshipped him, for, in some respects, I found his behaviour repulsive– his vivid descriptions of his sexual conquests, his brutal disdain for the victims, his habit of clawing at his genitals in the car. Yet I'd been attracted to his rebellious amorality, his cavalier disregard of authority and conventional values. It was liberating. It allowed me to shake off the harness of respectability with which I had been restrained by my parents. I was enjoying the freedom.

Besides, he liked me for some reason, and that was flattering.

'It's freezing out here,' she said, 'I'm going in. I'll wait for you inside.'

She walked away. I watched the small clouds of her breath fading in the streetlight and saw her glance back as she pushed open the hall doors. I didn't think that she would meet me again.

As I turned the corner into the car park, I saw her friend hurrying back to the hall. Spam was crouched in an open space between the cars, surrounded by four figures who were converging on him. My stomach shrank, squirting fear like a squid, but I sprinted towards the group, clenching my fists as I ran. At that moment, Spam sprang towards the leader, swinging what looked like a rope. It smacked across the boy's skull, and he cried out, clutching his head and doubling over to protect himself. As Spam swung the weapon a second time, it glittered in the amber gloom. A bicycle chain. The rest of the group stood transfixed, afraid to move, until they saw me running towards them. As the chain hit their leader for a third time and he collapsed at Spam's feet, they fled.

'Bit fuckin' late, Billy!' Spam snarled breathlessly as I reached him.

I looked down at the boy, recognising him as the creature who had prodded me in the chest. His sideburn was thick with blood, and his ear was split in half. His check lay open in a preposterous smile, exposing the bone beneath. I was horrified. I had seen noses broken and lips split, but I'd never seen a wound as severe as that gash. For a moment, I was transfixed by the cleanly sliced flesh, peeled back like raw liver, and the stream of dark blood until he moved and the awful magnitude of the violence swept over me.

'Jesus Christ, Spam,' I whispered, 'He'll need an ambulance.'

'Don't be daft. Fuck's sake, Billy, get a grip. C'mon, we'll need to get outa here.'

'Can't leave him here. Not like that.'

'His mates'll be back. C'mon. Get in the car, you clown.'

I did feel safer in the car and I was relieved to leave the car park and head into Belfast. A Simca, light green with leather seats, his father's car. I sat in silence as we raced through the empty streets, clattering over the cobbles in the docks. The ships for Liverpool, Heysham and Glasgow had left, and the quay lay empty. At that moment, I wished that I had sailed on one of them and avoided any part in the fight. I was sure that the boy was badly hurt. He lay so still on the frozen ground. I gazed down on the river as we crossed the bridge. Dark and still, the city lights flickering in the occasional ripple and patches of oil beneath the quay glimmering in the shadows. Gulls glided listlessly among the tall gantries, their wings flashing as they swung like trapeze artists in the tent of the night. I envied their remote ease and tranquillity.

I subsided gloomily into the car seat. I had probably lost Sarah, and if she were to hear of the assault, the loss would be certain. It was Spam's fault. His stupidity. A bloody bicycle chain, for God's sake! I was furious. I wanted Sarah. I wanted to take her to the pictures, buy two tickets, and be shown to our seats as a couple and slide my arm around her shoulder in the warm, flickering dark. I wanted to walk down the pier, sheltering her from the wind under my coat. I wanted to share those intimate moments when she combed her hair or put on her shoes. I wanted to walk down the street at night and watch my friends nod approvingly as we passed. I had to see her again.

'Light us a fag, Billy boy,' Spam muttered, shattering the fantasies. Obediently, I shook a Philip Morris from its packet, lit it and passed it to him. 'She's some ride, that red heifer. What a noise she makes!'

'Oh, aye? I didn't think you had time for that.' If he heard the challenge, he ignored it.

'Speedy Gonzales me. Here, smell her.'

He held his fingers under my nose.

'Fuck off!' I said, turning away in disgust. He laughed derisively.

'Jealous, eh? What about yours? What about Sarah? Did you get stuck into her?'

I did not want to think of her in that way, but, in spite of myself, I recalled the sensation of her skirt sliding over her stockings and the soft, smooth skin of her thigh. The flash of memory annoyed me. It felt like a betrayal.

'She's not like that,' I replied.

'They're all like that, Billy. If you handle them right.'

I knew then that I had to extricate myself from the friendship with Spam. Apart from the possibility of police action over the fight, I realised that the differences between us were too great to be sustained. He had no interest in the feelings of others, no sensitivity, no conscience. At least I could feel some remorse, some pity for the broken creature we had left to bleed in the car park, and I had some respect for the girls whose limits I tested in the dark. The respectable values of my parents, which I pretended to discard, had left an indelible mark, the stamp of our class, on my reflexes. I could never be like Spam. I realised that. It was time to part. Having taken the decision, I felt disloyal sitting beside him as the car raced wildly through the quiet suburbs. I didn't consider that there might be a cost to that retreat nor that it could be a prolonged and painful affair.

Chapter 2

I tried to find her on the Monday following the dance. I was working on a Canadian aircraft carrier far down the yard, a long way from the tracing office, but I was determined to reach the red brick building where she worked during the lunch break. I wanted to see her and reverse the impression that I had created at the dance, a task made more urgent by the rumour of police enquiries. Corky had heard of the fight, and if Corky knew, half the yard would know before the whistle blew.

The day had started badly. It was wet when I left the house in Bangor, wet and cold so that my fingers froze on the handlebars as I cycled to the train. I hated that, leaving in the dark at six, passing the ranks of smug terraced houses with their curtains still closed and their occupants warm in their beds. I felt as if I was the only person awake and smoldered with resentment, especially when the wind cut my face, and the rain soaked my knees. It wasn't true, of course.

Other folk had to rise for work but I saw myself as the only victim, dismissing any reminder that the discomfort was my own fault– I had chosen to go to the yard. The other boys had stayed at school, studying for leadership. I thought of them that morning and cursed my choice. To add to the misery, the front tyre of the bike was soft, so I had to pedal frantically to reach the station in time.

I tossed the bike into the ranks of others and ran for the train, collapsing breathless beside Corky in the guard's van.

I had travelled with Corky since my first day in the yard. A sturdy boy with copper hair and a foam-rubber face that he could twist into the most extraordinary expressions. We always travelled in the guard's van, just the two of us. The guard, at that time of the morning, chose to sit with the driver. We sat on the floor with our backs to the bulkhead.

'Christ, that was close,' I gasped.

'Lazy bastard,' he muttered, the endearment exploding from his thick lips, 'Should get up in time.'

The khaki gasmask bag that I used to carry my lunch dug into my buttock. I tried to slide it around to the front, but its sodden strap stuck to my donkey jacket. I wrestled with it angrily, raising my hips and twisting my body.

'What the fuck are you doing, Billy? Having a fit or something?'
'Trying to get this fuckin' piece bag off.'

Corky shook his head in mock despair, leaned across and hauled it round. 'Thanks.'

'Cost you a fag, Billy.'

'You never have fags, you bastard. When did you last buy a packet?'

'OP's are cheaper.'

I reached into my shirt pocket and pulled out a packet of Lucky Strike. It was crushed. 'Fuck me, my fags! Look at them.'

'They'll be okay. Don't fuss. Just get them out.'

I extracted two bent fags from the packet. At least the paper was intact.

With a flourish, Corky produced the lighter that he had made in the workshop from a cannon shell, and we lit up as the train left the platform with a jerk.

'Were you with Spam the other night? At the dance.'

I took a long, hard pull of the cigarette and inhaled the sour smoke slowly, frowning enigmatically like James Dean.

'Part of the time.'

'You were there when he chained your man, weren't you?'

'No. Heard about it, though.'

'Aye, you were. Don't be such a fuckin' liar.'

'I was with a woman round the back.'

'You were not, Billy. You don't need to lie to me. I know you were there. Your man works here, you know.'

'Who?'

'The guy that he chained.'

'Where? Where does he work?'

My sudden anxiety must have been apparent, for Corky grinned. 'Aye, you were there. I knew you were. He's up on the new frigate.'

The frigate berthed near the top of the yard, lay on the only route to the tracing office. I would have to pass it to reach Sarah.

'What's he do?'

'A helper of some kind. A catholic, anyway. With the welding crew, I think. Him and his mates.'

'His mates here too?'

'Aye, Billy boy. You'd better steer clear of the *Torquay.*'

He nicked the red end of his cigarette and stuck the butt behind his ear.

'Keep it for later,' he said, grinding the burning end into the floor with his boot.

We sat in silence, rocking in unison as the train swayed through the dark. I watched the rain streaking horizontally across the single window, wondering how I could reach Sarah without passing the frigate. If your man spotted me, I knew what would happen. I had seen fights in the yard– bare-knuckle battles at lunchtime with the two men surrounded by a predatory, cloth-capped crowd thirsty for blood. I imagined what it would feel like, locked in that pitiless circle, unable to escape, imprisoned by masculine pride in a brutal arena. No one would help, and no one would intervene till the combat ended as the loser collapsed like a stringless puppet, bleeding, broken and humiliated. I could feel the sickening, quivering excitement as the jackets peeled off, the astonishing pain of the first blow, the fearful intimacy of the clinch. I could smell the fear. I could hear the dull thud of knuckle on bone and the slithering of boots on the burnt ash surface of the jetty. I did not want to be part of that.

I had an image to maintain. No overalls or boiler suits like the others. A light blue denim shirt with breast pockets for the Lucky Strike or Phillip Morris and Number Eight jeans– not common trousers but soft blue denim swapped for British fags on an American ship. With these tucked into wellingtons carefully turned down to the ankle and a blue-striped white front from the Royal Navy, I tried to look like a seaman, a seasoned sailor accustomed to the blazing heat of the tropics or the piercing cold of the Baltic. I developed the rolling walk of the old salt and the habit of using naval slang in conversation. Part of the image had to be the projection of quiet strength, confident impregnability and wide experience in combat. If challenged, I could not escape from the consequences of that image.

'Who was the woman?' Corky asked suddenly, breaking the silence.

'What?'

'The woman. Who were you with?'

I looked around. Hunched inside the collar of his duffle coat, he gazed blankly at the ceiling as if it held the answer. He did not seem to be particularly interested in hearing a reply, so I said nothing.

'Who was it, Billy?' he repeated, clearly irritated by my silence. 'Sarah somebody.'

'Sarah McConnel?'

'Don't know her name.'

'Tall and dark with big, brown eyes.'

'No.'

I tried to hide my relief.

'Sarah Curran– small, blond with a cow's lick in her hair. Tracer in the office here.' 'No. She had auburn hair and green eyes. From Lisburn. Still at school. Friends' school, I think. Looks much older.'

'You're lying again, Billy. I can hear it in your voice.'

'I'm not, Corky. Honest to God. She's a real stunner.'

'Just as well, it's not Curran.'

He waited for a response, having set the trap. I kept silent and screwed out the cigarette on the floor.

'She's got a boyfriend,' he said, disappointed.

'Who has?'

'Curran has. An older guy with an MG sports car.'

'This Sarah has no one. She said, and I believe her.' He dropped the matter at last.

When the train reached Belfast, we separated. He worked in the generating hall and walked. I caught a bus to the bottom of Queen's Island, where the carrier was berthed.

There were no seats, so I had to stand, clinging to a chrome rail as the bus rattled over the cobbles. Men of all ages and shapes were squeezed together in the smoke, stunned into silence by the monotonous routine. I looked around, studying each young face in case one of the boys from the dance was among them. There was no obvious candidate, although one man with dark, crawling sideburns glared back at me. I thought I was safe. The bus swayed through the gloom, the windows black and streaming with moisture. It was like a submarine, the air fetid and thick, smelling of sweat and oil and damp clothes. Rows of caps nodded in unison as the wheels dipped in the gutters. Black caps, tweed caps, crimson caps. Small peaks, long peaks, curved peaks and peaks worn through to the leather. Wide flamboyant caps, neat impudent caps, tight aggressive caps, old caps limp with despair and caps glistening with years of grease, each revealing much about its wearer. I did not wear one, partly because it would spoil my hairstyle and partly because it did not fit the image. Instead, I kept a navy woollen cap in my pocket in case of heavy rain.

As we rolled deeper into the yard, the silhouettes of tall ships, still encased in their scaffolding, loomed out of the night, their black hulls flickering now and then in the cold light of welders' torches. It was still dark when we reached the timekeeper's office where the bus slowed to let some of us jump off. There were several of these offices scattered around the yard so that the massive workforce– twenty-seven thousand– could sign in and out. We filed slowly past a grimy window, calling out our work numbers to the sour-faced clerks who passed out our boards through the small arched opening. The boards– thin fillets of hardwood two inches by one stamped with our numbers– had to be returned at night when the scene was transformed with men rushing past the window, flinging in the boards and dashing for busses. An air of energy, relief, enthusiasm, banter, laughter and humour, unlike the lethargic trail in the morning.

I slipped the board into my breast pocket, buttoned it carefully and walked through the puddles to the carrier. She was an immense ship, towering over the quay. The anchors themselves seemed to dwarf the buildings below, their massive bulk protruding threateningly from the navels in the bow. In the winter dawn, lights glittered in the galleries that punctuated her long battleship-grey hull just below the flight deck, shining like secret caverns in a mountainside. That week, she was to undergo her tilting trials, so the flight deck listed alarmingly towards the quay and the superstructure, with its radar dishes and web of aerials, hung obliquely over the stores. It seemed as if the huge vessel, like a tumbling fortress, could keel over at any minute on top of the diminutive workers below. Heavy hawsers, taut with the strain, stretched from the top decks down to bollards on the ground. It was a strange world inside. In the enclosed corridors, without any reference to vertical lines outside, workers seemed to lean impossibly in one direction. If they forgot to lean, they slipped down the deck.

'Well, Billy. Good weekend?'

I met Jack at the foot of the gangway, and I followed him onto the carrier. At the top, he removed his cap and swept it down in a long arc over the deck to flick off the rain. A quiet man, dedicated to his work, he rarely complained except to gripe regularly about the incompetence of the draughtsmen. His massive hands were surprisingly dexterous, his thick fingers slipping into awkward corners as skillfully as those of a seamstress. With the shoulders and neck of a weightlifter, he could bend heavily armoured cable like liquorice. Gentle in spite of or maybe because of - his size, he was never aggressive. I was pleased that I had been assigned to work with him. He was patient and a great tutor, explaining every step of the work as it progressed. I should have chosen him as a role model rather than Spam, but I was drawn to excitement and the outrageous behaviour. In Jack's company I often felt ashamed of exploits with Spam. Certainly, I never told him of our habits.

'Aye. Good weekend, Jack. Could have done with more sleep, though.'

'Can't stand the pace, eh?'

I grinned, trying to compose an edited version of Saturday. 'Were you playing on Saturday?' he continued.

The town fielded four rugby teams, and I had played for the seconds, but since meeting Spam, I had not attended training and had been dropped from the team.

'No. Knee's still bad.'

'You should see the doctor about that. Been a long time.'

'Aye, you're right.'

He led the way along the deck, leaning heavily to his left to keep his balance. To our right, I looked down on the quay over the rail. We seemed to be suspended precariously above the buildings as if we were on a crane. Other men passed us, all sloping across the deck. Jack walked easily forward, apparently unaffected by the tilt. I tried to keep upright without reaching out to the bulkheads for support, keen to appear as experienced and confident as Jack. Twice, however, I leaned too far and had to steady myself, provoking a scornful grin on passing faces. The precious image temporarily shattered. I arrived at the cabin, embarrassed and annoyed.

Jack hung his piece bag and his jacket on one of the hooks and sat on the springs of a bunk. We had almost finished wiring the cabin, but the room was strewn with coils of cable, lengths of fishplate and tubes of conduit. Not a lot of space with four bunks and steel lockers.

'Tea?' I asked, hanging my bag beside his.

'Aye, why not?'

I retrieved the cans from beneath a bunk.

'Is there water in the galley yet?' I asked, hoping that I would not need to descend to the quay.

'Aye, I think so. Cold though.'

'Better than walking. I'll get a torch.'

'By the way, we're getting a shift.'

'Where to?'

'The tanker. The one that's just launched.'

I was horrified. The tanker lay next to the new frigate. 'What's wrong? Afraid of the cold?'

It would be cold. The freshly launched ship was essentially a floating refrigerator. Bare metal decks, bulkheads and ceilings. A steel hulk, sitting in freezing water. Yet it was not the cold that worried me but the proximity to the frigate.

'No. The noise. Bloody caulkers and rivetters. I hate the noise.' 'It's a shipyard, son,' he smiled indulgently, 'Better get used to it.' 'Suppose.'

I carried the cans to the galley, filled them and searched for a welding torch, following snakes of flexible tubing into the pantry next door. A welder was sitting on the deck, his back against the bulkhead and his heavy helmet tilted back like a knight after a battle apart from the cigarette. In his blackened face, the white tube trembled on his lips as he spoke.

'What you want, son?'

He studied me suspiciously. I had not seen the man before and was thrown by his hostility.

'The torch. Can I borrow the torch?'

'You a spark?'

'Aye.'

The fag tilted up towards his nose as he drew on it steadily. 'Who're with?'

'Jack. Big Jack Conway.'

'Big Jack, eh?'

He continued to study me, his red-rimmed eyes analysing every crease and seam of my clothing. I became distinctly uncomfortable.

'Can I have the torch?' He ignored the question.

'Big Jack, eh? Well, you go back and tell Big Jack to come and get his own fuckin' torch and not to send wee, soft-skinned schoolboys to beg me for it.'

A challenge. A challenge that I was to carry back to Jack. I felt that I should tell the welder to fuck off and convey his own messages, but there was something frightening about him, a latent violence, an instability flickering in his eyes, so I kept quiet, despising myself for the choice.

'Don't look at me like that, son. Go and do it.'

I knew that the message would test Jack's patience, and I didn't want to get caught up in a brawl between the welder and him. A flutter of panic seized my gut. I was Jack's mate. If the welder got the better of him, I would have to join in. I swallowed and turned to leave. Just as I reached the watertight door, he shouted behind me.

'Hey!'

I turned to find him grinning cruelly.

'I was only joking, son. Take the torch.'

He started to giggle and then cackled hilariously, inexplicably, insanely. I retreated, hauling the torch and its tubes with me.

'Who the fuck's that?' I whispered to Jack, 'He's crackers.' Jack smiled.

'Och, Mad Matt? He's harmless; thinks he's hard. Used to box, but now he couldn't box apples. Picked a fight with a caulker, and your man laid him out with a stilson. Broke his head open. Never the same since. Don't worry about him. Balance has gone.'

An image of the youth lying in the car park flashed across my vision, the splintered bone protruding through the split, crimson tissue. With the image, a spurt of fear.

'Was he charged– the caulker?' I asked anxiously.

'No charge. No witnesses. Plenty were there, but no one saw a thing. Typical. All too yellow to talk.'

Spam's victims had witnesses, but they wouldn't tell the police. They would deal with it in their own way. In the dark, silently. I longed to tell Jack about the incident and hear what he had to say. I couldn't. I had built an image for Jack of a sensible, considerate apprentice who handed over his wages to his mother.

I lit the torch and brought the water in the cans to the boil. Jack handed me the small oval tin containing the tea and sugar.

'Use mine,' he said, 'Yours at lunch.'

The tin had two lids - at one end the sugar, in the other the tea. Removing one of the lids, I shook the black tea leaves into the can and watched them spinning on the surface.

'All the sugar?' I asked, shaking the tin carefully.

'Aye. Heave it all in, Billy. To hell with poverty.'

Jack opened a small bottle of milk and poured a thin stream into each can. I broke the heads off two matches and dropped them into the water to gather the tea leaves, then held the cans over the flame again. The liquid bubbled, churning the tea and sugar into a dark, sweet brew. I let it simmer for a while, then set the cans on the deck and turned off the torch.

We settled with our backs against the bulkhead, and I shook out a cigarette. 'Matt's mates– did they not deal with the caulker?'

I tried to sound casual, but Jack was not deceived. 'You're awfully worried about Matt,' he said suspiciously.

'No, no. I just wondered.'

'Did he threaten you?'

'No,' I said quickly, 'No, honestly. He never said anything.'

I held the can by its wire handle and sipped the hot tea. Jack held his with his massive hands, apparently unaffected by the heat. It was wonderfully comfortable in the cabin, warm and safe, with the generators humming deep in the hull and the smell of new battleship grey paint. I thought about eating my Mars bar but decided to keep it till lunch. On the other hand lunch would be rushed if I was going to reach the tracing office.

'Jack, can I get to the tracing office without passing the frigate? Is there a back way?' He grinned over the black rim of the can.

'So you were out at the weekend then?'

'Aye. Saint Valentine's dance.'

'So who is she?'

'Sarah Curran.'

'Don't know her. Where's she from?'

'Bangor.'

'That's handy for you. Anyway, what's this about the frigate?'

'Nothing. It doesn't matter. I didn't want to go near the frigate. Her boyfriend– ex- boyfriend– works there,' Not sure that I had lied convincingly, I rummaged in the piece bag for the Mars bar to avoid his searching eyes.

'Young love, eh? You stole his girl, and now you're afraid to face him, eh?'

'I'm not scared of him. He's a weed.'

'Aye. I can see that. Anyway, there's no backway. Pass the frigate or forget about her. Right, it's time to get on.'

He heaved himself to his feet and laid the can in the corner, staggering as he forgot the tilt of the deck.

'Go down to the store, Billy, and get three boxes of four-way clips and more bolts. Need to get this cabin finished. Oh, and we'll need some glands for the switches.'

'What about the torch?' I mumbled, my mouth full of Mars bar. 'I'll see to that. You go. And hurry. I can't wait all day.'

I stood carefully and, leaning to my right, left the cabin.

At lunchtime, I hurried down to the jetty and joined the queue at the line of taps, where we filled our cans with steaming water from the pipes. I spilled too much of it on the way back and poured it all into Jack's can.

'Here, Jack, you have it. I'll not bother. I'm away up to the tracing office.'

'Take your piece, man. Bad for you that. Going without your food.'

'I'll live on love,' I grinned.

'Ballocks. Go then, for God's sake, before you burst your pants.'

I ran down the gangway and jogged past the crowd of men at the pitch and toss, attracting several suspicious glances. The rain had stopped, but it had left large black puddles gleaming with oil. I swerved around these, imagining I was on the rugby pitch, jinking skillfully around opponents. For a moment I was Jackie Kyle or Tony O'Reilly playing for Ireland. Slowing to walking pace as I approached the frigate, I managed to keep behind a row of crates but, when I reached the end, found that I could not avoid the open ground at the gangways. Crowds of men filled the space between the ship and the buildings on the quay. I stopped, wondering if it was wise to continue. The mates of Spain's victim could be in the crowd. I could be recognised. Yet I needed to see Sarah. I wanted to fix a time to meet so that no one else could step in. I wanted to stake a claim. That yearning was powerful enough to overwhelm the caution, and I stepped away from the crates, adopting the swaggering roll of an old salt.

I was, I thought, a picture of elegant composure with my blue denim shirt, faded American jeans and boots carefully turned down to match the height of cowboy boots. Different from the others, a splash of colour and refinement in the drab mass of workmen. Not a cut above the rest. I did not think that. No, not true. I *tried* not to think that, but the truth was that I had been fashioned by the privileges of my class and had chosen the yard. The others had not had a choice.

It was always a dilemma– the struggle between the need to identify with others and the wish to maintain my own fledgling identity.

As I edged my way through the crowd, taking care to avoid eye contact with anyone and nervously waiting for a shout, I felt that Sarah would approve of the image. I patted my pockets to make sure that I had my cigarettes and lighter. I planned to reach into my breast pocket, expertly shake out a Lucky Strike and offer her one. I planned to look relaxed and at ease with myself, unhurried, in control, a guy who could wait for a date, take it or leave it. I did not want to appear too eager. It did not work out that way.

Chapter 3

'Come and see, Sarah. You can see him from here.'

Nancy was leaning against the upstairs window of the tracing office, looking down on the road.

'I know what he looks like.'

Sarah drew a thin line with the pen along the sheet of tracing paper on her desk, carefully following the plan beneath. She could feel a faint flush on her cheeks. Why did he have to call at the office? Could he not wait till evening? He knew where she lived. He could have called at her house. Well, no. Perhaps not. She did not want her mother to know. Still, it was embarrassing to be told in front of the other girls that he wanted to speak to her.

'He's quite good-looking,' Nancy continued loudly, feigning a tone of surprise as if to suggest that Sarah was unlikely to attract handsome men.

Sarah did not look up but concentrated on her drawing. She tried to remain expressionless, but she was flattered by Nancy's appraisal.

'Come on, Sarah. He looks really anxious. Keeps glancing around the corner as if he was being followed. Don't be so hard-hearted. If you don't go down, I will. I wouldn't mind a bite of that cherry.'

'Oh, for heaven's sake, Nancy.'

She put down her pen, pretending to be cross, slipped her feet into her shoes and walked slowly over to the window.

'It is him. He's not that good-looking, Nancy. Looks different in the daylight. No more than a wee boy.'

'Bloody tasty wee boy, though. Old enough for a roll on the carpet.'

Sarah watched him, pacing up and down, clearly agitated, and she wondered if he had been involved in the fight. She had heard that Spam had used a bicycle chain on someone and that the boy was in hospital. Perhaps Billy had been involved. Yet, as she watched him, she felt that he was not that kind of boy. Certainly, she had been with him for only a few minutes outside the hall, but that was long enough as she had become quite adept at assessing the personality behind the bravado. There was something different about him– a carefully concealed gentleness, a sensitivity, an old-fashioned courtesy. Not like the others. They were always in such a rush, desperate to claw her breasts or scrape her thighs. He was more considerate and more respectful. His background, perhaps.

'I'd better go down before the guards appear. Don't you dare tell the others?'

'I wouldn't do that.'

'Yes, you would. Just don't.'

Sarah lifted her blue cardigan from the back of her chair, slung it over her shoulders and hurried down the stairs.

'What do you want?' She barked, trying to muster as much irritation in her voice as she could to establish immediate control over the situation and to test his response.

He smiled, clearly relieved and delighted to see her. 'I wanted to see you.'

'Why?'

Perhaps she had been a bit too abrupt. He seemed to be completely thrown by her feigned antagonism, but she waited, nevertheless, to see how he would cope. He frowned and, tilting his head forward slightly, looked at her from beneath his brows.

Oh God, she thought, *not another James Dean. Why do they all do that?* 'I wanted to ask you out,' he drawled.

'The answer's no.'

Another test. She wanted him to plead for the date.

He reached into his breast pocket, pulled out his American cigarettes and ostentatiously tried to shake one out. Unfortunately, he shook the packet too violently, and it fell onto the wet pavement at his feet. He did not bend to pick it up but shook his head and laughed.

'Serves me right.'

She liked his ability to laugh at himself. She smiled, inviting him to prolong the meeting.

'Have you always worked here?' he asked.

'Since I left school. I didn't want to work in the shop.'

'Which shop?'

'My Dad's shop. Well, it was his shop. He died ten years ago. My brother runs the shop. They wanted me to work there too.'

'You made up your own mind. Good for you. Sorry about your Dad, though.' She was right. There was something different about him.

'What kind of shop is it?'

'Hardware. Bags of nails, bolts, hinges, saws, axes, shovels, spades. Anything. Dark, dismal, covered in metal dust and spiders' webs.'

'You don't like it?' he smiled.

'No. I hate it. Never go there now. Dad took me when I was wee. I used to stay in the office, reading the ledgers and drawing on bits of paper.'

She didn't know why she was talking. It was so easy to talk to him. He seemed to listen.

Not many men listened to you.

'Anyway,' she continued, 'I can't stay here all day.'

'No. I'm sorry. I'll need to get back, too.'

For a moment, she thought that he was going to walk away. He glanced nervously towards the quay.

'That night at the dance,' she said, trying to delay his departure, 'did you see the fight?'

She saw him hesitate and waited to see how honest he could be.

'I was there. When I left you, I went to the car park to help Spam. I came round the corner, and I could see the gang about to attack him, so I ran towards them. Halfway there, I saw Spam hit the guy with a chain, and he fell. His mates ran. It was awful. I couldn't have stopped him. Honestly.'

She detested violence. Remembering how Billy had left her at the dance, her initial attraction to him began to fade. Perhaps he was like all the others but clever enough to conceal the similarity. Perhaps the charm was nothing but guile, And yet he had been honest about the fight. She was certain of that.

'What happened to him?'

'He went to the hospital, I think.'

'You think? You mean you left him there.'

She was horrified, imagining the boy lying unattended in a pool of blood. 'His mates would come back.'

'You didn't know that.'

She was furious, finding it incomprehensible that anyone could walk away so easily from an injured person. She had been brought up to admire the Good Samaritan.

'Spam was scared they would come back– your man's mates– and carve him up.' She could see that he was struggling to explain his failure.

'No excuse.'

'No. You're right. No excuse. I should have stayed, even if the peelers came.'

Contrite, she thought, *at least on the surface. That's something.*

'I'll have to get back,' she said, 'It's cold out here.'

'What are you doing tonight?'

'Rangers tonight. Sea Rangers.' He smiled.

'Nice uniform. It'll suit you. I was in the cadets.' She did not miss the attempt at flattery.

'The sea cadets?'

'Aye. Cadet corps in the school. Bell bottoms and collar.'

'I'll have to go.'

'Tomorrow night?'

'Choir practice.'

'Any night?'

'I don't know, Billy. I'll need to think about it.'

'How will I know the answer?'

'Meet me off the train Friday night.'

'Okay. It's a deal. Friday night.'

'Just to walk me home.'

'Okay. Just to walk you home.' He grinned happily.

Just a wee boy, she thought, *a wee boy with an irresistible smile.*

She turned and walked back towards the glass doors. She could see his reflection in the glass, watching her. He looked very young. The others would get a good laugh and accuse her of cradle snatching. Still...

She shivered as the bus drew away, its exhaust curling behind it in the freezing air.

She allowed the silence to wrap round her as the drone of its engine faded. She always enjoyed that moment. It signalled the end of her working day. She stood for a while in the street, feeling the frost on her lips and savouring the solitude. She knew that her mother would appear in the bay window of the front room at any minute, pressing her face against the glass and shading her eyes to see why she had not reached the front door. She imagined her silhouette, the hall light behind her like a halo. It was always like that. Sarah kept her back to the house, gazing up the street. The streetlights cast long umber shadows in the gardens of the houses opposite, all with privet hedges dividing each from its neighbour. Tall red-brick Victorian houses built for the middle classes with arched porches and bay windows, giving an air of lofty self-satisfaction. She visualised her garden behind her– the cherry tree so spectacular in Spring and dull for the rest of the year, the pampas grass which whispered in the wind, the regimental ranks of roses along the path, the clump of hydrangeas in the corner proudly hanging on to the last flowers of the season and the circular bed where father had managed to keep a flash of colour throughout the year.

She thought of him bending over the bed, his pipe in his mouth and his braces wrinkling his shirt. She missed him, his little glittering eyes and his short, muscular arms. She used to stroke the mat of hair on his forearms as she sat on his knee, pretending he was a bear. She felt a sudden surge of grief and turned quickly to avoid it.

As she expected, her mother was at the window. She saw her turn away towards the kitchen. She pulled the collar of her coat tight around her neck and walked towards the house. Her breath swirled in faint clouds in front of her nose. She imagined her mother lifting a saucepan off the gas stove and pouring the boiling water off the potatoes into the sink, her glasses opaque with steam in the warmth of the kitchen. Always busy, her short, thick arms thumping, squeezing, wringing, polishing, anything to pass the time, to stop her thinking of her husband.

She climbed the four steps to the tiled porch and wiped her feet on the mat. She could see the hall through the frosted panes of the half-glass front door and remembered a time when she had to stand on her toes to see over the oak panels. Opening the door, the warm air, perfumed with the familiar scent of Mansion polish, engulfed her. She shrugged off her coat and hung it on the hatstand above her father's walking stick. Unconsciously, she ran her fingers over the worn handle, remembering how her mother had resisted her attempts to remove his coats and tweed cap from their hooks and give them away. She had been reluctant herself to dispose of them, but she had found that every time she hung her coat beside them, the smell of the garments– pipe smoke and hair oil and hardware– sparked such painfully vivid images of the past that she had to cut off the source.

'Hello, Mum,' she said cheerily as she skipped down the stairs to the kitchen at the back of the house.

'Shut the door, love; I don't want the smell of cooking to go through the house.'

Her mother, stirring a white sauce with a wooden spoon, did not turn away from her task. 'Bus late?' she asked, again without looking around.

Sarah could sense the scarcely disguised criticism. It had become something of a ritual if she lingered in the street.

'Yes, I think so. I didn't look at my watch, though.' Her mother said nothing but nodded her head.

Sarah sat at the table, idly flicking through the Woman's Own, which her mother had been reading.

'Can I help at all?' she asked, knowing what the answer would be. 'No, no. Nearly ready. Clive phoned, by the way.'

His persistence annoyed Sarah. He had tried so many times in the back of the car to slide his hand up her thigh. Stopping him, breaking away, telling him nothing made any difference. Two minutes later, he would try again. She pictured him in the car, his pock-marked face grinning insolently in the gloom. Some of the girls envied her. He had plenty of money, a new MG, and parents rich enough to have a massive white house on the hill, but he had a reputation for flitting from one conquest to another, leaving a trail of distress. He had charm, though, and a sense of humour, features that she had found attractive, and when he asked her to dance, his style was exciting and masterful. Yet she had grown tired of his constant groping and monotonous pursuit of her virginity.

'What did he want?' she asked sourly, unable to keep the distaste out of her voice.

'Don't know. Said he would phone again later.'

'Well, I don't want to speak to him.'

'That's dreadful, Sarah. You can't do that. It's very rude.'

She watched her mother peel off a pat of butter and slide it into the hot potatoes.

'I don't know why you finished with him. Such a nice man. Nice family, too. They'll be disappointed.'

Her mother liked Clive. He flirted with her and played the role of a polite, generous, witty young gentleman when he was in the house. If only she knew. Seduced by his charm and, though she would have denied it vehemently, his wealth, she saw him as an ideal suitor for her daughter. Sarah, however, found his flamboyant performances intensely irritating and the more enthusiasm her mother expressed for Clive, the less Sarah liked him.

'He'll soon find someone else. He has had lots of girls already.'

Her mother plunged a masher into the potatoes and, thumping the pot rhythmically, crushed them into a dry pulp.

'I'm not surprised. Charming man like him. You're making a big mistake.'

'You don't know him.'

Sarah could feel a flush of anger in her cheeks. If her Dad was there, he would have defended her. He would have seen through Clive. He would have guessed why she wanted to finish with him.

'I suppose you've met someone else,' her mother persisted.

'There's no one else,' she said more sharply than she had intended. An image of Billy in his light blue denim flashed into her mind.

'Alright. Alright. No need to get ratty.'

Her mother noisily ladled a mound of steaming mash onto two plates and lifted a grill pan with three chops from the cooker, one of them for her brother, a suitable diversion from the intrusive conversation.

'Kenneth late tonight?' she asked lightly.

'Late again. Stocktaking. Works far too hard.'

Sarah could sense the criticism. She should be with him– that was the implication.

She should be with the firm. She ignored the remark. Kenneth would be bent over the ledgers, his little eyes peering through his thick wire-framed spectacles at the columns of figures and his blunt finger sliding like a slug from one item to the next. Slow but sure, pedantic but certain, his ponderous brain would digest, ruminate, regurgitate and chew the figures till they tallied.

'I've ironed your shirt,' her mother said, placing a plate of mash, sprouts and a lamb chop in front of her.

'Thanks, Mum. I would have done it myself.'

'No need. I had plenty of time.'

Sarah kicked off her shoes under the table and curled her toes in relief. Her mother carried her own plate to the table and sat beside her.

'That was a dreadful business at the dance the other night,' her mother said, carefully cutting the fat off her chop, 'Poor boy in hospital. Hit with a bicycle chain. Can you imagine? Scarred for life if he lives, that is.'

'If he lives?'

Sarah's fork, poised to stab a sprout, froze above her plate. She stared at her plate, avoiding her mother's eyes in order to conceal her anxiety. If the boy died, Billy might be charged as an accomplice. But why should she worry? He was not her boyfriend. Not yet, anyway. Perhaps she should turn him down. Have nothing to do with him.

'Had you not heard?' her mother asked, her tone of voice indicating that she knew Sarah would have heard and had failed to tell her.

'Of course I knew about it. I didn't think it was that serious. How did you hear?'

Sarah stabbed the sprout, dipped it in gravy, and placed it behind her teeth. She hated sprouts, their slimy leaves and bitter hearts, but she ate them to avoid the running battle with her mother. She was sure that her mother chose them to provoke her.'

'In the hairdresser's. They were talking about it in there. It was in the paper anyway.' Sarah saw a means of escape and examined her mother's perm.

'Really nice. She's made a grand job of it this time.'

'Not she. He. That man with the wig. I'm sure he's queer.'
'Mum!'

'Well, he's so effeminate, mincing round the shop like a ballerina. Little Lord Montague.'

They laughed together, and the rest of the meal passed without dispute.

She pulled the heavy brocade curtains across the bay window in her bedroom, shutting out the winter night. Since her father died, she had slept in the spacious double room above the lounge, the room which he had shared with her mother, the room which her mother had steadfastly refused to enter after she lost him. Sarah had disposed of his clothes and the other remnants of his life– his collar studs, his silver brush and comb, his braces and sock suspenders, his elastic armbands, his Waverley fountain pen and propelling pencil and his horn-rimmed spectacles. Of all his belongings, the most difficult to part with had been his shaving kit.

So often, she had watched him soap the shaving brush, work a thick white lather round his jaw and peel it off with the open blade of his razor. The foam came off like a second skin, curling in front of the steel to leave a smooth pink surface. The sheer precision of the blade had fascinated her, but it was the smell of the soap that she relished. It lingered with her throughout the day. It lay on her tongue when she sat on the train. It vapourised around her head, surrounding her in an aura of comfort and safety. His shaving had been a special time of intimacy, one of the few spaces in the day when she could have him to herself, watching him stand over the sink in his striped pyjamas, the hair on his arms glistening with moisture. When she had dropped the kit in the bin and closed the lid, the clang of the metal shocked her and she had stood transfixed and trembling, her fingers fluttering round her cheek, suddenly aware of what she had done. The only symbol of those precious moments had gone.

She sat on the chair beside the bed, loosened the suspenders and rolled off her stockings. Carefully slipping her hand into the nylon, she peeled them over her arm so that they were ready for the morning and hung them on the bed. Sitting back and hoisting up her skirt and slip, she examined her legs, stretching them out and pointing her toes. Not very muscular, she thought, but not a bad shape either. A bit more muscle on the calf would have made them quite shapely. The knees, though, were unsightly– hockey knees, although she had never played hockey. Still, they couldn't be changed. They would have to cling there like ugly limpets. She had thought about shaving her legs but decided that the razor would merely coarsen the fine, fair hair on her shins. Clive wasn't deterred by them. But Billy. She wondered what Billy liked about her. Not her figure, anyway. Her breasts were too small to excite the boys. They liked big breasts protruding provokingly from skin-tight jumpers. Perhaps Billy was different. He seemed different, but it was hard to tell. Maybe he liked her eyes. She had nice eyes. Her father had said that she had eyes the colour of cornflowers.

She changed into her Sea Rangers uniform, the dark skirt, the navy jersey over the white shirt, the scarf and the white lanyard and stood in front of the long mirror on the wardrobe to study the effect. Her hair was a mess. The jersey had pulled it down over her eyes. Still, it was strangely alluring like that. She turned her head sideways to the mirror and raised one eyebrow through the strands. Very sexy, but not like her, not the shy, respectable girl that she felt herself to be. She crossed to the dressing table, picked up her brush and carefully adjusted her hair, parting it on the side, then brushing the top forward and flicking it back to the side. Yes, that was her– neat, modest, restrained. She returned to the wardrobe and retrieved her white hat from the shelf. Like the wardrobe, it smelt of mothballs. Not wanting to spoil her hair, she tucked it under her arm, turned off the light and hurried downstairs.

'Bye, Mum,' she called as she opened the front door, 'See you later.'

'Straight home now,' the provocative reply filtered up from the kitchen.

Sarah tried to ignore it but was sufficiently annoyed to slam the door behind her as she hauled on her blue Burberry.

Straight home! She always came straight home. Only once, only once, had she been late and that was when Clive picked her up in the car and refused to take her home. She wished that his car would appear round the corner as she hurried up the road. It was much colder. The moisture on the pavement had frozen and glistened under the street lights. Her coat was too thin to keep her warm, and she could feel the frost nipping her lips. She had forgotten her gloves, so she kept her hands deep in her pockets as she walked, the click of her heels echoing in the empty street.

She longed for the summer– the long, warm evenings and the ripple of the sea against the hull of the dinghy. She imagined clipping the head of the jib to the halyard, hauling the sail to the masthead and fastening the rope to the pins on the thwart. She could hear the jib flapping in the wind and feel the dinghy dipping in the swell. She loved sailing, harnessing the wind and the tide to scud across the bay. It gave her a sense of power, a taste of freedom. She wished that she could have her own dinghy instead of relying on the men who, in spite of their protestations of pure friendship, could not control their appetites and invariably tried to seduce her when the boat was far from shore. One in particular she had had to fend off with the boat hook. She remembered his lascivious grin and trembling hands. A repulsive creature with flickering eyes. She shivered again, recalling him.

She was so absorbed in her recollections that she did not see the figure lurking in the shadows of a gateway.

42

Chapter 4

The sweat slid down Spam's nose and trickled down his armpits, but, with an immense effort, he hauled his chin up to his fists twice more to make fifty lifts. He had leaned a ladder against the rafters in the garage and, hanging from the higher rungs, used them to strengthen the muscles in his arms. A punchbag hung from the ceiling and still swayed after his session with the gloves. Determined to build up his fighting skills, he spent many evenings in the garage, skipping, punching, lifting and shadow boxing. He had made a set of weights using a car axle and wheels and often spent an hour pressing the bar above his head. All this effort, however, seemed to have little effect on his physique. He had not developed a Charles Atlas torso and arms. Not that he was the 'seven stone weakling' portrayed in the Charles Atlas advertisements, but when he flexed his muscles in front of the mirror, he was always disappointed by the rate of progress. Still, he could beat most of the boys at the boxing club and that gave him an incentive to carry on in the privacy of the garage. Billy was the only person who knew about the extra training. He trusted him.

He dropped down from the ladder, stretched his cramped fingers and drew his arm across his brow to remove the sweat. Then, clenching his fists, he crouched into a fighting position, his left arm forward to jab and defend his face and his right hand back near his chin, ready to hook. He had seen the position often on boxing posters and copied the stance of his hero, Sugar Ray Robinson. He danced forward, jabbing with his left hand as his left foot hit the floor so that his weight lay behind his fist. Three jabs, then a right hook, bringing his right foot forward to swing his body behind the punch. He bounced round the garage shadow-boxing, battering his imaginary opponent into submission and finally raising his fists in the air to proclaim his victory. 'Ray Robinson does it again!' he shouted breathlessly.

He left the garage and sprinted round to the front door, the heavy rain forcing him to duck his head. He slammed the door behind him as he entered the warmth of the house.

'Don't slam the door!' he heard his father shout from the sitting room. 'Fuck off,' he muttered in reply.

'And stop swearing.'

Spam picked up a towel from the bathroom and went through to his bedroom. The walls of the bungalow were so thin that sound carried easily from one room to another. When his parents had sex in the front bedroom, he could hear every grunt and moan from his bedroom at the back of the house. Fortunately, it was a rare occurrence and lasted only a few minutes. His brother used to time it, and they would giggle so much that they had to bury their heads in their pillows. It was one of the few times that he and his brother shared amusement. Usually, his brother's laughter was at his expense. Spam detested him. Ten years his senior, Robert had taken perverse pleasure in hurting him. For no reason. Spam had made every effort to avoid provoking him, but his brother always found some reason to be annoyed and would punch the flesh of his upper arms till they had permanent brown bruising.

There was a little more space in the house after Robert left, but it was barely noticeable. The bungalow in Donaghadee had always been too small. Built as a holiday house before the war, it crouched behind a tall privet hedge like a scruffy urchin overlooked by grander villas, an incongruous intrusion in the respectable avenue. The two rooms at the front– a bedroom and a sitting room– let in some light, but the rooms at the back– Spam's bedroom, bathroom and kitchenette– were gloomy and depressing. The back garden, also deprived of sunlight, was a patchwork of moss and bare soil, littered with the detritus of adolescent boys - a bent bicycle wheel, a burst leather football, a barrow without a wheel shipwrecked in the corner, a bin lid once used as a shield and a decaying football sock half buried in the mud. The contrast with the neat rows of roses and manicured lawns in the other gardens could not have been more marked. The small front garden, dwarfed by the hedge, bore the only signs of attention with a few limp geraniums planted by Mrs. Campbell, spreading tentatively across the narrow concrete path leading to the gate. In spite of the cramped conditions and all the evidence of neglect– the cracked window pasted with sunburnt sellotape, the paint peeling off the doors and windows, the gate leaning off its hinges - the family had no intention of moving, an inertia often regretted by the neighbours.

Spam slipped off his vest and rubbed himself down with the towel. The double bed occupied most of the space in the room, which was so small that the edge of the open door scraped against the bed cover. To pass the wardrobe and reach the far side of the bed, he had to crawl across the quilt. Not that the bed was unusually large, but it was too wide for the room.

Absurdly heavy, it had not been moved since the family had taken the lease of the house, and its broken casters had worn holes in the carpet. Its steel chassis, strong enough to carry a bus and bolted to the bed-ends, supported an oak frame covered in metal mesh, which could be tightened as the mesh stretched. As the mesh had never been altered, the bed sagged in the middle. For twelve years, Spam and his brother had shared the bed till Robert had left for the Head Line as a radio operator.

Twelve years. Spam stared at the bed and remembered with disgust, hoping that Robert would attempt to interfere with the wrong person in the navy and receive a beating for his perversion. He imagined Robert's nose flattened and bleeding and his eyes glistening with tears and enjoyed the vision. Spam hated queers and had battered an art student on the pier, convinced that he was one of them.

He sat on the bed, hauled off his boxing shorts and lay back with his hands behind his head, gazing at the pictures on the wall. Every space was covered with full-page photographs from magazines– boxers frowning aggressively behind their gloves, weight-lifters with rippling, oiled torsos, and smouldering film stars like Marilyn Monroe and Joan Collins in provocative poses. He remembered that he had seen an excellent picture of Rocky Marciano in one of the magazines in the paper shop and had just folded the paper to slip it into his jacket to pilfer it when he realised that he was being watched by the woman behind the counter. Careless that.

Usually, he was too slick to be caught. But he would be back. He would get the picture.

He reached across to the single chair and retrieved his packet of Capstan from his jacket. Only one left. Shit. He had forgotten that. The sixty that he had nicked from the Italian cafe had not lasted long. He would have to get some more. He lit the cigarette and lay back again, drawing the smoke into his mouth and blowing smoke rings towards the ceiling. He watched them drift towards the light. He wondered if Billy would be down the street. Billy would have fags. Save him having to nick them.

Good guy, Billy. Posh family right enough with a big house, but Billy was different.

Good fun. Carefree, a bit wild even, wild enough to dive off the top of a crane into the harbour in the pitch dark. Didn't mind a battle either. Fast on his feet and quick with his fists. A bit squeamish at times, but that would be his upbringing. A bit soft when it came to women. Still, a good mate. Nicking the top off his fag to keep the butt for later, he dressed to join the others down the street– the leather bomber jacket, the drainpipe trousers and the suede shoes. He rubbed some Brilliantine on his hands, rubbed it over his hair, and, bending in front of the mirror, picked up the brush– a small, round plastic affair with scattered teeth and a clip on the back for two fingers– and combed his crew cut so that it formed a smooth, level mat on top of his head. He did not approve of the Tony Curtis curl, claiming that it made you look like a queer, but he did make a modest DA at the back.

'I wish you'd clear the bloody garage,' his father muttered without raising his head from the racing pages of the paper.

Spam looked down on the bald head and was tempted to spit on it. 'You never use it.'

'Could have done with it in the frost the other night. The windscreen was thick with frost in the morning.'

'You've never put the car away. Even when it was empty, so don't talk shite.'

'Don't swear at your Dad!' his mother broke in without much conviction, continuing to darn the sock on her lap.

'Well, he's talking rubbish, Ma. He doesn't need the garage.'

'And you don't need it either,' his father said, 'all that stupid weight-lifting stuff. What do you want that for? Fancy yourself as a hard man? Trying to impress your mates?'

'Just fuck off!' Spam shouted and stormed out of the room.

'I wish you wouldn't annoy him,' his mother said calmly, breaking the silence that followed. She squinted through her spectacles, trying to see that the needle passed neatly over and under the woolen threads as she darned a new heel in the sock.

'He's an eejit. If he cared as much about his work as he does about his looks, he would do better.'

'He sells cars.'

'Aye, now and again. Not half often enough.'

'You never liked him.'

'What was there to like, eh? Tell me that. Every other day, down at the school with him in trouble and Johnston's daughter the teacher. How embarrassing was that? And now its the police. How could you like that, eh? Fuckin' hooligan.'

She stabbed the needle into the sock as if it was an image of her husband, stood, dropped the darning on to the chair and waddled angrily through to the kitchenette.

'I'm not going to stay and listen to that,' she barked over her shoulder.

'Aye, well.'

He lifted the poker and prodded the fire, but it remained as lifeless as it had been when he came in from work. It had been a bad day. Not a car sold, not even any genuine interest. Not really Spam's fault, though. Just no customers. He set down the poker and prodded the dog with the toe of his slipper, trying to create enough space in front of the fire to stretch his legs. The dog, a small, lank-haired Yorkshire terrier almost as irascible as its master, snarled and snapped at his foot.

'Get outa that, you wee bastard,' he snarled back, giving it a heave with his other foot, and the animal rose truculently and jumped on to the sofa.

'Are you annoying the dog again?' his wife called from the kitchen.

He ignored her and, stretching out his legs, lifted the paper again to study the racing page. He was sure that he had seen that Phil Drake, a horse that had come from the tail of the race to win the Derby the previous year, was to run again; that win against the odds had made him a hundred pounds– the only win of the season. Not that his wife knew about it. She was given her housekeeping money from his wages; the rest was his.

Betty, his wife, rinsed out a milk bottle ready for collection in the morning, half filling it with hot water, placing her palm over the neck and shaking it. She watched her reflection in the window behind the sink, noticing that her perm had collapsed, leaving her grey hair sagging over her ears. She could not afford to have the mess repaired. She remembered her hairdresser– what a nice, polite, attentive young man– even if he was queer. Well, if he wasn't queer, he certainly behaved like one, and she really didn't care. He was nice to her. Nicer than The Heap next door. She could imagine him stretched out in the chair, his feet crossed, his head leaning back on the chair, adding to the layer of grease on the fabric, and his paper held up in front of his face. His double chin would be resting on the hair on his chest like a hen in a nest, and his little blue eyes would be flitting over the page. She could see the light catching the fair hair on his arms and glistening on his head. What had she seen in him?

She remembered when they met in the dance hall in 1935. He had strolled across the floor, smiled engagingly and asked her to dance. The massive crystal ball, spinning from the ceiling, formed a glittering halo behind his head, but she could see his mischievous smile and sandy hair, carefully parted and smeared flat with Brylcreem. A brilliant and masterful dancer, he steered her round the floor like Fred Astaire, rising and falling gracefully to the rhythm of the foxtrot. 'Ain't She Sweet'. Their song after that. He seemed to be such a gentleman in his dark suit, white shirt with cufflinks and striped tie– navy, turquoise and white diagonal stripes– it still lay rolled in his drawer. A kind man, she thought, patient and considerate. What a mistake!

She had lost her virginity to him on the top deck of a double-deck bus, lying on one of the long seats. Not a service bus, but one of many parked for the night in the local bus station.

Frequently, the doors were left unlocked, and courting couples often found some privacy by picking one of the buses on winter nights. She remembered the cold leather on the back of her head, the sound of his shoes slipping on the floor as he fought to get a grip, and the dark silhouette of his head above her, heaving spasmodically as he grunted his way towards a climax. Fast and frantic. Over in seconds, he withdrew hurriedly before she could be impregnated.

Never any different after they were married. A bodily function for him, a quick burst of energy to relieve his instincts, passionless, insensitive. She tolerated it, faintly amused by his porcine snorting and the loud moan of relief at the end. They did not kiss. She found the smell of his breath offensive, and his bristles irritated her lips. Still, it rarely happened now, thank God.

Shaking her head as if to scatter the memories, she filled the kettle, lit a ring of the gas stove and placed the kettle over the blue flame.

'Tea,' she thought, 'No doubt he'll want tea. Doesn't deserve anything. Swearing like that.'

Still, swearing was better than the other. 'Do you want tea?' she called out.

'Aye.'

Not 'Yes, please' or 'Thanks, that would be nice'. What had happened to his manners, his common courtesy? A boor. That's what he was. Just a boor. She repeated the insult in her head several times, enjoying the explosive and derogatory sound of the word.

Opening one of the cupboards, she retrieved a packet of chocolate biscuits and squeezed four of them onto a side plate. She used to bake cakes for him and the boys, but Robert had left, and his young brother spent little time in the house. There was just The Heap and herself, and he never thanked her for her trouble, so she had abandoned the habit. In one way, however, she regretted giving it up because it had provided her with endless enjoyment in planning how she could poison him with impunity. She had even visited the library and read about deadly poisons that could not be traced. She knew that she would never make the attempt, but the planning gave her immeasurable satisfaction and a focus for her disaffection.

Biscuit crumbs had fallen on the worktop, so she wiped them away with her hand, noticing that there was another cut in the Fablon. How had that happened? She always used the breadboard. Perhaps, Patrick– he hated the nickname Spam– had cut a slice off the loaf in the morning. She wondered where he would be at that moment. Probably hanging about with those sluts down in the station. Since the railway closed, groups of teenagers gathered in the empty station to smoke and drink and generally misbehave in a manner designed to offend adults of her generation. It did annoy her and yet she envied their freedom, their determination to flout convention, but she worried about Patrick. She had heard two of the neighbours whispering that he was a delinquent and would end up in the Crumlin. He was a wild boy, certainly. She knew that, but he was not bad, not like that.

The kettle boiled, and she turned down the gas beneath it, lifted down the brown teapot and poured in a little hot water, swilling around to heat the pot. Dark brown with a yellow band, she had bought it in 1945 just after VE day. VE day. She smiled as she remembered the celebrations - the burning of the effigy of Hitler on the bonfire, the dancing on the pier, the long line of bonfires on the coast glittering in the night. The Heap had not joined her. Despised by many in the town because of his involvement in black market fuel deals, he avoided social gatherings of any kind. He had been attacked one night during the war, returning with a gaping wound on one eyebrow, a split and swollen lip and a broken nose. Since then he had stopped visiting the pubs in the town, drinking only in Belfast or in the house. The assault had left him with a festering, bitter resentment towards his own community. He had tried to prevent her from taking the children to join in the Victory celebrations, claiming that the war was not over, but she had, for once, defied him. She remembered Patrick dancing around the bonfire, his socks round his ankles and waving a miniature Union Jack.

Emptying the teapot, she lifted the lid of the tin tea caddy. The sweet scent of fresh tea always reminded her of the grocery shop where she used to work. She remembered the plywood tea chests behind the counter and the rustle of the black leaves as she ladled them into the scales. She was happy then, chatting with the customers and blethering with the other girls in the back shop. She should not have left the job, but, at that time, there was something to be gained by announcing an engagement. It lifted you above the other girls. You were given more respect.

Even the managers treated you differently, subtly absorbing you into their group. She had been the first of the girls to marry. What a mistake!

She dropped three heaped teaspoons of tea into the pot– one for each person and one for the pot– and filled it with hot water. Leaving it to draw, she fetched a bottle of milk from the yard, removed the round cardboard top and poured off the layer of cream into a jug for the morning. The Heap liked cream on his porridge. She poured a little milk into the cups, fitted the knitted tea cozy over the teapot and carried the tray through to the room.

'About time,' he muttered, 'What kept you?'

She ignored him and placed the tray on the low table.

He reached for a biscuit and broke off a corner for the dog, who jumped down from her chair and sat at his feet.

'The biscuits are soft,' he complained, 'Can you not keep them in the tin?'

'They were in the tin.'

She was tempted to lift the teapot and pour the scalding liquid over his head. She imagined him roaring in agony as his arms flailed fruitlessly around his head. She grinned as the vision rose in her head.

'What are you smiling for?' he snarled.

She poured the tea into the cups and handed him one of them, placing a teaspoon in the saucer, hoping to deter him from supping the last of his tea from the saucer as he normally did.

'I was thinking about VE day.'

'Not that oul' thing again. Have you nothing better to think about? Like what that boy of yours is doing down the street.'

She sat down, balancing her cup and saucer carefully as she subsided into the chair. 'He's your son too, you know.'

'Aye, but you spoilt him rotten. Doesn't listen to me now.'

She remembered the last time he argued with Patrick. They had growled and barked at each other like two dogs till he had pushed Patrick in the chest. Patrick had felled him with one blow and walked out. He had lain unconscious on the carpet till she had rushed from the kitchen with a cold, wet cloth and placed it on his brow. For a moment, she had thought he was dead. She remembered the panic, panic for her son in case he had killed his father. That was the source of her terror. True, she was worried about her man lying there with his mouth open and his eyes shut, but she had had a glimpse of Patrick in handcuffs, his frightened eyes glancing back at her as the police led him away. The relief that she felt as The Heap recovered was as much for Patrick as for her husband.

'He'll end up in the Crumlin. Mark my words.'

'Don't be silly,' she replied, sipping her tea.

'You wait.'

Spam swaggered into the abandoned railway station, his shoes echoing around the empty platforms. It had been the end of the line. The rusting buffers were still there, although the steel rails had been lifted. The gaps between the black sleepers were littered with discarded cigarette packets, sweet papers, sodden newspapers and broken beer bottles. It had been a busy station at one time when coal from Scotland was landed on the pier and carried in long, clattering lines of trucks to Belfast. The rails leading from the points outside the station down to the pier were still embedded in the roadway, a hazard which often brought cyclists crashing to the ground. The crane, which had lifted one-ton buckets of coal from the holds of Kelly's ships to the wooden trucks, still towered over the rusting bollards, its redundant hook swinging in the wind. In the vast cavern of the station, the platforms had been cleared of everything of value– the benches, the coin-operated weighing machine, the porters' barrows, the metal ticket barriers. Only the billboards remained, the tattered remnants of posters hanging like ripped garments from the wood.

Starlings, disturbed in their roosts by Spam's approach, fluttered among the steel roofbeams as he walked into a patch of pale light cast by the streetlights through the panes of broken glass. He was glad of the light. It enabled him to step over the line of bird droppings fallen from the beam above. He stopped, reached for his cigarettes and then remembered that he had none.

'Shit,' he whispered angrily.

He hoped that Billy would be in the street.

'Anyone here?' he called, wondering if any other youngsters were in the station.

His voice echoed nervously around the platforms, then faded into silence.

He thought he heard a movement in the shadows down by the old ticket office. He stared into the gloom, trying to make out the shape of the arched window.

'Anyone here?' he called again.

Still no reply. He stopped breathing and listened intently. Nothing. He must have imagined the sound, or perhaps one of the birds had moved. Yet he was sure that he heard something, like a shoe scuffing on skirting, a hollow sound. If someone was there, why did they not answer? The locals usually replied. Perhaps the boys from Belfast had come down. Perhaps they were waiting down there in the darkness and he had no chain, no blade, nothing. He crept to the edge of the platform, dropped down onto the sleepers and picked up a broken bottle.

Wielding this by the neck, he vaulted back to the platform and walked slowly towards the ticket office.

As he moved deeper into the darkness, he transferred his weight to the balls of his feet, ready to spring. Every sinew drew taught, and his breath trembled with tension. He saw the glow of a cigarette– not at the ticket office but further into the shadows near the toilets. He stopped again and listened. This time, he could hear voices murmuring indistinctly.

He crept silently towards the sound, the bottle ready to use as a weapon, until he realised that one of the voices was female. Not the Belfast boys, then.

'Who's that?' he whispered. A frantic scuffle followed.

'Jimmy. It's me. Jimmy. Who the fuck's that?' came the breathless reply.

'Jimmy Carson?'

'Aye. Who's that?'

'Who's with you, Jimmy?'

'Flo. Just Flo.'

'Thank fuck for that. I thought it was the neds from Belfast.'

Spam relaxed and flung the bottle away into the darkness, where it shattered on the concrete floor.

'Is that you, Spam?'

'Aye.'

'What was that?'

'My weapon. You were lucky not to get glassed. Why didn't you answer the first time?'

'I was busy.'

'In her knickers, eh? Have you any fags?'

'Sorry, no. Not one.'

'Have you, Flo?' he asked, peering towards the smaller figure in the gloom. 'I don't smoke. You should remember that.'

He had gone out with Florence for a couple of nights until he had tried to force his hand inside her thighs.

'I remember, honey. Have you seen Billy at all?'

'In the cafe.'

'Mencarelli's?'

'Aye.'

'Dead on. See you later.'

He hurried away in the direction of the main doorway.

'Horrible wee man,' Flo whispered to Jimmy, tightening her arms around his waist. 'Dangerous wee man. Yer man is still in hospital– the one that he chained.'

'Why does no one say? Why do they not tell the police?'

'He'd find out. As sure as God, he'd get the man who split. Chain, knife, bottle. He'd get him.'

'You're all scared.'

'Aye, Flo. Too right. All scared.'

'Maybe I'll tell them.'

'For Christ's sake, don't be stupid!' he shouted, gripping her arms and stepping back, 'He'd get me then and your brother and your old boy. Jesus, Flo have a titter o' wit. Come on, let's get outa here before he comes back.'

He took her hand and led her back towards the platforms away from the main door.

Spam emerged from the main doorway on to the street. On his right, the beam of the lighthouse at the end of the pier swept across the harbour, flashing over the boats moored at the north wall. Built to shelter square-rigged ships sailing to Scotland, the two arms of the north and south piers in Donaghadee stretched into the hostile sea to form a safe harbour. The village street ran along the shore with no houses between the roadway and the sea. The hotels, shops, restaurants and bars squeezed themselves close to the pier and railway station while, beyond them, the ancient single-story fishermens' cottages lay calmly facing the sea, their doors opening onto the pavement. When the maroons exploded over the harbour, it was from these doorways that the fisherman ran to man the lifeboat.

Spam found the street deserted. Turning up his collar to shield his neck from the cold wind, he slouched past the Royal Hotel towards the cafe. As he passed the public bar, the sour scent of Guinness swept past him. He was tempted to go in. A small Bushmills would have warmed his core but he had no cigarettes and had no intention of buying them when he could get them for nothing. He hauled on the brass handle of the double swinging doors of Mencarelli's cafe and stepped into the warm interior. The mirrors around the walls, reflecting the high glass display cabinets at the counter and the tables on the tiled floor, made the place look spacious.

Spam glanced around the room, carefully absorbing the identity of every individual to satisfy himself that there were no threats. Half a dozen young people crowded around the jukebox, gazing into the glowing glass and arguing over the next record. The room throbbed with the heartbeat of the music, the systolic thud of the drum rhythm and the thump of the guitar. 'You ain't nothin' but a hound dog...' Presley's voice mesmerised the group, apart from two who started to jive, the boy's eyes fixed on the floor and his Curtis curl nodding. None of them noticed Spam. Another clutch of four sat at one of the tables, empty coffee cups and milkshake glasses gathered around the overflowing ashtray. The boys looked up and dipped their heads reverentially towards Spam. The girls glanced at him and quickly looked away to avoid his attention.

'Fuck the bitches,' Spam said to himself.

One girl stood on her own, facing one of the mirrors and combing her dark hair. Spam watched her reflection for a moment, admiring her sensuous lips and breasts that protruded provocatively from her coat. Suddenly aware of his leering glance, she stuck out her tongue and strutted out of the cafe, swinging her hips.

'Hello, Davey,' he greeted the Italian proprietor with exaggerated warmth.

The old man, his head shining above silver wings of hair above his ears, was not deceived. Dipping deep into the ice cream maker, he lifted a scoop of his special gelato and dropped it into a tall glass. Spam noticed the thick, hairy forearms and wondered if Davey was stronger than he thought.

'What you want?' he growled aggressively.

'Nothing, Davey.'

'Get outa here then. I don't want you here. You come in here, one coffee and you stay all night. Go.'

Spam wanted to hit him in the teeth but hid his feelings behind a broad smile. 'Tell you what, Davey. Make me a knickerbocker glory. Your special. Best in the country.'

Davey poured cold milk into the glass, added a scarlet stream of strawberry cordial and stirred the mixture with a long spoon. He studied Spam suspiciously, his thick brows drawn in a frown.

'Knickerbocker glory, eh? You came into money or what?'

'Just feelin' generous. Generous to me.'

'Go and sit down. I bring it to you.'

'Thanks, Davey. Has Billy been in?'

'Yea. Ten minutes.'

Spam sat at the table in the corner where he could see everyone in the room. Still no fags. He glanced at the group of four at the next table, wondering if any of them would part with one. He wanted to ask but was inhibited by the embarrassment if he was refused. He leaned on the table and nibbled at the nail of his ring finger. He felt uncomfortable sitting on his own. The isolation suggested that he had no friends and that no one wanted to talk to him. Perhaps he could join the group at the jukebox. He looked over at them. No. All posers from the big houses. He despised their kind, playing at being rockers, pretending to be hard. Your man is jiving. Just a weed with his long curl bobbing and his fancy sideburns. Maybe he needed a lesson. Spam reached into his pocket and slipped his knuckle duster over his finger. Not much of a weapon, but all he had. He tightened his fist and was just about to stand when Billy flung the doors open and, assuming his James Dean frown, looked around the room.

'Billy boy!'

'Spam the man!'

They greeted each other. Billy crossed the room and joined him. Dressed in tight jeans, a black t-shirt and a black bomber jacket, Billy looked fit and bristling with energy.

'Any fags, Billy?'

They sat opposite each other and Billy fished out a crumpled packet, tossing it on the table.

'One. Last one. Share it.'

'We need more,' Spam said, nodding towards the counter. Billy sighed and shook his head.

'Not again, Spam. He's going to find out. Anyway, too many people here.'

'Let's get rid of some of them then.'

He stood and swaggered over to the jukebox, his confidence restored by Billy's company.

'Next one's mine,' he announced as a challenge. The jiving stopped.

'Who says?' the boy with the curl spoke first.

'I do,' Spam grinned, 'And it's going to be The Happy Wanderer.' Spam detested the song and knew it would annoy the others. 'You're joking.'

'I'm not, my friend. If you don't like it, you can fuck off.'

The boy dropped the girl's hand and stepped forward aggressively. His friends moved quickly to restrain him.

'C'mon chick. No trouble. We don't want no trouble,' one of them said urgently.

'Let's go,' murmured one of the girls, pushing past Spam, 'Let him have his housewives' choice. C'mon.'

They followed her out.

Still grinning, Spam inserted a coin and chose Heartbreak Hotel. 'You didn't need to do that,' Billy said as Spam returned to the table. 'They cleared off, didn't they?'

The other four rose and also left the cafe.

'Listen, Billy. When Davey brings me the Knickerbocker Glory, I'll ask him for chips. He'll have to go in the back for fresh ones. I'll keep watch at the counter. You nick the fags.'

'We're going to get caught one of these days. He's going to notice.'

'Don't be so yella, Billy. You need fags, don't you?'

Chapter 5

I waited for Sarah in the gateway on Laurel Avenue. I saw her coming and retreated into the shadows, uncertain of her reaction. After all, I had not arranged to meet her on her way to Rangers. She might have been so annoyed that any further approaches would be out of the question, and so I hesitated, watching her walk briskly towards me, her sailor's hat set at a slight angle and her Burberry belted tightly round her waist. I tried to think of a smooth opening greeting and various cliches came to mind, all of them unsuitable. She wasn't like the other girls. Much more reserved. Not supercilious but slightly strait-laced, a trifle over-cautious, a shield perhaps to protect her sensitivity. So I thought. The others were brash, extravert, impervious to male banter. We did not have to choose our words carefully for them. I wanted to impress Sarah, but I couldn't find an expression that would open the conversation with a flourish. I moved back silently and let her pass, but as I watched her figure vanish into the night, the urge to hold her again overcame my inhibitions.

'Sarah,' I called, leaving the gateway and hurrying after her.

Startled, she turned and peered nervously in my direction. Alone in the street, she must have felt dangerously exposed.

'Sorry if I frightened you,' I gasped as I caught up with her.

'Oh, it's you. I couldn't think who it was.'

She was frowning but much less annoyed than I expected. 'I'm on my way to Rangers. I'm late already, so I can't stop.'

'Can I walk with you?'

'I suppose so.'

She resumed her brisk march up the street, which I had to follow. 'You don't seem very pleased,' I said.

'I told you I had Rangers tonight.'

'I wanted to see you.'

'Well, you've seen me.'

'Can I walk you home after?'

'Clive might be picking me up in the car.'

'If he doesn't?'

'For heaven's sake, Billy! Do you never give up? You're so persistent.'

'Only when I've something to be persistent about.'

That was a good line, I thought, and I did mean it. The more I was with her, the more I wanted to repeat the embrace at the dance. She smiled and shook her head.

'You're a terrible man.'

My hopes rose, and I took her hand, fully expecting her to withdraw it. She allowed it to rest limply in mine, carefully uncommitted.

Leaving the avenue, we walked past the cinema and the park, exchanging trivial experiences. When we reached the drill hall, she withdrew her hand.

'If Clive doesn't turn up, can I walk you home then?'

'You don't give up, do you?'

I smiled engagingly.

She sighed.

'If Clive doesn't turn up, I'll see you at the cinema over there.'

'I'll be there. When do you finish?'

'Half nine.'

'Okay. See you then, I hope.'

I watched her walk away, her navy Burberry almost black under the streetlights, a slight figure in flat shoes. I wanted to hold her again, to feel her body against mine, but I was not sure how she felt. Clive was twenty-six and owned a car. It would be understandable were she to choose him. The embrace outside the dance might have been an aberration, a mistake which she regretted. I had two hours to wait. Just time to go home and borrow some money.

The house was a dismal Victorian building, three-storey tall and semi-detached. With few windows in front, its face was turned away disdainfully from its twin, claiming a superior view. Although the front of the house, which was really the side of the building, had been designed to overlook the sea, a row of meaner houses had been built below it, obscuring the view of the bay. The only rooms from which the sea could be seen were the two top bedrooms. A previous owner, determined to protect his property from damp, had had it rendered in concrete, so what was a mundane villa had been transformed into an edifice as elegant as a house of correction. Because it looked north, much of the rendering was green with a slimy lichen. The small garden, shaded from the sun, was barren and colourless, the grass struggling to conceal the dark and lifeless soil. Even in spring, the sporadic clumps of daffodils had a morbid transparency that merely added to the air of desolation. Besides, they rarely survived the ravages of my younger brothers and their football.

Set in the red tiles of the porch, there was a square hollow for a mat that had lain empty since our arrival, a trap for women with high heels. I had stood there once in high heels, dressed in a pleated skirt, a headscarf, a lady's overcoat, nylons and carrying a handbag. My sister had used her skills with make-up to disguise me as a woman and I had filled a bra with socks. Mother had advertised for a maid– we seemed to have a revolving door for domestic servants– and we thought it would be fun to impersonate an applicant. The inner door had a grooved ebony handle and a brass bell push, which occasionally gave callers an electric shock but never rang in the house. I knocked on the glass panel and stood demurely, waiting for an answer. The central frosted glass pane was surrounded by small red and blue windows etched with stars to make it impossible to see into the hall.

'Mrs Sproule?' I had asked politely in a falsetto voice and in a broad Donegal accent when my mother opened the door.

'Yes?'

She did not recognise me. 'You advertised for a maid?'

'Oh yes. Of course. I'm sorry. Do come in.'

It was a strange experience to see my mother as a stranger might see her: charming, courteous, dignified. She was not a tall woman but substantial like a Rubens female and endowed with a voluminous bust. Her well-shaped legs, however, indicated that she had been mildly athletic when young, although the heavy hips suggested a decline into a more decadent lifestyle. Her blond hair, falling in even, natural waves to her shoulders, framed a round face with a small, slightly porcine nose and striking azure eyes, which she emphasised carefully by choosing clothes of a matching tone. That day, she was wearing a smart navy skirt, a light blue silk scarf and a royal blue jumper to which she had pinned her circular sapphire brooch. As she led the way into the sitting room to the left of the hallway, I noticed for the first time that she waddled rather gracelessly.

'Come in,' she purred, 'Do sit down.'

She waved her hand regally in the direction of the sofa. Passing her, I sat as daintily as I could on the edge of the sofa with my high heels tucked discreetly under my knees.

'Would you like some tea?' she asked, looking straight into my face. At that point, I could see her struggling to place me. I think she felt that she had met me before but was too polite to mention it.

'Thank you, that would be nice.'

My voice cracked then, and a series of emotions erupted in her face– realisation, astonishment, amusement and finally, apoplectic fury. Her face turned puce and seemed to swell like an inflating bladder. Her blue eyes flickered wildly, and her lips trembled.

'How dare you!' she spat.

'For god's sake, only a joke, mother.'

'Don't ever do that again.'

She stormed out of the room and banged the door.

I never discovered the root of that fury. Any time the incident was mentioned, she flung a warning frown in my direction. Even my sister was forbidden to discuss it.

The sitting room was spacious, with a black marble fireplace, a thick purple carpet, red velvet curtains and a grand piano. Mother had studied at the Royal Academy and played with a passion that sometimes shook the vases on the mantle piece. The Steinway sat in the bay window, which looked out over a privet hedge to the road. I stared at its polished lid for some time on that occasion, watching the passing clouds reflected on its surface and stunned by the violence of her response.

Heartbreak House, we called it– my sister and I– a household that thrived on conflict as if the inhabitants were bound together in mutual disaffection, inescapably dependent on discord, trapped in the habit of dispute. An atmosphere charged with volatile fumes, ready to explode at any time given the smallest spark, but not always in antagonism, for sometimes it could erupt into a syrup of affected devotion, false, sentimental, suffocating. A mother left with two teenage children and two small boys. Father in England, pursuing his ambitions. A situation fraught with hazards.

There were no lights in the sitting room when I approached the house after leaving Sarah. That was worrying. Mother usually sat in there in the evening. Perhaps she had embarked on one of her fruitless economy drives and was saving coal. I opened the door and, turning right, was heading for the kitchen when a loud crash in the dining room stopped me in the hall. The boys were at it again.

The dining room was rarely used. At one time, when Father was at home, we had Sunday lunch in there once a week, the polished mahogany table covered with a freshly ironed linen cloth and places set formally with wine glasses and napkins in silver rings. After he left, we abandoned the ritual. The table was pushed into the window, and the room became a repository for discarded furniture and boxes. The boys adopted it as a rumpus room, scoring the table with the chairs as they converted it to an aircraft, pulling down the curtains as they parachuted to the ground. The room was in darkness when I opened the door, but I could hear whispering in the shadows. When I turned on the light, I found a scene of devastation. The old sofa lay on its back, the hessian on its base hanging in shreds, exposing its inner organs and its fractured arm twisted awkwardly to the side. Behind it, the boys were crouched among the broken glass of a fallen picture, trying to gather the shards with their bare hands.

They had been leaping from the high mantle piece on to the sofa again. No-one had thought to interfere. Another watercolour was ruined.

I left the room and followed the dark corridor along to the kitchen. There was a small dining room before the kitchen, a room that was also used as a living room. This was where we ate our meals and generally had our battles. One of the walls still bore the brown stain of a chocolate mousse that my sister had flung at me during an argument. The room was very cramped. A little more space might have allowed us to feel less imprisoned with each other.

Mother was sitting by the gas fire, reading a play.

'Well? Did you see her?' she asked, looking up from the script. 'Who?'

'The girl you went to meet.'

'I went to meet the boys.'

'That's not what Kathleen said.'

'Well, she was wrong. Anyway, what were the wee boys doing in the dining room? I thought they were banned.'

'I thought they were upstairs.'

'Could you not hear them? They were jumping from the mantlepiece again.'

'I had to read this play. I'll speak to them.'

You heard them perfectly well, I wanted to say, *but you were too involved in your bloody play.* However, needing to ask for some money, I refrained.

'Can you lend me some cash? Just till Thursday. I need cigarettes.'

'Not again, Billy. Two weeks digs you owe me. The butcher was here today– rude little man– demanding money and threatening to go to court. I'll have to pay him. The one in the square won't give us any more meat.'

I waited silently, hoping that my sympathetic expression would have some effect.

'Oh very well,' she sighed, 'Give me my purse. There's five shillings in it. No more mind. Promise to give it to me on Thursday.'

'Promise. I'll give you my pay packet unopened, and you can take it from the rest.'

Three pounds ten shillings less dig money of one pound ten less five shillings still left enough for Friday night. She handed me two half-crowns.

'Thanks. See you later.'

I kissed her on the forehead and fled.

'You're not going out again at this time of night?' she called after me. 'See you later,' I shouted from the front door.

I bought twenty Philip Morris on my way to meet Sarah. American packets were so much classier than British. When you shook them out, you felt like a GI in the films.

I waited outside the Rangers hut in case the arrangement to meet outside the cinema was a ploy to avoid me but moved across the road so that my presence was not too obvious. I leaned against the park railings under one of the trees and lit a cigarette, flicking the match expertly into the gutter. I wondered if I could persuade her to take a walk in the park. Probably not. It was one of the few places where a couple could find some privacy. A bit soon for that. I could hear the ducks complaining on one of the ponds, disturbed by someone passing, and imagined myself sitting with my arm round Sarah, watching the streetlights rippling on the water. I could impress her with florid observations on the effects of light on the dark water and the reflections of the trees.

Just then, the Rangers started to file out of the hut, hauling on their coats and shivering in the freezing air. A dozen appeared and set off in different directions at the gate but no sign of Sarah. Perhaps she had left early to meet me at the cinema. Perhaps I should have followed her instructions after all. I took a deep draw of the cigarette and blew the smoke casually towards the hut. I did not want to seem anxious in case one of the girls noticed me.

A car drew up at the curb beside the gate. An MG. I could not see the driver as the hood was pulled forward and cast a deep shadow over the seats. Sarah came out, bent to talk through the passenger window, held a brief conversation and climbed into the car. I watched it drive away, its spoked wheels shimmering in the light. I was stunned. How could she do that? I had misjudged her. I had been so sure that she was an honest girl and that she was keen to meet me that night. Clearly, I had made a mistake. I was devastated. I felt as if she had died. There was something painfully irreversible about her departure, a finality that sucked away any hope of persuasion. For a moment, I was too miserable to walk away, but then the grief was overtaken by humiliation, which, in turn, fired a blissful fury.

Flinging the cigarette butt into the street, I hurried back towards the town centre, away from the cinema, planning revenge. I would get hold of Spam's bicycle chain and split his face. I would pour petrol over his car and set it alight. Rage-fuelled fantasies were so extreme that I began to smile. Nursing the images— his cheek opened to the bone, his grey suit spattered with blood, the hood of his car blazing, his house burnt to the ground, his coffin decked with manure— I floated through the streets, past the town clock, along the esplanade, past the swimming pool and into the darkness where the streetlights ended.

The narrow path towards the point was tarred and twisted round the headlands above the sea. It was not completely dark, for a full moon lit the shore and cast a long, glittering blade on the sea. I ran along the path, leaping high into the air like a dancer. Every leap seemed to be higher and longer. I felt that I could fly. I started spinning in the air, exhilarated, almost ecstatic, watching the moon flitting past my eyes. Untouchable, indestructible, I spun like a dervish, driven by a primeval power. Moon-child, witch-boy. Dark of the moon, whirling into oblivion, defying gravity, defying the earth, gripped by a dark energy. I felt free, unfettered, uninhibited. The sarcophagus in which I had been entombed had burst apart. The god of my childhood and his sterile commandments had been overthrown, littering the church floors with splinters of stained glass. I could do anything. Every moral could be cast aside. I could curse the Trinity, fornicate on the altar, and summon the Devil from his blazing depths. I leapt and whirled in the darkness until I crashed off the path, breathless and delirious. The grass, crisp with frost, melted under my cheek.

'To the Devil a Daughter,' I remember the title. Excited by its exotic and erotic detail, I had become obsessed with the occult. I had drawn a pentagram on my bedroom floor and moved my bed into the centre. I had climbed a statue of the Virgin Mary and had kissed her stone lips sensually. I had read Crowley's 'Moonchild' and Fraser's 'Golden Bough' in a thirst for knowledge. But this was a secret, a wisdom unknown to the people around me that I could nourish and enjoy, knowing that it was undetected.

I lay on the ground, gazing at the moon and imagining myself rescuing Sarah from the clutches of an evil cabal, snatching her from their altar where she lay naked, drugged and prepared for sacrifice. I lay till the sweat on my back turned cold and the frost bit into my face. Shivering, I staggered to my feet and jogged back along the path.

When I reached the house, I hurried quietly upstairs to my room and shut the door. I had left a bar of the electric fire burning so the room was warm. The small fire was far from efficient as the curved reflector was badly marked with spilled coffee, but, in the enclosed space, it managed to heat the air surprisingly well. Set under the roof with a coomb ceiling and two exterior walls, the room would have been unbearably cold without the fire, so I left it to burn most of the winter, regardless of the cost. The room was my space, my sanctuary where I could indulge in fantasies about the occult or attractive women. It had a blue chair– a carver from the dining room– and a card table with a green baize top pitted with cigarette burns. Far from steady, the table rocked under the weight of a heavy typewriter inherited from a literary but helplessly inebriate aunt.

At the time, I dreamt of being a famous poet and sat poetically by the window, gazing over the small patch of sea visible from the room and waiting for inspiration. I did write and, after laboriously typing the verse, sent samples off to publishers, confident that one of them would recognise the talent. The profusion of rejection slips should have convinced me that the whole activity was misguided, if not ridiculous, but I carried on regardless.

The room was cluttered with sheets of paper; books spread open and face-down on the floor, erupting ashtrays, milk jugs solid with biology, drumsticks and drum brushes, EP vinyl records, a record player and a radio– all the detritus of a 1950's adolescent. I used to listen to the charts on Sunday nights - Radio Luxemburg 208 metres– hoping for something more exciting than the bland, vacuous, sentimental music of the post-war stars, but I was usually disappointed. Instead, I had to rely on traditional Dixieland jazz and beat out the rhythm furiously on a bentwood chair, pretending to be Kruppa or Baby Dodds.

I wondered if I could ever lure her to my room, and that, at the time, seemed to be unlikely. Yet I yearned to have here there, to enclose her in the space that was mine, to possess her, to act like a couple and lie together in the bed under the painting. The image was so vivid that I had to try again to win her over.

Chapter 6

'I waited for half an hour, in the freezing cold.'

'You poor soul. They're not worth it, are they? Men. They're all the same. Find me one you can trust.'

'Clive took me to the Tonic in the car. I should have gone straight home when Billy wasn't there, but I waited for him. Stupid, really, but I thought he was different.'

Sarah stared out of the office window over the shipyard. Although it faced south towards the sun, the view was dismal. Ranks of shed roofs - a sea of black metal ridges - and the grubby walls of the main generating house filled the foreground, while, in the distance, the smog of the city obscured the hills. If she pressed her face against the glass and looked to her right, she could just see the dark shapes of the great hulls of ships under construction.

She could not understand it. Billy had taken the trouble to follow her and had seemed really anxious to meet her. Perhaps something had happened. Perhaps he still wanted to see her. She searched for an excuse, hoping that she could find one that was plausible. She did want to see him again. She was sure that he was different.

Nancy put her arm over her shoulder and squeezed. 'Forget him, girl. Plenty of other fish in the sea.'

'Yes, I suppose so.'

Nancy turned her round so that she could look straight into her eyes. 'God, you really like him, don't you?'

'I don't know.'

'Aye, you do. Admit it.'

'No. Really. I don't know. There's something about him that I like and something that I'm not sure of. He's a bit wild. He hangs about with Spam. I don't like that. I think he thinks he's a hard man.'

'If you fly with the crows…'

'I know. Still, maybe he's not like that, really.'

'Maybe he'll come up at lunch-time.'

'Don't think so. Anyway, we'd better get back to work. We're being watched.'

'Miss Quasimodo? Old bitch. She's always watching.'

'She can't help it. Being bent, I mean.'

'No wonder she's a spinster. No man would have her. She's an alcoholic, you know.'

'You're joking. She can't be. She couldn't keep her job.'

'She can, and she does. A half bottle of brandy in the drawer. You watch. Every so often, out to the bog. You can smell it on her breath. Never really drunk though– just topped up.'

'But she's a supervisor. Surely the manager would guess?'

'Runs to him with all her tales about us. His eyes and ears in the office.'

'Better go then. She's standing up.'

They returned to their desks. Sarah rolled out a new sheet of tracing paper and clipped it down. The plan below of a ship's stern shone through the light blue paper. She picked up her fine pen and ruler and started to trace the outline. She enjoyed her work. Her perfect control of the pen and the steady lines of her drawing gave her a sense of satisfaction. The plan seemed to grow under her hand as if she had drawn it as if it were her creation. Often, when a ship was launched, she could identify the parts that she had traced and felt that the vessel was hers, that she had designed it. She thought about Nancy's comment on Miss Capper and looked over at her, only to find that the supervisor was staring through her thick spectacles in her direction. She re-focussed on her plan quickly.

The little woman was not as bent as Nancy's nickname suggested, but she had a slight stoop as if the years of bending over the drawing board had welded the top of her spine into that position. Her long knitted cardigans, sagging from her shoulders, hung shapelessly round her hips, the pockets drooping open like toothless mouths, one of them always stuffed with a hankie. She seemed to suffer from a constant cold, the edges of her nose scarlet and her nostrils moist.

Her lifeless grey hair was drawn back into a taut bun to ensure that no stray locks could create an impression of slovenliness. Her spectacles were perched on a nose that was very close to being a beak and, magnifying the size of her eyes, gave her face a predatory appearance as she scanned her office like an owl searching for prey. When she caught a girl slacking, she would swoop on the victim, her beak chattering angrily in her ear before strutting back to her desk.

Sarah wondered about her drinking. Surely, if she had been tippling in the office, more of the girls would have spoken about it and she herself would have detected it. Besides, Nancy was suspected as the source of many poisonous rumours that circulated in the office. Still, it might be true. She felt sorry for the woman. Nancy's description of her appearance was unkind, however close to the truth. There were times when she seemed to be in pain, grimacing as she rose from her seat at the top of the office. Perhaps that was why she drank– to relieve the aches associated with her slight deformity. In such circumstances, Sarah could understand her addiction, though she couldn't imagine how people allowed themselves to be controlled by alcohol. She had been drunk a few times– not incapable, but unsteady, what she called 'tipsy,' but the experience had always left her feeling so dreadful the following morning that she refused drinks for weeks.

Besides, her mother and brother were strictly opposed to alcohol. Not her father, though, for he had often enjoyed a visit to the pub on a Saturday, returning with an inebriate glow and a Saturnine grin. She smiled as she remembered him.

'And what do you find so amusing, Miss Curran?'

She was so startled by the voice in her ear that she smeared the tracing. 'Not thinking about your work anyway,' Miss Capper continued.

Sarah did not turn round but stared at the long, black smear, waiting for the next complaint. She had not heard the supervisor approach, and if the other girls had warned her in the usual way by coughing loudly, she had been so absorbed in her thoughts that she had been oblivious to them.

'Quite a mess, Sarah. The standard of your work leaves a lot to be desired. Perhaps if you spent less time gazing out of the window and chatting to Nancy, it would improve.'

Sarah was about to argue but realised that it would be pointless. That was the reason she gave herself. In fact, she was too timid to argue, too scared of confrontation, a weakness of which she was ashamed. Faced with authority, she shrank or, subjected to injustice, suppressed her fury till she exploded in inarticulate and ineffective invective. Whether she retreated or whether she lost her temper, she loathed herself afterwards. She had tried to find the origin of that weakness, but the search had been fruitless.

'I can sort the mistake,' she murmured submissively.

'Indeed you will. In this office, we pride ourselves on the quality of the tracing. If you are more interested in gossip than attending to your work, there is no place for you in this firm. Now carry on with the rest of the drawing, and you can correct the error at lunchtime.'

Sarah, fighting to control her temper, bent over the drawing and traced a fine line along the parallel ruler. She could feel the flush of embarrassment in her cheeks and down her neck and vowed to find a way of hurting Miss Curran in return. She knew that the other girls would be watching her humiliation over their desks, quickly returning to their tasks when Miss Curran looked round.

With a final sniff of disapproval, the supervisor returned to her desk. Sarah wanted to turn and stick out her tongue at the woman's back but chose to retain her dignity and concentrate on her work. She did not feel sorry for the creature any longer. She hated her at that moment. Miss Quasimodo. Old bitch. As she worked, she tried to think of a way of reporting her drinking. Who was above the manager? She had no idea. The bosses. A nameless, faceless squad of men who ran the yard from their invisible heights, controlling every workshop and skeleton ship, ordering the lives and destinies of more than twenty thousand men and women.

She had seen some of them at launches– men in dark suits with white starched collars and expensive overcoats– but they were as remote from her world as Holywood stars. She could never approach them. What would they care anyway? Miss Curran did her job. Speak to one of them and she herself would end up being dismissed. The union. She could speak to the union, but who was her shop steward? She had no idea. She wasn't interested in unions or politics. She paid her dues, and that was it. Anyway, they wouldn't care about her problems. She was stuck with Miss Curran.

'Just stick it out, girl,' her father would say, 'She'll get what she deserves in the end, don't worry. You're worth twenty of her.'

She could hear his voice and feel his hand on her shoulder. She smiled and carried on.

At lunchtime, the other girls left their desks and headed for the canteen. Sarah carefully worked at the smudge on the paper.

At one point, she looked up and saw Nancy waving her over to the window and pointing to the yard below.

'She's at the toilet,' she hissed. Sure enough, Miss Curran's desk was empty. 'He's here,' Nancy insisted, 'Billy's here. Come on over.'

'No! She might come back.'

'She's just gone. She won't be back for ages.'

'No. You go down and tell him to wait. I won't be long. I have to finish this.' Nancy grinned and patted her hair into place.

'Be delighted,' she purred provocatively and stepped out of the office, exaggerating the swing of her hips.

Sarah was not sure what she felt about Billy. There were things about him that she liked.

He was polite, funny, and patient, and yet she was not completely certain that these qualities were genuine. There seemed to be something hidden, something she could not quite define, but its shadow was there like a figure behind frosted glass. And why did he hang about with Spam? Spam was different– a different class, for a start. Billy's father was in business. True, his parents were not together, but the money was there, and you could see that Billy had been raised in comfort and sophistication. He had that air of self-assurance and ease in company. Why would he choose such a friend– a violent hooligan with a bad reputation? Excitement? The thrill of breaking the law? He could end up in prison. She didn't want to be seen with a criminal.

And yet, there was the other side. The way that he kissed her that night– gently, respectfully, without that voracious gnawing of her lips that the others felt they could inflict on her. She remembered his fingers on her thigh, tentative, trembling slightly as if they expected a rejection. She should have pushed them away. She should not have allowed it, but she enjoyed the sensation, and she would have reacted if he had tried a change in direction. She was quite sure of that. She was going to be a virgin when she got married. She was going to save herself for that. For Billy? Could she marry Billy? He was just a wee boy, really. But then a wee boy would grow, and maybe she could help him to grow into a man, nourish his better qualities and steer him away from danger. Maybe she could look after him. She liked the idea. It made her feel tender and warm.

She finished her correction and left the office. As she came down the stairs, she could see Nancy and Billy on the pavement. She stopped and watched them for a moment to see if Billy behaved differently when she was not there. He was smiling amiably at Nancy, not leering seductively and peering at her full bosom as so many of the boys were prone to do. She liked the way he brushed his fingers nervously through his hair and seemed slightly ill at ease as if he was hiding a natural timidity. He dipped two fingers into his breast pocket and fished out a packet of American cigarettes, offering one to Nancy, who shook her head. She remembered the sweet smell of the tobacco on his clothes.

She stepped forward, pushed the glass door open and joined. 'Hello, Sarah,' he said quietly, clearly not sure of her reaction. 'Hello, Billy.'

'I'll be off then,' Nancy announced, sliding back through the door, 'Leave the happy couple alone.'

For a moment, an awkward silence stood between them. He shook a cigarette from the packet and hung it between his lips. Forming a cup with his fingers and a matchbox to shelter the flame from the wind, he lit a match and bent his head over his fists. She watched the end of the cigarette glow as he sucked in the smoke. Quite a ritual, she thought, waiting to see what he would say. He flicked the match away and returned the box to his pocket. Holding the cigarette between his fingers, he took a deep draw and spoke as he exhaled the smoke.

'I hope you don't mind me coming up here.'

'No.' She forced him to lead, testing his commitment.

'I waited for you, you know.'

'Not at the Tonic.'

'I saw you get in the car.'

'Clive drove me to the Tonic, and you weren't there.'

'Are you going with him?'

'Not really.'

'I'm sorry I was in the wrong place. I wanted to see you.'

She was impressed. Boys of that age rarely apologised, but she wanted him to make the first move.

'Can I see you tonight?' he asked eventually.

'I don't know, Billy. Are you not meeting Spam?'

'No. I don't see him that often. He's not that important.'

'Yes, he is. He's your friend. He doesn't have many others.'

'I would sooner see you.'

'No, you wouldn't. Be honest.'

'I am. Really, I am. Please.'

'Okay then. Phone me at six thirty, and I'll see.'

'Great, Sarah! Dead on! I'll phone at half six.'

The hooter howled across the yard, signalling the end of lunchtime.

'I'll have to go,' he said, 'See you later.'

'Maybe. I said I'll see.'

He grinned, nicked his cigarette, placed the butt-end behind his ear and hurried away.

She watched him dodge through a crowd of men heading for the frigate and wondered why he seemed to glance nervously around him and why he did not turn and wave. She felt a bit disappointed. She had hoped that he would look back, a small gesture of appreciation.

'Have nothing to do with him,' her brother said, chewing a sausage as he spoke.

He really has no manners, she thought, as he stabbed a piece of potato and ate it off his fork like a lollipop. His thick, round spectacles steamed over as he bent over the plate across the kitchen table from her. *Coarse,* she said to herself. *I know two things about a horse, and one of them is rather coarse,* her father used to say. How could his son be so different? Kenneth, her brother, rarely smiled, a morose, detached little man, always finding fault with other people. He had always been like that. She remembered her father clowning around the kitchen in her mother's hat and coat, trying to make Kenneth smile. She watched him stick his fork in a potato, peel off its skin and swill it round the Bisto gravy on his plate.

'You don't know him. You know nothing about him,' she replied. 'I know more than you do anyway.'

'No, you don't. You're just saying that. You've never met him.'

'I know all about him, though. I know his father.'

He picked up the potato on his fork and started to chew it.

'For heaven's sake, Kenneth,' her mother interrupted, 'Do you have to eat like a savage?' He ignored her.

'I know his father.'

'No, you don't. You've never met him either.'

'You're wrong. I sat next to him on the train.'

'And you spoke to him?'

'He was with his mistress.'

'His mistress?' her mother asked, clearly shocked.

Sarah glared at her brother. He was deliberately causing trouble. She wanted to slap his face.

'They've been separated for years,' she explained calmly, although she was furious, 'He lives in England. I daresay he has a girl friend. So what?'

'Does his wife know?'

'Of course, she knows. Anyway, it's none of your business, Kenneth.'

'It might be. If he comes to the wedding.'

'Oh for God's sake! I've only met him. And where's your girl friend? You never mention her, do you? You hav'n't got one, have you? You can't find one. No right-minded girl would have you,' she rattled angrily.

'That's enough, you two,' her mother said firmly, 'Eat your tea and stop arguing.'

'He's trying to annoy me.'

'Just ignore him. Tell me more about Billy. Did he go to the Grammar school?'

'No. I told you. He went to Campbell.'

'So you did. So why's he in the yard? I don't follow that. Most of those boys go on to Queen's or Trinity or even Oxford.'

'He wanted to work in the yard.'

'Really strange and strange his father let him.'

'I told you he was odd, something not quite right about him,' Kenneth intervened, 'Trying to be something he's not.'

'Will you shut up?' Sarah hissed and, placing her knife and fork neatly on her plate and folding her napkin, she rose and left the table.

'Just ignore him, Sarah. Come and have your pudding. I made it especially for you. Apple crumble and Birds custard. It's just about ready.'

'I'll have it later.'

Sarah left the kitchen and, kicking off her shoes in the hall, ran up to her room and sat on the bed. Gripping her small fingers into fists, she thumped the coverlet beside her.

'Pig!' she exploded, 'What a pig!'

She hated her brother. A nasty toad. Always making trouble, knowing precisely how to worry her mother. She wished that there was some way that she could annoy him in return, but his interests outside work were few, and he had no close friends. He seemed to be impregnable. It was so frustrating. He went to the pictures occasionally, never to the dances and never to the pubs. Sad really.

She could feel her anger subsiding, diluted by sympathy. She tried to resist the sentiment, wanting to hold on to the warmth of her fury, but it seeped into the simmering flux and calmed its surface. She shivered and realised how cold it was in the room. *Better draw the curtains,* she thought, but stayed where she was, feeling the warmth of the eiderdown through her skirt.

She thought about Nancy and the way she flirted with Billy. Not much of a friend, really.

She would steal your boyfriend without hesitation. No conscience, Nancy. One of those who lived for the moment. Perhaps Billy liked her. Perhaps he wouldn't phone. She found herself feeling jealous and possessive. She did not want Nancy to have him, and that annoyed her. She shouldn't feel like that. She hardly knew him– as Kenneth had said.

She stood, walked over to the windows, feeling the cold linoleum through her stocking soles, and drew the heavy curtains across the bay window. The room seemed cosier immediately, the echo less pronounced. She sat at the dressing table and casually examined herself in the mirror. The cold sore in the corner of her mouth had almost disappeared. She didn't like her mouth. The lips were too thin, and she was sure that her top teeth protruded slightly. Her sharp nose made her look like a ferret, but her eyes were a beautiful blue.

'Bonny blue eyes,' her father used to say.

She remembered when he took her to see Moira Shearer in 'The Red Shoes' and how she wept uncontrollably when the young ballerina, having plunged off a balcony, lay on a stretcher fatally injured. The memory of the film still stirred the sorrow that had made her weep then. She could still see the final scene as the spotlight wove through the dancers, following the empty space on the stage where the ballerina would have danced. You were left to imagine her, her grace, her pain, her exhaustion as, clothed in rags, she is driven until she collapses to dance in the red shoes. She was no longer there, a silver circle on the stage, a memory of her brilliance enough to tell the story. The empty space. Sarah could feel that space behind her again. The place where her father used to be.

'Bonny blue eyes all red,' he said as the house lights went up in the cinema and gave her his clean white handkerchief.

He had passed his fingers through her hair and smiled down at her; his eyes, she remembered, full of compassion and love.

'It's only a film,' he said, 'Not a true story.'

The heavy, scarlet curtains had come across the screen, and the music had been replaced by the thud of tipping seats and the murmur of the shuffling crowd.

She remembered his hand on her shoulder, a broad, thick hand with scars on the knuckles, the fingers like sausages and the skin stretched and worn. The gold ring glittered in the dim light. The hand had guided her out through the swing doors into the cold night air and the harsh reality of the street.

Just the two of them. The other two had stayed at home. A special night. The Red Shoes. 'Sloppy, sentimental stuff,' Kenneth had said.

She leaned forward so that she could see the reflection in the side mirror. The kidney-shaped dressing table had three mirrors– a large central one and one on each side. When she was a child she had discovered that, if she set the side mirrors to reflect each other, she could see a long hall of mirrors like a green corridor stretching into infinity. The effect still fascinated her.

The corridor seemed so stately and still, a passage leading to a magic world. She used to imagine herself walking down it, her shoes echoing on the tiles and her tiara glittering in the emerald light. It was still there. She smiled and sat back.

It was her mother's dressing table. She remembered her sitting on the stool, her hair in a hair net, ready for bed. Their room. Their bed. Her mother had never entered it after he died. She had moved to a back bedroom and persuaded Sarah to sleep in their double bed. That had been an uncomfortable experience. Her mother had placed a hot water bottle between the sheets and wrapped her pyjamas around it, but Sarah had changed in the bathroom and had stood in the doorway for some time before approaching the bed. Although she had often crept into it on a Sunday morning, cuddling up to her father, on that occasion, as a young woman, she felt like an intruder. Their bed. Sometimes, she had thought of them making love in the bed but found the vision so appalling that had swept it violently out of her mind, disgusted. The idea of her father behaving like a dog with a bitch, his bare backside thrusting obscenely between her mother's thighs, was too dreadful to contemplate. She knew that they must have engaged in the act, but she did not want to think about it.

She wondered what it would be like the first time. Painful. She was quite sure of that. Nancy said it was brilliant, electrifying, like a bolt of lightning that set every cell jangling with ecstasy but Nancy would say that. Probably all lies. Nancy always exaggerated. Maybe she had never done it at all. Still, perhaps it was wonderful. She tried to imagine being married to Billy, lying in bed with him, feeling his skin next to hers and hearing his breathing on the pillow beside her.

If he touched her, would he be gentle, would he be content to hold her in his arms and wait, or would he be swept away by his passion and force himself on her? Many husbands were like that. She had read about them in magazines. She did not want that. Such brutality would be terrifying. If she were to make love, it would have to be gentle and slow and under her control.

She tried to make her body feel what it would be like opening her legs slightly and imagining the sensation of him inside her. It might be brilliant, as Nancy had said. She began to enjoy the sensation and then saw herself in the mirror, her lips parted and a silly expression on her face. She closed her legs tightly and sat up straight. Dirty thoughts. Her mother would be horrified if she knew what she had been thinking. She dismissed them quickly.

She looked at the bed in the mirror. The depression where she had been sitting distorted the delicate floral design embroidered by her mother before their marriage. She could imagine her patiently and diligently sewing the tiny leaves and shoots as she now darned socks. Behind the bed the heavy mahogany wardrobe reached almost to the picture rail, the row of hatboxes above the cornice adding to its dominance of the room. She remembered removing her father's clothes and folding them into a laundry basket, rolling his ties and his socks, folding his trousers and jackets and bending the starched white collars of his Sunday shirts. Some things she could not give away. Hidden from her mother, she had kept his collar-studs and cuff-links and the comb that silver comb that he had used to part her hair. She swung round and opened the drawer of her bedside table to make sure that the mementoes were there. Sliding her fingers to the back of the drawer, she felt the soft tissue paper in which she had wrapped the precious items. They were still there.

She turned back to the mirror, wondering what to wear if she were to meet Billy. The royal blue polo neck was too tight, too provocative, and her mother detested it.

'Makes you look like a tart, ' she said.

Sometimes, she wore it anyway. It made her feel smart and drew attention to her figure. Yet her mother's comment had sown a doubt which she could not shake off and which always scratched at her thoughts during the evening.

She had a light blue cardigan that matched her eyes and a navy circular skirt. That would be better, she decided, for the first proper meeting. But was she going to meet him? She had not agreed to see him after all. It was not too late to hold back, to let him wait for an answer. Yet she might lose him, and there was something about him that she found intriguing, something attractive purely because of its uncertainty. The moment of doubt passed. She rose from the stool and, crossing to the wardrobe, opened the door. The smell of tobacco surprised her again. It never failed to have that effect. It was fading, but every time she opened the door, it hit her like a pillow, shocking her senses. She recovered quickly, but it annoyed her that it took her by surprise every time. All her clothes had a faint scent of it in spite of the mothballs hung on the rail and the perfume she used, but she refused to use the cupboard in her old room.

She had just removed her cardigan and blouse when the phone rang downstairs. She was tempted to hurry down but heard her mother answer it.

She slipped off her cardigan and blouse, shivering in the cold air, and put on a new white shirt. She unfastened the eyes on her working skirt, stepped out of it and hung it on its hanger.

She always enjoyed that moment in the evening. She felt that she was hanging the working day on a hook and closing it behind the door. If only she could hang Miss Capper in a cupboard, lock the door and leave her to decompose. She felt better immediately when she pulled on the circular skirt. It gave her a sense of freedom. She twirled in front of the mirror to see it spinning.

'Its Auntie Belle,' her mother croaked breathlessly after hurrying up the stairs, 'She's fallen in the bathroom and hurt her arm. Pop round and see she's alright, will you?'

'But Billy'

Seeing the stern expression in her mother's eyes and the slightly raised eyebrow, she abandoned her resistance and nodded.

'There's no one else, and she is on her own,' her mother reminded her.

'I know. I know. I'll go. But listen. If Billy phones, tell him I'll meet him another night.'

'Yes, yes. Now hurry, please. I'm worried about her.'

Sarah straightened her stockings and slotted her toes into her shoes.

She suspected that her mother had not listened to her message for Billy and that she would deal with his call in her own way. If he called…

Aunt Belle was not her aunt but an aged friend of the family. Frail but formidable, a former school teacher with a remarkable memory and a disturbing ability to see through the affectations of other people. Sarah found her perception alarming at times. Yet, because it was expressed with such disarming kindness, she never felt hurt by it. Many people found her far too direct and abrasive, a reason perhaps for her isolation. Sarah liked her, however. The old lady, with extraordinary subtlety, had always built up her confidence, encouraging her to think independently and to assert herself in the family. She had taught her to play the piano and to listen to operatic arias on the wireless. She could see her at that moment, one thin hand raised as if conducting the orchestra and her eyes brimming with tears behind her gold spectacles, lost in the magnificent firmament of music. She had been a tall woman, slim and elegant, but, in recent years, she had seemed to totter and tremble like a high building with cracked foundations, losing her sure stride and vitality. She still dressed carefully, always in high-necked frocks with a brooch below her chin, and had her grey hair permed and dyed blue.

'Remember to tell Billy,' Sarah called from the hall as she hauled on her coat and left the house.

She knocked firmly on Aunt Belle's door and, receiving no reply, stepped into the narrow corridor. The lack of response was worrying. Normally, the old lady heard her knock and called out immediately. Sarah wondered if she was still upstairs in the bathroom and, holding the bannister, shouted for her. No reply. She climbed the stairs nervously, afraid that she might find the old lady comatose on the bathroom floor, but then she remembered that she had used the phone and turned back towards the kitchen.

'Aunt Belle,' she called again. Her voice echoed in the stairwell, but there was no reply.

It was a semi-detached house, and she did not want to disturb the neighbours, who often complained about the noise of Aunt Belle's record player. The walls were not thin, but when Aunt Belle played Gigli or Tebaldi, she twisted the volume control on her new player as far as it would turn.

Although the hall corridor and stairs were narrow, the rooms were spacious. The villa had belonged to an ancient spinster, and the décor had not been changed since it was built in 1895. Dark shellac varnish covered the patterned wallpaper as high as the dado rail. Glass bead curtains shielded the windows of the front room from the curiosity of pedestrians who, because of the minute front garden, passed within feet of the door. In daylight, the room was dark and depressing, the stern leather armchairs adding to the gloom, but in the evening, with the brass fender glittering in the firelight and the standard lamps bringing some life to the sterile décor, it could feel almost cosy. The bedroom above was a different matter, a complete contrast to the rest of the house. This was Aunt Belle's room, bright and colourful with vibrant landscape paintings and prints and a brilliant scarlet counterpane embroidered with fiery Chinese dragons. The furniture was royal blue, and the curtains turquoise. This was where she played her music.

Sarah opened the kitchen door to find her aunt struggling in from the yard with a bucket of coal.

'Aunt Belle! You shouldn't be doing that. Here, give it to me.'

'Its alright, love. I used my good arm.'

'What happened?'

Sarah took the brass coal bucket from her hand.

'I slipped in the bathroom and broke the fall with my left hand. Silly, really.'

'It's not broken, is it?'

'No, no. Pulled the tendons or something. It's nothing, but I need someone to fill my hot water bottle. Can't use my left hand at the minute. Anyway, you were going out, weren't you?'

'No. I wasn't doing anything.'

'That's why you have your blue skirt on. Of course, you were going out. Don't pretend. Who is he?'

'It might be a girl friend.'

'I'll ignore that. Put down the bucket and sit down.'

Sarah was quite pleased to put the bucket on the floor and sit at the table. Her aunt pulled out a chair with her right hand and sat down.

'Fix a ciggy in my holder for me and give me a light.'

Sarah opened the packet of Du Maurier, fixed a cigarette in the long blue holder and passed it across the table. She watched her aunt place it between her teeth and point to the lamp- shaped lighter on the table. Sarah flicked up a flame and held it towards the holder,

Her aunt drew in deeply and smiled. 'Who is he then? Tell me.'
'Billy. His name is Billy.'

'Protestant then?'

'Not anything really. I think his family is from the Church of Ireland.'

'What are they like?'

'His mum and dad are separated or divorced. I'm not sure which. Only his mum and sister are at home. I haven't met them.'

'What's he like?'

'Not very tall. Fairish hair in a kind of crew cut.'

'I don't mean his appearance, Sarah. What is he like as a person?'
'Kind, I think. Good fun. Considerate.'

'Oh dear.'

'What do you mean, oh dear?'

'You like him.'

'Yes, I do, but there's one thing that puts me off. His friend. He hangs about with Spam, Patrick, whatever his name is, the boy who is always in trouble.'

'Rebellion, love. Nothing to worry about. He'll grow out of it. His family have money I take it.'

'I think so. He went to a posh school anyway.'

'There you are then,' she said, not hiding her triumph, 'I was right. Rebellion.' She tapped her cigarette holder over the ash tray.

'Your mother likes Clive.'

'He has a car, a good job, prospects and a stable family.'

'How boring! You need something more exciting, something creative, something with a bit of flair, a bit of panache.'

'There is something about Billy. I don't know what it is. Something different.'

'A bit dangerous even?'

'No. Not dangerous, exactly. I don't know how to describe it. Something going on under the surface, like a shape under the water. Something you can't quite define.'

'Sounds fascinating. Worth exploring, Sarah. If it was me, I would have a go.'

'You think so?'

'Yes. As long as you're careful. Where did you meet him?'

'At the last dance in Belfast.'

'Did he try it on?'

'Aunt Belle! That's terrible. Of course not. He's not like that.' The immediate blush in her cheeks told the truth.

'Just be careful, Sarah love. Now, can you fill the kettle and put it on the gas for me?'

Sarah filled the kettle over the deep sink, watching the bubbles rise through the water.

She felt better about Billy. Aunt Belle's encouragement had diluted her doubts.

'Did Billy phone?' she asked as soon as she returned.

Her mother, absorbed in Woman's Own, barely noticed her arrival in the kitchen. 'Yes, I think so. Is Aunt Belle alright?'

'How do you mean you think so? Did he phone, or did he not?'

'Kenneth answered it.'

'You let him answer it? So Billy didn't get my message.' She was furious. God knows what Kenneth would have said.

'I'm more concerned about Aunt Belle. How is she?'

'She's fine. If you were so worried, why didn't you go yourself?'

'Sarah!'

She looked up from her magazine, suddenly realising that her daughter was unusually annoyed, and decided not to pursue the argument.

'Kenneth is in the sitting room. Go and ask him what he said.'

Sarah turned and flounced out of the room.

Kenneth was bent over the piano stool, trying to fix new screws in the loose hinge of the piano stool.

'Damn!' he swore as the screwdriver slipped and pierced his finger. He shook his hand violently and then tried to suck the pain from the injury.

'What did you say to Billy?' she demanded. 'Who?'

He stared blankly at her through his thick glasses.

'Billy!' she repeated angrily, 'You answered the phone. What did you say?'

'Oh, him. I told him you were out.'

'That's all? Just out. You didn't say where I was. You didn't explain. You didn't give him my message?'

'What message?'

'I gave Mum a message to give to him.'

'She didn't say. Anyway, you should have told me.'

Finding the logic of that merely added to her frustration, she left him, hurried up the stairs and sat on her bed, gripping the counterpane in her fists.

Billy would be put off. She was sure of that. He would think that she was trying to avoid him. She wanted to speak to him, but she didn't have his telephone number, she didn't know where he lived, she wasn't sure where he worked in the yard. She really knew very little about him. Yet she wanted to see him again. She wanted to see the silly James Dean look again. She clutched the bed clothes and willed him to call at the office again.

Chapter 7

'It's the fuckin' peelers for you. What the hell have you done this time?'

Spam glared at his father as he returned to the room after answering the staccato knock on the front door. Spam wondered what the police thought of the dishevelled little man with his trousers hanging open at the waist, one strap of his braces off his shoulder and his grubby vest exposing his flab.

'Nothing,' he grunted, pushing past and deliberately nudging him out of the way.

'Aye. Nothing. Always nothing.'

Spam ignored him and left the room, shutting the door firmly behind him. He could see the two policemen in the shadows outside. He hated policemen ever since one of them had gripped him firmly by the arm in front of his friends and taken him to the barracks for a lecture. His twelfth birthday and he had been flinging fireworks at passing cars in the street. The same man, catching him stealing stout from a crate behind a pub the following spring, had slapped his ear so hard that he had wept, and the blow rang in his head for days. He detested them all after that but also feared them. They were big men and knew how to deal with aggression.

He wondered why they had come to the door. Had someone split on him? Did they know he had chained the boy at the dance? Maybe he had died. Christ, he thought, maybe he was dead. Maybe they were going to charge him for murder. He could feel his stomach shrinking with terror, but he had to behave casually. He stopped in front of the mirror in the hall and combed his hair, watching his reflection for signs of panic. His slight frown betrayed worry, so he relaxed his face and smiled as he walked to the door, his hands in his pockets.

'You wanted to see me, gentlemen?' he said jauntily. 'Yes, Patrick. Mr. Mencarelli's cafe.'

He fought to control his relief.

'Great place. Good music. Nice man, old Davey.'

'Mr. Mencarelli says you've been stealing cigarettes.' Spam laughed.

'I don't need to nick fags.'

The faces of the policemen remained impassive. Spam looked down at their holsters and wondered if the revolvers were loaded and whether the men would use them. He had seen the older man occasionally in the street, puzzled by his kind eyes and stern voice. The two did not seem to fit as though the voice belonged to another face. The younger man glared at him from the shadow beneath his peaked hat, his dark eyes cold with distaste. Above his long chin, the thin lips were pursed like an asshole. Beside him, the older man appeared as a figure of amiable benevolence.

'No,' the younger said coldly, 'Then why do you do it, son? Just for kicks?'

'I don't.'

'You won't mind showing us your room then? Just to be sure.'

Spam tried to remember if he had thrown out the empty packets and emptied the ashtray.

'No, come on in. Fire away. I'll show you.'

He led them down the narrow passage into his bedroom and stood aside to let them squeeze past.

'Not much room in here,' the older one remarked, 'John, have a look on the other side of the bed.'

His colleague frowned but crawled across the quilt. Spam suppressed a grin as he watched the dark green buttocks swaying across the squeaking bed until he remembered that he might have left fag ends or empty packets on the floor. He scratched himself nervously, studying the policeman for signs of discovery.

'You a boxing fan then?' the older man asked, nodding towards the posters.

'Aye.'

Spam smiled, relieved to find a hint of humanity. 'In the club?'

'Aye.'

'Do you win?'

'Most times.'

'Must be quite good. You won't need a weapon in a fight then.'

A spasm of panic forced Spam to hold his breath as he remembered his chain in the garage, but he looked the policeman straight in the eye as he spoke.

'Only fight in the ring. Rule of the club– if you get in a fight, you're barred. Unless its self-defence.'

'Good rule, son. Stick to it.'

Spam tried to see through the calm, grey eyes. Did he know about the chain? Did he know about the boy at the dance? Nothing in the man's expression hinted that his remark about the weapon was set to test his response, but he was studying him carefully as he spoke the words. On the other hand, it might have been merely a casual piece of conversation.

Suddenly, the head of the younger officer, who had been searching under the bed, appeared above the covers and tossed an empty cigarette packet on to the creased and grubby sheet. His narrow mouth split in a triumphant grin. He was clearly delighted with his discovery. The three of them stared at the packet.

'Gallahers blue,' the older man sighed patiently, 'Its Senior Service we're looking for, John.'

'Oh, aye. So it is.'

He could not hide his disappointment and continued his search. Spam relaxed, trying not to smile.

'Fan of Joan Collins, then?' the older man asked, nodding towards the poster.

'Aye. Hot stuff, eh?'

Spam noticed the slight frown of disapproval and knew that he had crossed the line of acceptable familiarity.

'Good actress, isn't she?' he continued quickly, trying to repair the damage. The officer did not reply.

'You at the Valentine's dance in Belfast?' he asked instead. Startled by the sudden change in direction, Spam swallowed.

'Aye.'

'Good night?'

'Dead on. Great band, Dave Glover.'

'You'll know about the fight then.'

'I heard about it. A boy in the hospital. Terrible that. I hate chains.'

'A chain was it?'

'So I heard.'

'You'd be in the hall all night?'

'Aye. All night.'

'With Billy?'

'Aye.'

How the fuck does he know about Billy? He thought, *Must have spoken to him. Christ Billy. He's that fuckin' green. God knows what he's said.*

'Billy went out with a girl.'

He tested the man to see if he had spoken to Billy. He did not reply.

'Nothing here,' his colleague announced, standing up and dusting down the knees of his uniform.

'No. He's too careful, is our Patrick. Right then. We'll be off. C'mon John.'

Spam led them along the narrow passage to the front door and stood aside to let them pass. The faint scent of the police cells– Lysol and green soap - floated past, reminding him of the night he had spent in the barracks. An image of the rubber mattress and the spy-hole in the door flashed into his mind.

'Right, Patrick. We're away then. Keep up the club. It's good for young men like yourself,' the older man said, straightening his hat.

'I will. Don't worry. You'll see me in the Ulster Hall yet.'

'Rinty Monaghan the second, eh?'

'I won't sing after the fight, though.'

'Oh?'

'When I sing, the dog whines.'

'As bad as that? Anyway, we'll watch for your name in the papers and hope that it's for boxing. In the meantime, stay away from the cafe, son. Mr. Mencarelli's a good man. I wouldn't want to see anyone taking advantage of him.'

'I wouldn't do that. I like him. He's a nice man.'

'Just a word of warning. Watch your step. We'll be back some other night for a wee blether. See you then.'

The two policemen melted into the gloom. Spam watched their silhouettes fade as they passed the arc of the streetlight. He leaned his shoulder on the door-post and chewed his lower lip. Shaken by the visit, he tried to fathom what they knew about the night of the dance. They knew that he was there and that he was with Billy. And he had made a bad mistake when he mentioned the chain.

'Silly bastard!' he whispered, thumping the door with his fist, 'What a clown!'

Maybe they knew already, though, from the wound. Aye, they could work that out. What it was. Why did your man say that, then? What was it? *A chain was it?* Aye, that's what he said. Why did he say that? He wanted him to think that he had given the game away. That was it. Wanted him to think that they didn't know already. Clever bastard, that old boy. Trying to confuse. Hoping that he would say the wrong thing.

He thought of the boy lying in the hospital, his head swathed in bandages, and his Tony Curtis curl matted with blood.

'Taught him anyway,' he muttered to himself. 'Won't try that again. Who did he think he was? Dancing about on his crepe soles, acting the hard man. I'll kill him the next time.'

He cleared his throat and spat across the garden. He was an expert in spitting. He could aim the gob of phlegm at a flower and hit it dead centre. He took pleasure in the accuracy.

What if the boy died? He frowned. Christ. He could be done for murder. Dismissing the thought, he turned away and walked back to the living room.

'What did they want this time?' his father asked without raising his head from the racing column.

'Nothing. Your man who escaped from the Crumlin. They wanted to know if I'd seen him.'

'You're a fuckin' liar.'

'Will you stop swearing!' his wife shouted. 'You got the car keys?' Spam asked.

'What do you want the car for at this time of night?'

'Where are they?'

'Why do you want the car?'

Spam stepped forward menacingly and snatched the paper out of his hands.

'For heaven's sake, give him the keys,' his mother pleaded, trying to avoid a battle.

'They're in the hall.'

Spam looked down at his father, a smile of triumph creasing his cheeks. His eyes were not smiling, though. They were grim with contempt.

'Back later, Mum,' he announced cheerily as he left the room.

He started the Simca and drove it slowly along the avenue, watching for the police.

Once he reached the high road to Bangor, he pressed the accelerator and felt the car leap forward into the night.

Stopping the car outside Billy's house, he ran up the steps and pressed the bell. He hoped that Billy would answer the door and not his mother. He knew that she disliked him but was far too polite to show it. She had told Billy to stay away from him. A bad influence. He grinned. A bad influence. What an accolade! He enjoyed the thought but hid his smile as the light was switched on in the hall. He could tell by the shape that it was Billy's mother. She was a big lady, unlike his mother, and he was afraid of her. He could not work out why. She had never tried to intimidate or humiliate him, never been antagonistic or forceful, but she had an air of confidence that he found disturbing. He felt that if she was provoked, she could strip him naked with her words, savage him with her mouth like a hound with a fox, and he was ashamed of his fear. He claimed to be afraid of no one and, in a sense, that was true, for, in a fight, he had never felt fear.

He braced himself to face her as she opened the door.

'Good evening, Mrs. Sproule,' he said politely, choosing a greeting which he thought might impress, 'Sorry to trouble you. Is Billy in?'

'Hello, Patrick. It's a bit late, but I think he's in his room. Will you come in?' She left the door open and crossed to the foot of the stairs.

'Billy!' she called, her hand on the carved newel post.

Spam stepped into the hall and waited. The smell of the house was so different from that of his own bungalow. A scent of furniture polish and flowers and cleanliness. There was a spring in the fitted carpet under his shoes.

'Billy!' she shouted again, starting to climb the stairs. There was no response. 'He must be playing his records, Patrick. Hold on a minute.'

She climbed to the next landing and shouted again.

'What is it?' he heard Billy's voice in the distance.

'Patricks here.'

'Just coming.'

She came down slowly. 'Like waking the dead,' She smiled.

'Her face changes when she smiles', Spam said to himself. *'Her eyes light up, and she looks pleased to see me.'* But he did not trust her.

'When he plays his records, he can't hear anything,' she continued, 'Bill Haley night after night. Gets a bit wearing.'

'I bet it does. Can't stand Bill Haley myself,' he lied, 'I'd sooner have Rosemary Clooney.'

'Really? She has a great voice. But I thought you'd prefer something more vigorous.'

'I like Ronnie Carrol too and Michael Holliday.'

He could see from her expression that she suspected he was lying and that she was on the point of challenging him when Billy rushed down the stairs.

'Spam the man!'

'Billy boy!'

'I'm away out, Mum. Back soon.'

Hurrying past her, Billy grabbed his arm and led him towards the door. 'Don't be late, Billy,' she called after him.

'G'night Mrs. Sproule.'

Spam glanced back over his shoulder and was astonished to see her face change again, the smile replaced by an expression of cold distaste, her lips pursed, and her eyes grim. *Jealous,* Spam thought,

Jealous of me! Her wee boy wants to be with me and not with her. Silly cow!

'In the car, Billy. Hurry up.'

They banged the doors shut and sank into the leather seats, Spam whistling in relief. 'Fucks sake!' Spam muttered.

'What? What's wrong?'

'Some lady, your old dear.'

'Why? What did she say?'

'Nothing. She doesn't like me. I can tell. Anyway, that's not what I came to see you about.'

He started the engine and turned on the headlights, lighting the hedge-lined avenue. 'Oh?'

'Have the peelers been round?'

'At my place? No. Why should they?'

'Thank fuck for that anyway. We'll need to get our stories to match.' He slotted the car into gear and drove off towards the town.

'What stories? What are you talking about?'

'The dance, you daft bastard. You were with me at the dance. We never saw those boys, right? When I left that ginger cow, we went back to the hall, you and me.'

'His mates'll swear it was you, though.'

'Their word against ours.'

'And what about the girl? She saw what happened.'

'No. She went back to the hall. She saw nothing. You saw her leave, came down to the car, and we walked back together. Simple.'

He was suspicious of Billy's silence and wondered for a moment if he could count on his loyalty. He turned the car down onto the seafront and cruised along the esplanade, his elbow out of the window.

'Did you get rid of the chain?' Billy asked.

'Christ, aye. It's in the sea.'

He thought of the weapon lying in the tool drawer in the garage. He had squeezed it in the vice and, using a fine file, had sharpened every link at one end. He remembered the way the dark metal glistened in the light. It was safe in the drawer. Unless the peelers came back. He would have to find a better hiding place.

He spotted two girls on the pavement and slowed down.

'Wind down the window, Billy, and ask them if they want a ride.' Billy reluctantly opened the window.

'You ask them. I can't be bothered. They're just schoolgirls anyway.'

'Young enough to bloom, young enough to pluck.'

'You want me to lie for you.' Billy had returned to the story.

'What's wrong with you, Billy? You're a mate, aren't you? That's what mates do. Shut the window a minute.'

He stopped the car, leaned towards Billy and, gripping his shoulder, turned him to face him. He wanted to see his eyes. Surely Billy hadn't a yellow streak. He wouldn't let him down, would he?

He was smiling nervously, but he met his gaze steadily. Spam didn't trust smiles. Yet Billy had always been loyal before. What was wrong this time?

'Are you going to tell them or not?'

'Who?'

'The peelers, for fucks sake!' he shouted,'Who do you think?'

'Aye. Course. Course, I'll tell them.'

Spam relaxed but was not entirely convinced.

'Light us a fag, Billy boy. Anyway, you were there. You were an accomplice.'

'Fucks sake, Spam! I was nowhere near you. I didn't know you had a chain.'

'Calm down, Billy. I was only joking. Get the fags out.'

Joking perhaps, but he had conveyed the warning. He could make life difficult for Billy if he failed to corroborate his story. He did not want to do that, of course. He liked Billy. He was great in a fight, and he could run like a whippet, but apart from that, he felt that Billy respected him and looked up to him even. No one else treated him in that way. Besides, Billy had a great laugh with an infectious giggle. He liked to see him laugh. His eyes lit up, and his cheeks folded. He was really fond of him when he laughed. He felt close to him, warmed by an affection for him that he had to control. He did not want to fancy him. That would be disgusting. He wasn't a queer, nothing like that. He just wanted to be with him, to have him all to himself.

He started the car and waited while Billy shook a cigarette from the packet and passed it to him. He enjoyed the rich taste of American tobacco as he sparked his lighter and lit the end.

He turned and looked through the rear window. 'They've gone.'

'Who?'

'The girls.'

He drove off down the esplanade towards the town clock, noticing that it was ten o'clock. Most of the shops along the front were closed, their dark windows reflecting their headlights as they passed. The streets were almost empty. A man was walking his dog on the pavement next to the sea, a small group of youngsters under the canopy outside the dance hall, and a woman in an overall locking a shop door. Bangor in the winter. Dismal and dull.

Spam accelerated and raced towards the clock where the main street joined the esplanade.

Spinning the car round the corner, he turned right up the main street towards the station.

'Where are we going?' Billy asked.

'Wait and see.'

At the top of the hill, he turned right again past the Widow's pub and down Central Avenue. He parked near the Rediffusion building and switched off the engine. Reaching under the seat, he lifted a small wrecking bar from the floor and slid it down his trouser leg, hooking the curved end over his belt.

'Why here?' Billy asked.

'A wee walk. Come on.'

He swung out of his seat, shut the door and started to walk up the hill in front of the car.

Billy followed.

'Where to?'

'A wee present for you, Billy boy.'

They stopped at the corner shop at the top of the hill where five roads met. During the day, this was a busy junction, but at that moment, it was deserted and silent.

Spam moved into the shadows in the doorway of the shop and listened. Billy moved in beside him, flicking his fag-end into the gutter.

'Pick it up,' Spam ordered urgently.

'Why?'

'Just fuckin' do it!' he whispered. Confused, Billy picked up the wet fag-end.

Spam did not feel nervous before he did a job. Not normally. On this occasion, however, his stomach began to shrink, and he could feel his heart pounding in his chest as it did before a fight. He could see Billy's eyes in the amber streetlights, watching him anxiously.

'You're not going to break in, are you?' Billy whispered, 'These people know me, for fucks sake.'

'Come round here.'

They moved round to the side of the shop where there was a high blank wall. 'Give us a leg up.'

'What if somebody comes?'

'You walk away whistling until they're past. Hurry up for Christ's sake.' Billy leaned his back against the wall and cupped his hands.

Spam leaped up, caught the parapet, hauled himself to the top and crouched, listening for movement. If a car came down the hill, its headlights would illuminate him like a rabbit in a spotlight. He dropped down and, in the dim reflected light, searched for the wooden shed.

McAteer, a delivery boy, had told him about the shed. It was nowhere to be seen. The small yard, enclosed by buildings, was cluttered with empty boxes and bins, but there was no shed.

'Fuckin' McAteer!' he swore and lifted an empty tea chest across so that he could climb the wall again.

Then he saw it. Not a shed but a brick-built lean-to against the shop. He crept over to the door, removing the wrecking bar from his trousers. The lock was forced easily, and there they were. Boxes of cigarettes. Quickly, he lifted two boxes and carried them over to the wall.

'Billy!' he whispered loudly.

'Aye. I'm here.'

'Catch.'

He tossed a box over the wall and heard it land on the ground. The second followed quietly.

Leaping on the tea chest, he scrambled over the wall and dropped to the pavement. 'Fucks sake, Spam. What'll we do with these?'

They heard a car coming over the hill. 'Into the doorway. Quick.'

They dived into the doorway, each with a box, and the car passed.

Spam was delighted. It had gone like a dream, like a commando raid. Silent, efficient.

He felt exhilarated, powerful, intoxicated with success.

'Stay here with the fags,' he commanded, 'If anyone comes, walk round the corner. Don't be seen. I'll get the car.'

He strolled casually back towards the car. The avenue was deserted, but he watched the windows of the terraced houses for the twitch of a curtain or a face against the glass.

The road dipped down and rose again steeply towards the main street. He could see the car in the hollow. He wanted to run and escape quickly from the area, but he controlled the urge and continued to amble along the pavement, his shadow growing and shrinking as he passed under the street lights.

Reaching the car, he drove slowly up the hill, stopped at the shop and wound down the window. Billy emerged furtively from the doorway.

'I thought you were never coming,' he whispered.

'Get the fags in the back and hurry up, for Christ's sake.'

Billy opened the back door and bundled the boxes onto the back seat. 'Don't slam it!' Spam hissed just as Billy was about to fling the door shut. Billy closed it quietly and slipped into the seat, breathing heavily.

Spam drove off, grinning.

'These are for you, Billy boy,' he announced benevolently, 'I smoke yours all the time. You have these.'

'You don't need to.'

'Aye, I do,' he interrupted, 'We're a team, aren't we?'

'Aye.'

'Well then '

Spam drove carefully round in a circle by Maxwell Road. He felt fulfilled, inflated by a sense of well-being. He clenched his left fist and punched Billy hard on the upper arm.

'You and me, Billy, a team. A quare fuckin' team, eh?'

'Yep. Bonnie and Clyde.'

Spam laughed, dismissing the brief memory of their fate. 'Aye, and you're Bonnie, eh?' he giggled.

They laughed together, sharing much more than the joke: companionship, affection, triumph.

Spam thought of his brother, his round, fat face and developing a double chin, his hairy belly hanging over his belt and his thin, weak legs. How he despised him. He couldn't have done the job.

'Fat bastard!' he growled.

'What?' Billy replied, alarmed by the venom in his voice. 'Not you, silly cunt. Not you.'

Chapter 8

I rang the bell nervously, hoping that Sarah would answer and that I would not have to speak to her mother or, worse still, her brother.

It was a relief to see Sarah's shape through the glass. 'Come in, Billy.'

She had a way of opening the door that made her seem shy and timid, standing behind it and peeping around the edge like a child.

'Is it okay?'

'Course it is. Come in.'

I stepped past her into the hall. 'Come and meet my Mum.'

I frowned, feigning terror, although I was merely apprehensive.

'Come on,' she said, closing the door and leading me by the hand towards the kitchen.

She let go, though, as we descended the four steps to the back of the house.

'Mum, this is Billy,' she announced gaily.

Her mother, bent over a slab of pastry on the table, was clearly displeased, flicking a quick glance of annoyance in Sarah's direction. She slammed down the slab and wiped her hands on her apron.

'Hello, Mrs Curran,' I said cheerily, crossing the room and holding out my hand.

She did not smile, and behind her spectacles, her small eyes peered at me suspiciously. She did not offer her hand in return but shook her head and held both hands up in front of her, palms facing me, indicating that they were covered in flour, but also, I felt, as a gesture of rejection, as if she was pushing me away. I was not used to such hostility and was thrown by her response.

'So you're Billy,' she said.

'Yes.' I smiled amiably, trying to dilute the antagonism, and dropped my hand.

'And you work in the yard.'

'I do.'

'An electrician,' Sarah said. 'An apprentice.'

'Bit of a come-down after Campbell College.'

'I really wanted to go to sea– the Royal Navy– but I failed the eye test. The shipyard was the next best thing.'

'You won't see the world from Queen's Island.'

'No, I suppose not.'

The conversation sagged into silence.

She did not invite me to sit or offer to make tea but turned away, lifted a rolling pin, smoothed it with flour and started to roll the pastry. I watched the roller squeeze the buff pastry into shape, pressing a ripple of dough ahead of it as it flattened the slab across the table. My mother did not bake. The maid occasionally made scones or syrup sponge for pudding, but cakes and pies were bought in, so I was fascinated by Mrs Curran's expertise. The muscles in her arms slithered under the skin as she rolled out the pastry into a flat circle. I could not help feeling that she was rolling me out of the house.

It is said that if you want to know what a girl will look like in middle age, study her mother, but I could see little resemblance between Sarah and the squat housewife at the table.

Sarah was slim and slight with soft fair hair over a wedge-shaped face; her mother was small and sturdy with a crop of thick yellow hair and a round, folded face like a half-blown bladder. Her amber spectacles sat askew on her nose as if one ear was lower than the other. I could not imagine Sarah looking like her at any time.

'Are you baking a cake?' I asked to break the silence.

'This is pastry. For a pie. Does your mother not bake, then?'

'No, I don't think so. Baking all comes from the shops.'

'More money than sense.'

'True enough.'

In the long pause, I looked around the kitchen. It was very different from ours, larger, more like a place of work. A range, set in the chimney space, took up most of the back wall. Its handles and hinges, polished scrupulously, gleamed like silver in the light, and a copper boiler on top, burnished to perfection, reflected the scene in the room. An immense pine dresser filled the second wall, its top shelves decorated with willow-pattern salvers and plates, assorted jugs, three Coronation mugs beside a miniature Coronation coach with horses and several copper jelly moulds. Beneath the shelves on the wide top, three items, evenly spaced, were carefully placed to form a line– a white enamel bread-bin, an art deco chiming clock and a wireless. Everything had its place, and everything was scrubbed, polished, dusted or wiped. There was something disturbing about the strict order and cleanliness as if, should one part of it be moved or marred or broken, her part of the universe would spin out of control. Yet, when I compared it all to the chaos of Heartbreak House, her efficiency had to be admired.

'Are you two not going out?' she grunted over the roller.

'Yes, Mum. I just wanted you to meet Billy.'

'Well, I've met him.'

'Okay, okay. We can take a hint. Come one, Billy. Let's go.'

'I'm sorry,' her mother said, regretting perhaps her hostile approach, 'I should have offered you tea, but I'm trying to get the baking done for the church. It was rude of me.'

It was a remarkable transformation, quite bizarre, really. The antagonism was suddenly replaced by what appeared to be genuine friendliness.

'Perfectly okay, Mrs Curran. Don't worry. I shouldn't have interrupted,' I said.

'Nice to meet you, Billy. Don't be too late, Sarah.'

As we left the room, her face resumed its original stern expression, frowning at her pancake of pastry. It was confusing. I was not sure how to deal with her.

'I don't think she likes me,' I said to Sarah as we walked down the path towards the road. 'She's always like that at first. Don't worry about it.'

She took my hand and squeezed my fingers reassuringly.

'She's like that with all our friends at the beginning. I think she's shy and covers it up with that gruff way of talking. I should have warned you.'

'No, no. It's okay. Doesn't matter.'

We turned right at the gate, crossed the road and walked down the avenue towards the bay. Above the shore, there was a wide public park with a shelter, an isolated wooden building consisting of four porches facing in four different directions, north, south, east and west, so that you could always escape from the wind. Well-used in the summer, it was usually deserted in the winter, particularly at night. Each porch had a bench along the back wall, ideal for courting couples. The green paint on the benches was scarred with the initials of lovers who had recorded their bond for posterity, some of the letters already indistinguishable with age.

I steered Sarah towards the shelter. She did not object nor ask where we were going.

She seemed to know.

There was no wind that night, and it was not as cold as the evening of the dance. We could hear the sea rippling quietly along the tide edge behind us. We sat on the lea-side of the shelter facing the road. It was not completely dark, for the moon, almost invisible behind the low clouds, lit the park with a spectral glimmer, and the distant street lights shone on the houses along the esplanade.

We talked about films we had seen, and I wondered why she had become so emotional in her description of *The Red Shoes* when she had seen it so many years ago. The slight tremor in her voice and the sadness in her eyes suggested that there was more to the memory than the film itself. I felt an intense tenderness for her, an overwhelming urge to protect her from harm, a sensation so extreme that I gasped. It burned, it flowed through me like an irresistible current, flooding every vein, swelling the tissues till I felt myself drowning in a deluge of compassion. I wanted to grow, to expand so that I could envelop her, wrap her in an impregnable mantle, possess her. Yes, there was that. Mingled with the tenderness, the will to be the sole protector, the desire to claim her for myself. Yet there was a strange sorrow, too, a sense of loss as if I knew that the moment was ephemeral, the great surge of emotion transitory.

My first experience of love, I suppose. When I kissed her, I tried to express what I felt, touching her cheek gently with my fingertips and caressing her lips with mine. I remember the soft down around her jaw and the taste of her mouth. In spite of the passion, there was an urge to slip my hand over her breast or slide my fingers over her thigh. Such a step, I felt, would mar the perfection of that moment, sully its purity. Perhaps I was right. That surge of selfless compassion never returned. I tried to revive it, to recapture its brilliance, but its essence always eluded me. It vanished as quickly as it came that last remnant of innocence supplanted by the tempestuous torrents of desire.

'Will I see you tomorrow?' I asked as I left her at her gate.

The soft quiff of hair glistened under the streetlights, hiding one of her eyes in shadow. She glanced back towards the house to make sure, perhaps, that her mother was not watching.

'If you want to.'

'Course I want to.'

'Not at work, though. Don't come to the office. Meet me at the station after work.'

'In Belfast?'

'Yes. I'll wait at the ticket office.'

I pulled her towards me but she placed a finger on my lips and shook her head. 'See you tomorrow,' she said coyly and walked away.

I watched her till she turned at the steps, where she stopped and waved, a small figure in the gloom beside the house.

I stood for a while at the gate after she disappeared, so delighted with the result of the evening that I grinned. I was almost certain that Sarah would see me as her boyfriend and that we would become a couple. I enjoyed the prospect of being seen in that way.

I walked back through the empty streets with a new sense of maturity, glancing at my reflection in the shop windows to see if it showed. I was pleased to see a lithe figure in a leather jacket striding athletically past with a cigarette in his mouth. Definitely a young man and not a boy, the kind of man that others would not challenge readily, the kind of man who would fell anyone who touched his girl– the Marlon Brando of Bangor.

I walked down the main street towards the clock, along the seafront and past Pickie Pool, thinking of the summer when tanned bodies, glistening with olive oil, would swagger out of the changing rooms into the sunlight. I remembered the sweet smell of the oil and the shrieks of the children as they plunged into the freezing water. It was always cold. The pool was filled with salt water and jutted out into the sea. I wondered if Sarah could swim. I knew that she sailed but there was something about her physique that suggested she might not be keen on sport.

Perhaps I wouldn't be able to parade her in the pool in the summer. Still, she could dance, and her balance on the floor was superb.

As I reached Heartbreak House, I saw a bicycle leaning against the hedge. I stopped, suddenly alarmed. It was a peeler's bike. No doubt. A heavy frame and a large lamp. I turned quickly and retreated back down the avenue so that I could watch the gate without being seen.

'Jesus Christ!' I muttered breathlessly, crouching behind a hedge.

It couldn't be! How could they know I was there? No one had seen me at the shop. I was sure of that. The car. Maybe someone saw the car. But they couldn't connect me with the car. Spam, yes, but not me. Unless Spam split on me. No, he wouldn't do that. The dance!

Maybe it was the dance. But they didn't know me, those guys. They might have found out about Spam– he had a reputation– but not me. They wouldn't know me.

What would Sarah think now? The police at my door, maybe a charge. What a fuckin' mess!

Chapter 9

'Stupid fuckin' bastard!' Spam swore at himself.

He had nothing. No chain, no knife, no duster, no bottle. Nothing. He glanced round the close. Sodden cardboard boxes, limp newspapers, flattened fag packets, nothing solid, nothing for a weapon. He had dodged into the yard to avoid them, thinking it was a lane, but it was a cul-de-sac, and now the three men stood at the entrance, waiting. He looked down at the ground, hoping to find a stone, but the cobbles fitted too neatly together to prise out a missile. There were no doors in the high brick walls and no means of escape. They started to walk towards him, their crepe soles silent on the cobbles. He tightened his fists and shifted his weight onto the balls of his feet, ready to spring. It was dark, and against the dim light from the street, he couldn't see their faces, just three silhouettes approaching menacingly.

He wondered what weapons they were carrying. They would have something. They would come prepared. He wished Billy was with him. Three to two, that would be okay. He was glad that he didn't wear crepe soles. They were no good in a fight. Stout shoes. He always wore stout shoes. His mother liked that. 'Smart,' she said and always shone them for him. He thought of her in her kitchen, making tea.

He was not afraid but he felt his stomach shrinking and his heart racing. Nerves, just nerves, thinking of the pain ahead. Not fear.

As they approached, he heard a click and saw the silver flicker of a blade. The middle one had a knife, then. The one on the right had a bar. Left-handed, Spam noticed. He could just see their faces but not their eyes. That was a pity. He could tell a lot from their eyes. The one on the left seemed to hesitate. The weakest link.

Spam smiled.

'Well, boys,' he said and instantly flew at the middle man, springing off his feet and kicking him hard in the crotch. He felt the kick landing in the right place, heard a gasp and a moan and saw him double over. He landed skillfully on his feet and swung round to face the bar, which landed on his forearm. A flash of pain shot across his eyes, and he knew that his arm was useless. He could not feel his fist. There was another blow coming. He saw the bar raised and lifted the crushed arm to defend his face, lashing out with his foot towards the shins. He missed, but the bar crashed against his ribs. He winced and felt sick, but, with his good hand, he caught the bar, wrenched it away from his attacker, and swung it at the head of the crouched knifeman. He felt it crunch against his skull and saw him drop to the ground, the knife spinning across the cobbles. One down, he thought.

Spinning round, he swung the bar at the head of the one who carried it, and, for a moment, he saw his face in the dim light. A mate of the boy he had chained. He knew then why they were there. The bar hit him low on the ribs. Spam heard him grunt and bend over, clutching his side.

Flinging the weapon aside, he leapt across the yard and snatched up the knife. The third man fled past him towards the street.

Breathless and aching, Spam pounced on the bent figure, knocked him to the ground and knelt on his arms.

'Next time, I'll kill you,' he whispered.

Holding the knife as if he were about to stab him, he ran the blade down the boy's cheek. The skin opened in a red streak. Spam enjoyed the sensation. It gave him a feeling of power as blood trickled into the dark sideburn. The terror in his eyes enhanced the pleasure.

'No, next time!' the boy begged, 'Promise. No next time. Fucks sake. No more.' Spam pressed the point of the knife into his throat.

'You lie there till I reach the street. Right? One move, and I'll come back and cut your throat.'

'Okay, okay.'

Spam rose slowly, pointing the knife steadily at his victim. He stood over him, kicked him hard in the place where the bar had landed and hurried away. The pain in his arm was excruciating, and his ribs seemed to crack as he breathed. He held his arm against his chest, trying to keep it still as he walked. The bone was broken; he knew that. He couldn't move his fingers. He would have to leave the car and get a bus home.

He walked past the City Hall and down Chicester Steet towards the river, wondering if the boy with the knife would recover. He had lain very still, his mouth open and his face in a puddle. Still, he deserved it, the bastard. He wouldn't tackle him again. In spite of the pain, he felt elated. Three to one. He had taken them on and smashed them. They would not try that again. Not on him anyway. Too good for them. The bastards. Too good for them all. Let them all come. He would take them on. Any of them. He was good. Fast and deadly, like a panther, like an Apache. He started to walk like an Indian, pacing lightly on his feet as if he wore moccasins, as if he was in the forest, leaving no trail, flitting silently through the trees, A warrior, a leader of the tribe.

'What happened?'

Billy was visibly upset when he showed him the plaster. 'Four of them. Set on me in a close in Belfast.'

'For nothing? Just set on you. In broad daylight?'

'No, no. Monday night. In a close. Mates of the bastard I chained. Followed me up Anne Street. Knives and a steel bar.'

'Jesus! You could have been killed.'

'Other way round, Billy boy. I beat the whole fuckin' lot of them.'

'You didn't! Four of them. How?'

Billy's astonishment and admiration gave him limitless satisfaction.

'Yanked the bar off them and laid them out. One after the other. You should have seen me, Billy. One, two, three, four. Flat out.'

'And your arm? What happened to your arm?'

'Caught the first whack. Fought them with one hand.'

'Jesus. You're a hard man, Spam.'

He didn't tell him about the boy who lay supine on the cobbles. Billy was squeamish. He saw it in his face at the dance. One was enough. He knew that Billy watched the papers for reports from the hospital.

'Is it sore?'

'Not now. Fuckin' agony at the time. Anyway, come to the car. I've a plan.'

'Can you drive?'

'Aye, aye. C'mon.'

They were outside Billy's house, and he could see Billy's mother in the front room.

Fortunately, she hadn't answered when he rang the doorbell. He hadn't been forced to make up another story.

'Light us a fag, Billy boy,' he ordered as they settled into the seats.

No argument this time. Billy slipped a new packet of Capstan out of pocket and lit two fags with his lighter.

'Stolen goods, eh?' Spam asked, nodding towards the packet. 'Aye.'

'I thought they were American.'

'No. Capstan.'

'Sorry about that. Do better next time.'

They laughed together in the gloom, the two red ends of the fags glowing enthusiastically.

'Anyway,' Spam continued, 'This war in Suez.'

'We going to join up?'

'We're not fuckin' eejits. Listen, there's going to be rationing, petrol rationing. I'll bet you a fiver they'll ration it. If they do, we get rubber tubes and petrol cans, and we go round the cars at night, siphon off petrol and sell it on the black market. A fortune, Billy. A fuckin' fortune.'

'Sounds great.'

He could sense that Billy had reservations and waited for the questions. 'If we get caught?'

'We won't get caught. I can sell it at the showroom. No trouble. Offer to fill the tank for a few quid. A nod and a wink. No trouble.'

'You're some man. Never miss a trick, eh?'

'Keep your eye on the main chance, Billy Boy. That's how you get places. Are you game?'

'Aye. Course.'

Spam could still sense a slight reluctance, a lack of enthusiasm, but put it down to Billy's entanglement with Sarah. He reckoned that it wouldn't last. Sarah was far too conventional for Billy, far too quiet and unexciting. Still, he did not want to interfere. In fact, he decided to encourage the affair. If it made Billy happy, that was a good thing.

'You want a run over to Sarah's?' he asked.

'I don't know. I was supposed to take her to the pictures and I can't.'

'Why not?'

'I'm skint. Nothing till pay-day. Even then, I owe my old dear most of it.'

Spam reached into his inside pocket, slipped out his wallet and handed Billy a ten-shilling note.

'No, Spam. I can't take that.'

'Don't be such a fuckin' eejit. Take it. I've plenty. Take her to the pictures.'

He replaced the wallet and started the car. He could see that Billy was delighted and that pleased him, made him feel warm and generous.

'I'd better tell the old dear where I'm going.'

'Fuck the old dear! Well, not literally!'

He drove round to Sarah's and stopped at the gate.

'Go on! Go in and get her, and I'll drive you to the Tonic.' Billy opened the door and hurried towards the house.

Spam gazed at the building. Ten times bigger than his bungalow. One day, he thought, I'll have a place like that– bigger even, with a garden and a garage and apple trees and a huge bedroom with a fitted carpet; one day I'll be somebody, a big shot, with a Jaguar and a bank account in Jersey; move away from this fuckin' hole, away to London or New York. He saw himself in flash suits with loud ties and shoes that shone in the sunlight, ordering a table in a top restaurant, showing off his elegant lady-friend to the whole room; every male in the room would steal an envious glance in his direction. One day, he promised himself. He reached for his cigarettes and lit one as Billy and Sarah hurried down the steps.

Spam watched them walking up the path and noticed that her figure was better than he remembered. Quite a neat wee woman, in fact. Perhaps Billy had done better than he thought. He wound down the window and leaned his elbow casually on the sill.

'Hi, Sarah,' he said cheerily, 'How are you?'

'Very well, thanks. Good of you to give us a lift.'

'No trouble, Sarah. In you get.'

Thin lips, he thought, not his type. He liked big, soft lips that fitted over his like inner tubes, thick, voluptuous lips that threatened to suffocate him, lips like Marilyn Monroe's.

Billy and Sarah sat in the back and Spam drove sedately to the cinema, determined to create a good impression.

'Enjoy yourselves,' he called magnanimously as they left the car. 'She hasn't even nice legs,' he said to himself.

Still, she was a female, and he would have groped her happily in the back seat had he been given a chance. He sat in the car park for a while, imagining what it would be like to have sex with her. She was not the kind to get carried away, thrashing and groaning in ecstasy. She would lie there passively and let you do it. Not much fun in that. On the other hand, maybe that was the challenge– to handle her slowly and patiently till she finally gave way and let her passion rip. He became aroused just thinking about it, imagining himself bringing Sarah to a wild climax, and it was pure imagination, for he had sex only once, and that was with a girl known as 'The Tricycle', the local tart renowned for her generosity. It had been a disappointing and unsatisfactory experience that made him feel grubby after the event. He drove off before the temptation to masturbate became irresistible. He did not want to wet his flannels, and Sarah, after all, was Billy's girl. Besides, he had promised himself to refrain because he had read that it weakened you, and he needed his strength for the ring.

He left the cinema and drove towards Donaghadee on the high road. Pleased with himself for helping Billy, he did not hurry but allowed the Simca to cruise through the night in top gear, casually planning how to siphon and sell petrol. The car parks at dances would be an ideal place, dark, often deserted till late in the evening. You would have to watch for courting couples, though, and choose the bigger cars. He saw himself getting rich, escaping from home and living luxuriously in a spacious house with a large garden and a private beach, a house like Sinton's. Sinton had made a fortune in the carpet trade and lived on the shore road, a millionaire, some said. Spam remembered his speedboat, the sleek mahogany hull, gleaming chrome deck fittings and powerful engines and the way it glided over the waves like a seaplane. Its bow sliced through the sea, opening it out like a blade and leaving a twisting, boiling ribbon of white water astern. He remembered the wind in his face and the thrust of the engines, tilting him backwards as they gripped the sea. One day, he promised himself he would have a speedboat and a white cruiser in Cannes.

Sinton's daughter, Stephanie. She had invited him for a trip in the boat. A short, pneumatic girl with heavy breasts and lips like doughnuts, she had shown an interest in him after he had seen him climbing the lighthouse on the pier. He had been flattered by the attention. An heiress, a toff, a girl from a level normally out of reach for the likes of him. She was attractive, too. Plump but agile and effervescent. He remembered her long brown hair blowing in the wind and her brown eyes shining with excitement as she swerved the boat around the bay. He had been sure that he would get off with her, but when he tried to slide his hand up her jersey, she had pushed him away aggressively. Kissing was fine. She didn't seem to mind that, and he enjoyed the feeling of her thick lips against his and the expensive scent of her perfume, but he wanted more than that and saw little point in long embraces that led no further. Perhaps he should have persevered. Perhaps she would have surrendered in the end. After all, she was rich. Marry her, and you will never need to work again.

'Slipped up there, Spam boy,' he muttered aloud, 'All that money and those big tits. You could have had your lips round the nipples and your prick in her fanny.'

He imagined her strong thighs gripping his and her mouth open in ecstasy as he played her like a violin.

Suddenly, the vision snapped shut. As the car came over the crest of a hill, its headlights shone on a bicycle lying halfway across the road. His right foot shot to the brake, and he swerved to the other side. There was a figure on the verge, sitting with its head in its hands. Spam stopped the car, the lights still shining on the scene and hauled on the handbrake. Leaving the engine running, he opened the door and knelt by the figure. Blood was streaming through the fingers, hiding his face.

'You okay?'

'Aye. Fine.'

'You're not. Let's see.'

Spam pulled the fingers away to reveal a gash where the tarmac had torn the flesh from his skull.

'Jesus! You'll need to see a doctor.'

Just a boy, younger than Billy. He had seen him before but couldn't remember where. A long, thin face with eyes that shrank back into the skull like hermit crabs, fearful, watching for a blow. Spam was sorry for him.

'C'mon. I'll take you back to Bangor.'

'No. Be okay.'

'Will you fuck? C'mon.'

Spam hoisted him to his feet, astonished to find him lighter than a child, and helped him towards the car.

'My bike, mister,' the boy muttered.

'I'll get the bike. Tie it on the boot. Don't worry.'

Spam noticed that the knee of the boy's trouser leg was shredded, and there was blood around the tear. His clothes smelt of fried lard and stale sweat as if the flesh inside them was rancid and decaying. Spam tried to remember where he had encountered the nauseous odour before. There was something familiar about it, something that hovered on the edge of his memory.

'In you get,' he said, opening the passenger door.

The boy slumped into the seat, again holding his head.

Spam opened the boot, tied the twisted bike across the door with his tow rope and hurried round to the driver's seat.

'What happened, anyway?' he asked, turning the car and heading back to Bangor. 'The bus. The double-decker. Knocked me off.'

'Bastard. And he didn't stop.'

'Don't know if he knew.'

'Course he fuckin' knew.'

The heat of the car intensified the smell of the boy's clothes, and Spam searched for his cigarettes, hoping the taste would overwhelm it.

'You want a fag?'

The boy shook his head.

Spam lit one, drawing as much smoke down his throat as he could. The end of the cigarette sputtered and sparked like a firework. The harsh taste brought relief and he exhaled the smoke down his nose. He pressed the accelerator and watched the needle hit sixty. The verges flew past as he aimed the bonnet down the tunnel lit by the headlights. He felt like an ambulance driver on an emergency call, a good citizen performing his duty. The casualty in his hands, depending on his skills at the wheel. The siren clearing the traffic, cars swerving out of his path. A hero hurrying through the night to save a life.

The boy coughed suddenly and did not seem able to stop, his shoulders heaving as he gasped for breath between each spasm.

Spam slowed the car.

'Are you okay?'

The boy nodded vigorously as the fit subsided, his head almost between his knees.

Spam stared at him anxiously, wondering if he had internal injuries. He did not want him to die in the car. How would he explain that? A corpse in the car and badly hurt, too. What would the peelers say? Christ, it could mean real trouble. He would have to dump the body and fling the bike into the sea. Perhaps he should get rid of the boy anyway. Perhaps he was making trouble for himself as it was. Yet the boy needed help and might even need a transfusion. He accelerated again, hurrying towards the glow of the town lights.

He drove past the Tonic and round to the hospital.

'I'll take you to the door and leave your bike outside. After that, you're on your own. Okay?'

'Aye. Thanks, mister.'

Spam helped him out of the car and left him at the main door. 'Thanks, mister. God bless you.'

Spam, slightly disturbed by the blessing, returned to the car, untied the bike and left it against the wall. Not often folk blessed you. What kind of creep was he? A Mormon or something? Maybe in the Sally Army. Where had he seen him before? It annoyed him intensely, his failure to remember. He was good with faces. And that smell. He knew that smell.

He shut the boot and drove away.

'I know who it was!' Billy announced after hearing the description.

'Who?'

'Yer man from the caravans. He came to the dodgems. The caravans out past the putting green. Remember. You flattened him outside the amusement place.'

'Jesus Christ! Him! Fucks sake. You're right, Billy Boy. No fuckin' wonder he smelled.'

'He did take a swing at you.'

'So he did! The bastard. And came in close. I remember. And the smell. I remember the smell. Stinkin' bastard.'

'I think he went to hospital.'

'I didn't hurt him that bad.'

'Not that kind of hospital. The sanitorium.'

'What?'

Alarmed, Spam swung around and caught Billy's sleeve.

'He had TB. So they say. Anyway, he was there with Sailor. Sailor blamed him for spreading it. Tried to get him in the hospital, but the guy ran away.'

Spam was horrified. That cough. And he had held him close. He imagined the germs crawling from the boy's clothes to his own, wriggling like red worms, slithering up his chest and into his mouth, fixing themselves in his lungs, their fangs gripping the soft tissue. He saw himself coughing up blood, dying in his bed, the white pillowcase stained scarlet.

'Jesus, Billy. I helped him into the car. I was really close to him. Do you think I could get it off him? He was coughing in the car. A real fit. Do you think he still has it? He was awful white and thin.'

'No, no. Don't worry. You can't catch it as easily as that.'

But Spam caught a hint of worry in Billy's voice, a reassurance that was not quite genuine.

'Fucks sake Billy. What'll I do?'

Fear caught in his throat and made him swallow. The germs might be in his chest already, eating away at his lungs.

'Get an X-ray if you're worried, but there's no need.'

'I had an X-ray. When the vans came around. Jesus, do you remember Big Trevor? They took him away. Great big guy and fit, too. Played for the seconds. What a lock he was. Who would have guessed he had it? It must have been a year away. Christ, Billy. I don't fancy that. A year in a fuckin' sanitorium. A year out of my life.'

'Calm down, for fucks sake. You won't get it. Much more likely to get clap or syphilis.' 'Fuck off!'

Relieved to escape from the gloomy track of thought, he punched Billy on the arm and laughed.

Chapter 10

The Adelphi cinema was on the promenade near the town clock, always regarded as inferior to the Tonic. The Tonic was grander, set in isolation back from the road with an imposing Deco façade and a large red illuminated sign. The Adelphi was more modest, crushed between other buildings with its swing doors opening onto the street. On the edge of being shabby inside, its projectors failed occasionally and, during intervals, its staff came round with hand sprays, squirting DDT into the smoky atmosphere to kill parasites. Not the place to take a girl on a first date.

That night, however, there was a queue of teenagers waiting for the doors to open. Sarah was not happy. There had been trouble in Belfast when the film was shown, and the crowd of youngsters outside the Adelphi was already unusually excited.

'Let's go back,' she said, 'I don't want to go.'

'It'll be great. Don't worry. It's a brilliant film. We can't miss it.'

I could see that she was apprehensive. She had a way of pursing her lips and frowning when she was doubtful.

'Look. Let's go in and, if you don't like it, we'll leave. Okay?' She hesitated.

'You promise?'

'I promise.'

I put my arm around her and joined the queue. My girl. She was wearing a half-length navy woolen coat with a high collar, slightly incongruous among the skin-tight sweaters and cardigans of the other girls. But, in many ways, she was strangely old-fashioned, a quality that I admired. She had her own values which, at that time, she refused to dilute.

Blackboard Jungle. Bill Haley and the Comets. *Rock Around the Clock* stunned the crowd into silence. Not many film scores had that effect in the first few minutes. The crack of the snare drum and the thud of the heavy bass blasted out of the darkness, sparking a conflagration in the senses like a match in petrol, exciting, visceral, rebellious, liberating, unlike the bland crooning in Top Twenty. It finished too quickly, the opening music, and the film at first seemed to be a bit tame after the strident start, and some of the boys in the front seats started to make loud wisecracks about Anne Francis, Glenn Ford's insipid wife. The usherettes had to hurry down the aisles, the beams of their torches searching fruitlessly for the ringleaders. Sporadic cries of 'Get them off, Mrs!' and 'Get stuck into her, Glenn boy!' continued, but gradually the interruptions subsided.

We were in the back row under the flickering beam from the projector. Rising smoke curled into the beam from the seats below. I put my arm around Sarah, and she lifted her face towards me for a kiss. That was always her most enthusiastic gesture, other movements hinted at mere acquiescence, submission almost. She allowed me to explore her breasts beneath her coat but pushed my hand away if I tried to slip it under her sweater to touch her skin. I had to be content with the feeling of hard bra fabric under her clothes. I did not mind. It was enough to work myself into a passion through the long, masticating kisses.

A dark, wet slum alley in an American inner city with one dim streetlight reflected in the puddles. Glenn Ford, the teacher, took a shortcut home after school. You knew what was coming. A group of delinquents from his class leapt from the shadows and set upon him silently, punching, kicking and leaving him lying in the gutter. Ford, or Mr Dadier, had dared to intervene when one of the boys tried to rape a new teacher. The assault was his punishment for interfering.

There was silence during the scene. Every face around us was fixed on the screen, the boys mesmerized by the violence. Each of us, I'm sure, thought of teachers who had humiliated us and who might have benefited from such a lesson. Yet Ford had not deserved it. That was the dilemma. Part of you punched and kicked with the boys, expressing the rage and resentment left from school, and part of you sympathized with Ford, who was only trying to do his best.

'Horrible,' Sarah said, turning away as the blows landed, 'I hate fights.'

'So do I.'

Time for a fag break. I removed my arm from her shoulder, shook out a cigarette and offered her one, knowing that she would refuse. She smoked very rarely, and when she did, she held the cigarette awkwardly with the tip of her fingers and did not inhale as if the whole ritual was distasteful, slightly slovenly even. I lit up and blew the smoke towards the beam of light above us.

Youth violence on the screen was not a novelty to us. Spam and I had seen a British film called *Cosh Boy* but James Kenney was such an unpleasant and cowardly character neither of us could identify with him. Coshing old ladies or prostitutes was outside our code, and although Spam's scruples were to slip beyond my comprehension later, he still had limits at that time.

When Kenney organized a raid on the takings of the Palindrome, Spam watched the boys' planning intently, concluding that they had no idea how to organize a robbery. Kenney was useless. He despised him, particularly at the end when he submitted to a thrashing from his stepfather. God help Spam's Dad if he tried that. Spam had no inhibitions. He would have used any weapon on his 'old man'. *Cosh Boy* had little effect on us other than inspiring Spam to make a cosh.

Blackboard Jungle was different. The young guys were slicker, more successful as criminals, able to survive in a lawless underworld. When one of them drew a knife on Glenn Ford in the classroom and slashed his arm, Ford, an army veteran, retaliated. As they circled each other, Ford, shielding himself with his wounded arm, forced the boy into a corner, disarmed him and beat his head against the wall. The tension in that scene was extreme, with Ford crouched like a panther, challenging, provoking, and smiling confidently while the boy, his blade glittering and pointed with blood, searched for the right moment to attack. Once again, you were torn between wanting Ford to win and, on the other hand, taking the side of the youth. Ford was a teacher, one of the men in white hats, one of the good guys. The boy was an Apache, a brave of the city jungle, living by its rules.

Two loyalties, two forces, stretching you apart, the bow and the bowstring quivering with tension. With the first beat of the rock music at the end it exploded.

The boys in the front rows leaped to their feet, hauling their girls into the space in front of the seats, jiving to the irresistible rhythm, their curls bobbing, their feet stamping.

One o'clock, two o'clock, three o'clock rock

The usherettes left their posts at the back and tried to reach the dancers, but soon, every aisle was full of couples swinging, swirling, pirouetting, stomping with an energy and abandon that nothing would stop. Couples in the middle of the rows were standing on their seats, swaying, clapping, driven by an inexorable force. The whole crowd erupted, bouncing in time to the hypnotic beat, bewitched by the rhythm, in thrall to the drum. A wild primeval celebration. Walpurgisnacht. A revel with the Devil. I could feel it. The force. The feeling of release, of abandon. Like swimming naked. Like breaking windows. The tearing of the veil. And we were all together. Our night. And no fuckin' adult was going to stop us.

Even Sarah was infected. I took her hand and led her into the aisle. We had just started to dance when the house lights were switched on, and the music stopped.

It was a mistake. The manager, in trying to stop the dancing by cutting short the credit titles, provoked a reaction that he did not anticipate– a savage anger. Two boys leaped onto the stage and ripped down the curtains; others jumped hard on the seats and broke the hinges; others slashed the seat covers, raising clouds of dust. The usherettes fled, leaving the manager to deal with the chaos he had created.

'Come on,' Sarah shouted to me above the noise, 'Let's go.'

I led her out past the manager, who was instructing the girl in the ticket office to phone the police.

I was sorry for him in a way. His voice trembled as he spoke, and his face was pale. A little, portly man in a black suit with a thin, twitching moustache and a shining bald head as smooth as his worn suit. He was clearly bewildered and shaken.

Sarah was very subdued as we walked home.

'Crowd of hooligans,' she said as the black police car drove past. 'Suppose so. They shouldn't have cut it short, though. That was stupid.'

'No excuse.'

'Aye. You're right.'

I slipped my arm around her and pulled her against me. I did not want her to think that I was on the side of the boys she was criticizing, but I was. Had she not been there, I would have joined them. I knew how they felt, furious with the adults who dared to interfere. Dried-up old sods were spoiling the fun.

I could still hear it– *One, two, three o'clock, four o'clock rock.*

I had to get hold of the record.

It was still light as we walked along the promenade. A warm summer evening with a purple sky. Out in the bay, the lights of an anchored aircraft carrier glittered on the calm water. Her arm was round my waist. It was the first time she had sent a signal of that kind, a symbol of togetherness. It made me feel a sudden tenderness for her, dispelling the lingering resentment from the cinema and the attachment to the rioters. I glanced at her, admiring her blue eyes and the wisp of hair over her brow. I squeezed her waist and she looked at me, holding my eyes, searching behind them as if she had lost something, as if she was trying to reach someone else inside me. A strange and uncomfortable sensation and yet one that drew me towards her irresistibly. I leaned over and kissed her brow, knowing that a kiss on the lips in the street would upset her.

For the first time I was intensely aware of her as a person rather than an accessory, an extension of myself, a territory to be occupied. She was something astonishing, another being with thoughts of her own, mysteries, and memories beyond my reach. I wanted to enfold her, to crush her against me till we merged, to be part of her. It was not an erotic sensation. It transcended the lust for her body, which had driven me till then. Almost a form of worship. It did not last long.

At that moment, the Simca drew up beside us, its engine still running, and Spam opened the door.

'Young love, eh?'

Sarah glared at him.

'It's Spam, the man!' I greeted him.

He stepped out of the car and leaned on the roof.

'Billy boy! Friday night. Dance in Donaghadee. Got all the gear. Are you on, Billy boy?'

Siphoning petrol. That's what he meant. I wanted to get out of the job. The taste of petrol lingered in your mouth for days, spoiling the taste of everything you ate or drank. You couldn't avoid it, though. The only way to get the siphon working was to suck the petrol through the tube. Besides, there was a high risk of being caught. Yet he was my mate, and somehow, I could not resist his demands. I still needed his approval but that need was diminishing as Sarah's opinion became more important. I did not need to look at her to know what her reaction would be if I showed any sign of agreement.

'Not this Friday, Spam. Got a rehearsal that night.'

'A what?'

'A rehearsal. I've joined the drama club. I told you.'

'Jesus Christ, Billy. You'll be joining Lord Montague next. Fucks sake, this is a great chance, Billy. A lot of money.'

I wanted him to shut up. The more he spoke, the more he gave away. I could not tell him that the police had been in the house. Not while she was there.

'I can't go. Really. Another time, maybe.'

'Suit yourself then.'

He climbed back into the car and drove away aggressively. 'What was that about?'

'He's selling some fags at the dance. Smuggled fags from the South. He wants a hand.'

'He's a spiv. I hope you'll have nothing to do with it.'

'I said I'd a rehearsal.'

'But you haven't. Why don't you tell the truth? Just say you don't want to? Are you afraid of him? Afraid he'll think you're soft?'

'Course not.'

'Well then.'

We walked on in silence, I took her hand but it lay limply in mine. I knew that she wanted me to choose– Spam or her.

'Look. I'll tell him. If you'll meet me on Friday night, I'll tell him that I'm not getting involved. No more carry on.'

'I don't care what you do, Billy, but for your own sake, stay away from him.'

'So you won't come out on Friday.'

'You've got a rehearsal. Remember?'

'That was a lie.'

'It came out too easily, Billy. It worries me. You might be lying to me sometimes.'

'Never. I promise. Never to you.'

I stopped and looked straight into her eyes. Tilting back her head, she gazed at me suspiciously for a moment and then smiled.

'I believe you. Thousands wouldn't, but I'll take a risk.'

'Risk it for a biscuit.'

I laughed with relief. 'Friday night?'

She shook her head.

'You never give up, do you?'

I put my arm around her waist and hugged her.

Like a ripple of pastry in front of a rolling pin, the skin on her back slid upwards before his fingers. She lay on the bed like a beached porpoise, her face buried in the pillow and her clothes rolled up to her shoulders, naked from her hips to her neck. He bent over her, concentrating on his task, the skin of his head glistening through the thin grey hair. The doctor massaged my mother's back. Nothing remarkable about that. But there was. There was more than professional application in the movement of his fingers and something distinctly defensive in his reaction to my appearance in the bedroom. He sprang backwards, his hands fluttering over his head, brushing back his hair.

'Your mother is not well,' he said accusingly.

Hearing him speak she rolled over quickly, hauling down her clothes, her face flushing with embarrassment.

'You should knock before you come in.'

I didn't answer but stood quietly watching them.

He continued to stroke his head as if it would help him to disappear. A small man dressed in a tweed sports jacket and grey flannels, his little moustache twitched excitedly above his lips as his mouth searched for the right words. I could see the back of his head in the mirror of the dressing table, his neck shrinking into his shoulders like that of a turtle in its shell. Behind him, on the kidney-shaped stool, his black case hung open, revealing the paraphernalia of his profession– the stethoscope, the cotton wool, the linctus bottles, the slim chrome case of the thermometer, the instrument for aural examination. The room smelled of his antiseptic aura.

I turned and left, shutting the door behind me.

'I told you,' my sister said as I entered the living room. 'What?'

'I told you they were having an affair.'

'Rubbish.'

I lowered myself into the armchair by the gas fire. Leaning over the ironing board, she ran the iron over her white blouse. The lock of her hair hanging over her face did not hide the mischievous glance in my direction.

'I saw them kissing at the front door.'

'Nonsense. You're making it up. Again. You're always making things up. One day, it'll get you into trouble. Real trouble.'

'I'm not. I swear. I saw them.'

'So she kissed him goodbye. What's wrong with that.'

'Wasn't that kind of kiss.'

'God's sake. He's her doctor. He wouldn't do that. More than his job was worth. Anyway, he's wee, he's nearly bald, and he's not Errol Flynn.'

'I'm telling you. You watch.'

She shook some water over the arm of the blouse and pressed it flat. I shook out a cigarette and lit it from the gas fire. Gazing into the glow, I thought about what she had seen. Perhaps she was right. After what I had seen in the bedroom, it was possible. The idea was repulsive. Until that moment, I had never seen my mother as a sexual being, a woman having appetites or interests outside the family. She ran the household. That was her job. She ordered the food, paid the bills, mended our clothes, darned our socks, organized the maid and made my sandwiches. I could not imagine her making love or having sex. That had to be a different person, not the mother I knew. The thought of the doctor touching her made me squirm.

'Give me a fag, Billy.'

'You're too young.'

'And when did you start, may I ask?'

She knew that I had started when I was seven. In a tree hut. Woodbine with an older boy from the prefabs. The first one made me boak, but with his encouragement, I persevered and became an accomplished smoker by Christmas.

I shook out another, lit it and handed it to her.

She laid down the iron and, taking a deep draw, gazed at me steadily. 'Is Spam in trouble, Billy?'

'No. Why?'

'You know that policeman who was here? I heard him mention Patrick's name.'

'What did he want anyway?'

'I don't know. That's all I heard.'

I had forgotten about the visit. The reminder was uncoiled in my stomach. I would have to find out why the peeler came, carefully though, cunningly, without letting mother know.

'Do you know your lines now?' I asked to divert the conversation.

Kathleen had been given the part of Lotus Blossom, a geisha, in *Teahouse of the August Moon*, a play based on the American occupation of Okinawa immediately after the war. She had to practice walking with tiny, delicate steps, floating across the room as if she were on wheels and speaking broken English. It was the leading female role. I had secured only a minor part as an American sergeant. She had talent. Mine proved to be more limited than I thought. Still, the magic of applying Leichner 5 and 9 grease paint and tracing lines of Lake and Grey with white highlights was perversely exciting. I could transform my whole appearance, become a different person, a different gender even, and the musky smell of the greasepaint was strangely seductive and exotic.

'Most of them,' she replied, 'Why?'

'I just wondered.'

'Changing the subject, you mean. You should stay away from him.'

'Who?'

'Spam. You know who I mean.'

'You're beginning to sound like mother. Anyway, what about Derek? He's no angel, is he?'

Derek, a man locally renowned for his sexual adventures with nubile females, had enticed her into bed at a party. Noticing their absence, I searched for them and hauled her out of bed just in time. She had been furious and flushed with humiliation while I, on the other hand, inflated myself with righteous outrage and brotherly protectiveness. His sneering indifference to the intrusion reminded me of Spam– that would have been his response– and I had to resist the temptation to flatten the curl on his lip. Yet he looked so ridiculous with his flannels round his thighs and his shabby underpants exposed to the view that an assault was unnecessary.

'You always bring that up.'

'Well, it was pretty stupid.'

She lifted the iron again and pressed down angrily on the blouse.

She had dyed her fair hair black for the role. A bit excessive, I thought, as a black wig would have served the purpose. I watched her pressing the iron along the sleeve, the tip of her tongue curled over her upper lip in concentration, and her large brown eyes fixed on the task. An attractive girl now. The plump little sister was becoming a young woman, proud of her new breasts, which she hoisted provocatively upwards to walk down the street.

'Do you think she is having an affair?' I asked.

'Yes. You watch them.'

I started to giggle. On reflection, it was an amusing picture, the little bald doctor and the great whale of a woman. Moby Dick and a limp mackerel.

'Hello, Mrs Curran. Is Sarah in?'

'She's not well, Billy. Come in anyway.' I stepped past her into the hall.

'Is she okay?'

'I think it's that flu, but yes, she'll be fine in a couple of days.'

'Is she in bed?'

'She is, but just go up and see her if you like.'

I was astonished. The invitation showed a level of trust that I had not expected. I had to hide my surprise.

'Can I take anything up to her?'

'I don't think so. On you go up and give me a shout in the kitchen before you go.'

'I'll do that.'

I walked up the stairs casually.

'I wondered who it was,' Sarah said as I peered round the door. 'Can I come in?'

'I suppose so.'

'How are you feeling?'

'Better tonight. I slept most of the day. Take the chair from the dressing table.'

I sat beside the bed and took her hand. She looked so petite and defenceless in the massive bed as she turned towards me with her head on the pillow. I stroked her brow tenderly with my fingers and leaned over to lay my head beside hers.

'It's like being married, being so close,' I whispered.

'Not with mother downstairs.'

'One day '

'When you're rich and famous, maybe.'

I kissed her and felt her lips quiver in response, supple with an urgency that I had not met before. At least, that's what I thought it was. I slipped my hand under her pyjama top and felt her skin smooth and warm. She did not stop my hand as it moved over her breast. I could barely breathe with sudden excitement as she arched towards me. The fantasies imagined before sleep, the dreams which left the dawns so desolate, flickered past, vibrant with potent vitality. My breath trembled with anticipation.

As I slid my hand down over her belly, expecting a jerk of resistance, her lips held mine steadily. I could not believe what was happening. It was new territory, frightening yet electrifying. I moved my hand gently and rhythmically across her skin, wondering how she might respond if my fingers crept downwards, testing her lips, listening to her breath, feeling her body, measuring her compliance. My inhibitions were crumbling before a storm of emotions, all the taboos instilled from childhood melting.

'Do not touch... Dirty... Not in the bathroom... Not when she's dressing.'

I could hear the voices. *'Bad to do that... That would be awful... disgusting.'*

They were wrong, though. They had to be. The urge to touch her was so compelling and so natural that it swamped the past. Desperate to slide into the dark, forbidden cleft, I could wait no longer and, for the first time, felt the soft, moist flesh of womanhood. She did not move. Frantic with passion, I allowed my thumb to enter her. The sensation was so exciting that the ecstasy erupted in my groin. At the same time, she twisted away from me, flinging my hand out of the bed.

'Bastard!' she hissed, 'Get out of here! Go away!' Startled, I sat back in the chair.

'What's wrong, Sarah?'

'Just get out of here! Go on, for God's sake! Go!'

'I thought . . .. .'

'Go!'

I stood and left the room. I could hear her sobs as I closed the door.

Utterly confused, I stood on the landing, trying to work out what had happened. I thought that she had allowed me to touch her and that she was showing enthusiasm even, but clearly, I had been wrong. I had misread the signals. I walked slowly down the stairs, tempted to return and apologise, but decided that it was best to leave her.

'I'm away now, Mrs Curran,' I called round the kitchen door, taking care to hide my trousers in case a wet stain betrayed that moment of pleasure.

'So soon, Billy, I've just made some tea. Will you not stay?'

'Thanks, but no, Mrs Currran. I have to get home. I have work tomorrow.'

'Oh aye, I'd forgotten with her in bed. Is she alright?'

'She's grand. She'll be better in no time. Goodnight now. I'll see you soon.'

'Goodnight, Billy. God bless.'

Chapter 11

She could still feel him inside her, an outrageous intrusion, a violation of her body, piercing the sanctuary of her inner being. She sat on the train on the way to work, staring out at the brown mudflats near Belfast and leaning against the window, furious that it had happened. Still angry with Billy but more annoyed with herself, she pursed her lips, squeezing them into a knot till she felt the pressure. She had wanted him not to invade her but to lie beside her and love her gently. She had not wanted anyone to touch her there till she was married. She should have stopped him and pushed his hand away the moment it touched her belly, but the feeling of his fingers on her skin had been exciting. She watched a gull wading in the black, slimy pools, its white feathers soiled by the mud. That was how she felt–sullied, defiled.

Yet she felt also that he was bound to her now, that he owed her reparation.

If they were married, that would set things right. She tried to imagine him as a husband. If he served his time in the yard, he could be an electrician. Not a bad trade; well paid and secure. A good living if he had his own business, but she could not see him in that role. Restless, idealistic, and artistic, flitting from one grandiose scheme to the next, Billy was too impulsive to settle into a monotonous job. Still, it was that uncertainty, that aura of danger around him, which she found attractive. She wondered what her father would think of him. He would, no doubt, hide any critical views from her if he knew that she liked him. He would even support the marriage if it was her wish. Not much help, really.

Sydenham station flew past. She unclipped her bag and took out her compact. For a moment, she gazed at her face in its mirror. Had she changed? Would they be able to tell at work? Nancy would know. Nancy would watch every expression, listen carefully to every inflexion and discover the truth. Even Miss Capper might guess. She did not want to go to work. She loathed Miss Capper. Dried up old bag. She would have to keep her mind on her work, keep her head down and hope that she would ignore her. Yet she had to explain her absence. She would have to face her.

She screwed out her lipstick and applied it carefully. A quiet coral colour, not too loud.

She remembered the first time she put on lipstick. Her mother had been horrified.

'Do you want to look like a whore?' she croaked, 'Take it off for God's sake!'

She had defied her mother, though, and worn it to the dance. Sixteen. Old enough to make her own decisions.

She did not defy her often. She did not like to see her upset. She was an old woman, after all, a widow and had lost her husband. She tried to remember that when, in those moments of grief, the pain of missing her father struck suddenly and unprompted like a blade in her side.

She finished with the lipstick, crimped her lips together and padded a little powder onto her nose and cheeks. She felt ready to face Miss Quasimodo.

'Well, Miss Curran. Back at last. We have no time for malingerers in this office.' Sarah glared at the hard little eyes. Eyes like a snowman, brittle, lifeless.

'If you care to consult personnel, Miss Capper, you will find that I provided a medical certificate. I was not well, and I was not malingering.'

She was surprised by her own confidence and the forceful tone of her voice. Several of the girls at desks nearby looked up. She was no longer frightened of the woman and, for some reason, felt slightly superior.

'In thirty years with the firm, I have never missed a day,' Miss Capper continued disdainfully.

'That's not true, Miss Capper. You were off sick for a week last year.' The girls, clearly shocked, turned to watch the response.

'You are calling me a liar, young lady?'

'No. I am stating a fact.'

'I have never heard such insolence! I will report you to the manager. There is no room in this office for troublemakers. And your work is sloppy and slow.'

Sarah watched the thin lips trembling with fury and two white patches bloom under the taut cheeks.

'There is nothing wrong with my work. It is as good as any other work in the office.'

'Go to your desk, Miss Curran. You will be hearing from the management.'

Sarah turned and walked calmly between the desks, conscious of the attention of almost a hundred other girls.

'Jesus, Sarah, What have you done? You'll get your books,' Nancy whispered out of the corner of her mouth without raising her head from her work.

'I don't think so. She's a bully. She won't do anything.'

'Some risk, though.'

'I don't care.'

'God, what's happened to you? Won the pools or something?'

'Just fed up with her picking on me.'

'Good for you.'

Sarah rolled out the plan, fixed the corners and picked up her pen. At the tea break, Nancy turned to face her.

'Were you ill right enough?'

'Yes, I was. I felt really dreadful. I couldn't come to work. I just couldn't.'

'Some of the others been off too. Billy's been around every lunchtime– even Thursday when it was pouring. Stood outside in the rain. Did he not know you were sick?'

'Course he knew.' She hoped that she was not blushing.

'You've fallen out, haven't you? What's happened? He's tried it on, hasn't he? Come on, Sarah. Tell me what's happened. I won't breathe a word.'

'Nothing has happened. We had a row, that's all.'

'You've had a ride, haven't you?'

'No! Nothing like that. He's not like that.'

'I don't believe you. They're all like that– given the chance.'

'He's not. We had a row about Clive. He doesn't want me to see him. Not at all. He's far too possessive and jealous. Anyway, I don't want to talk about him. I want to forget about him.'

'Okay. Okay. I bet he comes at lunchtime again.'

'Too bad. I'm away to the toilet.'

Sarah was furious. How did Nancy know these things? Did it show? She should not have challenged Miss Capper, drawing attention to herself like that. Yet she was glad that she had done it. As she walked across the office, she could sense the other girls watching her. She locked the toilet door, hitched up her skirt, hauled down her pants and sat down. Again, that feeling, the feeling of him inside her.

'Bastard!' she hissed, 'Bloody bastard!'

She wanted to shout it in his face, tell him how she felt. Lunchtime. If he came at lunchtime, she would go down and yell at him. Let Nancy see her from the window. She would be watching. No doubt. Nosey Nancy.

'He's there again. I told you he would come.' Nancy spoke over her shoulder from the window.

Sarah bit into her banana sandwich and shook her head. The notion of shouting at him had faded. She did not like banana sandwiches; they were too sweet, and the mush stuck to her palate.

She thought of her mother in the kitchen, making sandwiches, squeezing banana in a bowl and spreading it on the bread.

'Good for you, bananas,' she said every time, 'Never got them in wartime.'

Bananas. What a disappointment they were! She remembered her father peeling the first one and handing it to her, the white flesh erect in its cluster of skins, like eating blotting paper. She had tried to enjoy it for him. That was her mistake.

She drank some tea to wash away the mush that clung to her palate.

'Come on, Sarah,' Nancy cajoled, 'The poor wee fella's freezing out there.'

'You go if you're so sorry for him.'

'It's not me he wants to see.'

She lifted the bread paper in which her sandwiches had been wrapped, smoothed it out on her knee and folded it carefully. She like the edges to meet exactly. Perhaps she should speak to him. It was not polite to ignore him.

She swung her cardigan around her shoulders and, studiously avoiding Nancy, left the office.

'What do you want, Billy?' she asked more aggressively than she intended.

'To say sorry. Really. I'm sorry, Sarah.'

She looked into his eyes to see if he meant it. She had not noticed that his eyes were different colours and was quite taken aback by her failure to see it before. One eye was hazel, and the other almost blue. How strange. Why had she not noticed? She glanced from one eye to the other, wondering if they revealed different mysteries, but she could not penetrate their depths. She felt that there was a hint of sincerity there, an earnest attempt to convince her that he regretted what he had done.

'I want to see you again,' he pleaded.

She remembered her fury and disgust and how she had sworn at the time never to see him again, but it seemed suddenly remote as if a gauze had fallen between her and her anger. She studied his face, trying to see behind the eyes and hear the truth in his voice, trying to decide whether to trust him. He had cut his chin shaving, and there was a pimple of dried blood where the blade had slipped. Her father sometimes cut himself and left for work with a snowflake of paper on his face. She dropped her eyes and stared at his boots, breaking the contact so that she could think.

She had trusted him before, and he had taken advantage of her. In her bed, the one place where she had felt safe. She should not have allowed him near her. Perhaps it was all her fault. Perhaps she should forgive him, at least give him another chance.

The riveters were working already in the ribs of the new tanker, the clattering echoing around the yard.

She looked up at his face again. His expression had not changed, serious, worried, imploring. There was no sign of attempt to emulate James Dean. He seemed to be genuine, and there was a gentleness there, a sensitivity that few other men dared to betray. Besides, he was quite handsome. Perhaps she could love him.

'Meet me in the shelter tonight, the one in the park,' she said, trying to speak with a coolness in her tone, 'We can talk about it then.'

She was startled by his response. Before she could stop him, he threw his arms around her, crushing her against his chest. She was horrified, knowing that Nancy– and maybe others– would be watching upstairs. He smelled of American tobacco and shipyard dust. She pushed him away.

'No, Billy! Not here, for heaven's sake.'

He was so obviously delighted that she did not want to puncture his enthusiasm. Like a child really with an innocence, a naivety, that she found irresistible. He was almost dancing with happiness, unable to contain or conceal his relief.

'I said we would talk about it. No more than that.'

'That's okay, Sarah. That's all I wanted.'

'See you tonight then.'

'Aye. Great. See you then.'

She turned away quickly and walked back through the swing doors to the stairway.

Chapter 12

Spam sat on the tram, nursing the paper bag of liquorice comfits, his grandmother's favourite sweet. He thought of the miniature torpedoes with their tart, dark thread of liquorice and their coloured coats of crunchy sugar, and he was tempted to open the bag and take a couple, but he was sure that she would know. She had an uncanny ability to detect his misdeeds. Yet she was the only person in the family for whom he had any respect and who, he felt, liked him, perhaps even loved him. He imagined her grin and the way she shook her head when she was pleased. Some folk found her stern and intimidating but he had never seen that side of her character.

He had visited her regularly since her husband died four years beforehand.

There was a coolness between her and his mother, her only daughter, and he had suspected that his mother would not make an effort to visit her in Belfast. He had been right. She did visit a couple of times in the beginning but soon abandoned the commitment. He was sure that the rift related to his father and that the old lady felt that her daughter had married beneath her. She never expressed her contempt for his father - she was too much of a lady to be so direct— but she could not conceal it completely, and it escaped in little barbed comments. He was certain that her opinion lay behind the friction. Whatever the cause, he had taken on the responsibility of visiting his Gran.

He remembered the funeral and the great hiccough of grief that had almost wrecked his composure in the church. It came so suddenly and inexplicably that he had almost allowed it to escape. Until that point, he had not felt any sorrow apart from the sympathy for his Gran. It was the glimpse of the coffin that triggered it and the thought of his Grandpa lying under the lid.

Fortunately, the feeling subsided as quickly as it erupted, and he could survive the rest of the funeral dispassionately. Nevertheless it did make him think about death and wonder about its finality.

He had lain on his bed that night, a fag balanced between his lips, thinking deep thoughts about the question. He knew that hell was a lot of fuckin' nonsense, a ruse conjured up by priests to make you be good, but he reckoned that there might be something in the idea of heaven, somewhere nice to go after you died, somewhere to meet with old friends and relatives that you liked, a vast, warm space where you could avoid folk that you hated. He thought of it like a Garden of Eden, which he had seen in Bibles, a paradise with palm trees and sunlight and placid animals. Not cats, though. He hated fuckin' cats, the way they sidled up to you and curled their tails around your legs, sleek, sly parasites. No cats in heaven. He still felt that way about cats and about heaven.

He left the tram on the Lisburn Road and crossed into Ulsterville Avenue. His Gran, his mother's mother, lived in one of the three-storey terraced houses, much grander than her daughter's shabby bungalow. The small front garden was always neat and vibrant with colour in the summer, unlike the dismal waste-ground round his house. As he stepped up towards the front door, he watched for the twitch of the bead curtains on the bay window, but there was no movement. Perhaps she was in the kitchen. He raised the brass knocker and tapped on the open storm door. He heard her shoes on the tiled floor. He imagined them, their black pointed toes glittering and their laces precisely tied to match each other, twin bows perched on her thick fawn stockings.

'Hello, Gran,' he called as her shape appeared behind the frosted glass panel of the inner door, 'It's me.'

'I know it's you, silly boy,' she grinned as she opened the door, 'I saw you coming.'

He held out the bag of sweets, watching for her response.

'You shouldn't have,' she said, shaking her head. He could see that she was pleased. She hooked her arm around his neck and kissed him on the cheek. He could feel the bristles on her chin.

'Go on in, Patrick. You know where to go, and I'll put the kettle on.'

He turned into the front room while she scuttled through to the back kitchen. He sat in his grandfather's armchair, its leather still smelling of his pipe and its headrest stained with his hair cream in spite of the embroidered antimacassar. The brass fender in front of the fire was still marked where he rested his feet in the evenings. His pipe lay in the ashtray beside the chair. Spam picked it up and hooked it between his teeth. It gave him a feeling of maturity and authority, and he pretended to light it, sucking and popping his lips as his grandfather did, but as the bitter taste of burnt tobacco touched his tongue, Spam tugged out his cigarettes and lit one with his new lighter. He liked its smooth click action and the way it fitted neatly into his hand. It had not cost him anything. He blew the smoke towards the ceiling and looked around the room.

The glass bead curtains excluded most of the daylight, yet they cast an array of colours across the room when the sun was shining.

He remembered trying to catch the dancing rays of light on the wall when he was a child. His mother detested the room– dark, dismal and smelly, she said, like a dungeon– but he had always felt comfortable in it. It was dark, certainly. The tawny parquet-patterned linoleum, the umber wallpaper, the tall mahogany display cabinet nursing its precious porcelain and the black marble mantelpiece all added to the gloom, but the blaze of the coal fire with its flames reflected in the fender made the room feel homely. He liked the home-made screen with its multitude of pictures cut from magazines– a roaring stag, a sailing ship sinking in a storm, a monkey dressed as a sailor and a whiskered man in a straw boater– images which he had often studied as a child while the adults talked.

'How is business then?' she asked, setting down a three-tiered cake stand with buttered scones, chocolate biscuits and fairy cakes.

'Kept busy, Gran. You should see the queues at the license office, hurrying to get their license before the test.'

'I can imagine.'

'Ladies older than you even.'

'Surely not. Who would want to drive at my age? Nothing wrong with the trains or the buses. I'll just get the tea. Oh, and the jam. I forgot the jam.'

She left the room, tutting at her forgetfulness.

He reached out and took a biscuit from the stand, crunching it quickly to finish it before she returned. Billy's favourite, he remembered. Chocolate wafer. He thought of Billy grinning at his mother, charming her with his eyes.

'Billy boy,' he whispered to himself.

And then it happened. The image exploded again into his mind. It had returned suddenly several times, the vision of the boy he had chained. He saw the skin split open along his jaw and the white, bare bone. The sideburn gleaming with the blood in the gloom. The horror in Billy's eyes. It annoyed him. He had no remorse or sympathy for the boy. Why did he keep seeing the scene? True, it would worry him if he died and if the police somehow connected him with his death, but he could deal with that. Billy would back his story.

'How is Billy?' she asked, sitting in her chair to pour the tea. How did she know he was thinking of Billy? It was uncanny.

'He's grand. Joined the drama and talks about nothing else.'

'He'll be good at that. Nice boy, Billy. And what about you? What are you going to do in the evenings?'

'Training, Gran. Getting fit.'

'You're not still at the boxing, Patrick. You'll lose your good looks, you know. End up with a boxer's nose and cauliflower ears and half a brain.'

'Rinty Monaghan did alright.'

'Going to be a world champion then?'

'Not as good as that, Gran, but you never know.'

He watched as she poured his tea. A steady hand for an old lady. He noticed the transparency of her skin over the blue network of veins and the liver marks on the surface.

'I suppose it keeps you out of mischief. Have you seen that film yet?'

She handed him his tea in a delicate china cup and saucer decorated with climbing roses.

He took it nervously.

'The King and I?'

'No, no. The Rock film. You know the one.'

'Rock Around the Clock?'

'Yes. That's the one. Did you go?'

'Aye. Couldn't miss that, Gran.'

'Hope you weren't one of those who tore up the seats.'

'Course not,' he lied, 'Dreadful that.'

'Indeed. We didn't dare behave like that when we were young. We had respect for our elders.'

A silence crept between them. He could feel it frowning.

She handed him a scone on a side plate, the yellow butter oozing from its waist. 'There is something you could do for me, Patrick.'

'Certainly. Anything I can.'

'One of my neighbours, Mrs. Grainger, is in hospital. I have a wee bag of things that she asked me to fetch from her house. Could you take it to her? I would go myself, but corns are bad just now, and it's a bit of a walk.'

The hospital. Which hospital? He had just taken a bite of a scone, and he stopped chewing, his expression frozen as he tried to conceal the knot of panic forming in his belly. It might be the same hospital, the one where his victim lay. Jesus! He couldn't refuse.

'What's wrong, Patrick? Do you not want to go?'

'I hate hospitals, Gran, but for you, I'll do it.'

'Good, man yourself, and thanks. I appreciate it. It's the City Hospital. Not too far away.' What a mess! He tried to think of an escape, but there seemed to be no solution. He couldn't dump the bag and lie. She was sure to check, and if he found someone else to go, she would hear of it. He had to deliver the bag and hope that the boy was in another hospital or another corridor. At least it would not be the same ward. That was a comfort. 'You're very quiet today, Patrick.'

'I'm enjoying your scone. Best scones in Belfast.'

'Just in Belfast?'

'In the world, Gran.'

Her head shook with pleasure, and she grinned at him over her cup.

Chapter 13

She tried to understand when I left the yard and found work in a theatre in Belfast. I saw the disappointment in her eyes. We had spoken of the day when we would live in our own house, how she would decorate it and we would cook meals together. She saw the future in terms of her past - her family before her father died.

I had an appetite for excitement, something different from what I saw as the banal existence of the masses. Theatre. Even the word was seductive. To be on a stage, under the lights, stirring an audience, being admired was thrilling and more seductive than petty crime with Spam. That world of blinding lights, trembling flats, dimmer boards, cables, pulleys, stage props, gelatines– all the paraphernalia of theatre was more enticing than the filth and noise of the yard. The scent of grease paint, liquid paraffin, dusty costumes, and face powder more attractive. Voluptuous shadows, furtive movements, nervous whisperings. I wanted to be part of it.

She did not express her disappointment. It leaked out in questions about how we would meet.

'You'll be working every night. When will I see you?'

'All day Sunday. I'll come down to Bangor, and I can see you at lunchtime.'

'How?'

'Get a bus down to your office.'

'Why do you have to go professional? Why not a hobby?'

Why indeed? The glamour, the chance of fame, the association with the famous. 'I want to do it full time, as a career.'

'The yard's not good enough.'

'It's not that. I hate the noise, the cold, the early mornings.'

'Other boys do it and don't moan about it.'

'Maybe they've no choice.'

'You're better than them?'

'No. I don't think that. I need to do something creative.'

She gave up after a while, resigned to the uncertainty. I thought that she might look for someone else or go back to Clive, but she waited for me to tire of the enthusiasm.

The rooms where the sets were made were dark and smelt of glue and size and paint.

Bizarre props from almost forgotten plays littered the cupboards and costumes, filmed with dust, hung like paralyzed actors along one wall. The bare wooden floor was spattered with ancient paint.

I slept there, rolling myself in discarded theatre curtains to keep warm. My first job was helping to make flats and paint scenery– not even a walk-on part, but a start, nevertheless.

I was placed in the care of George, tall and thin with long grey hair and a stoop meant to conceal his height. The long overcoat, which might at one time have been camel hair, hung from his shoulders like a cape, the empty arms flapping limply by his side. His fingers and the hair above his right eye were stained yellow with tar from the cigarettes, which he smoked one after the other. His chin displayed the carelessness that was an endearing aspect of his character, as it was constantly decorated with bloody pieces of tissue and clumps of silver beard that had escaped the trembling razor.

He was what Protestants describe as a 'relic of auld decency.' Clearly, from a wealthy, landowning family that had fallen on hard times, his accent would not have been out of place in an Oxford college. He had indeed been a teacher of art in a boys' prep school somewhere in England, but his revolutionary views and outrageous behaviour when inebriated proved to be too shocking for the staff. His uninhibited use of coarse language in the classroom amused the boys but filtered out to the parents.

A skilled painter, nevertheless, but every now and again, he would have a bonfire of every recent canvas. Never satisfied. In the theatre rooms, he had an uncanny knack for transferring small set designs to tall flats without squaring off. With his cigarette in his mouth and a brush in his hand, he would perform wide sweeps on the canvas, always with a flourish, and create a perfect scene.

He taught me to make flats, melting glue over a gas ring and stretching the canvas over the frame. He showed me how to mix colours and how different stage lighting could enhance or kill them.

'Now, dear boy,' he would say after a couple of hours in the morning, 'Time for lunch.'

Flinging his coat over his shoulders, he would stride across the street to the pub. There we would remain till the late afternoon, George insisting that he bought the drinks. He knew that my three pounds did not stretch to sessions of that length. His prodigious consumption had no effect on his work. I could never understand that.

He would stagger across the street and still manage to paint with extraordinary accuracy.

Everyone adored him except the director, who found his casual approach to deadlines infuriating. I found his carefree attitude infectious and liberating. I swam into it with relish, learning to enjoy the self-indulgence. We spent hours sitting by the gas ring, drinking coffee, smoking, and gossiping about characters he had known in the theatre. Never malicious, he always balanced scurrilous tales about people with generous remarks on their better nature. A kind man, really. My affection for him grew as he talked. I found myself copying his aristocratic drawl and languid manner. He was the father that I should have had.

It was through him that I met Kathleen.

We had made and painted a set for *Summer of the Seventeenth Doll*, a play about rough cane cutters in Australia and their women. The first night was the world premiere, so the theatre was packed with celebrities, and there was an extravagance of champagne back stage after the show. Kathleen was an art student and helped to design the set. George introduced us.

Most of the crowd were dressed formally in dark suits or glittering dresses and stood round the stage with glasses in their hands. Kathleen wore a long navy sweater and jeans spattered with paint. Her thick, auburn hair flowed in waves over her shoulders, and she had a habit of flicking her head to toss it back from her face. Green eyes in a field of freckles. Irresistible.

'I'm going back to Mark's,' she said after the small talk, 'You want to come?' No preliminaries. No conversational foreplay.

'Of course,' I replied casually in George's accent, 'How do I get there? Is it far?'

'Mark has a car. I'll speak to him. Need to rescue him from the vultures anyway. Wait here.'

I watched her walk towards the crowd.

'Splendid girl,' George murmured over my shoulder.

'Christ, George! You startled me.'

I had not realized that he was behind me.

'Great talent, dear boy. Draws like a master. Ask to see her drawings.'

'That good?'

'Unquestionably. Best in the year. I've seen her work.'

'Oh yes? And what else have you seen?'

'Too young and thin for me, dear boy. Prefer the voluptuous kind like Rubens. Besides, Lucy would cut my balls off if I betrayed her. You have your fun when you're young and free.'

He took a long draw of his cigarette, followed by the usual fit of cancerous coughing, and walked away.

'This is Billy,' she said as she returned.

Mark, about ten years older than us, clearly wanted people to guess that he was a designer. A yellow cravat, brown corduroy jacket, suede shoes, and a cigarette holder announced his creative interests. I disliked him instantly. Spam would have slashed his face without a thought. Pretentious, conceited, effete. So I thought.

'Ah, Billy. I've heard about you from George. Wonderful character, George. Not many like him around. Great painter, too– when he can see straight. Anyway, do come with us. We'll give you a lift.'

'Is there room?'

'Of course.'

The three of us left the theatre and stepped out into the street. After the bright stage lights, the street lights were dim and misted with drizzle. Mark slipped off his jacket and lifted it over his head. His dark hair was swept back in tight little wavelets as if it were permed. He did not want it to get wet.

The car was a Citroen 'deux cheveux'. I was surprised, expecting something a little more elegant than what Spam called a toaster on wheels. We rattled through the empty streets heading south, Kathleen beside me in the back.

'How long have you been with that lot?' she asked.

'Three weeks now. I'm helping George at the minute, but Harry has promised me small parts.'

'You don't need to speak in that voice. Be yourself. Drop the posh accent. I can tell it's not your own. You believe Harry?'

'Yes.'

Obediently, I lapsed into my own accent. Perplexed and slightly hurt, I wondered how she had noticed the assumed voice. I'd considered it to be quite convincing, not identical to George's refined speech but sufficiently authentic to fool most people. I had underestimated her. Perhaps I had ruined any chances of getting off with her.

'George tells me you're the best in your year,' I continued, trying to smooth over the bad impression, 'I'd like to see your work sometime.'

'George always exaggerates. He drinks too much and talks nonsense. He has talent, though. Have you seen his paintings?'

'No. Not yet, They say he burns them, sets fire to them once he has a collection.'

'Never good enough, I suppose. I can understand that.'

'You don't burn yours?' She laughed.

'Not in the same league, dear boy.'

A perfect imitation of George, better than my attempt.

The third-floor flat was more modest than I expected– two bedrooms, a sitting room, kitchen and bathroom. There was little there to indicate that it was the home of a flamboyant designer. Drab moquette suite, a faded green carpet, and a standard lamp with a saffron shade. More like a student flat, except for the painting above the yellow tiled fireplace. James Craig's original landscape with those exuberant post-impressionist brush strokes, vivid colours, and vibrant skies. I was impressed.

'You like it?' he asked, handing me a glass of red wine.

'Superb.'

We stood in front of it. I caught the scent of the brilliantine on his hair and the Gauloise on his clothes.

'Yes. Very French and yet very Irish.'

'I prefer Chagall,' Kathleen said from behind us, 'or Magritte– a bit of mystery, something to make you think.'

'Can't afford that, darling,' Mark replied, 'Wait till I'm rich and famous, and I'll buy you one.'

I joined Kathleen on the sofa as the front door opened, and a small, dumpy lady with long black hair removed her coat and flung it across the chair.

'Dismal,' she said, 'Damp and cold.'

Jewish, I thought. A Rachel or a Ruth. I looked at Mark, wondering if he was Jewish too. I was wrong on both counts. She turned out to be a lapsed Catholic from Roscrea and a staunch Republican.

'Kathleen, love. Good to see you. How did it go? Did they like the set?'

'Raved about it,' Mark interrupted before Kathleen could speak, 'Simply raved about it. Even your man from *The Whig.*'

'I didn't ask you. You're biased. All your work's brilliant in your eyes.'

'They loved it, Maggie,' Kathleen replied, 'Really. You should go and see it.'

'Better things to do. Two classes of papers to mark. Who's your friend?'

'Billy. Sorry, Maggie. Billy, this is Maggie, Mark's wife. Billy works with George. Thinks he's going to be an actor.'

'In Belfast? Never. If you want to act, Billy, go to Dublin or London. Belfast's a graveyard. Kitchen sink comedy. That's all they want. That's all they put on. Trash.'

'*Summer of the Seventeenth Doll* is okay. Something different anyway,' I dared to argue.

'Give it a week.'

Mark handed her a glass of wine, and she stretched out in one of the armchairs.

We finished a second bottle and talked about theatre and art. Mark asked me about my background and plans, showing a genuine interest in my adventures with Spam. My first impressions began to fade. Perhaps he was not as shallow as I thought. As the wine took effect, I warmed to him. His hair seemed more natural, his clothes less flamboyant, his cigarette holder more casual. After the third bottle, he rose unsteadily and, hauling Maggie from her chair, pointed to the second bedroom.

'You two are in there. Small bed but I'm sure you'll manage. We have an early start, I'm afraid. Maggie is working, and I'm off to London. May have a contract in the West End. Night, night, mes enfants. Dormez bien.'

'Night, you two,' Maggie said, 'Help yourselves to coffee in the morning.'

They disappeared into their bedroom. I did not look at Kathleen, but I was anxious to know what she was thinking. Mark and Maggie seemed to assume that we would be sleeping together. Did Kathleen? Was it too much to hope for?

I shook out a Phillip Morris and offered it to Kathleen. She shook her head. 'I'm kippered. Tired too. Are you coming?'

I tried not to look surprised and casually fitted the cigarette back into the packet. I glanced at her face, searching for signals. Did she really want to sleep with me? Did she like me at all? Her green eyes were steady and calm, revealing nothing, neither affection nor desire nor amusement. I was relieved in a way, and yet it would have been reassuring to have some indication of what lay ahead. I thought it best to appear as casual as she was.

She rose, and I followed her into the bedroom. As I stood, I realized that the wine had seeped into my head. For a moment, the room swirled around me. Without looking back, she stripped to her bra and pants and climbed into the bed.

'Turn off the light,' she said as she turned on her side.

I peeled off my shirt, stripped to my underpants, and turned off the light.

The whole thing was unreal as if it was not happening to me, like a scene from a film, a bohemian fantasy.

I climbed into bed beside her. She had not turned to the wall. I could feel her breath on my cheek. I wanted to reach out and touch her but could not predict her reaction. She was the kind of girl who would tell you to fuck off and knee you in the groin if you insulted her. On the other hand, she might scoff at my hesitation and naivety. I did not want her to think that I was inhibited or inexperienced. I turned towards her and ran my fingers through her hair. She did not move. That was a relief. At least she did not pull away. She seemed to be waiting, but I was not sure. It was like lying next to a panther. If

I tried to kiss her, she might sink her teeth in my throat. Yet the surge of desire for her was irresistible.

I found her lips and kissed her. They were soft and welcoming. I relaxed.

It was going to be okay. Her tongue flickered round my mouth. My God! Sarah had never done that. In our first kiss she had held her lips as tight as a purse.

There was little flesh over her bones. I could feel her ribs, and her breasts might have been those of a pubescent girl. When I lay between her thighs, I could feel the rim of her hip bone.

She raised her hands behind her head and raised her hips off the sheet, waiting for me. The pants were in the way. I should have thought of that before I rolled over. I did not want her to think that I had little experience, so I stretched the elastic to one side with my finger and pressed forward. It did not last long. Fearful of causing conception, I pulled away before the climax.

'Silly boy,' she whispered, 'It was quite safe.'

The second time, I swam in an ecstasy that I never thought was possible.

I could taste the passion on her breath and feel it in the writhing of her lips. Her lithe body seemed to envelope me, drawing me into the warmth of her womb. We seemed to swirl together like eels, entwined in a glittering stream. I wanted to say that I loved her but could not bear to leave her lips even for a moment. When the surge came, I shuddered. An agony or ecstasy, cracking my spine, drawing the chord like a worm from the bone, hauling my entrails out through my groin, flowing into the voluptuous recesses of her being.

We slept wrapped together in the small bed.

Kathleen demanded nothing, expected nothing from the encounter. It was as casual as shaking hands. We did meet a few times afterwards but it transpired that she had been offered a scholarship and was leaving for London. I did see her drawings, though. We met several times in the Piccolo, a fashionable new coffee house in Belfast frequented by art students. Neither of us dared to suggest that we should repeat the experience of the night together. There seemed to be a silent recognition that its casual nature was sacrosanct, that we should not seek to transform it into something permanent, as if the desire to repeat it might create expectations of the other partner. I did ask to see her drawings, however, and she took me to her house in East Belfast where she lived with her grandmother.

A modest, red-brick, terraced building with a small patch of grass at the front, it hinted at the solid, protestant, sterile, middle-class values of my father's foremen. Inside, it was amazing. Her grandmother had collected artifacts from across the globe– Japanese prints, Chinese jade ornaments and porcelain, American Indian beading, and French painting. I could guess the source of Kathleen's inspiration. Her drawings were superb. She had spent time at the zoo, and many of them were of primates, but her collection included exotic plants and strange rocks, all drawn with a wonderful balance between panache and attention to detail, freedom, and discipline. I envied her talent and the casual modesty with which she regarded it.

'Brilliant,' I said, 'I wish I could draw like that.'

'Maybe you can. How would I know?'

'Believe me. I can't.'

'Its all her fault really,' she nodded towards the bedroom upstairs where her grandmother slept, 'She dragged me round galleries and bought armfuls of paper and pads and paints and books on art. Never said good or bad when I drew, but I could always tell. She made me who I am.'

'Not your parents?'

'What do they have to do with it?'

'I don't know. I just thought.'

'Well, don't think. None of your business.'

'Fair enough.'

I never knew how she would react, but it was her unpredictable nature that made her exciting.

That night, we walked along the east bank of the river. The city lights shimmered on the black surface of the water. A train puffed fire quietly on the far side, and a pair of swans glided through its reflection. It was not cold, but her hands were tucked together in the sleeves of her duffle coat. We sat on a bench, watching the river. Only the distant hum of traffic disturbed the silence. I had my arm around her, and she leaned her head on my shoulder.

'I am leaving tomorrow,' she said.

'By boat?'

'Of course. How else?'

'Can I come and see you off?'

'No. I hate goodbyes.'

'Will you write?'

'No. When I go, I go.'

'Never come back?'

'Maybe never. Well, perhaps to see my Gran.'

I was tempted to ask, 'So we may not meet again?' but that would have put into words what we knew to be the truth and might have spoiled the undemanding nature of the friendship. It was, after all, ephemeral and I valued that. Yet, as I held her, a part of me wanted that moment to last forever. Enveloped in the warm summer night beneath the amber glow of the city lights, I knew that there was something precious about the scene, something that I should capture and preserve, something that I should never forget. No passion, no intense emotion. Just supreme contentment shared with another.

We never met again.

I did think about Sarah, wondering if I should confess, but decided against it, telling myself that it would only hurt her. Besides, it was different, belonging to a new world, a new play with a fascinating set, sophisticated, subversive, and amoral. Greedy for excitement but still attached to the comfort of familiar roles, I wanted to keep both– Sarah and theatre– stretching the elastic between them to the limit.

The next intimate encounter was very different.

Once again it was George who introduced us. Michael Forbes-Robertson was an architect with his own practice in the city. One of his main interests, however, was set design and he had been asked to design and make sets for a production of Carmen and Rigoletto. George, keen, I think, to make mischief, offered my services.

'You will enjoy it, dear boy. An education for you. Splendid chap, Michael. Beautiful house on the shore of Strangford Lough. Elegant, gleaming with light and tiled floors. You should see it. Besides, Michael has contacts in Dublin. Better than this shit-hole, dear boy.'

'But Harry has promised me parts here.'

'Ballocks, Billy. Painting scenery, brushing floors, moving sets, maybe even prompt but no parts, boy. Go south, young man. Dublin is the place. Centre of the universe. The Gate Theatre. Groome's hotel. Michael will fix it.'

Michael was not what I expected when we met. Tall, gaunt, delicate, like a Jesuit Inquisitor, with lank, dark hair carefully oiled and brushed flat. The tailored suit hung clung to his ascetic frame like a second skin, emphasizing the slim hips and long legs. Two inches of starched white cuff showed below his sleeve. Wisps of black hair sprouted from the pale fingers, which were curled decorously around a wine glass.

'Well, Willie, I refuse to call you Billy; it sounds so common and Protestant. George tells me you would like to help with the scenery.'

'It was George's idea.'

'I see. So you're not as keen as he makes out?' '

'No. I mean, yes, I would like to help.'

'Good. Good. We would love to have you. We are working in the Opera House. Come tomorrow. Stage door. Ten o'clock?'

'Ten is fine.'

'Splendid. Look forward to seeing you then, Willie.'

His fingers touched my arm, and he moved away. I was sure he left a scent of perfume behind.

The Opera House was the only theatre with a painting gallery where tall flats could be hung from the flies. Michael believed in tall flats. His design for Carmen included a Spanish square with all the houses in perfect perspective and with every detail shadowed for depth.

Michael introduced me to his friend, Frank, who studied me suspiciously, regarding me apparently as a rival for Michael's affections. A waiter in a hotel, he fluttered around Michael with a sycophancy perfected in his trade. His little, quick steps rattled along the gallery as he mixed paints.

With a red chalked string, we snapped out squares on the twenty-foot flat and then transferred Michael's small drawing to the tall canvas. Starting at the top, we began to paint the scene. Behind us, at the front of the stage, there was a cinema screen so, when the matinee started, we had to work quietly. Day after day, we listened to Frank Sinatra in 'The Joker is Wild' till we knew his script line by line.

'You must come for dinner, Willie,' Michael announced one evening as we cleaned the brushes, 'I want to show you the rest of the drawings.'

'I'd like to see them. That would be great.'

'Excellent. Tomorrow night, then.'

He removed his overall coat and left me with Frank.

'Such a kind man,' Frank said, 'Generous to a fault. People take advantage of him, you know.'

'I can imagine.'

He was referring to me.

Michael drove me to the house in his Jaguar. It was indeed an impressive property with a garden sloping down to the shore and immense picture windows in the sitting room. Inside, the stark white walls were relieved by original oil paintings– a William Conor landscape, a vivid seascape by James Dixon, and a green Daniel O'Neill. The bare, polished parquet floor reflected the light from the windows and created a feeling of space. No ornaments but vases of fresh flowers, and these splashes of warm colour saved the long sitting room from seeming cold and Spartan. The whole effect showed taste and creativity.

'You like it?' Michael asked, handing me a glass of sherry.

'Wonderful. I like the view.'

'Only the view?'

'No, no. I like the house. Your own design?'

'Naturally. Do sit down.'

I sank into the cushions of the vast sofa. Michael crossed to the radiogram and chose a record from the cabinet.

'You can relax while I see to the meal. I presume you like opera.'

'Yes, of course.'

He left the room as it filled with the first notes of an aria that I had heard but could not place. Anxious to impress, I walked quietly across to the radiogram and read the sleeve.

When he returned with an apron around his waist, I was reclining on the sofa, sipping the sherry, and commenting casually on the recording.

'Wonderful tone, Bjorling, but a bit lifeless, don't you think? Technically perfect but lacking in emotion. Cold.'

'You recognized him?'

'I would know his voice anywhere.'

'I'm impressed.'

'I prefer Gigli.'

'I have some of his if you would prefer that.'

'No, no. Please. Leave it on.'

He fetched some crystal glasses and laid the table.

The meal was exceptional– halibut cooked to perfection, potato rosti, asparagus tips, and a dry white wine. I had never tasted food like it. Silver cutlery, fine porcelain plates, linen napkins with embossed napkin rings. An introduction to a different lifestyle– elegant, exciting, cultured. I noticed the way his gold cufflinks glittered in the candlelight and the way he dabbed delicately with his napkin at the edge of his mouth.

'Can I help with the washing-up?' I asked after the meal.

'No, no, dear boy. The housekeeper sees to that. Sit back and have some port. Or would you prefer brandy? A little fire in the tummy?'

'No. Port would be lovely, thanks.'

He poured two glasses and, handing one to me, sat beside me on the sofa.

'Ciggies in the box,' he said, nodding towards the silver casket on the coffee table, 'Help yourself.'

I leaned across and opened the lid. A multi-coloured array in pastel shades.

I picked a blue one, slid my glass onto the table, and fitted it to my cigarette holder. No longer the Phillip Morris or Lucky Strike in the breast pocket. A different image. A long blue cigarette holder with a gilt crown halfway down the hilt.

'Very elegant,' he said, 'Very Noel Coward. Would you like to see the drawings?'

'Of course. I want to see how it's done.'

He fetched a portfolio case from the bookshelves and opened it on the desk.

'These are brilliant, Michael. The perspective is amazing. From these small sketches to the full plan. Wonderful. All the colours too. Have you been to Seville?'

'No. Madrid, yes. I went to see Lorca's statue in Madrid. You've heard of Lorca?'

'The poet?'

'Much more than a poet, dear boy. They shot him, you know, Franco's men. Shot for loving other men. The love that dare not speak its name. A deep and intense love for Dali. A very beautiful young man, a mouth not unlike yours.'

'I've never read his poems, I'm afraid.'

'What do you think? Do you think it is possible for men to love one another?'

'Why not? It's dreadful that men like Wildeblood are locked up for it.'

'Or humiliated like Gielguid. You don't disapprove?'

'Of course not.'

He smiled, studying me silently.

'You must read Lorca, dear boy. I have a copy. His work was banned in Spain, you know. Come, I want to show my model for the sets.' Touching my elbow, he led me through to his study.

The model was astonishing. The stage was set to scale, and every flat was reproduced exactly and in colour. He showed me how the sets changed and used small lamps with coloured gelatine to imitate the lighting. His long, delicate fingers handled the pieces with the precision of a surgeon. I noticed the perfectly manicured nails and the mat of black hair under the cuffs.

Returning to the sitting room, we sat till midnight, sipping port and listening to opera. 'What will you do when we're finished with Carmen?' he asked.

'Don't know. Can't go back to Goldblatt.'

'A friend of mine is staging a restoration comedy in Dublin. *The Way of the World* in the Gate. I think I could get you a part, if you are a good boy.'

Dublin. The Gate Theatre. What a chance! I wanted that, more than anything, to be a great actor, hypnotizing an audience with passion and sincerity, holding the crowd in suspense as it waited for every gesture, every word, every expression. I wanted the grease paint, the costumes, the wigs, and the excitement of being different. I wanted recognition and acclaim.

'That would be wonderful, Michael. I've never been to Dublin.'

'I'll see what I can do.'

He rose and changed the record on the radiogram. Tosca was replaced by a Strauss waltz.

'Come, Willie, you must dance with me.'

'I can't dance. Not like that, anyway. Jive maybe, but not ballroom.'

'Of course you can. Anyone can, and if you can't, it is time you learnt. An actor must be able to dance.'

He took me by the hand and led me towards the middle of the floor. I wanted to refuse, to dismiss the idea as preposterous, but I felt trapped into complying. I had agreed to be there to eat and drink with him. I must have known that he would expect repayment. I had wandered casually into the situation without considering the consequences. Not naïve but thoughtless, callously insensitive to the effect that rejection might have on him. I could not retreat. Besides, he had friends in Dublin. As we waltzed around the room, I thought of Sarah and wondered what she would think. The elastic was about to snap.

Chapter 14

The first night in Dublin we shared a double room in an elegant hotel in one of the Georgian squares near the centre. Polished brass, echoing tiles, corniced ceilings, and uniformed staff, all designed to portray a sense of luxury and discretion. In the bedroom, a deep-fitted carpet, velvet curtains, and an en-suite bathroom– all very different from my squat in Belfast.

'Bath before dinner, dear boy. Can't have stale odours at the table.'

Michael slipped off his jacket and went through to run a bath. Yellow tiles on the floor and gleaming taps with a shower fitting. The rush of water echoed around the tiled walls. Michael was bent over the bath, his fingers still on the taps. The sleeves of his shirt were slightly creased from the journey. I wondered what was in his mind. I wandered over to the window and gazed out over the square. The trees in the centre garden were still green, although a fine carpet of fallen leaves covered the grass. Beyond the trees, the fanlights of the Georgian terrace glistened in the evening sun. I watched an Armstrong Siddeley glide up to the hotel and its chauffeur open the rear door to a lady in a fur coat. An affluent, exotic world, irresistible and rich with possibilities.

When I turned, it was to see Michael naked by the bed with his back to me, shaking out a pristine towel. Pale, tight buttocks, bald, were worn with sitting, topped lank legs clearly unused to activity, and black hair shaded the crevice at the base of his spine. A picture of frailty, a creature unaccustomed to exposure, in no sense attractive. He looked around and caught me studying his body and smiled.

'Your turn next.'

He disappeared into the bathroom.

The horns of a dilemma brushed against my back. On the one hand, unhappy about where the situation was heading; on the other, keen to appear bohemian and open-minded. I sat in one of the velvet-clad chairs to remove my shoes and socks, wondering whether Michael was planning to invite me into his bath. All his clothes were laid out neatly on the bed beside me– the silk vest, the gold cufflinks, the tailored suit, the carefully ironed handkerchief, the white shirt, and the underpants. He was going to emerge naked from the bathroom. I could hear him splashing water on his head.

Spam would have detested the man– the kind of specimen he would target, a queer. He would kick his shins and break his nose.

'I hate fuckin' queers.' He had said that often. 'I would castrate every fuckin' one of them. Jam a plug up their arses so that they drown in their shit.'

He relished jokes about Lord Montagu and Peter Wildeblood. And there I was– 'Billy Boy'– sharing a room with Michael. I removed my cravat and folded it neatly.

I remembered pale bodies like pink seals slithering and squirming in the showers. In the chrome pipes, their elongated reflections moving sensuously up and down the metal. Young male bodies, hairless and smooth, shining in the haze, hot water streaming from their chins, elbows, and little male organs- the blunt bulbs of the circumcised and the pinched nozzles of the intact- Roundheads and Cavaliers in the school language. Ripples of white soap suds sliding like snakes across the red-tiled floor. Thirty boys, fighting for six

showers, shoving and nudging for space under the sprays. My friend
Mac and I leaning against each other, back to back, with our feet
spread wide, forming a pyramid that was hard to dislodge. Around us,
a cacophony of strident voices, taut with the excitement of the rugby
pitch, echoing from the tiles. Shrieks, when showers were turned to
cold or bare legs, were flicked with towels. We loved each other,
never touching like lovers but held together by the intense pleasure of
each other's presence, the bond of intimate knowledge and trust.

The space between Michael and I was not of that kind. I wondered
if that was what he had in mind, a platonic friendship, a benign
association between a youth and an older man.

I heard him step out of the bath. I was still sitting in my shirt and
trousers when he glanced round the door.

'Come, come, dear boy. Can't bathe in your clothes.'

I rose and slipped them off, standing naked beside the bed.

'Beautiful body,' he said, 'Classical. Like the Florentine David.
Even the pubic hair curving deliciously downward like the tip of a
fern.'

Grinning foolishly, I walked past him into the bathroom. Lying in
the steam, I remembered.

A figure kneeling beside my bed in the dorm, forearms resting on
my blanket. I was petrified. I could just see the head and shoulders in
the gloom. It was not a ghost, but there was something unnatural about
its presence. I wanted to wake someone but was afraid to move. I lay
as still as I could, scarcely daring to breathe. It was very late. There
was not a sound in the dormitory.

The figure moved an arm, and I was about to cry out when a cool finger was placed gently on my lips, and the head of the intruder loomed over my face. I thought that I was going to die.

The head descended till it lay beside me on the pillow.

'Shush,' it whispered so quietly as to be almost inaudible, 'It's me. Lie still. I will not harm you.'

I relaxed. I knew the voice. The prefect who had protected me. I couldn't understand why he had come to my bed in the night, although, on the edges of my mind, there lurked an anxiety - formless, wordless, but still an entity, a shadow.

When his cool fingers slid across my pyjamas and over the smooth skin of my lower belly, I did not move.

'Disgusting,' my mother's voice had echoed in my head and her frowning face had flashed through the darkness.

Part of me, infected by her horror, recoiled. Yet I felt safe in his hands, and the rhythmic movement of his fingers produced waves of intense pleasure, hints of ecstasy that stemmed from something in my memory, something just out of reach. It moved up from my loins, burning like a lance. Pain and pleasure, fear and fascination, thirst and submersion - a cauldron of sensations.

'Lie still, lie still, beautiful boy. I will be your teacher. I will show you wonderful things,' he whispered breathlessly.

As his fingers moved more rapidly, I winced and gasped. Pain burst in my groin, flashing up my spine, sparking from bone to bone. I found lips on my own and felt the rough bristle of a shaven face. I was kissed hungrily as a vast lava flow of ecstasy followed the pain. The prefect shuddered and collapsed on my shoulder.

'More. Much more. I will show you. Another time.' He slid away from the bed and vanished into the dark.

I lay stunned, tumult and confusion tumbling like clouds inside me. I could still feel his lips, but although I had kissed them passionately only a few moments beforehand, I suddenly found the memory of it repulsive. The tide of pleasure retreated, leaving bleak mud-flats of remorse and disgust in its wake.

'Lie still, lie still, beautiful boy.'

I could hear his voice as I stepped into the bath.

We dined with the celebrated director, Teddy Masterson, whose long clandestine affair with James O'Brien was in the last sad stages of decay. I had heard that O'Brien's skill with make-up had deserted him, and he was seen in public with smeared mascara and lipstick which strayed so far from his lips that it curled his mouth into a permanent expression of disdain. No longer a beautiful youth, he was finding it difficult to find a replacement for Teddy and was forced into sordid promiscuity. Teddy, on the other hand, had a handsome young actor on his arm.

'Michael,' he said, striding across the lounge, 'Wonderful to see you again. I want you to meet Maurice, our new juvenile lead.'

Maurice, dressed impeccably in a dark suit, moved gracefully forward to take Michael's hand. The white cuff, I noticed, was slightly frayed, but he grasped Michael's hand firmly and held it while he smiled mischievously, clearly aware of the effect of his good looks.

'Teddy has told me much about you. Best designer in the north, he says.' A blush travelled up Michael's scrawny neck.

'He always exaggerates. This is Willie. He's been working with the Group in Belfast.'

'Has he now? Welcome to Dublin, Willie.'

He bowed theatrically as he took my hand, his dark eyes flirting, trying to embarrass me with his pouting lips. It was hard to believe that he should behave so provocatively in front of Teddy. I did not find him attractive. Handsome certainly with an uncanny resemblance to photographs of James when he was young. The same sensual mouth the same expressive eyes, the same perfect profile but not the voice. James possessed a voice that drew the eyes of any crowd in his direction: melodious, resonating, with a range as wide as a piano, a captivating musical instrument. When Maurice spoke, there was nothing unusual in the timbre. Mundane, really, with the slight nasal whine of the Dublin suburbs.

Michael moved to rescue me from Maurice's attention. 'What would you like to drink, Maurice?'

'No. Let me get these,' Teddy intervened, 'I insist. You are the visitors.'

'In that case, Teddy dear, I'll have a very large G and T,' Maurice said, subsiding smoothly into an armchair and settling himself into a suitably elegant pose. The sharp crease in the trousers contrasted with the shabby shoes.

'Come, Willie, sit beside me here. Not often, I meet beautiful young men from the North.' I glanced at Michael, who, with a balletic gesture with his long fingers and a wry smile, gave his permission.

I felt I was betraying him by responding to the invitation. Yet he didn't seem to mind, seating himself opposite Maurice and brushing invisible dust from his trousers.

'Rehearsing, Maurice?' he said.

'The Informer'. Have you not heard?'

'We don't hear much in the north.'

'Of course. Belfast. Kitchen comedy and banal theatre.' I rose to the defence of the Group.

'We've just done 'Summer of the Seventeenth Doll,' I said, immediately regretting the intervention. Why I had felt it necessary to step into the arena, I could not understand. It was bound to lead to exposure.

'Indeed, Willie? Gritty Australian stuff, I believe. What part did you have?'

'I helped with the scenery.'

'A noble start to the profession,' he said, squeezing my knee in a condescending manner just as Teddy returned.

'I see you are getting to know each other.'

'Are you jealous, darling?' Maurice asked.

'Not at all. Should I be?'

Teddy's reptilian eyes, magnified by his horn-rimmed spectacles, glared venomously at his partner.

'Never know, Teddy. Perhaps Willie and I will arrange a secret assignation when you're away.'

I began to wish I wasn't there. I couldn't decide whether Maurice was intending to make me uncomfortable or trying to annoy Teddy. I had hoped to impress Teddy or at least exploit his contacts in Dublin. Michael came to the rescue.

'I'm not sure that Willie will have too much time on his hands. He's to meet Eve tonight for a chat about her new production. I was saving that up till later, Willie. A small surprise.'

'Eve Williamson?' asked Teddy, 'She's putting on a show?'

'Yes. Restoration comedy.'

'The Way of the World'.'

'Of course. She's always wanted to play in Millamant. Must have some money behind her. It can't possibly be a success. Dublin doesn't take to Congreve.'

'Shelagh Richards as Lady Wishfort– the 'old peeled wall.' I don't know. Dublin might flock to it.'

I wondered what Spam would make of the trio. Probably zip open Maurice's face with his chain merely for being effeminate. I could hear him scolding me for being there– 'What the fuck are you doing with them, Billy Boy? They're as queer as coots.' The memory of the slashed face outside the dance hall flashed past and, with it, a moment of dread, a premonition of discovery and arrest. A brief distraction. And Sarah. What would she say? She seemed so far away, in another world. For a moment, I remembered the taste of her lipstick and the shape of her smile. The scene would probably confirm her worst suspicions of me. Not the man she hoped for. She would purse her lips like a cow's hole on entering the lounge, disapproving of the gilded furniture, the velvet curtains, the French mirrors, the luxurious carpets, and the fish tank on the wall from which guests chose their trout for dinner.

'Eve's a delight, Willie. You'll love her. Where will you be staying?' Maurice asked. 'I don't know yet. I haven't thought. I don't have a part so far.'

'I thought he could stay with Freddy.' Michael intervened.

'The Queen of Dun Laoghaire. Don't think you'll be safe there, Willie.'

'He'd be perfectly safe. Freddy is a gentleman.'

'Of course he would,' said Teddy.

'An old chum of yours, Teddy?' Maurice smirked.

'I wish he had been. He was the most beautiful creature when he was young. Most handsome juvenile lead in Ireland.'

'More handsome than James?'

Teddy visibly winced. I decided that Maurice was a person to be avoided. A man with a poisonous tongue. Yet I had to get past him to speak to Teddy on his own.

'What did you think of Maurice?' Michael asked me as he tied his pyjama cord.

'A bit of a vixen, really.'

'Yes. I really don't know why Teddy tolerates his vitriol.'

'He's young and handsome.'

'An eye-catching accessory. You didn't fancy him then.'

'Certainly not.'

'Good. Come to bed.'

That was the moment I was dreading. How could I share the bed and resist his advances?

Did I really want to avoid them? The glasses of expensive Burgundy and port had flooded me with such a warm sensation of contentment and liberation that anything was possible. I did not want to hurt his feelings or appear to be a prude. I joined him in bed, looking up at the intricate plasterwork of the ceiling rose.

Chapter 15

'Is that you, son?'

Spam heard his mother's voice as he was heading quietly to his room. 'Aye. What is it?'

He turned back and put his head round the living room door.

She was sitting back in her chair, wiping her eyes with her apron. Her knitting lay on the floor beside her slippers.

'Your gran's fallen. She's in the hospital.'

'Jesus. Is she bad?'

'They don't know yet. You'd better go up to Belfast.'

'Where's my Da?'

'He's gone up.'

'Oh, aye? That's great. She'll know that she's at death's door if he appears.'

'Don't be so nasty. She'll want to see you.'

'What about you? Do you not want to go?'

'Not yet. Maybe tomorrow. Once they know.'

'Which hospital?'

'The City.'

The City. The one where his victim lay. The one he had promised to visit for his Gran.

The bag for her neighbour was still in the garage. He would have to go, though. For her, he would take the risk. The boy was bound to be in a different part, surely.

'Okay. I'll go. Can I give her a message?'

'Maybe she won't hear. But aye, give her my love and say I'll be tomorrow.'

'Sure. I'll be off then.'

He bent down and kissed her on the head. 'Don't worry. She'll be fine.'

He sat in the front seat on the top deck of the bus, mindlessly rolling the bus ticket into a tube. He stretched out his legs and rested his shoes on the front shelf, thinking that the relaxed pose would ease the worry. What if he met his victim in the corridor? Would the guy recognise him? It had been dark in the car park. Maybe the blow would have blanked out the memory. He was kidding himself. Of course, he would know him. Unless he changed his appearance - grow a beard, wear specs. He could do that. Aye, he could nick a pair of specs in Belfast. And a cap. He never wore a cap, so that would help. A master of disguise. The Scarlet Pimpernel. But what was the point? The guy's mates knew him anyway. It was the mother he was afraid to meet.

He stuck the ticket in his pocket and lit a cigarette. Maybe he should leave the country.

Join the army. Why had he not thought of that before? Join the Paras, the Red Berets, hard men, the best soldiers in the world. Fuckin' brilliant. Unarmed combat, kill with one blow. Blackened faces behind enemy lines. Strip a Bren in the dark. The more he thought about it, the more excited he became. Come back and kill every one of those bastards, striking silently and efficiently without warning. One hand over the mouth, commando knife in the back. Stab upwards through the ribs into the heart.

'Can I see your ticket, please?' The inspector stood over him.

'And take your feet off the shelf, please.'

Spam delved in his pocket for the ticket but left his shoes where they were. He handed over the crushed tube. The inspector unrolled it, clearly annoyed by Spam's contempt for his company's property.

'Could you take your feet off the shelf, please?'

Spam was about to confront him, cut him down to size, grab him by the lapels, and knee him where it hurt when he remembered the Paras. An assault on an official would not go down well in the recruiting office and there were other folk on the bus to act as witnesses.

He swung his feet to the floor.

'Thank you, sir,' the inspector sarcastically and walked away.

Spam took out his flick knife, sliced a long, neat incision in the seat, and returned his feet to the shelf.

He hated hospitals– the smell of carbolic and Dettol, the echoing corridors, the nurses who could pass him without a glance. He climbed the stairs slowly, sliding his hand up the bannister, feeling the shape. A chaplain passed him, his silver Lloyd George moustache stained with tobacco. Perhaps he had been at his victim's bedside, giving the last rites or whatever they did in his church. Jesus, maybe the guy was dead. He stopped on the top step, tempted to go back, to escape from the place, tell his Ma that he had not been allowed to see her. But his Da might be there already, and anyway, it was his Gran, the only person who really liked him.

He found the ward and looked around the beds. Some dreadful sights. An old woman sleeping with her mouth open, her face as pale as the sheets but slightly yellow. Nothing of her under the bed cover, just a torso like a Punch and Judy show. Death had claimed her already, although she was breathing. Another in a chair, her chin on her chest, her claws clamped to the arm, clinging to life. They scared him. He turned away and searched the beds for his Gran, eventually spotting his Da sitting by a bed, holding her hand.

'How is she?'

'Grand. Just grand. How do you think she is?'

'Christ's sake! I only asked.'

Spam stared at her. So frail and tired. He had never seen her without her false teeth. Her face seemed to be eating itself.

'What happened?'

'She fell down the stairs. Lay in the hall. Neighbour found her.'

'Will she be okay?'

'How the hell would I know?'

'Have you spoken to anyone? A doctor. A nurse.'

'Nurse says she's comfortable. They gave her something to make her sleep. They don't know yet.'

'Are there bones broken?'

'They don't fuckin' know I said. Are you deaf or something?' The woman in the next bed tutted.

Spam turned and walked away, afraid that he would smack his Da in the mouth. 'Come back here! It'll be you she wants to see.'

Spam kept walking, clenching the knife in his pocket.

When he reached home, they were there. The two peelers had just emerged from the garage, the younger grinning when he saw the shock on Spam's face.

'What's this then, eh?' he said, swinging the chain.

'Looks like a bike chain, but then it might be a pair of drawers.'

'Don't be so bloody cheeky. What's it for? There's no bike in there.'

'Aye, that's a sad story. Some bastard stole my bike. Left the spare chain, though.'

'Always an answer, eh?' the older one said, 'We'll take it with us and give it to the boffins. See what they make of it. You won't need it anyway, will you?'

'No. You're welcome to it. Rusty ol' chain. Not much good for anything.'

'That's the odd thing, Patrick. It's not rusty. It's in grand order. Looks as though it's been used recently.'

'You're wrong there. I kept it oiled in case the force managed to find my bike. I don't hold out much hope of that, though. Not a high priority, my bike.'

'And did you report it missing?'

'Do you know? I'm not sure. I was that upset; maybe I didn't. I can't remember.'

'Well, we'll have a look at the book when we get back. When was it?'

'I just can't remember.'

'If it's in the book, we'll find it, and we'll organise a nationwide search for your bike when we find the details. In the meantime, Patrick, you'd be wise to stay out of Belfast. They say that the mates of the boy who was chained have a big posse together, a kind of lynch mob, out for vengeance.'

'Nothing to do with me.'

'Oh aye, I was forgetting. Anyway, there are you now. We'll be off. Stick to the boxing ring, Patrick. It's less dangerous than the street. We'll be back if the boffins find anything.'

They rode off on their bikes. As he lit a fag he found that his fingers were shaking.

Fuckin' bastards. What made them look in the garage? They might find blood on the chain or even bits of skin. Jesus. He might end up inside. Couldn't stand that, locked in a cell day after day. And if yer man dies… Christ almighty! Murder. Done for murder. Fucksake. Threw away the fag and headed for the house. The Paras. Next stop…

'I've joined up,' Spam announced, marching into the room and coming to attention with a salute.

His father, lounging in his chair, shifted his stockinged feet along the fender but did not look up from the racing page of the paper.

'Oh aye?' he said.

His mother laid her knitting on her lap. 'What do you mean, joined up?'

'What do you think he means, stupid woman?' his father growled, 'He's joined the army. About bloody time he did something useful. Knock some sense into him and discipline him. Have to do what he's told for a change.'

'Fuck off, you lazy bastard. Look at you. Never did a stroke of work in your life.'

'For heaven's sake, stop it, you two,' his mother shouted, ' What are you saying, Patrick?'

'I've joined the army. Going into the Paras. The Red Berets. Have to start with the infantry, though, for basic training and all that.'

'When do you start?'

'Soon. They'll let me know when and where?'

'Where? Not Belfast then? Not here?'

'England likely.'

'He's running from something,' his father folded the paper and looked at him, 'You're in trouble, aren't you? I can tell. All this hurry to get away and the police searching the garage. You don't kid me, boy.'

'Nothing like that. I want to make something of my life. Not selling clapped out cars for the rest of my days. What kind of life is that?'

'Good enough for your Dad,' his mother said, 'But you could have joined the merchant navy. That's what the others round here do. Sail all over the world, they do. Shell tankers and Head Line. Like your big brother.'

'That's why I joined the army. To steer clear of that bastard.'

'Patrick! He's your brother.'

'He's a queer like Lord Montagu.'

'That's a terrible thing to say.'

'Takes one to know one,' his father muttered.

Spam clenched his fist to smash his mouth but, remembering the army turned and left the room, slamming his knuckles through the door panel on the way.

He strolled up to the camp gates, his hands in his pockets. He had walked the two miles from the station, enjoying the sun and the smell of the English countryside. Not a single car or lorry had passed him. The single soldier on duty was not armed but studied him with suspicion and disapproval.

'Can I help you, sir?'

Who the hell are you, and what are you doing here? Was that what he meant?

Spam reached into his pocket to retrieve the letter. The soldier stiffened and shouted over his shoulder to the guardroom.

'Corporal Bates!'

Spam unfolded the letter and handed it over.

A corporal stepped out of the guardroom and strutted across. Spam noted the neatly pressed uniform, the glittering cap badge, the gleaming boots, and the beret carefully moulded into a smart peak at the front.

'Who's this then?'

The soldier passed over the letter. Bates read it and frowned.

'There's a mistake here, another balls up. You're a week late, son. The rest of the recruits are kitted out and on parade.'

'What'll I do?'

'You'd better come in.'

Spam followed the corporal into the guardroom.

A sergeant was sitting at the desk, adjusting his red beret as Spam came in.

'Another fuckin' shambles, Sarge,' Bates said, handing over the letter, 'They've got the wrong date.'

'A Paddy, eh? A bog-trotter? All the way from Tipperary.'

'From the north, near Belfast.'

'No difference. What's your name, Paddy? We'd better fill in the details. Name and home address. You'll get your number later.'

'Patrick Simpson.'

'Patrick Simpson, *sergeant*. Better get used to it.'

'Yes, sergeant.'

'Take him to the store, Corporal, and get him kitted out. See that he gets bedding, too.'

Spam staggered away from the store with a pile of kit in his arms, trying to see where he was going as he followed the corporal. The billet was a brick building set in a dismal group of other brick buildings. Windows high in the wall to maximise the gloom inside. Eight iron beds in each of the two rooms, the eight divided by four tall steel lockers. At the top of every bed, the blankets are neatly 'boxed,' each one folded precisely on top of the next. In the middle of the room, an iron stove with its flue reaching to the roof. Spam imagined the men bunched around it with blankets around their shoulders, trying to keep warm, the billet being so cold that frost still clung to the windows.

'That's yours,' the corporal said, pointing to the one empty bed, 'The others'll be back shortly. They'll tell you the drill and show you around. You could maybe get the fire going for them. Pile of coke out the back.'

'Okay. Thanks. Thanks, corporal.' He stared at the kit as the NCO left.

A great coat, a battledress blouse and trousers, gaiters and belt, boots and grey socks, a black beret and cap badge, ammunition pouches, a large pack, a housewife, eating irons, and mess tins. He had hoped to be handed a rifle, that his soldiering would begin immediately.

He lit a cigarette and left to search for kindling. He was met at the door by the returning squad, all in uniform.

'What are you doing in there?' the leader asked, a tall young man whose lank dark hair had been shaven above his ears.

Spam did not like his manner and, in any other circumstances, would have smacked him in the mouth.

'My kit's in there. My bed's in there. I'm going to be in there.'

'In our squad?'

'I don't know whose fuckin' squad. I just do what I'm told.'

'You're a recruit then?'

'Christ's sake, get inside. It's fuckin' freezing out here,' the man behind the leader said. A small, sturdy soldier with a pock-marked face and glasses as thick as oyster shells. 'You'd better go in,' the leader said, 'You're a Paddy, aren't you?'

'Aye. A small place near Belfast.'

The seven men gathered around the stove. 'What's your right name?'

'Patrick. They call me Spam.'

'You a Tim then?' the small man asked.

'No. Does it matter?'

'Yeh. It does. I hate Tims. Lazy bastards. Like you. You could have lit the stove.'

'You're a smart guy. You do it.'

The tall man stepped between them.

'Don't mind him. He's from Manchester, so he can't help it. My name's Joe. From Yorkshire, the civilised part of the North. Somebody can light the stove while I show Spam the ropes. Open your locker, and I'll show you how to stow your kit. They inspect the lockers, everything, so it has to be right. Don't want you on jankers.'

Spam learnt quickly. Burn down the pimples on his boots with a hot spoon to get a smooth surface for a deep, dark shine. Soap the inside of the creases on his trousers to get them razor-sharp. Buff the cap badge flat so that it glittered in the sun. Polish the brasses with Duraglit. He became part of the team in spite of Kelly the Mancunian and his constant provocation. He kept control of his anger, waiting for a time when he could deal with Kelly.

On parade, he was soon the best in the platoon, drilling with precision and dressing meticulously. He picked up the arms drill with his Lee-Enfield 303 rifle immediately. He handled the rifle like a lover, caressing the butt like a woman's thigh, thrusting the bolt forward, and feeling its metal slide sensually into place. Even the glint of the dark steel gave him pleasure. He used the pull-through to clean the barrel till the rifling inside shone like a mirror. The recruits were not issued with full bayonets but with spikes that allowed them to drill as if they had real blades. Spam hoped that they would be given bayonets and that he would be taught how to use them as they did in films.

His favourite weapon, however, was the sten gun. He learnt how to strip and re-assemble the weapon while blindfolded. He could feel every part and loved the kick of the barrel when he used it on the range. It's not at all accurate at long range but deadly in close quarters. He imagined the expression on the faces of the neds back home when he produced it in a street fight and sprayed them with bullets. What a feeling of power!

'I don't know how you can do that so fast,' Joe said as Spam stripped and re-assembled in front of the squad.

'Cause he's a brown nose,' Kelly muttered.

'Cause he's a fuckin' soldier, Kelly,' said the corporal instructor, 'Not a wanker from Manchester. Could mean life or death in the jungle. Gooks won't wait for you to clean your specs before they cut your throat, you know.'

Spam did not need a weapon to deal with Kelly. He planned the attack carefully so that there would be no witnesses.

Chapter 16

I watched the rehearsals of 'The Way of the World' in the Gate Theatre with awe. The interaction between Shelagh Richards as Lady Wishfort, the lascivious old aristocrat, and Dermot Touhy as her rough bucolic nephew Sir Wilfull Witwoud was an inspiration. I never tired of Shelagh's delivery of Wishfort's line, 'I look like an old peeled wall.' She always managed to express in her cracked voice the essence of the crumbling old lady in those words.

Aiden Grenell played Witwoud, a fop, with such panache and versatility that I copied him in the privacy of my digs at night, twirling a handkerchief effeminately and swooping a gracious bow to a chair. I pictured myself in the part of a cavalier rake with a long curling wig, extravagant shirt cuffs, a velvet coat, tight white breeches, and buckled shoes. I was determined to be an actor like Aiden. It was exciting to be part of that theatrical world, mixing with such talented people. Sadly, I was not on stage but was in charge of the prompt script and all the lighting and curtain cues, a humble role but a step on the way, I thought, to certain stardom.

Dermot, a hefty, sandy-haired Dubliner, invited me to see 'Under Milk Wood' staged in the Gate at night, where he was playing blind Captain Cat. During the performance he was placed in the shadows in front of the proscenium, isolated with his dreams of Rosie Probert. It was the most moving performance I had seen, wringing tears from my eyes in the darkness. Absolutely wonderful. I didn't know what to say to him in the dressing room after the show for fear of sounding sycophantic. It was a humbling experience, too, reminding me that my ambitions to be a great actor might be misplaced. I felt like a wee boy in the company of men, but Dermot treated me with kindness and respect and invited me to Groom's hotel after the show.

After rehearsals, evenings were free, and many of them spent drinking in hotels or in the front rooms of theatre people. Sleep became something that happened just before it was time to rise. On the last free evening before our show opened, Dermot took me out to a little theatre above a gas showroom in Dun Laoghaire to see 'Murder Mistaken.' The theatre was indeed tiny, with the space in the wings acting as dressing rooms, but the actors seemed to be oblivious to the difficulties. After the show, I met Pauline Delaney, one of the kindest and warmest actresses in Dublin, and her husband, Norman Rodway. I loved Pauline from that first encounter, a love that hovered in the air but never landed, undeclared and unrequited. I don't suppose she even noticed.

It was into this milieu that Spam suddenly intruded. When a girl from the ticket office interrupted a rehearsal to tell me that I had a visitor at the door, at first I thought it might be Michael but then remembered he had returned north. I could not hide my horror when I saw Spam.

'Billy Boy!'

'Spam the Man,' I replied without the usual enthusiasm.

'Not pleased to see me?'

'Course I am.'

'Jesus. You even speak differently. Where did that BBC accent come from?'

'I'm still the same.'

'Look at you, for Christ's sake. Long hair, cravat, suede shoes, and is that the hint of a beard, or is it bum-fluff on your chin?'

'And what about your blazer and flannels and shining shoes? What's happened to you?'

'I've joined up. I'm in the army. Leave for training again in England on Wednesday.'

'You're joking.'

'No. A fact. I came to see you before I left. Come for a pint?'

'I'm working, Spam. Have to get back in. I'll meet you at lunchtime.'

'Come on. Never mind them queers inside, Billy.'

'No, really. I've got to finish this scene. Come back at lunch. I'll meet you here.'

'Right. One o'clock. No later.'

He turned and grinned at the girl in the ticket office. 'Thanks, darlin'. Fancy a wee gargle in the hotel?' She smiled patiently and shook her head.

He left with his usual insolent gait, and I returned to the gloom of the auditorium, dreading the prospect of Spam meeting some of the cast. I was tempted to avoid him at lunchtime and sneak out well before he arrived, but shreds of the old loyalty stuck like flypaper. His carefree, hedonistic attitude to life had been infectious. He really didn't care what other people thought of him and now I found myself addicted to pleasing or impressing my new circle of friends. I felt guilty about the wish to disown him, but I did not want him to destroy my new image. I wanted to be an actor, and I did not want him to get in the way of that, and I did not want my colleagues to know anything of my reckless plebeian past. Besides, I was suspicious. He would not have driven all the way from Belfast just to say farewell. There must be another reason.

In the auditorium, John, the director, was talking to a burly man with tousled dark hair, heavy, unshaven jowls, a grubby shirt, and eyes rimmed with sleep– everything suggesting debauchery. Yet John was treating him with respect…

'Just a couple of quid, John boy. A couple of quid till the money comes in.'

'And what will Beatrice say? I'll be crucified.'

'She'll never know.'

'She'll know when you roll in the door. Like the last time when we took you home in a taxi, and she attacked me with an umbrella and blamed me for your inebriation. A fierce woman, your wife.'

'I won't mention your name. Jesus, John, what's a couple of quid between friends?'

'Oh, very well. Here. Now go away and leave me in peace.'

'God love you, John boy. And who's this fine-looking young man.' The dark eyes swung in my direction, squinting in the poor light. 'Willie, our ASM. Learning the trade. Down from the North.'

'The North, is it? Well, with a name like Willie from the North, he must be a Prod. A Prod are you, Willie?'

'Not anything.'

'You're a fuckin' liar, Willie. You're brought up a Prod, and you'll never shake that off. Where are you from?'

'Bangor.'

'Fuckin' Bangor, eh? The arsehole of the world. Now Donaghadee– there's a tidy wee place. I painted the lighthouse there one summer. Fuckin' bastard of a boss tried to get me dismissed. Blakely by name. Do you know him?' I shook my head.

'Just as well. Do you know Mrs Morrison? Now there's a lady.'

'I don't live in Donaghadee.'

I was about to mention Spam but thought it wise to keep quiet.

'Thirteen pubs, John. Thirteen Fuckin' pubs in Donaghadee. A lot of hostelries in a wee village. The Royal. Drank there with Kicker Nelson, skipper of the lifeboat. A real gentleman, Kicker.'

'I know him, right enough. I saw him bring in survivors from the 'Princess Victoria.'

'Brave man. That was a terrible tragedy. Here, seeing you know Kicker. Couple of tickets to my play at Damer Hall tonight. Come along. Must toddle on now. A date with Mt Neary. Thanks, John.'

He handed me the tickets as he passed.

'What a boor,' I said to John as the door closed behind him.'

'On the exterior perhaps, but that is one of the most erudite, creative, and wittiest men in Dublin. Don't be deceived, Willie. Go along tonight. The play is in Gaelic, but you will be able to follow the drift. 'An Giall'. In twenty years time you'll be able to boast that you met him.'

'Really?'

'Oh yes. And he has a book coming out at the end of the year. Look at his name on the ticket and remember it. Now, back to the script. I've cut a bit of Witwoud's speech when you were out, so make sure it's clearly marked.'

The name of the playwright was Brendan Behan. I had no idea who he was.

John called Lady Wishfort on stage for Sir Wilful's entrance, and I sat in the stalls with the script on my knee.

At lunchtime, I dropped the script on the seat and hurried out of the theatre. Just as I reached the street at the bottom of the steps outside, Maurice appeared.

'Willie. I was on my way to see you. I thought you'd be here.'

Knowing that Spam might appear at any minute, I could not hide my anxiety.

'What's wrong, dear boy? Are you not pleased to see me?'

'Of course I am, but I was expecting a friend of mine.'

'Ah. A special friend?'

'Not that kind of friend.'

'I must meet him if he is as handsome as young and handsome as you...' At that point, Spam appeared.

'Billy Boy!'

'This is Maurice,' I said, omitting the usual greeting, 'And this is Spam.'

'A great delicacy, dear boy. Spam and beans.'

'And who the fuck are you, dear boy?'

'Maurice, as Willie said.'

'His name's Billy.'

'Far too common. He's not a Billy. Beautiful boy can't be called Billy.'

'He's Billy. And you, my friend, can fuck off unless you want your good looks spoiled altogether.'

'Oh, we are course, aren't we?'

I knew what was about to happen. The image that I had tried to build in Dublin was about to be shattered. I tried to think of something to say or do that would prevent the inevitable but stood helplessly in the middle.

Spam grabbed Maurice by the throat, forcing him back against the wall.

'Course am I? You fuckin' pansy. One more word and your face'll look like something from a butcher's slab.'

'For God's sake, Spam. Leave him. You'll have the police on us.'

Maurice's face was white, and his lip was quivering with terror. Spam did not turn around.

I noticed the knuckle duster on his finger and imagined what it could do to Maurice. 'Leave him, Spam.'

I didn't dare touch Spam's arm or try to restrain him in case he turned on me, but he did release Maurice and walked away, pulling me by the arm. I looked back, and Maurice was hurrying away up the street. I was relieved that he did not go into the theatre or across the road to the hotel.

'Why the fuck do you have anything to do with creeps like that?'

'I don't. He's not a friend. He's just one of the theatre crowd.'

'And they're a right bunch. For fuck's sake, Billy, go back and get a job. A proper job.'

'Like a car salesman. No thanks. Not on your life. I want to be an actor. Anyway, what's the point of going back? You won't be there.'

'And what about Sarah? You couldn't get enough of her.'

'She'll wait.'

'Will she now? I wonder.'

'Did you come all that way to give me a lecture?'

'No. I wanted to see you before I go. Make sure you and I had the right story about the night of the dance.'

'We've been over that a hundred times.'

'And to give you this.'

He slipped notes from his pocket and handed me twenty Irish pounds. 'I can't take that.'

'You can. You'll need it if you're going to be an actor. Just take it and go and join your friends for lunch. Go on. I've got to leave. I'm catching the Heysham boat tonight.'

I was astonished. He seemed to be giving me permission to be an actor and I couldn't help wondering why he had changed his mind.

'Go before I give you kicking.'

He threw his arms around me, gave me a hug, and walked away. I spent the next few days worrying about meeting Maurice or finding that he had reported his encounter with Spam, embellished no doubt with lurid and fanciful detail.

The day before the opening night, a report in the Irish Times, 'WELL-DRESSED THIEF ESCAPES WITH TWO HUNDRED POUNDS.'

A thief carrying what appeared to be a firearm held up a post office in Pearse Street and escaped in a green Simca car. He was dressed in a blazer and flannels and covered his face and head with a scarf. The number of the car is not known, but the Garda are trying to trace the vehicle.

I took out my wallet and looked at the money. Irish pounds. Spam's generosity was not so extravagant after all.

When we opened, the show as a whole did not receive outstanding reviews. 'It was not perfect Restoration comedy,' the Irish Times commented, 'with many minor weaknesses' 'Dermot Tuohy's otherwise admirable Wilful Witwoud loses something by occasional woolly dialogue' I thought this was unfair and told Dermot that the reviewer must have forgotten his ear trumpet.

'He had a point, dear boy. I was pissed on the first night.'

Sitting in the wings with the script, I had not noticed, but then the drunkenness fitted perfectly with the character.

Shelagh, I read with delight, was hailed as 'a triumph.' Raddled, addled, and plastered (cosmetically speaking), she dominated every scene she was in.' She was the star of the show.

Every day, I scanned the newspapers to see if Spam had been identified, and I worried about spending the money in case it was recognised.

As the show ran on, I became anxious about the next step. I frequented places such as Grooms Hotel or the Theatre Club on Gardner Street, where there was a chance to meet producers and other actors in the hope of securing a small part. I knew that the Globe Theatre Company was due to stage Anouilh's 'Dinner with the Family' in the Gate and spoke to Aiden, who said that he would do what he could. I met Maurice O'Brien, who was producing 'A Lady Mislaid' at the Gas Company Theatre, but his rehearsals were already well underway. I even tried the Abbey where 'A Change of Mind' was due to open. As the days passed I began to despair of finding a part in Dublin or anywhere else. The more desperate I became, the more I invited myself to every theatrical party in the city, lingering there in the hope of meeting someone who could be persuaded to find me a part. It was humiliating to beg, but the distress caused by the prospect of failure was greater than the mortification. It seemed as though a return to the north and mundane employment was inevitable. There was always Michael, of course, but this time, any help might incur a greater expense. I remembered his embrace and shuddered.

Sarah's lips would be soft and feminine. I had forgotten about her and felt guilty about that. I had not written since the play opened. Perhaps she would have found someone else or gone back to Clive. She had not promised to wait. The thought of losing her just added to the misery.

Chapter 17

'I miss him, you know.'

'For God's sake, Sarah, forget him. He'll have had all kinds of floosies down there.'

'He writes twice a week sometimes.'

'Guilty conscience.'

'Really poetic letters.'

'Even worse. You can't trust that kind of man.'

The two girls stared out over the shipyard, watching the mass of workmen as a spate of cloth caps streaming towards the gates.

'He's probably queer,' Nancy continued, 'him being an actor.' 'He is not. Don't be disgusting.'

'If he's not now, he will be. Mark my words. They're all like that. Better off with Clive.'

'You sound like my mother.'

'Maybe she's got sense. You can't wait on Billy forever.'

'Three weeks. Only three weeks.'

'You're daft, Sarah. Anyway, I'm late. Big dance tonight. Dave Glover's band. Be good. You should come.'

Nancy lifted her coat from the rack and shook it on. 'Church choir tonight,' Sarah said.

'Goody two shoes. See you later, alligator.'

'Bye, Nancy.'

Sarah turned and gazed over the empty office, the rows of tracing desks, the compasses, curves, squares, and inks, still and silent. She looked at the high stools and imagined the ranks of girls bent over the plans, each with her shoe heel clipped over the bottom bar. All away to their separate homes - some to husbands and children, some to parents, some, like Miss Capper, to the loneliness of a single household with an anaemic gas fire.

She walked up to Miss Capper's desk and sat down.

What would she be doing at that minute? Closing the door, shivering as she hung up her coat, her shoes clattering on the lino as she walked towards the living room. No mail to pick up. No voice from the kitchen. Bending to light the gas fire, her fingers blue with cold. An ashtray of curled, black, spent matches like an empty nest in the tiled fireplace. Holding the flickering match to the grill, fearful of the first pop of the gas. Through to the kitchen to wet the tea. Fill the kettle, light the gas, and place it on the ring. A cup and saucer from the cupboard and a bottle of milk from the pantry. Squeeze the cardboard top to open. Warm the brown pot with the chipped spout with water from the kettle. Open the tin with the picture of the Coronation and ladle it in two spoonfuls– one for each person and one for the pot. Watch the dry tea spinning on the surface as you fill the pot. The routine of a spinster in the crushing silence of the house. Only the gentle roar of the gas.

Sarah shivered. She did not want to end up like that. She thought of Billy. If they were married, would he be there to meet her when she came home? Would he wash the dishes and change nappies? She tried hard to visualise him at the sink with a dishtowel in his hands.

No, not domesticated. Not him. Used to having his mother or the maid see to his needs. Yet he might change. Everyone can change. If he loved her, he could change. Be a father and a husband. Yet where was he now? Chasing the bright lights. Wanting to be a star. He was quite good. Quite good, but not a Dirk Bogarde. Maybe, if he failed, he would settle, but who would want a failure in the house, a man twisted by rejection and bitter with envy of those who succeeded?

'Why can he not be ordinary?' she said aloud.

Yet it was his difference that was attractive, the way he used words, the way he would suddenly say something extraordinary or do something surprising like bring roses to the office.

'What are you doing here, young lady?'

She was so shocked that she fell sideways as she turned, just managing to catch the edge of the desk to stop herself from landing on the floor.

The owner of the yard. She had seen him at launches. 'Sorry, I didn't mean to startle you.'

'No… No sir… I was… There was no… I'm sorry, sir.' She felt her neck and cheeks glowing.

'You would like to take Miss Capper's place? I like a bit of ambition. Perhaps one day you will. Miss…?'

'Curran, sir. Sarah Curran. I didn't mean any harm.'

'Of course not. No harm done. You're late finishing this evening.'
'I wanted to finish the section. The tracing.'

'What part are you working on?'

'The lounge, sir. Of the Canberra, that is.'

'You don't need to call me "sir" all the time. My name is David.'

She knew that. More like Goliath, she thought. Tall with broad shoulders. A rugby player, no doubt. She didn't like the way his eyebrows were raised as if he was slightly amused by her embarrassment, laughing at her behind his dark brown eyes. Clearly used to being admired, justifiable so. Very handsome, charming, and furnished with the confidence of his class.

'Do you live in Belfast, Sarah?'

'No, sir. Bangor. I catch the train home.'

'I'll give you a lift to the station. The car is just outside. Get your coat and handbag.'

'No, sir. Really. I was going to walk.'

'Nonsense. I won't hear of it. Do we need to turn off the lights?'
'No. The cleaners do that.'

She was conscious of the frayed cuffs on her coat as they walked towards the car– a sleek, grey Humber Snipe– Clive had taught her to recognise the expensive cars to which he aspired. Mr Becker opened the door for her, and she sank into the leather seat, trying to hide the ladder in her stocking.

'How long have you been with us, Sarah?' he asked as the car slid smoothly into the roadway.

'Four years, sir.'

'No. Not sir.'

'Sorry. Four years.'

'You enjoy the work?'

'Yes. Very much.'

'Truthfully? You don't need to pretend on my behalf.'

'I'm not. I like the work.'

She did not tell him off the sharp pain in her wrist with the strain of holding the pens or the oppressive silence of Miss Capper's regime.

'Have you ever been on board any of the ships, ones for which you have drawn the tracings?'

'No. Not yet, anyway.'

'Tell you what. Meet me at the gangway of the Reina Del Mar at lunchtime tomorrow, and I'll show you around. She's due to go into service soon.'

'I couldn't do that, sir. What would Miss Capper say?'

What would Nancy and the others say? 'Sarah's a gold-digger.' 'Who does she think she is?' She could hear the bitching.

'Never mind, Miss Capper. I'll deal with her. It's time the tracers saw the results of all their hard work. You said you were working on the Canberra at the moment?'

'Yes.'

'When she's finished, I'll take the whole team round– all the tracers.'

'That would be wonderful. We've been to launches but never been around a finished ship.'

'Good. That's a promise. You can tell the girls.'

The car swung into the station, and Sarah opened the door quickly. 'Thanks very much for the lift, sir. Saved me a walk.'

'You're welcome, Sarah. See you tomorrow at the gangway.' 'Yes. See you then.'

She managed to find a seat by herself on the train. It was dark, and she watched the lights of the aircraft factory fly past. The window had been wiped, and droplets of brown water slid down the glass. She saw her reflection, surprised by the frown and the tight lips, the fear in her eyes. And she was afraid. A man with more power than anyone she knew was showing interest in her. Why should he? A married man with the pick of any woman in Belfast was meeting her at lunchtime. Surely, she was misreading the situation. Surely, he had merely taken pity on her and was making amends for startling her. Yet she was certain that she had seen something more than casual interest in the way he glanced at her figure, and he was very handsome and charming. If he did make advances, what would she do? If she refused, she could lose her job. Would she want to refuse?

She imagined her mother's face if she confessed that she was dating Mr. Becker and giggled, the humour breaking the rising tide of apprehension and confusion. She reached into her bag and opened Woman's Own to read her horoscope.

He was waiting at the gangway as promised. Two men leaving the ship touched their caps to him as they passed.'

'Ah, Sarah. I'm so glad you were able to come. I hope Miss Capper didn't cause any difficulties.'

She had not told Miss Capper nor Nancy, or anyone else.

'No, sir. No difficulties.'

'Splendid. Come aboard.'

He steered her towards the gangway.

'I'm really pleased with this ship. Built for Pacific Steam. Just think, Sarah, in a few months, she'll be sailing through the Panama Canal and down to Peru and Chile. Wouldn't you like to go?'

'I can't afford to go to Portrush, let alone America.'

She blushed, thinking the reply might be taken as a criticism of her wages.

'Who knows, Sarah, what the future holds. Never dismiss any of your dreams. Through this way. This is the cocktail bar. What do you think?'

Her lips parted in amazement. The brilliant colours and lighting gave the room a feeling of modern luxury. The blue and red leather armchairs, the light oak panelling, the wide circle of downlights, and the central rose all looked like something from a film.

'So light and tasteful,' she said, 'Not fussy like the Queens.'

'I'm glad you like it. We tried to move away from ostentation to a sort of quiet, comfortable display of affluence if you see what I mean.'

'Yes. I see.' She didn't.

'Come, I want to show you the lido deck.'

They climbed the wide stairway together. His black shoes were highly polished, glinting beneath the sharp creases in his trousers, and she supposed he had maids to see to these tasks.

'What do you think?' he said, his arm sweeping round the scene. 'A swimming pool!'

'Yes, and each table will have a parasol when the sun shines.' 'Brilliant.'

'Tempt you to go on a cruise?'

'Yes, but I wouldn't want to be away from home for all that time.' 'Miss your boyfriend?'

She recognised the probe. 'Yes. Probably.'

'He from Bangor too?'

'How do you know that?'

'I try to know a little about my staff.'

'All twenty-seven thousand.'

'No. Of course not. Selected ones.'

'You've been spying on me.'

'I suppose I have. I was interested. I called in with personnel.' 'Really?'

'I wanted to know a little more.'

'They won't know much. I haven't seen them since the day I started. There's not much to know anyway. I don't do anything exciting.'

'Yes, but you could. You could go on a cruise. Think of that– the wide ocean, the clear blue skies, the sun by day, the moonlight on the water.'

'You make it sound so romantic.'

'Think about it. I'm serious. You would love it. A free cruise.'
'Why me? I'm just a tracer, sir. What would the others say?'

'They'd be as jealous as hell, wouldn't they? Look, I want to reward one of my staff, one who turns up day after day to do the same humdrum work, one who doesn't stand out from the crowd, an ordinary, honest, reliable, loyal member of the workforce. We applaud engineers, designers, managers, and salesmen, but we don't recognise the work done by anonymous workers like yourself who toil away for modest rewards but without whom we could not succeed. If you accept the offer and enjoy the experience, I will make the same offer next year to one of the draughtsmen. What do you think, Sarah?'

'I don't know. It's really kind, but not me. Someone else. I would never hear the end of it. "What's she done to deserve it?" that's what they would say, "Got off with the boss or something?" I can just hear them. No, sir. It's a wonderful offer, but I can't accept it. Anyway, I can't leave my Mum… or my boyfriend.'

'Fair enough, Sarah, but don't turn it down immediately. Think about it, as I say. I'll leave it on the table for a week or two.'

Chapter 18

She was reading her horoscope in Woman's Own on the kitchen table when the doorbell rang. Thinking her mother was in the sitting room, she waited for her voice in the hall. The bell rang a second time.

'Damn,' she said and closed the magazine. Her mother must have been upstairs. As she approached the door, she instantly knew the figure on the porch.

'Billy!'

Billy, but not quite the same. Longer hair, a hint of a beard, a polo-neck sweater, and slacks.

She threw her arms around his neck and reached up to kiss him, opening her lips and pressing her body against his. He smelled different and unfamiliar, and the soft beard touched her face as she pulled back to speak.

He seemed to be a bit shocked by her enthusiasm, shocked but pleased, 'I thought you were never coming back.'

'Of course, I was coming back. Did you really think I wouldn't?'

'I thought you might get carried away by the life down there. All those actresses and admiring females.'

'It wasn't like that. Just hard work. Did you miss me?'
'Sometimes. Not all the time.'

She didn't want to tell him that she had thought of him every night, that she had longed for him to be in bed beside her, that she had remembered his fingers on her skin, recalling the touch so vividly that she gasped. She had lain in the dark, moving her hips on the sheet, feeling the fabric flowing across her skin, imagining his lips on hers and his weight on her body. All the disgust she felt when he had taken advantage of her illness had dissipated and been replaced by a yearning for repetition. She wanted him as a lover, a husband. She wanted to be his wife, to surrender to him, to open herself to him, and to share every moment of her life with him, but she didn't want him to know her thoughts. Not yet, anyway. She still needed to trust him, to know his feelings, and be sure that he loved her.

'I missed you,' he said.

'Sometimes. I'll bet you were far too busy impressing the ladies to think of me.'

'No, really. It wasn't like that. I bought you a present.'

'You shouldn't have. I don't need a present.'

'It's at the house. Come over, and I'll give it to you.'

'What now?'

'Yes. Why not?'

'But I'm not dressed, and what will I tell Mum?'

'Tell her it's my sister's birthday, and you're invited to the party.'
'That's a lie, isn't it?'

'Yeh.'

'You're wicked. Okay. Come in and wait. I think Mum's gone for a bath. Wait in the kitchen while I get dressed.'

She hurried upstairs and, in her bedroom, stood by the wardrobe wondering what to wear and trying to gather her scattered thoughts. So many uncertainties. Could she really trust Billy, who lied so easily? Should she tell him about her boss? Was Billy mature enough to settle down and get a proper job? Was he being honest about Dublin? Her horoscope had warned her not to be too trusting. But then she remembered what Aunt Belle had said– 'something more exciting, creative, a bit of flair, panache.' Compared with Clive, Billy had all of those. Aunt Belle would approve of Billy.

She dressed in her tightest sweater, her blue circular skirt, and high heels. Passing the bathroom, she called her mother.

'I'm going over to Billy's. His sister's birthday. Be back later.'
'Don't be late. You have work tomorrow.'

'Bye.'

She walked hand in hand with Billy across the town, past the cinema, and through the main street towards the railway station. She enjoyed being seen with him. He was quite handsome, and girls often turned to look at him. He stopped in the shadows of Dufferin Avenue, and, gently turning her face towards his, he kissed her. There was a tenderness there which made her feel safe, cared for, and nurtured as if he were holding a nestling. Different from the way he kissed outside the dance hall.

'I missed you,' he said as they walked on. She took his arm and snuggled up to him.

When they reached the house, he led her towards the stairs. She hesitated, wondering where he was trying to take her.

'It's okay,' he said, 'My room is at the top.'

'What about your Mum and your sister?'

'They're out, and Mother won't mind anyway. It's my kingdom up there. None of them are allowed on the top floor. You'll be quite safe.'

'I don't know. Can we not stay in the sitting room?'

'Your present is upstairs. Don't you trust me?'

'Course I do. But what will your Mum think when she comes back?'

'She won't mind. Really. I've had lots of friends up there.'

She had felt safe with him earlier, but she thought it was wrong to go to his room… She liked his mother and didn't want to offend her or create an impression of herself as a girl of loose morals, a hussy. She wanted his family to think well of her and respect her. She had spent time with his mother when he was away and knew that she worried about him. They had shared their concerns, but his mother was pleased that he was in the theatre and that he was involved in something artistic. For some reason, she did not approve of his work in the yard, thinking perhaps that her son was too good for manual labour. She did indulge all the children. Indeed, they seemed to have no rules or discipline. Maybe she wouldn't mind. Maybe Billy was right.

She followed him to the top of the house. The small room was cluttered with scripts, clothes, papers, and towels. On the slope of the coomb ceiling, a massive painting of a cornfield and crows copied from Van Gogh made the room feel even smaller. Beneath it, the single bed occupied a third of the space. At least the bed was tidy. Nothing else. On the small table, a typewriter spewed a half-finished sheet of paper. This must be what any young man's room looks like, she thought.

'Sit,' he said, pointing to the only chair, 'Cigarette?'

Not the American ones now, she noted, but coloured cocktail tubes. 'You know I don't.'

'I forgot.'

'Must get a bit stuffy in here.'

He returned the cigarette to its packet and placed it on the table beside what appeared to be a very long cigarette holder.

'That yours?' she said.

'Yes. Used it to swan about like an actor in Dublin.'

Some honesty there, then. She wondered what Spam would think of it. 'Did you paint that?' she asked, nodding at the sloped ceiling.

'After we went to that Kirk Douglas film. You don't like it.'

'Not up there. No.'

'I'll paint it out. Just for you.'

'Don't be silly.'

He lifted a brown paper bag from the corner and sat on the bed. 'Your present. Come and sit here.'

She was reluctant to sit beside him, worried that he would use the position to lay her on the quilt.

'Come on. Do you not want it?'

Not wanting to offend him, she sat stiffly on the edge, leaving a space between them.

He retrieved a brightly coloured woven band with tasselled ends from the bag and handed it to her.

'Beautiful. What is it?'

'A crios. Traditional Irish belt thing. I'll show you how to tie it. Stand up.'

She stood in front of him, and he looped it around her waist, tying it together at her side. 'There. An Irish Caileen.'

He pulled her towards him. Standing between his knees, she could feel his thighs against hers. Quite spontaneously, she slid her hands behind his head and cradled it against her body like a child. Just a boy. She stroked his hair and could feel him breathing and his arms around her waist. She was happy to stay like that, rocking him gently below her breasts, but sensed that it would not last. She was right. His hands slid down to hold her thighs, and his fingers, deftly raising her skirt, found the bare flesh above her stockings. She did not pull away. She liked the sensation.

He raised his head and looked at her. 'I love you,' he said.

She smiled as the words flowed through her, warm, kind, a flush of contentment like she used to feel in her father's arms. She allowed him to move her sideways onto the bed. It felt safe. They lay together under the cornfield, barely moving, until he grew restless and slid his hand under her sweater and up to her breast. His gentle kiss developed an urgency, a mounting passion which might prove to be uncontrollable. Yet she still trusted him and his hand on her skin. Twin sensations curled up from her womb– pleasure and a feeling of guilt– one tempting her forward, telling her to enjoy the ecstasy that hovered inside, that she had a right to it, the other reminding her that passion was not polite, that intimacy should go no further than a kiss. Her body yearned to taste the pleasure, and she passed it to him through her lips. Above her, the sun shone on the ripe corn, and she floated in a sky of contentment. Until his hand moved to her thigh and his fingers slid under her pants.

She stiffened and pushed his hand away. The kiss ended, and he looked down at her. 'What's wrong?'

'Not now.'

He was frowning. 'Why?'

'Just.'

She could see the frustration in his eyes. She did not want to hurt him.

'One day,' she said, gripping his hair and pulling his head down to kiss him. This time, she led him, letting loose his desire, feeling his hands on her body under her control. She felt his body squirming snake-like in his clothes, his breath quivering in hers, his hips thrusting until, in a final spasm, he collapsed on her. She cradled his head on her shoulder and stroked his hair. She felt maternal and pleased with herself. She had mastered his passion and enjoyed it safely, and she had controlled it on her own.

'Are you going back?' she asked.

'To Dublin?'

'No. The theatre. Back to acting?'

'If I can. Yes. There's a visiting rep company coming here. I'm going down to see them, see if I can get a part.'

'Could you not go back to the yard?'

'Good God, no! They would never have me back.'

'Not as an apprentice, but there are other jobs. I know someone who could help. I could ask him.'

'Who? Who do you know?' He sat up, clearly suspicious.

'One of the bosses. He comes into the office a lot. I could ask him.'

'No. I don't want to go back anyway. I hate the work.'

'Other boys stick it. Become tradesmen. Start their own business.'
'I don't care about that. I love the theatre, Sarah.'

'And what about me? You'll never be at home. Always away somewhere.'

He stood and crossed to the table, fiddling with the scripts.

'Plenty of theatres here– Group, Arts, Lyric. And the BBC. I might not have to be away.'

'Yes, but always at night. I'll never see you.'

'You will. I promise. I'll see you as often as I can.'

He came back to her and held her in his arms. She had wanted to tell him about Becker and his proposal to show him that she could attract other men, men of influence and wealth. She had wanted to make him jealous but realised that the revelation would only make him angry. She would have to share him with the theatre. Perhaps he would be famous one day, famous enough to make other girls envy her. Anyway, she loved him with all his faults.

247

Chapter 19

I tried to get work in Ulster to please Sarah and was given the part of the 'mobiliser' in 'Juno and the Paycock' with the travelling company in Bangor and a small part in 'Jane Eyre' but, after that, disappointment. I did consider abandoning the whole idea of acting, but having seen Gerald McLarnon's 'The Bonfire' in Belfast, I was inspired to persist. The timid governors of the Group Theatre, finding the play about bigotry too controversial, decided not to stage it, so a new company was formed and took it to the Grand Opera House. It sold out.

It was a powerful play set on the night before the Twelfth of July, with mob violence, rhythmic chanting, primitive drumbeats, and sensational effects, such as the twin pillars of orange fire bursting from the stage. Colin Blakely's brilliant portrayal of a young Catholic street fighter was so gripping that I wanted to be up there beside him, to be part of it. I had to be an actor.

I wrote to Teddy, who suggested getting in touch with Anew McMaster, an actor-manager who ran a touring company in Dublin. I was astonished when a letter from the great man arrived offering me work. So it was back to Dublin for rehearsal. I dreaded the prospect of confessing the plan to Sarah but was surprised when she accepted it– not willingly but with a resigned shake of her head.

A shabby room above a café called the Dog and Waffle. An iron bedstead, sagging in the middle, a single cane chair, a chest of drawers with broken handles, a threadbare mat on the linoleum floor, and frayed curtains. In the bathroom, a toilet with a cracked Bakelite seat and an antique bath stained green beneath the leaking tap. Behind the building is a slaughterhouse and stockyard. The cattle to be killed roar through the night, but just before dawn, when the slaughter commences, an uncanny silence settles over the pens. That silence is more disturbing than the noise. Still, the room was cheap, at £ 2.19.

When Maurice takes me home, I am too inebriated to care about the place. We have been in Davey Byrnes till closing time.

'Where are you staying, beautiful boy?' he says as we leave. 'Dog and Waffle.'

My mouth chews the words.

'Mother of God! Still, it's not far. I'll see you home.'

He holds my arm, and we stagger across the street, my feet somewhere far below and detached from my head. I am flattered by the attention and mutter compliments on his acting as we head for Chatham Street. Light rain casts haloes around the street lights.

When we reach the café, I expect him to walk away, but he steered me through the door and up the stairs. I'm not happy about this, but to seem suspicious might insult him, so I don't object when he comes into the room and shuts the door.

'Sit,' he says, 'You can't sleep in your shoes.'

I obey, glad to anchor myself on something solid.

He kneels and unties my laces. I look down on his Brylcreemed hair, glittering with raindrops, wondering about his intentions, but can't organise the swirl of thoughts in my head.

I try to think of an escape from the developing predicament.

'Where's the bathroom? I take it there is one in these dreadful premises.'

'Next door.'

'So you can hear every piddle of the other dregs of humanity through the wall. How squalid! Nevertheless, I will go next door while you undress and get into bed.'

I am tempted to lock the door when he leaves the room, but I don't want to appear ungracious. After all, it is possible that he's being considerate and merely wants to see me safely in bed. Besides, he is Teddy's partner. Surely, he would not be disloyal to him. Teddy and James had been together for years– until Maurice came along. There is something about Maurice that suggests dishonesty, a hint of amorality, and depravity.

Very different from Michael, who is something of a gentleman. He had kissed me in bed, but as I shrank from the contact, he patted my cheek and rolled away. I did feel sorry for him and a bit guilty, but I disliked the sensation of an embrace with an unshaven mouth.

I undress as hurriedly as the alcohol allows and fall into bed in a vest and underpants, conscious of the grubby sheets and blankets.

When he returns, he switches off the light. I hear him removing his clothes. The hiss of his shirt over his head, the clink of coins in his trouser pockets, the thud of his shoes on the floor.

'Move over, beautiful boy,' he says, lifting the blankets.

I squeeze up against the wall in the narrow bed with my back to him. I can smell his sweat and the wine he has been drinking. Unlike Michael he will not respect any protests. I could tell him to leave. I could leap out of bed and turn on the light, but in this state of intoxication, it is easier to acquiesce, to lie here and see what happens. The need to be liked, to prove that I am liberated and unconventional, smothers my inhibitions.

His fingers slide across my belly and down to my groin. I lie very still, hoping that the lack of response will discourage him, but he presses against me and tries to arouse the limp thing in his fingers. I'm relieved that it doesn't respond. He tries to enter me from behind, but his prick is too large. It stabs at me relentlessly like an enormous blind maggot.

'You're very tight,' he said, 'Have you no Vaseline?' I say nothing, pretending to be asleep.

He uses his fingers to widen the entrance and tries again. This time, there is some success. The maggot forces its slimy head inside and thrusts a few times till, with one last spasm, it spurts its entrails into the orifice.

I wonder what Spam would do in these circumstances. I imagine him bursting into the room and whipping his chain across Maurice's face. The sallow skin slices open like seal blubber, blood pulsing onto the pillow. I'm delighted. Spam has the strength to deal with such things. I lie here, weak, sickened, and emasculated, trying to understand how I could have allowed such a thing to happen. I will never tell anyone of this. No one must know. The shame of it terrifies me.

Maurice has fallen asleep. His grip on me relaxes.

I think of Sarah. She seems so remote, so untouchable, clean, and pristine. I want her more than ever, but I am a different person. I picture the person I was, walking through the shipyard with that confident, affected seaman's gait, denim with a Phillip Morris packet in the breast pocket, a young man who thought the world of himself.

I wait till he is sound asleep, slide out of bed, find my clothes, dress, and leave the Dog and Waffle as the first lorry load of cattle arrives to be slaughtered.

The sea glitters in the dawn. Cool, clean, cleansing. Down there, the dark weed sways over the sand, its fingers touching the seabed elegantly like a dancer's. A green, silent world. Floating through it would be like flying, soaring like a gull, wings still, weightless, born by the thermals. Free to glide where you will. Under the sea, twisting, turning like a seal, sliding through forests of kelp, shadow on the sand, green sun overhead, warm on the back. Over ribs of wrecks, barnacled, fluttering with small fish. A different world, clean, cool, cleansing. A corpse on the seabed, rocking gently, smiling, shreds of silk skin floating from the skull, eels in the eye sockets, blind, speechless, senseless, unashamed. The pain is over.

Shame is not a dark vortex spiralling downward. It's a fire, a blaze of indescribable heat, white-hot in the core, an explosion of molten lava, ignited by the memory, unquenchable. The uncontainable flow, cremating, consuming, vaporising, roaring as it hits the sea, glowing as it sinks, resting on the seabed, solidifying. Cooled, cleansed, inert.

One step forward. Breathe water not fire. Intense pain. Soon over…

We rehearsed in a shabby top-floor room in Frederick Street, an elegant Georgian avenue that lapsed into disrepair a little like the old actor-manager directing the company. Making an entrance deliberately later than the rest of us, he strode into the room with his long overcoat flying melodramatically behind him.

'What are you waiting for, dears? Manage without me. Come, come. Vesti La Guibba.'

A tall man with a stentorian voice which could sweep from deep bass to falsetto, from whisper to clamour, from simper to snarl with such ease that seasoned actors were startled. His kind face concealed a temper which could be unleashed on colleagues who dared to upstage him. I was to watch several over-ambitious thespians deflate after an attack from The Master.

We had three weeks to rehearse six plays, which was not a problem to McMaster, who knew every part by heart, but a challenge to the rest of the cast, particularly the other leads. He played every lead, of course, including juvenile parts, appearing in 'Rebecca,' 'Ideal Husband,' 'As You Like It,' 'Macbeth' and crime dramas such 'Dear Delinquent' and 'Murder Mistaken'– all to be ready in three weeks. I was relieved to be given only minor parts, so I sat and watched, entranced by the speed with which the actors could pick up the essence of their parts and envious of their opportunities.

The evenings passed in a blur of different hotels and bars, swallowing spirits as if the supplies were about to run out but avoiding Davey Byrnes in case I met Maurice. In spite of the spirits, memories of him kept flashing into my head when least expected. I would freeze with a glass halfway to my lips, paralysed with shame and fear of exposure. His image appeared behind pillars, in the snugs, at the far end of a bar. I was sure that he would tell his friends of our encounter, laughing as he boasted of his success. Yet there was another fear that flickered in the murk; an apprehension tinted with temptation, for there was a part of the intimacy that I enjoyed. To imagine holding another man did not feel repugnant, and the thought of touching him aroused a sensation of excitement. Fleeting fantasies scotched before they grew, but enough to cause confusion and doubt. I was not one of them, I told myself, and yet…

There were many in Dublin who would not have been surprised or upset by the incident and, indeed, a few who might have envied me. I had arrived in the city in the company of a respected homosexual, and everyone naturally assumed I was of that persuasion, too. I had been introduced to a hidden stratum of Dublin society, a fellowship which met in recognised rendezvous– lawyers, politicians, actors, singers, doctors– men whose desire was only for lovers of their own gender. Some of them had been a couple for many years, and their affection for each other was clear to everyone. All of them are forced into that sad, covert world by the laws of the land. In theatrical circles, however, there was more freedom, although Maurice's more predatory behaviour would not have been admired. Nevertheless, I was worried that I might meet him again. In every bar and hotel lounge, I watched for him.

On the nightly tour of the hostelries, I was usually with the company - McMaster and his diminutive wife, a couple who had been recruited from a travelling circus, an English couple (Lady Macbeth and Banquo) clearly refugees from the seaside rep, a young couple freshly out of drama college and a completely hairless actor from Yorkshire (MacDuff) called Roland. Roland decided that, as an innocent abroad, I needed a mentor and assumed that role ostentatiously. The others grinned knowingly as I succumbed uncomfortably, not wishing to offend him yet afraid that he might be as predatory as Maurice. A superb actor; I could not hide my admiration for his extraordinary flexibility, his ability to flit from one character to another, and the small movements with which he could capture a roll. I watched him eagerly, yearning to be like him, a leading man, an actor who could hold an audience in awe.

When I told him of my digs in the Dog and Waffle, he was outraged.

'No, no, my dear. Can't have that. I have a friend in Monkstown who would be delighted to have you– not in the carnal sense, my dear. An old queen but absolutely harmless. One of the kindest and most gentle people I know. I will take you to meet him tonight.'

That evening, we took a bus out to Monkstown.

'You must not be deterred by his appearance,' Roland said as we neared the stop, 'When he was young, Freddy was one of the most handsome actors in Dublin, a truly beautiful boy– I have seen the photographs. He could command any juvenile part in theatre, but cruelly, oh so cruelly, my dear, the sword of fate sliced through his career. A tumour grew on his temple, and after surgery, the whole side of his face collapsed. He never appeared on stage again.'

'Good God. How dreadful.'

'Tragic, dear boy. In fact, he has become something of a recluse. Delightful, though. You will like him.'

I did. I was glad that Roland had warned me. Freddy's affliction would have been a shock otherwise. The contrast between the two sides of his face was extraordinary, one clearly showing the handsome star worshipped by the public, the other the devastating results of surgery. The twisted mouth affected his speech but not the theatrical timbre of his voice or the warmth of his smile. The courtesy of his welcome dispelled all my worries.

'Come in, come in, young man. Roland has told me all about you on the phone. He didn't tell me you were such a handsome boy, though. I was handsome once, too, you know. I expect Roland has prepared you to meet the monster of Monkstown. How are the rehearsals, Roland?'

He showed us into a comfortable living room lined with books and posters of his performances.

'As ever, Freddy. The Master knows all the lines, and we struggle to learn them in an evening.'

'He's such a ham. All the lines are in his head, but not a clue about the character. Splendid voice, though. Commands the stage with the voice. But I tell you this. Don't ever upstage him, Willie. Throws caution to the wind and throws a tantrum on stage. Never mind the public, dear. Public's there merely to applaud. Anyway, enough of that. Tell me about you, dear boy.'

And he was interested. Most actors, when they ask that, listen only to detect a point at which they can interrupt and use it to expand on their own fascinating experiences. Freddy actually listened. I knew I was going to like him.

We could not wait on that occasion, and having satisfied Freddy that I was a suitable visitor, I returned to Dublin to retrieve my belongings from the Dog and Waffle. Entering the room brought back the memories, and before the feelings of distaste and shame could erupt, I flung the few belongings into a bag and fled. Outside in the street, I took a deep breath and savoured the scent of traffic and the brewery on the river. I thought of Sarah and, for a moment, wished that I had never come to Dublin. I should have stayed with her and remained in the yard. And what would Spam think of me now? A faggot, a weakling who had allowed himself to be seduced by a 'queer.' He would take one look at my green corduroy jacket, suede shoes, and yellow cravat and turn away. Even Sarah would shake her head in despair. The more I thought of her, the more I longed to be with her, to hold her, to taste her lipstick, and breathe her clean breath. I made up my mind to return to her after the tour.

The intention was soon swept away in the whirl of evenings after rehearsal and became a fleeting memory in the fuzzy awakenings. So many people to impress so many places to admire. We went to see David Bell in 'View from the Bridge,' at the time causing horror in polite Dublin society by showing two men kissing on stage. You could hear the gasp in the auditorium when the embrace was seen. This was the era in which J.P Dunleavy's book 'The Ginger Man' was banned in Ireland. We spent an evening with Christopher Casson in Strand Road as he played the harp while reciting Yeats, a combination which spun an unforgettable magic around the words. We seemed to spend night after night at parties with people from the theatre. So far from the shipyards and the stifling culture of the North. Freddy tolerated my late nights with understanding and enjoyed the gossip.

I was sorry to leave him when we went out on tour, the first show being in Kilkenny.

Carlow, Furmoy, Ennis, Hospital, and Limerick followed. When we arrived in a town, we had to find our own digs in the morning, set up a stage in the afternoon, and run a performance that night, often striking the set after the show. Hauling laundry baskets of costumes, drapes, and bundles of black borders on and off the lorry, carrying coils of cables and heavy switchboards, and climbing ladders on empty stages was exhausting work, but I relished every minute of it.

Sitting in front of a mirror, blanking one's face with pale No.5 greasepaint and rebuilding it as a different character with No.9 and shadows and lines of lake, grey and white, donning a costume and finally appearing on stage made up for the fatigue. The chaotic life of a travelling player held a magic that the dull routine of less disreputable professions could not offer.

We normally found digs in council houses where the folk were most welcoming and tolerant of our hours. In one of these, we arrived late at night and found the host sitting at the kitchen table with a bottle and three cups. He insisted that we had a drink with him, and Roland, in his usual extravagant fashion, threw back two cups of the blazing liquid. I knew that poteen had to be treated with caution, so I sipped mine tenderly. In the morning, Roland staggered downstairs and left without breakfast. On the spot where the bottle had been sitting, there was a dark ring burnt in the wood on the scrubbed table.

Television had not invaded the living rooms of the West, and we filled theatres everywhere, with audiences thrilled by the performances. Even in the matinees, children threw Polo mints at Macbeth and hooted when he was killed. In a place called Hospital, we arrived to find that the village hall had no stage and no electricity, so we had to build a stage with tea chests and run electrical cables from the house next door. Local people did all they could to help, and we performed Macbeth and Rebecca on a tea chest stage.

The dream ended in Limerick. McMaster cut short the tour and sped back to Dublin, forgetting to hand over our meagre wages. So there we were– Roland and I– stuck in Limerick without the fare to reach home.

'What will we do?' asked Roland, for the first time looking helpless and dismayed.

'Hitch-hike.'

'Hitch-hike?'

'Yes. You know. Get on the road and hold out our thumbs.'

'And what if it rains?'

'We get wet.'

'Good God! Has it come to this? All because of the thieves.'

'What?'

'The break-in, dear boy. The Master's house was ransacked. That's why he sped back to Sandymount. To rescue his most precious possession– a gold cigarette case given to him by Ivor Novello. He lived with him, you know.'

'Who?'

'McMaster lived with Ivor in England, so they say. Rumour has it that he had to flee from England when the police were alerted to their intimacy.'

'How dramatic. Still, he didn't have to leave us here without a penny.'

'Perhaps if you had been a little less profligate in the hostelries, we might have taken a train.'

'And you more prudent, of course.'

'I sent money home, dear boy. My poor sick mother, you know.'
'What rubbish! And there is nothing wrong with your mother.'

'You have such a cold heart, William.'

'We need to retrieve our cases from the digs. Sneak out quickly before we are asked for rent.'

'Indeed? Who is being dramatic now?'

'Are you going to pay?'

He did not reply, so we walked back towards the digs. I knew that Spam would have approved the strategy but not of my hairless companion.

We hitch-hiked back to Dublin. We did manage lifts for the first half of the trek, but as the light faded to sepulchral darkness outside a village called Moone, it started to rain. We kept ourselves going by reciting pieces from plays, sometimes roaring at imaginary actors. In spite of the histrionics, we became increasingly depressed as cars and lorries swept past without stopping, their tail lights gleaming red on the wet road behind them. We discussed the wisdom of lying down in front of a driver but decided that it was beneath our dignity. Besides, on a dark, wet night, the driver might not notice the carcass in the headlights.

It was midnight when a lorry stopped and drove us to Dublin, where we contacted Freddy and headed out to Monkstown.

'You poor darlings,' he said, opening the door, 'Come in; you're drenched. You will catch pneumonia. Come. I'll run a bath and find a change of clothes.'

It was indeed bliss to be welcomed in such a manner.

Chapter 20

The streets shone black in the rain, and the wind ripped sodden paper from the gutters as Sarah left the cinema. She pulled a scarf from her pocket and tied it over her head. She had gone alone to the film, for none of her friends was interested in seeing Kirk Douglas cut off his ear as Van Gogh. Billy enjoyed it He often talked about Van Gogh and his dark, depressing paintings of working people. She had not heard from him for some time and wondered if he had become so absorbed in the theatre that he had forgotten about her. He had changed. She could tell that from his letters, full of flowery descriptions of Dublin and names of famous actors whom she was supposed to recognise. Very little about him or his feelings for her– if he still had any. She didn't want it to end. She still wanted him to come home and settle into a safe job.

Mr Becker still accosted her at work. It was becoming embarrassing as he came to the office, walking nonchalantly around the desks and talking to the girls but stopping at her desk too frequently and for too long. There were times when she thought of the cruise and imagined herself reclining in a swimsuit beside the pool or waltzing with him in the ballroom, but she knew that all he wanted was a fling, an 'extra-marital affair' as they called it. Yet his attention was causing problems. The girls had noticed. Nancy, naturally, concluded that he was in love with her and tried to persuade her to seduce him.

'Gee whizz, Sarah. He's worth thousands. Be his mistress, and you'll have a penthouse flat, cruises in the Caribbean, a gleaming new car, and glittering jewellery. Think about it.'

'I'm not a prostitute, and he's married.'

'You do fancy him then?'

'No, I don't, Nancy. For heaven's sake, leave it alone.'

But she did fancy him in a way. He was mature, courteous, considerate, a real gentleman. Billy seemed like a little boy beside him, but that's what she liked about Billy– his naivety, his impulsiveness, his unpredictable nature, and his 'Lust for Life.' Yes, a bit like Van Gogh, a bit dangerous. She wanted to capture the wild boy and tame him. Not lock him in a cage where he would pace up and down like a panther but have on a long leash so that she could hold him close when she needed him. She remembered the time when he had come to her bedroom when she was ill and the feeling of his hand on her skin. The fury fired by his invasion of her body had faded, and she was left with a longing for him.

A car swerved across the road and drew up beside her. As the driver wound down the window, she recognised Spam's grin.

'Terrible night, Sarah. Jump in, and I'll take you home.'

'No thanks. I'll walk.'

'Don't be daft. You'll be quite safe. I'm going steady.'

'That'll be a first.'

'Come on. I won't try it on. Promise.'

He looked as though he meant it, and he was Billy's friend after all. She walked around the car and slid into the passenger seat.

'You're soaked already. You'd have been drenched by the time you got home.'

The car smelt of polish and tobacco smoke. It was warm and comfortable. Spam swung it expertly across the road.

'I thought you'd joined the army.'

'I did. I'm home on leave.'

'Didn't think you'd like the discipline.'

'I don't, but I can see why it's there. To be a good soldier, you have to learn to act quickly and obey orders– for your own safety as much as for your comrade's sake. Teamwork. It's all about teamwork, Sarah. Tough too. Twenty-mile route marches, assault courses in the dark, live ammo overhead.'

'Yes, I can see that appealing to you. Having to be tough, violent even.'

'All under control now. I'm a changed man.'

She wondered if that was true. Maybe her picture of him was based on his past. He had a reputation, but people could change. Perhaps he had grown out of all that. The army could have that effect.

'Let me take you for a drink, Sarah, for old time's sake. I know that Billy's down south. An actor. I never thought he was like that. Still, good luck to him if that's what he wants. I'm sure he wouldn't mind you coming for a drink with his old mucker.'

'No thanks, Spam. I have to get home.'

'Am I not good enough then? Bad for the reputation to be seen with me, eh?'

'Don't be silly. Mum will worry if I'm not home.'

'If you'd been walking home, you wouldn't be there for ages. Come on, Sarah, be a devil.'

'Okay. One drink. No more.'

She had given in too easily, but she didn't want to go home. She hadn't been out since Billy left. Not once, except to Sea Rangers. And he would be out enjoying himself with his actor friends. Maybe even with one of the girls, for all she knew. Only his letters to go by, and they could be all lies or stories made up to keep her happy. Why shouldn't she go out for a drink with his old friend?

She liked The Widows, an old-fashioned cocktail bar with dark wood, leather armchairs, and brass table-tops. Spam seemed to admire her figure as she slipped off her coat and sat down.

'What would you like, Sarah?'

'Sherry, please.'

She watched him swagger up to the bar. He did dress differently now. Smart, with a crease in his trousers, a blazer with a regimental badge, and highly polished shoes. He returned with the drinks, and, opening a silver cigarette case, he offered her one, but she shook her head, remembering Billy's crumpled American packets. She lifted her glass and felt the warmth of the spirit on her tongue, sweet and comforting. Spam talked about the army, emphasising his physical achievements and describing in detail the weapons. She didn't really listen but punctuated the conversation with appropriate admiration. Before she realised it, she had finished the sherry, and Spam had bought another. She felt it swirling inside her like a slack tide, neither ebbing nor flowing but lapping gently against the edges of her inhibitions, and she started to relax.

'Maybe I'll have a fag after all,' she said.

'You don't smoke really, do you?'

'Now and again,' but she choked on the smoke. Spam laughed and bought her another sherry.

She drank it aggressively as if the fire of the spirit could burn what she didn't like about herself, destroy her naivety, her shyness, and her submission to the will of her mother and brother. She swallowed it to smother them, to drown them and their expectations of her, to cleanse herself of their influence, to strip off the respectability and the need to conform. She drank to hurt her brother and his habit of interfering, to steam over his little round specs so that he couldn't see.

She drank to annoy her mother and her spiteful remarks about Billy. She felt a flow of anger and allowed it to flood through her. Fuck them, she said to herself, relishing the freedom to think the words.

'What about the boy that you chained?' she found herself saying suddenly. He was shocked.

'I never chained anyone, Sarah.'

'Aye, you did. At the dance that time.'

'Is that what Billy said?'

'No, no. not Billy. All round the yard. Gonna get that bastard Spam, that fuckin' bastard Spam, he was saying. The boy that you chained.'

She enjoyed the chance to swear, but she found that her tongue was rolling around in her mouth., twisting the words. She couldn't speak properly, but it was funny. She didn't care. She blew the smoke into the air and laughed. Spam was sitting silently, staring at his drink.

'I swear to God, Sarah. I didn't do it. I couldn't do that. Look. I've been in a fight or two– everyone knows that– but I fight clean. Always clean. No blades, no dusters, no chains. Ask Billy.'

'Billy's in Dublin. I don't care anyway. Forget it. Get me another sherry.'

'You sure?'

'Course I'm sure.'

She watched him making his way to the bar, but when she looked for the sign for the ladies' toilet, her eyes seemed to swing sluggishly across the room as if there was a great weight attached to them. Eventually, she found the sign and rose to cross the floor but swayed against her chair. Whoops, she whispered and walked unsteadily towards the door.

When she looked in the mirror, the reflection confirmed the image of herself that she always carried– a plain, weasel-faced creature whom no one would notice in a dance hall. Yet this time, there was a change. The complexion had more colour; the eyes were brighter, and the lips more pronounced. You're drunk, you clown, she said and grinned at herself. Don't care.

Don't give a toss. Be careful, though. Spam out there. He doesn't care, either. Treats women like shit. Being nice to me. Looking after me. Billy's friend, too. Maybe he's okay.

The Army has changed him, maybe. A soldier now has to behave himself. Making sure the tail of her skirt was not tucked into her pants, she swayed out into the smoke and sat down.

'Okay?' he asked.

'Course. Sorry, I said about the chain. Must have been someone else. Yard's bad for rumours.'

'I wouldn't do that kind of thing. Ask Billy.'

'Don't care about Billy. He's probably out with some theatre floosie in Dublin.'

'You're right, Sarah. Not good at resisting temptation, our Billy.'

She finished her sherry and said that he had to go. Spam tried to help her into her coat, but she kept missing the sleeve till he took her hand and guided it in.

It was still raining outside, and Spam threw his blazer over her head, and they hurried to the car. Once inside, he threw the blazer in the back, unfastened his cufflinks, and rolled up his sleeves. She noticed the muscles in his arm and a tattoo. He pressed the starter, and the car moved smoothly away from the curb. She sat back and watched the wipers clearing the screen. To and fro, left and right. Rhythmic and restful. In the warmth, she could feel sleep behind her eyes. Just a wee doze would be nice. At one point, she saw trees through the wipers and wondered where she was. No trees on the way home. She didn't care.

When the car stopped, it was dark. Dark and silent except for Spam's breathing. What happened next was a terrifying blur as if she was tumbling down a cliff face in the dark, over and over, thumping off the rock, blades of pain slicing, tearing, splitting. When she tried to remember it later, a door slammed shut in her head.

She remembered the car stopping near her house and him leaning across to open her door.

She was standing in the road as he drove away without a word. The rain was cold on her face, and she was shivering. She looked down, and her pants were around one ankle. She was wondering why they were there, lying on the wet tarmac, bent down, kicked off her shoe, and, stepping out of them, stuffed them in her pocket. There was a taste of blood in her mouth. Her handbag lay in a puddle where he had flung it.

She staggered into the house and upstairs to the bathroom. Locking the door, she ran a bath using only the hot tap. As steam rose from the water, she stripped off her clothes and stepped in. The shock of the scalding water almost forced her to withdraw, but relishing the pain, she submerged her body beneath the surface. The blistering heat made her gasp, but she clenched her fists and endured it. The more it hurt, the more it would clean her flesh. She opened her thighs, hoping it would seep into the open wound left by the attack. She could not bring herself to use her hands to wash it.

As the water cooled, she slid down the bath, allowing the water to cover her face.

Chapter 21

Freddy gave me the fare home to Bangor. I called for Sarah, but her mother answered the door.

'She doesn't want to see you.' I was shocked.

'Why? Why not?'

'She doesn't want to see you, and that's that.'

Her eyes stared at me as if I had raped her daughter. 'Is she seeing Clive again?'

'None of your business. Now please leave. Unlike you, I have work to do.' She shut the door and left me standing on the porch, bewildered and hurt.

I tried to meet Sarah several times, waiting at the train station or outside Sea Rangers, but she never appeared. I wondered if she had left the yard or had found a place to stay in Belfast. I even asked my sister to search for her, persuading her to visit Sarah's church on Sunday, but she was no more successful.

I put on my old working denim and visited the yard, taking a late train to avoid Corky. I waited around the tracing office till one of the girls appeared.

'Is Sarah in there?'

'Sarah left. Did you not know? You're Billy, aren't you?'

'Yes. When did she leave?'

'About a week ago. She just didn't come in, and then we were told that she'd left.'

'Why?'

'God knows. Very sudden anyway.'

'Is Nancy still here?'

'Aye. Nancy's here. She doesn't seem to know either, but she gone very quiet so maybe she knows more than she's letting on.'

'Could you ask her to come down? I'd really like to speak to her.'
'I'll go back up and ask, but she might not come.'

As soon as Nancy appeared at the door, I knew that something was wrong. Normally ebullient and cheeky, she was so subdued I suspected something had happened to Sarah at work.

'Why did she leave, Nancy? You're her best friend. You must have some idea.'

'I don't. I know that Becker was pestering her, but I don't think it was that.'

'The big boss?'

'Yeah. He fancied her, but she knew it would come to nothing. Anyway, she said she was waiting for you.'

'For me?'

'That's what she said.'

'You sound a bit doubtful.'

'There's something I heard, Billy. It may not be true, but my friend in Bangor told me.'

'What? I need to know Nancy.'

'She went out with Spam.'

'What?'

'She left the pub with Spam and went in his car.'

'Jesus Christ.'

'Sorry, Billy. It's maybe not true.'

I turned away and walked back into the yard past the new frigate. I couldn't believe it.

Anyone but Spam. The thought of them together made me squirm. Spam who had no respect for women, who treated them like pieces of meat, who asked me to smell his fingers after he had seduced one of them. And he was supposed to be my mate. The bastard. The fuckin' bastard. And Sarah. What was she thinking of? She knew what he was like, what I thought of him. I felt as if I'd been stabbed, the knife turning in my guts, winding my entrails round the blade. I wanted to cry and I wanted to roar in anger at the same time. Hate her and love her.

Rage and grief in a soup of misery.

As I passed the frigate, one of the helpers grabbed my arm. 'You're Spam's pal, aren't you?'

I remembered him from the dance.

'Get your fuckin' hand off my arm, or I'll fuckin' kill you!'

Clearly, he saw the fury in my eyes, reckoned that I might explode, and backed off.

'We'll get you, Billy.'

I heard him shout as I walked on, too submerged in my own turmoil to care.

I took to sitting in my room, gazing out of the window but seeing only what was in my head and oppressed by a shroud of desolation. Haunted by images of Sarah and Spam and visions of Maurice, I sank slowly into a morass of misery. I rose some mornings brimming with intentions to write to rep companies or compose poems to express the grief, but instead, I sat at the desk or lay on the bed listening to the wireless. Sometimes, I sat in the gloom, the room lit only be the glow of the small electric fire, feeling that there was something behind me, something malevolent and shapeless. At such times, my palms were damp with sweat and my mouth dry. When I appeared downstairs at mealtimes, they would comment on my appearance.

'Why don't you go out for a walk?' 'You can't be up there all day, wasting electricity.' 'You could go to the library.' 'There's a good film on at the Tonic.' 'What happened to Sarah?' 'There's a job going at the architect's office– you were good at drawing' Prodding, goading, stirring with the best of intentions but really to heal their discomfort. My sister searching my eyes for a reason, and my mother trying to find a solution. At times, I answered with humour, trying to divert their attention; at other times, remaining silent, locked in myself.

I tried to explain, to describe the turmoil, the moments of inexplicable terror, the melting away of physical surroundings, the fluidity of solid matter, the beast that tore at my entrails and left me shaking. How could I explain the moments of fury when I sliced my arm with a knife and pierced my chest with the point but was too timid to dig it right into the flesh? I lifted the chair and smashed everything breakable in the room, filling the air with rage and the scent of broken wood. One moment hating myself, the next sinking down into a pit of self-pity. The world around me is cracking, fading, withdrawing into disjointed, unrelated events, losing its meaning.

How do you explain running through the streets trying to escape the fear, the indefinable, indescribable terror, as if the pain in the lungs and the legs would diminish the horror? How do you put into words the dread of the endless night, the darkness that might never end? And, if you could, who would believe you? In that space there is no meaning, no sense of who you are or what is happening to you. Unending seismic fracturing and convulsion.

'What are you afraid of?'

'I don't know.'

'There must be something. Is there somebody threatening you?'

'No, no. Not like that. Not something physical.' You could see the despair in their eyes.

A scream inside 'What is happening to me? Will no one tell me?'

It is better to sit in my room alone than to witness the hopelessness in their face, the shrugs when you turn your back, the shake of the head.

One day, I sliced the skin too deeply and fell to the floor in a faint. In the waking, for one moment, there was peace, a swirling, sickly sensation but peace. With my arm streaming blood, I staggered downstairs into the sitting room and asked for a doctor. Stunned, my mother stayed in her chair.

'A doctor,' I repeated and collapsed on the floor as she ran past.

I lay there waiting, waiting, desperate for medical help, waiting and singing, singing to make the seconds pass.

'Wait till the sun shines, Nellie. When the clouds go drifting by, we will be happy, Nellie. Don't you sigh. Down Lover's Lane, we'll wander like sweethearts, you and I.'

Over and over again.

Keeping the darkness at bay, keeping the claws of the fear away. How long, though? Sing again; it is the needle that ends it all. Swim into a warm, mellow twilight with voices far away, murmuring wordlessly in quiet tones, the carpet on my cheek soft and purple, fists opening like flowers, petals drifting by, sweethearts you and I…

Chapter 22

SARAH.

She met Robert at a dance. Same sort of place where she met Billy, but years later. She had been watching him from the seats as he danced, admiring his fluttering feet and willowy limbs, his glistening black hair and pale face. He was lost in the rhythm, never glancing at his partner, frowning at the floor as if he were performing for a crowd beneath his feet. She was stunned when he asked her to dance after the interval.

He moved so fast on the floor that she was quite dizzy, twirling her round so that her skirt spun out like a hat-brim and lifting her above his head. In spite of the energy, he never lost control, moving exactly in time to the drums. People stopped to watch them as he threw her between his legs and swung her over his hips. Bobbing and whirling with him, she spun into a kind of trance, circling in the air above the crowd like an eagle, lifted on the thermals, gliding under the great crystal ball near the ceiling. Ecstasy. She did not want it to end. She wanted to spin and spin into the night till her feet burned and her arms stretched like wings.

When the music stopped, he held onto her hand and led her out into the cold air. 'You're good,' he said.

'No. You're good.'

'I've seen you before. In my father's bar. A bit the worse for wear.'

'Really?'

'Your name's Sarah, isn't it? You're a tracer in Harland and Woolf's.'

She didn't tell him that she had left the yard. She could not face Nancy's inquisition nor Becker's attention.

'You seem to know all about me, and I know nothing about you, not even your name.'

'Robert. I'm Robert. Dad has the Sefton.'

'I've never been in there.'

'You have, you know. Maybe you don't remember. You were wearing that blue circular skirt and a white cardigan.'

She thought it better not to argue. It was possible that she had been too drunk to remember. Besides, she liked him. He was handsome in a sort of gypsy way with neat sideburns and an impudent smile. She shivered, and he placed his arm over her shoulder.

'You're cold. Let's go back in.'

'No. I'm okay.'

'You'll catch a cold.'

'I like the fresh air.'

'Have you a coat? I could fetch it for you.'

'No. You'd never find it in there. I'm perfectly okay.'

'Do you live in Bangor?'

'Yes. In Ballyholme.'

'Did you walk here?'

'Course.'

'Can I give you a lift home after?'

'That would be nice. Yes.'

That's how it began. His car was a Humber with soft leather seats and a wooden dashboard. It didn't smell of tobacco like Clive's but had an air of cleanliness, a scent of polish, a surgical sterility, an indication of the fastidious care lavished upon it. As they stopped under the streetlight outside the house, she hoped that her mother was watching. She would be impressed. As he leant across to kiss her, she drew back instinctively. It would have been the first since the nameless, formless thing, the monstrous darkness enclosed in a fragile shell, the place where she did not dare to go.

'What's wrong? Never been kissed?'

'Nothing. No, nothing really. Sorry.'

She couldn't explain. Yet she didn't want to lose him. She leaned her head against his shoulder.

'I'd like to see you again,' she said.

'Good. That's good. I thought maybe you had gone off me.'

'No. Not at all.'

He arranged to call for her the following afternoon and kissed her forehead as she left the car. His patience and understanding were so different from other men.

As she walked up the path to the house, she saw the glint of her mother's glasses in the shadows of the front room, so she sat on the steps and waited for her to go to bed.

She wondered what Nancy would make of Robert. She would admire his good looks, his car, his skill on the dance floor, and, most of all, his money and independence. Nancy would have offered him everything in the car– well, not quite everything, for she would never have allowed herself to become pregnant. 'Heavy petting' was as far as she would go. 'Keeping it for Mr Right,' she said. Sarah wondered if Robert was her Mr. Right. Too soon to say. He seemed to accept her avoidance of his kiss as if he understood. How could he understand? Maybe he had been with someone like her, someone as terrified. Maybe he knew. Maybe Spam…

With a clap of thunder, the door in her head comes down. Bang. Don't look, don't move, don't breathe, don't break the shell, don't let it out. Dig nails into palms till the blood seeps out. Pain is the answer. Pain keeps it in its place. Swerve away. Think of the sea and sailing, hauling up the gaff, tightening the jib sheets, leaving the mooring, watching the wind. Anything. A reef knot, not a granny knot. Right over left, left over right. Anything. Think of Monday. In her brother's shop. No 8 countersunk screws. GKN bolts. Washers. 6 inch nails. Chisels. Braces and bits. Sweep the floor. Shake water on the boards to keep the dust down.

Little drops shivering like mercury in the dust, shivering like her shoulders. It will pass. Till the next time. Always there, waiting, lurking.

Flashes. Pictures and feelings. Him heavy on top thrusting, great black bull on top crushing. His belt buckle scraping her thigh. Mouth searching for hers, snuffling, flesh-eating rodent, searching. Impaled naked on a lance razor-sharp into hips, into the spine, into the skull, screaming. Darkness, warm slime, pain. Car engine starting, windscreen wipers over and back, over and back, breathing the rain.

Out on a wet road under street lights at home. Red tail lights and smell of exhaust. Two stagger steps and pants fall on the shoe, torn. Heaving sick. Silence. No words. Nothing. The End.

Her brother's shop was her prison, her punishment for leaving the yard. She chose to travel on a different train to avoid him. What could we have said to each other anyway? He led his own life with its rigid routine. Up at half-past six and into the bathroom to shave, always banging the door so that it woke her. Downstairs by seven to porridge and toast, mother shuffling round the kitchen in her slippers and dressing gown, ministering to her favourite child. Fried sausage, potato bread, an egg, tea with two sugars, and off he went. Sarah never rose till she heard the front door bang behind him. Then she had to face her.

'You have Rangers tonight.' 'You have choir tonight.' 'You'd better go down and see your Aunt tonight.' Short, staccato sentences like bullets aimed at her self-esteem, intending to wound and humiliate. Never asked after Billy or even Clive. After she left the yard, she ceased showing any interest in her. Sarah thought she would be pleased when she offered to work in the shop, but even that seemed to be a fault, and when she insisted on a wage similar to her usual, her mother was outraged. In spite of the fury, Sarah stuck to the demand. She was proud of herself for showing some strength for once.

She didn't ask about Robert or his car, although Sarah was sure she had seen them. She thought about Robert as she lay in bed that night, wondering if he could provide an escape from the prison. If she married him, she would not need to work. She could help in the hotel, greeting guests, answering the phone, arranging bookings, ordering supplies, and organising staff. She saw herself as the proprietrix, enclosed in comfort with soft, thick carpets and the scent of polish, everything gleaming and clean. A warm tiled bathroom with fluffy towels and bath salts. Robert by her side, a handsome, courteous host, articulate, intelligent, and able to engage the most sophisticated guests in conversation. How they would admire us as a couple! And how Nancy would envy her. A dream, perhaps. After all, Robert might never call, and if he did, it might lead to nothing. Why would he want damaged goods?

Chapter 23

BILLY

Imprisoned in a fish bowl of sedatives, swimming in a soup of opiates, seeing the world outside distorted by the glass and dulled by elixirs, I knew that I had to escape, yet the prospect of leaving was terrifying. Day by day, I was decaying, slowly rotting from the skin inwards, suspended in a globe above an abyss of fear. There seemed to be no solution. It was tempting to end it all, to let go and fall into the dark, hoping that there would be comfort somewhere at the bottom, but the letting go needed strength and courage, which I did not possess.

The family did their best to help, but when I tried to describe the turmoil, I could see their incomprehension. Even my sister seemed to back away, perhaps in awe of the darkness.

'Come to the drama club' 'Pickie Pool is opening soon.' 'Why don't you go for a walk?' 'Perhaps Reverend Quinn could help– he's a great listener.' They meant well but I heard the suggestions as you would hear distant thunder, faintly disturbing, slightly threatening. My sister left to work in England that summer and the house closed even further around me, its tentacles smothering attempts to escape.

I heard my mother on the telephone trying to persuade Sarah to call, but I knew that she wouldn't come. Spam never came, either. I was not sorry about that, as he reminded me of Dublin. He seemed to belong to a distant part of my life, a time when I could control what I felt, a time when I slept at night and woke looking forward to the day.

My mother had contracted religion. From declaring herself to be a 'rational agnostic' to assuming the role of faith healer was a breathtaking transition. I suspected that the change was related to her intimacy with the little doctor whose remedy for her psychosomatic illnesses was regular visits with him to prayer meetings. When my demons were at their worst, and I lay curled and terrified on my bed, she laid her hands on my head and prayed. I did not object. The presence of another human being outside the mental sarcophagus in which I was enclosed was a comfort. The touch of hands was a reminder of another reality, but the demons remained, unafraid of her deity, and lurked in the catacombs of my skull, waiting to pounce.

One day, I read of a monastic community on a remote Scottish island where healing was a central part of its philosophy. Anything had to be better than the suffocating vacuum of home and the prospect of finding an alternative to the chemical morass in which I was sinking was intensely appealing. An island on the edge of the ocean with clean air and a simple life, however romantic, promised escape to a different reality. I wrote to the leader immediately enquiring about a visit and, when he replied to say that all the places had been taken for that year, I wrote back warning that I was coming anyway, such was the extent of my desperation. Mother was hurt by my decision to leave, believing that her faith could cure all illnesses, but could not object to the move to a religious community.

As the boat left the Belfast docks I stood in the stern watching the harbour lights fade into the night and the wake spreading out across the still water. Leaving on a ship evokes a strange turmoil of emotions. Sorrow, as you let go of the land of your birth, a sentimental longing for a past that might have been the Celtic yearning for Tir NanOg. Relief, as the churning wake drowns memories best forgotten. Apprehension, as the bow forges into the unknown, and hope, as you imagine the fresh dawn over a new land. As we sailed past the shipyards, I thought of Sarah and wished that she could be with me, leaning on the rail and watching the dark silhouettes of half-built ships slide past, but the chances were that I would never see her again. I loved her, I think. At least that painful yearning to hold her, to brush that quiff of hair from her face, to see the sun glisten through the fine hair on her jaw, to feel her hip against mine as we walked in the street, that might have been love. Leaving her, even though she had rejected me, was the hardest part.

When I first saw the island, I was sure that I had been there before, an irrational conviction but a strong sensation nevertheless. The square, squat tower of the abbey, the brilliant white sands on the shore, the pink granite of the rocks, and the azure sea all seemed strangely familiar. So much so that I felt as if I had come home, that I would find peace of mind there.

The steamer anchored off the island, and we had to scramble onto small boats to ferry us ashore. I must have appeared as a pathetic figure, arriving on the island on a glorious day dressed in a thick overcoat, suede shoes, and a cravate, unable to shed the skin of an actor.

Incongruous. Other young people were in shorts and vests, and some of the boys were stripped to the waist and tanned. I asked the way to the leader's house and walked up the single street, passing roofless stone houses, their empty windows green with moss. The leader, tall and lean with a face as weathered as the ancient cross behind him, met me at the gate, his long silver hair blowing in the breeze. Xavier Martin exuded a mixture of kindness and authority, gentleness and strength, convention and anarchy. I was not sure whether to like him or to be wary of his façade.

'As I warned you, there is no room in the abbey just now. I'm afraid you will have to stay with me and my family in the meantime.'

'I had to come.'

'I see. Well, you are welcome anyway. Come away in and share our humble fare.' He showed me to a small room upstairs from which I could see the abbey.

'I hope you'll be comfortable here. Dinner will be in half an hour. I'll call you when we're ready.'

'Many thanks. It's very good of you.'

So there I was, on a small island three miles by one, knowing nothing of its people, its history, or its culture, yet hoping that it would provide an answer to my troubles.

I ate with the family that night– his wife and two children who asked me about Belfast and the shipyard which had built the Titanic. They seemed to know better than to ask the reason for my visit as if they were used to guests whose past was not to be discussed. The topic of the shipyard outlasted the meal.

'Im going down for evening prayers if you would like to come.'

It would have been churlish to refuse, so I followed him down to the abbey, passing an ancient graveyard.

'They say that there are forty-eight Kings of Scotland buried there and four Kings of |Ireland.'

Surrounded by a low stone wall, the grass mounds of the graves and a few scattered stones were all that remained of that royalty. The open door of the small chapel was enclosed in the jagged teeth of a Norman arch.

'Eleventh century,' he announced, 'A bit before my time.'

Sheep scuttled away as we approached the abbey. The evening sun glistened on the pink granite walls and cast long shadows from the medieval Celtic crosses at the door.

'A fellow countryman of yours founded the community here. Like you, he had turned his back on Ireland. There's a hill at the south end known as Carn Cuil ri Eirinn– the hill of the back to Erin. Maybe he left for the same reason as you have. I want to hear your story sometime, seeing you were so anxious to come.'

Our footsteps echoed on the schist floor as we entered the long nave. At the far end, a simple silver cross shone above the altar, and as we descended into the choir, the cross flashed as the setting sun shone down the aisle.

'You can sit here,' he said, indicating a seat in the choir stalls, 'others will be here in a minute.'

I sat alone for some time, enthralled by the surroundings. Ancient pillars, green with moss, carved with images of the Crucifixion and Judgement Day. The cool air smelling of stone. A doorway with a carved arch worn almost smooth by the storms. I could imagine cassocked monks in the choir stalls chanting vespers, the echoes of their worship resounding in the roof timbers. For the first time in months, I felt safe but a little anxious, too, remembering that Xavier had asked to hear my story. How much should I reveal? Would he despise me for that drunken evening in Dublin? Would it have happened at all if I had remained sober? And my crimes with Spam, did he need to know about those? I did not want him to think ill of me, and yet I was desperate to find healing, to escape from the terrors and the grip of medication.

The short service started with ritual short prayers and responses, followed by psalms chanted in harmony, which, echoing around the ancient walls, resonated with medieval simplicity. It was like floating back to blend with the voices of the monks who built the place. You could imagine them standing in the choir, their fingers rough with labour, their heads tanned with the sun, the hems of their habits frayed with use. These would not be the pale, ascetic creatures of strictly disciplined seminaries but working men with wives and children. The labourers standing in the choir that evening were of that kind too.

Xavier came to my room that night. 'Tell me, Billy.'

'What?'

'Why you had to come.'

'I've had a breakdown.'

'Who told you that?'

'Doctors, psychiatrists, family.'

'What do you think?'

'I don't know. Don't know what it is except that it's frightening, terrifying at times, as if you are about to disintegrate, shatter into pieces, as if there is something about to destroy you. Sometimes, I run through the streets to escape, running till I collapse.'

'Sounds really dreadful. When did it begin?'

'After I came back from Dublin.'

'What were you doing in Dublin?'

'In the theatre.'

'An actor?'

'Sort of. Small parts. Mainly assistant stage manager. A touring company, so we staged a different play every night and moved from town every week.'

'Hard work, I would think.'

'Exhausting.'

'Is that what went wrong? Exhaustion?'

Here it comes. The moment of decision. Whether to trust this man whom I have hardly met with the truth. I looked into his eyes and saw only kindness and strength.

'I was raped.'

He said nothing but waited for me to explain.

'I got very drunk one night, and this other actor came back to my digs. All very sordid.'

'You blame yourself for this?'

'If I had not got drunk, if I had not been so desperate to impress, to persuade people to like me, perhaps…'

'There was another person involved, though. He took advantage of the situation, did he not?'

'I submitted. For that, I despise myself. I feel sick just thinking of it.'

'Where does the fear come from? Fear of discovery, of being exposed?'

'No. Well, maybe a bit. But mostly, I don't know. It's just there, always lurking, waiting to leap on me, massive, black, ravenous.'

'And the medication helps?'

'It gets me through the night.'

'Right. Tonight, I will make you a cup of cocoa and you will lie down and sleep– without the pill– and I will sit here and keep the beast at bay.'

He did. He sat there all night. When I woke trembling and terrified through the dark hours, he was always there, reassuring me quietly. Once, I thought he was praying but he never spoke about that. I was not convinced that his approach was going to work. The shadow of fear still lingered.

In the dawn, he announced that I would be helping with the hay, so after a breakfast of porridge and toast, we stepped out into a blaze of sunshine.

The other men were already in the field, turning over the cut hay with pitchforks. I was surprised to see that the brothers wore no uniform, no dark habits or hoods, but were in shirt sleeves and flannels. As we passed the gate, Xavier lifted a fork and handed it to me.

'You will feel better after a day's work in the fields.' I was not convinced.

My hands soon blistered, first shaking out the grass to dry in the sun and then raking it in as the men started building rucks. In spite of the blisters, I began to enjoy the work, immersed in the sweet scent of meadow hay, cuffed by the crisp breeze from the north and feeling the strength in my arms. Keen to prove that I was no weakling, I lifted heavier and heavier forkfuls onto the ruck as it grew. At times the fork handle bent with the weight.

'We have all day, my friend,' one of the men said to me, 'This is not a competition. Take your time. We will be here till the sun goes down.'

'I'm enjoying the work.'

'I can see that. Keeping the demons at bay. I know. I have walked through the canyon's shadows, too.'

He smiled and returned to his work.

At ten o'clock, Xavier's wife and children carried tea and buttered scones to the field. 'There's a jug of buttermilk there if anyone would like a cold drink,' she said.

I sat with my back against a ruck. The man who had spoken joined me with a mug of tea in one hand and a scone in the other.

'You're here for healing?'

He was not looking at me but was gazing across the sea towards the horizon.

'I hope so.'

'This is a good place, quiet, peaceful, remote. You can find God here easily. His spirit is in every rock, every wave, every bird, every ear of corn. Everywhere. You don't have to look. We don't need a church here, walls to enclose and incarcerate the spirit, stone floors to keep us from the earth. We find the spirit in everything around us and in the work we do. You will find healing here.'

I sipped my tea, wondering if I would. What he said seemed to be distinctly fanciful, hand-knitted, too remote from the serpents that squirmed in my inner caverns to have any relevance. The cobra of despair began to rise from its basket and dance to his words.

'Xavier is an amazing man,' I said.

'A man of vision and intense spirituality. He sees the Holy Spirit in the most extraordinary places, even in the H bomb, in the fusion of atoms that that make the explosion, as well as in the blossoming of wildflowers on the shore. In him and in visionaries of his kind lies the hope of survival of the human race.'

I found his hyperbole distasteful and changed the subject. 'Why did you come here?'

He was shocked and turned to look at me for the first time.

'Me? I hated the way the world was heading– the self-indulgence, the materialism, the rejection of God, the obsession with sex, the nihilism, the iconoclasm, the destruction of Christian values. My friends turned to rock music, dancing, jukeboxes, Tony Curtis hair, and girls with tight sweaters. They despised me for going to church, not smoking or drinking, and avoiding the dances. Even in church, people disliked my devotion to the word of God. I had to search elsewhere. Tried all kinds of churches– Witnesses, Quakers, Methodists, Baptists, Brethren– and found no answer. So I came here and found peace.'

Yet there was something unsettled in him, a dispute taking place behind the façade, a conflict which caused his eyes to flit around the world before him as if it was on the point of disintegration, a fearfulness that appeared in his trembling foot. A man not at peace.

'That must have been a relief.'

'Yes. What is your name, by the way?'

'Billy.'

'Mine's Simon.'

He held out his hand. His handshake was weak and slippery like fresh haddock.

'You must come to my room sometime so that we can talk,' he said as he rose to return to work. I had no intention of accepting his invitation,

We worked till the sun dipped towards the western horizon, and a dampness fell on the hay. By that time, most of the crop had been lifted into rucks.

Xavier stayed with me again that night while I fought with the formless beasts that reared up from the quagmire of my dreams. Yet they were less threatening that night, and there were periods of calm sleep.

The following day dawned bright and dry, and I rose refreshed for the first time in months.

'Shearing today, Billy,' Xavier announced, 'Do you know anything about sheep?'

'They're good with mint sauce.'

A thin smile.

'Nothing then. Come with me. We have a flock of blackface sheep. I expect you have seen them round the abbey. We shear the ewes with lambs just now and send the wool away.'

We walked over the bare fields towards a ruined house. I could hear the lambs bleating for their mothers long before I could see them. Small tufts of white wool blew across the grass as we approached. One of the men was sitting astride a long stool with his back against the wall and a pipe in his teeth. Sharing his stool with its legs in the air between his knees, a ewe lay as if hypnotised by the trauma. As he clipped with his shears, the wool seemed to fall off easily. Simon was bent over, shearing a ewe on the ground. Their expertise was astonishing. The razor-sharp shears glided over the skin without cutting.

'You go in the pen, Billy, and pass the sheep out to the shearers. Easy. Come. I'll show you.'

We squeezed in among the bleating ewes.

'Catch it by the horn, right in at the base, and grip the ear as well. Horns look sturdy, but they're not, and if they break, the wound is a target for maggots. Grip the horn and the back end and haul the ewe out through the gate.'

Xavier caught one of them, pulled it out, and passed it to Simon, who turned it on its tail. I was surprised by his expertise as I thought him a bit of a weed.

'When it comes to Pierre on the stool. You pass him the head and help him lift the ewe onto the stool. There you are. I'll leave you to it.'

It was heavy work at first, particularly when another of the brothers joined the squad, but I grasped the technique fairly quickly and kept up with them. One of the older men came to roll the fleeces.

'You're from Ireland, are you?' Pierre asked at one point. 'Yes. From the North.'

'Far from home then. What brings you here?'

'Peace and quiet.'

'You would find peace on the shore of Lough Gill or on the top of Errigal. Why cross the water?'

'I read about this place and was sure that I would find healing here.'

'Ah. Healing is it? Wherever you go, only you can do that. And you can. Believe me. Find yourself first and learn to like that person with all the faults. Start there, Billy. Now are you going to bring another beast, or do I have to rise off my arse?'

His profanity shocked me, and yet, with the mischief in his eyes, I should not have been surprised. I like him immediately.

By the end of the day, my thumbs were blistered from the horns, and my back ached, but I knew that I would sleep.

Xavier suggested that I should join the others in the abbey as a room had become available so I moved that night to a small single cell in the ancient building. The narrow arched window looked out over a field of corn and across the sound to the distant mainland. As the sun set, the creaking call of corncrakes started in the corn and persisted through the night. Like a rusty bicycle turning endlessly in a circle, the sound at first annoyed and then infuriated, but once I accepted that it was not going to stop, it became quite soporific, lulling me towards sleep.

Perhaps, I thought, I could find healing after all.

Chapter 24

She was dreading it– the first night of the honeymoon. She sat beside Robert at the head of the table during the reception and tried to appear happy. She wasn't miserable, just shaking with worry. She knew her mother was watching her. Every time she glanced at her, their eyes met, and she could see the warning behind her glasses, the instruction to conform and behave herself. Her mother was delighted with the match. She looked at Robert with pride and affection and smiled when he turned in her direction. It was as if she was marrying hm and Sarah was a maid of honour. Sarah couldn't say she loved hm. He was kind and patient and gentle, but she never felt the spark that lit her time with Billy. She was marrying him because he offered her the chance of a different life, away from the shop, away from her mother and brother, away from the memories.

Some of the guests around the table were strangers to her, friends of his family who had flown from England, but most were from the church, invited by her mother, reserved, polite, with strict limits to their enjoyment. There would be no drunken hilarity at that wedding. They sipped the wine as if they were at communion. She swallowed hers as a gesture of defiance. Her mother frowned as she lifted the glass and tipped it back. She felt the ring on her finger, an alien attachment, a reminder of the ritual in the church, and spun it round with her thumb. She watched his hand on the white tablecloth crawl like a hairy crab towards hers. Not the hand of a working man, delicate with groomed fingernails. She imagined it moving over her skin and quickly shifted hers under the table, pretending she hadn't seen his move.

'Are you alright, Sarah?'

'Yes, I'm fine.'

'You look a bit sad.'

'Sorry. I just wish my Dad could have been here.'

'Of course. He would have been very proud of you.'

She had not thought of him till that moment. Proud of her? No. Not if he knew the truth.

The truth. Did she have to tell Robert the truth? Did she have to carry that black secret into her marriage? She lifted the napkin from her lap, placed it on the table, and began to fold it meticulously, smoothing out each fold with her fingers. She did not want him to notice the trembling.

'Leave that to the staff. You don't need to do that.'

'I do.'

'Are you nervous?'

'What? About what?'

'About . . . about me?'

'Course not. Don't be silly.'

'Good. That's good. We could go and change now. Get out of these stupid clothes.'

'I rather like mine.'

'You look gorgeous.'

Her mother had insisted on a white dress and had fallen out with Auntie Belle who said she should wear what she liked. She had wanted to get married in a registry office, wearing a blue suit to match her eyes. Outraged, mother had forbidden it.

'Never,' she shouted, 'What will the folk at the church think? They'll think you're pregnant, that's what. Absolutely not. Over my dead body. What would your father think?

He would turn in his grave if you went to the registry office. Never, never, never. In the church or not at all.'

She always brought her father into it, knowing it would hurt. She employed a seamstress to make the dress. A high neck modesty, for of course– 'just like Princess Grace'– and a white tulle with a ballerina skirt and a lace bodice. She insisted on white gloves and a veil. Sarah felt like a turkey trussed up for Christmas, and yet, when she saw herself in the mirror that morning, she was pleasantly surprised. The dress fitted perfectly and made her look quite elegant. Nancy would have envied her.

'I forgot,' he said, 'we have to cut the cake.'

'Where is it?'

'I think they're going to bring it in. Mum baked it herself and iced it. She's really good at that kind of thing, although her hands are nearly crippled with rheumatics. I haven't seen it yet.'

'It's amazing.'

She adored Robert, her only son and clearly a very late baby. It was hard to imagine her giving birth. So slim that the baby must have been visible. You must have been able to see every limb and curve of his body. A tall lady, she used her height to look down on people she regarded as inferior- such as Sarah and her mother. Clearly, she felt that her son was marrying beneath him and that we were of a different class. She never said anything to that effect- she was far too polite- but her opinions escaped in other ways. She insisted on a limousine to take them from the church and a Belfast photographer. The reception had to be in the best hotel at her expense and the honeymoon in Dublin in the Shelbourne Hotel.

As the cake was wheeled in, all the guests rose and applauded. Robert led Sarah from the top table into the space below. As she stood she could feel the effects of the wine and had to walk carefully, resisting Robert's tug on her arm. The cake was indeed a splendid creation with three tiers, glittering with silver and gold. She had no idea how to cut it and stood awkwardly, waiting for Robert to take the initiative. The waitress came to the rescue and lifted the top layers aside. Sarah rested her hand on his as he sliced into the icing, the first joint task of their life together. That's when the panic started. 'Let's go and change,' she said.

'Wait for the photographer. He won't be a minute.'

'No. I have to go.'

She didn't wait.

'Please excuse us, ladies and gentlemen. We have to change for the journey. Mother here will see that you all have some of this magnificent wedding cake.'

She was in tears when he joined her upstairs. 'Sarah, love, what's wrong?'

'All too much. All these people.'

'Never mind. We'll be leaving soon.'

Leaving. The prospect of being shut in a hotel bedroom with hm terrified her, not because he might be forceful or violent but because she would have to find a credible excuse to reject his advances, a way of dealing with his quite legitimate expectations.

She carried her case through to the bathroom and changed there, glad to be rid of the tight-fitting wedding dress and to slip on the blue lamb's wool sweater and cardigan. Without thinking, she had locked the door. When she came back to the room, he was wearing a sports jacket and flannels.

'Where's your dress?'

'In the bathroom. Mum's going to collect it.'

'All organised.'

'That's me.'

'You alright to go down?'

'And face the wolf pack? I suppose so.'

'They're not that bad. I'll take your case.'

His mother actually sobbed as he said goodbye. Hers gave her a cursory hug and whispered in her ear,

'See and behave yourself. He's your husband, remember.' As if she would forget.

They were all out on the steps as they drove off, waving and smiling– even her mother.

As they travelled south, she tried to work out a plan for the evening, but just as she gathered the threads together in her head, they unravelled and fell into a mess. She thought of getting very drunk so that she wouldn't care what happened but knew that she would still feel every movement of his body on hers. The prospect made her shiver.

'Are you warm enough?' he asked.

'Yes, yes. I'm fine, thanks.'

She thought of feigning her periods but reckoned that he would suspect the deceit. She imagined herself lying in bed in her pyjamas– at least she had brought them and not a nightie - and felt his fingers creeping under the top. She remembered Billy's first intrusion and wished it was him beside her in the car and that she had not rejected him so violently. She wanted to jump out and run back to him.

'Remember, he's your husband,' her mother said. What was she supposed to do? Pretend she was a virgin and squeal when he entered her? Leave a patch of blood on the sheet? Pretend to have a climax so that he would feel good, moan and squirm, and breathe heavily? Submit to his clumsy fumblings and bestial thrusting? She wondered what her mother did on her first night.

She could not imagine Daddy behaving like that. The more she thought, the angrier she became and the more determined to resist his advances.

Yet, when they sat in the hotel lounge before dinner, it was the gin that calmed her down. She looked around at the other guests in the spacious lounge and felt completely out of place. The ladies were in their elegant dinner dresses, fur stoles, glittering jewellery, and high heels, and she was in her skirt and cardigan. Robert seemed quite at home, though, swilling his brandy round in a glass and sniffing its 'nose'. Pretentious dope.

She sipped the gin and held it in her mouth, savouring the sharp sensation. She swallowed and it slipped down easily, nicely, gently warming her inside. Draining the glass, she asked for another and Robert beckoned one of the waters to order, begging her with his steady gaze to behave. That's when it started, her loving affair with alcohol. She can pin it down to that night, that second drink, and the others that followed.

Suddenly, she made a decision. She was watching a couple across the way. He was dressed in a dinner suit with a dickie-bow tie and red socks, but his costume fitted awkwardly on him as if it had once been his size and had just been taken out of the closet after a year in the wardrobe. A countryman with hands like hams, he was clearly annoyed with his partner. He leaned across, plucked the cigarette from her mouth, and stubbed it in the ashtray. She took a moment to react but then rose slowly from her seat, lifted her fur stole, and walked out. Sarah watched her go, admiring her elegance, the set of her shoulders, her swaying silken hair, her athletic legs, and not just admiring but envying her style and confidence. If she could do it, Sarah reckoned, then so could she.

Robert left to visit the toilet, and she lifted her handbag and walked out through the revolving doors. She felt free, as if she had just been released from a cage, as if she had slipped the leash held by her mother, by Robert, by her brother, by all those people who held her by the throat. She followed the pavement to the end of the square and turned towards the centre of the city, heading for the river. She knew he would look in the park, hunting around the pond and among the trees. She didn't want to think about him. Every time he came into her mind, she closed her eyes tight and shook her head. She found a street packed with people, their faces lit by the shop windows, and reckoned that she would be safe among the crowd. Walked down past Woolworth's and Lipton's. It was not like Belfast. There were rows of bicycles parked by the kerb, a horse and cart clattered up the street, a covey of nuns hurried past the shops, a girl was playing a fiddle with her child, fast asleep slung from her shoulders, a couple of youths on Vespas sped through the traffic, their bravado designed to attract attention. Their display reminded her of Billy and she stopped still in the middle of the pavement. Billy. This was his city, the place where he had worked, the place which he had described in his letters with such enthusiasm. The Gate Theatre. She had stopped so suddenly that someone bumped into her. She turned to see a young man, no more than a teenager, frowning at her.

'Sorry. Really sorry,' she said.

'No, no. My fault. I was looking in the shop window. Are you alright?'

The frown faded, and he smiled. Long, blond hair and blue eyes. Pretty rather than handsome but very attractive.

'I just remembered something.'

'Yeh, I know how it is. Me Ma asks me to get something halfway home; I suddenly remember and stop in the street and think oh Jesus, not again, and have to go back to the shops. Hellish.'

'You live here, do you? In Dublin, I mean.'

'Yeh. Dublin's Fair City. You're not from here, though. The north, maybe.'

'How do you know?'

'Our neighbours are from Derry. You speak like them. A bit more refined.'

'Refined?'

'Well, polite then.'

'Posh you mean.'

'No, no. I didn't mean that. Well-spoken me Ma would say.'

She laughed. Well-spoken. She'd never been accused of that before. 'Can you tell me where to find the Gate Theatre?'

'It's miles from here. Away at the top of O'Connell Street. You'd need to get a bus or a taxi or something.'

'It doesn't matter, really. I just wondered where it was. A friend of mine used to work there.'

'An actor?'

'No. A girlfriend, an actress.'

'She's famous?'

'No, no. Small parts. She was there only a couple of weeks.'

'I'd love to be an actor. Up on the stage under the spotlights, name in lights, picture in the in the papers and all that.'

'If you make it to the top.'

'Oh I'd make it to the top. Nothing less for me. I can see the headlines "Slaughter Boy Goes to Holywood".'

'Slaughter boy?'

'Yeh. I work in the abattoir.'

'That's awful. What a horrible job.'

'Not that bad. Good money. Listen, I was just going round to Davey Byrne's for a jar. Why don't you come? It's quite a place. All the actors go there. Come on, why don't you? My name's Connor, by the way.'

'I don't know. I have to get back to the hotel.'

'Which hotel's that?'

'The Sherbourne.'

'Oh. Very posh. But it's just around the corner. Won't take a minute to get back. Come on. Come and see Dubln's celebrities.'

'Okay. Just for a few minutes, though.'

'Well done. It's just down the street.'

She liked the boy - and he was just a boy. She didn't think he had been shaving for many years. Maybe that's why she went with him, like going with a child. Baby-snatching Nancy would call it. He was courteous, considerate, and patient. He would not let her buy a drink.

She didn't remember much about the pub except the sour smell of stout and a man coming to the bar beside her wearing make-up. Eyeliner tan foundation and lipstick. He smiled at Connor and raised his eyebrows in appreciation. Connor was amused rather than embarrassed. He seemed to be used to that sort of admiration, but she didn't like it. She was glad when the man– if that's what he was– ordered a port and left the bar.

'He's a famous actor,' Connor said, 'Queer as a coot.'

She drank a lot of gin that night. Every time Robert came into her head, she swallowed a large mouthful until it didn't matter. She told Connor a lot of lies, pretending to be Nancy.

Acting like her, she flirted with him, using her lips like she would and fluttering her eyelashes. She became Nancy. No, not Nancy. Someone far more outrageous. She bought some Sobranie and smoked like a film star. She felt amazing inside that person, wild, careless, mature, confident. When she spilled some gin on her skirt, Connor took her glass and put it back on the counter.

'Let me take you back to the hotel,' he said.

'Not going back there. Somewhere else. Let's go somewhere else. A nightclub, a party, or something.'

When they left, she had her arm around his waist to steady her. Her feet seemed a long way off, as if they were working by themselves. They went down to the river near the bridge, where the lights glittered on the black water. They went to his aunt's house. He said it was his aunt's and he had a key, but there was no one else there.

His body was smooth like silk, warm and smooth, moving gently over her in waves, washing over her, through her, lying on the tide edge in a sunlit sea. Slow and tender like he loved her. Like she was floating on her back, held safely in his arms. Daddy's arms teaching her to swim. There were tears slipping into her hair, happy tears. The wee boy between her thighs stroking his blond hair as he lay spent with his head on her shoulder.

Chapter 25

BILLY

Dawn on the island was spectacular. From the summit of the only hill, the tip of the sun rose over a mantle of mist covering everything except the tops of the mountains on the mainland, which seemed to float like ships in a white sea. The hill was not particularly high but high enough to rise above the mist. I had taken a sleeping bag and spent the night by the cairn, watching shooting stars flitting across the sky and listening to the murmur of the swell on the western shore.

I woke to find I was not alone. Wearing only a pair of shorts, his bronzed athletic torso gleaming in the amber light, he did not move but sat completely still, gazing over the sea. It seemed as if he had just materialised, a young god transported from his heaven to that spot, his blond hair reflecting the light like a halo. He turned slowly and stared at me with a hint of amusement.

'You from the abbey?'

'I'm staying there. Yes.'

'You a Christian?'

'Depends what you mean.'

'What's your interpretation?'

'I don't know, really. I suppose there must have been a man, Jesus, at one time but the son of God and all that and his resurrection. God knows. Maybe an idea dreamt up by his followers. Had to say something after believing he was immortal.'

'Bit of a cynic then. Not one of the crowd in the abbey.'

'No. Not really. Not one of them.'

'Why are you here then?'

'Came up to watch the sunset and the dawn.'

'You know that's not what I meant, but if you don't want to give the reason, just say. Be truthful.'

'I was looking for healing.'

'See. Wasn't hard to say it, was it?'

'No, I suppose not.'

I stood and shook off the sleeping bag

. 'Are you on holiday here?' I asked.

'I run camps for young people. Just down there.'

He pointed to the north, and I could see a large tent and several small ones around it.

Beside them, there was a stone barn with a rusty tin roof. A thin column of smoke snaked from the chimney.

'All summer?'

'I'm here all summer. Different groups come every week. You should visit– when you're not busy being healed.'

He smiled and walked away down the hill. I noticed that he had bare feet yet walked with ease between the rocks. Not a god after all, but an unusual person with a magnificent physique and an attractive smile. I found myself admiring his self-assurance, his harmony with the earth, his way of life. I rolled up the sleeping bag, tugged on my shoes, and headed back towards the abbey. I knew that I would visit him later.

That evening, having blistered my hands trying to use a scythe, I walked up to the camp.

He was in the barn, sewing the hem of a sail. I could hear singing in the main tent. 'I knew you'd come.'

'Second sight?'

'No. I know about people, how they work.'

'A psychologist then.'

'No. Just a human being. Sit down.'

'Thanks. How did you get this job?'

'Long story. What's your name, by the way?'

'Billy.'

'Billy from Ireland. You'll not be a Catholic then.'

'No. Not anything, really.'

'Floundering or a searcher after truth? Some tea?'

He swung a blackened kettle across the fire. The ancient fireplace still had its swee and a massive granite lintel.

'Yes, please. What about you? A searcher?'

'I know where it is. I don't need to look.'

'I see.'

He sat down again, returning to his sewing, his palm protected by a leather strap. 'Do you come every summer?'

'This is the third. I was a youth worker in Glasgow, and someone told me about the job here, and it sounded interesting, so I'm here.'

'That's not a long story.'

'I'll tell you the rest one day. I'm Mark, by the way.'

I watched him working the sail needle deftly along the seam. 'How many young folks are here?'

'Twenty-five, though sometimes it feels like sixty. They're all from the city and go a bit wild at times. Never seen a cow or a sheep or been in a boat. Took some of them fishing last night and caught a big lithe. You should have seen the excitement. Two of them were really terrified. They cooked it for tea. That was an experience for them. They'd only had fish suppers before. Fish in batter. Maybe this'll change their lives and help them to see a way out of their personal prisons. They're criminal kids mainly from Borstal.'

'What do the abbey folk think of it?'

'Most of them seem to appreciate what we're doing. Some of the kids actually go to the abbey services. With their officers, of course.'

'Do you go?'

'No. I don't need to. I told you. I know where the truth is.'
'Where's that then?'

Gautama Buddha said, "Look within. Thou art Buddha."

'You're a Buddhist?'

'I follow my own path. The truth is inside you. You have all the answers.'

'Oh yes? And if the inside is darkness and chaos and confusion?'

'You turn on the light and calm things down.'

'Easier said than done.'

'It can be done. Believe me. You don't have to be a Buddhist, a Hindu, or a Christian. You can learn to let go, release yourself, surrender to the life force.'

'Have you done this?'

'I met a man in England, in Coombe Springs. A man called Pak Subuh, an Indonesian mystic was over here on a visit. A most remarkable person, a visionary. You know he is enlightened as soon as you meet him. He has many followers now on a path they call Subud, which is short for Susila, Budhi, and Dharma. Susila stands for the behaviour of a good human being, budhi for the life force in each of us, and dharma for submission to the life force. There's a kind of ritual you go through, a sort of physical release, a cleansing– we call a latihan. Wonderful experience. You feel completely different after it, as if you have sloughed off old skin.'

'Sounds fascinating. Can you do that here, on the island?'

'You're supposed to have a teacher, but I practice it on my own every day. I could show you sometime if you're interested.'

'That would be great…'

I was interrupted by the clatter of a cooking pot on the floor and the breathless entrance of a girl.

'Bloody heavy,' she said.

'This is Billy.'

She, too, had bare feet and blackened where she had come through the bog. Her jeans were rolled up to her knees, and her navy sweater hung down over her hips. Long dark hair adorned with a white gull's feather completed the image, clearly contrived to convey contempt for convention.

'Hi Billy,' she said, raising her eyebrows to Mark for an explanation of my presence.

'He's at the abbey.'

'Oh, one of them.'

'No, actually. He's staying there, but not one of them. Not yet, anyway. We met at the top of the hill.'

I was pleased that he had defended me from her cynicism.

'You should throw away your shoes,' she said, 'Feel Mother Earth between your toes. You're not in the city now.'

'Maybe I will. Anyway, I'll need to get back. Chores to do.'

'Tea won't be minute,' Mark said.

'Next time. See you then.'

On the path back to the abbey, I thought about Mark and his ideas. I admired his strength, his certainty, and his outlook on life. I stopped to remove my shoes and socks. The ground felt cold and wet and hurt my tender soles as I walked, but I resolved to persist, to transform myself, to cast off the detritus of the old life, to feel strength in my limbs, to expose the decadent pale flesh to the sun and to be at one with the earth like Mark. He was my new idol, the latest father figure. I had not yet discovered his flaws.

The ancient chapel's walls were green with damp and white lime seeped from the mortar seams. Although the chapel was small, the schist flagstone floor and absence of pews sent an echo into the roof above. It was empty apart from a single silver cross high on the gable. Mark closed the oak door behind us, and we stood together in the gloom.

'This is a good place,' he said, 'The thick stone walls hold us in the centre and shut out the movement of the world outside. The stone is near the centre of the wheel. Feel the skin of the stones under your feet. Be still. Listen to your breath. Feel it cool in your nose and on your lips. Be aware of your limbs, your arms, your legs. Listen to your heart. That is you. Let your thoughts pass through you. Do not hold them. Let your body do what it wants to do. Let it shake, leap, collapse, dance, curl. You can moan, shout, sing, whistle– any sound coming from the depths of your being. I will behave in the same way. Pay no attention.'

At first, I found his bizarre actions astonishing. He groaned and shook and spoke in a strange language. Yet, when I chose to discard my scepticism and participate, I found it exhilarating. Letting go physically seemed to help a surrender of the mind, a release of subconscious tension and stress. My arms and hands flung off shreds of my fears, my throat roared out my rage, and my feet drummed on the flagstones in a primordial dance. Swinging through infancy, childhood, and adolescence and expelling the darkest memories of the years, I seemed to float away from myself and soar into a strange cloud of consciousness, a different realm of being. Gradually descending, I found myself curled on the floor in a foetal position with my thumb in my mouth. I had no idea how I came to be there.

Mark was standing against the wall.

'That is your first latihan kejiwaan, your first surrender. Now, when you go from here, you will carry that with you and try to follow a new path, a different way of life, respecting others, the creatures of the earth, the things that grow, and the earth itself. Remember what I said, "Look within. Thou art Buddha." You are your own god. How do you feel?'

'Weird. I feel as if I had lost something.'

'Good. It will be calmer next time and eventually a time of peace. Now we'll go back to the world.'

As I sat in the choir of the abbey that evening, not really listening to others chanting responses to Xavier's prayers. I wondered what he would think of Subud and the bizarre ritual of the latihan. I imagined the disdainful smile, the slightly patronising expression in the eyes. I thought of Sarah and remembered my obsession with the occult, the night of dancing and leaping along the road in the moonlight. That was before . . . .

In a moment of panic, I stood up and fled from the service. The terror and darkness, for no apparent reason, had suddenly returned like a thunderstorm. In my bare feet, I ran across the island, fleeing from the indescribable demon behind me. The more my feet hurt, the more, the more I could keep it at bay. Across the machair and up onto the cliff, staring down on the surf below and wondering if the cool water would cool the blazing turmoil in my head. The great swell from the Atlantic breaking over the rocks, surging, breaking, retreating, sucking the weed back into its depths. I thought of a body sinking down towards the seabed, pirouetting gracefully in the calm waters, free, languid, released from the turbulence above…

Chapter 26

'For Christ's sake, Sarah! Where have you been? I looked for you everywhere– all over the hotel, out in the park, in the streets. I had to call the police. Where were you?'

Robert stood with his back to reception. Not 'Are you okay?' He looked annoyed rather than upset or concerned.

'I'll need to phone the police and tell them. Everyone's been looking for you. The staff have been all over the hotel. I phoned your Mum to see if you'd gone home and her Dad. They're out of their minds with worry. Where did you go?'

'For a walk.'

'All night?'

'Yes.'

'Why did you not say?'

'You weren't here.'

'You could have told someone, Sarah. You can't just walk out like that. I'll need to phone the police.'

He turned his back and asked for the phone at the desk.

She walked past him, up the broad staircase, and ran a bath in their suite. She lay in the luxury of the hot water, relaxing, allowing her fingers to float lazily like palm leaves in its warmth. She didn't really care what they thought– him, her mother, his mother. She drifted away from them. The night with the wee boy– what was his name?– Connor, that's right– the night with Connor had changed everything.

She was not frightened anymore. She no longer felt ashamed. He had loved her, slowly, carefully. And they would never know. Her space, her own secret.

She heard Robert come into the room and rattle clothes hangers in the wardrobe. She lay in the warmth and watched the suds bubbling around her knees, listening to him moving around the room. He meant as much to her as one of the bell boys.

'You'd better get dressed,' he called.

'Really?'

'Yes. We're leaving today.'

They had booked for another night but she wasn't going to satisfy him by questioning his decision. She wondered what had prompted it– embarrassment? Fury? Humiliation? Confusion? She tried to remember his face when she strolled into the foyer but could only see the small tuft of white toilet roll stuck to his chin where his razor had nicked the skin. He had taken time to shave, time which might have been spent searching for his missing bride.

She climbed out of the bath and lifted the brass plunger, admiring the gleaming taps.

The towel was soft and fluffy and smelt of Lux flakes. She sat on the toilet seat to dry her legs, remembering that she had returned to the hotel without her stockings. She must have left them and her suspender belt in Connor's place.

She watched Robert struggling to close his suitcase, trying to force the clasps into the lock sockets. The clothes, packed in a hurry, would never allow the lid to close. The more he fought with it, the more obvious it became that he would be defeated. He lifted the case onto the floor and knelt on it. Still no success. Finally, he stood up, his face puce with the effort.

'You will have to take some of mine in yours,' he announced. 'Yes. I can see that.'

He hauled out his pyjamas and a Fair Isle jumper, threw them on the bed, closed the case, and left the room.

'Leaving in half an hour,' he said as he shut the door.

He didn't ask anything more about the previous night. Nothing. Not a word. Not ever.

Very strange. Did he not care? Did he just crush it into a tin and slam the lid? She began to think that he had no feelings, that he was emotionally neutered.

He barely spoke on the way home.

'Say nothing about the episode,' he announced when they reached Bangor, 'Nothing. They paid for the hotel and I don't want them upset. We left early because you weren't feeling well. Is that clear?'

'Completely.'

So it continued, the ritual, the years of deception.

His mother was sufficiently polite not to ask about children. Little humorous hints, now and then, but no searching enquiry. Sarah thought that she spoke to her mother because she confronted her. Sarah told her that she had a medical problem.

'You've been to the doctor then?'

'Of course.'

'What's the problem?'

'I don't want to discuss it.'

'It's him, isn't it?'

'No, it's not. Now, just leave it. I'm not going to talk about it.'
'You could adopt,' she suggested.

'We're trying to run a business. We really don't have time. You can't bring up kids and run a hotel.'

She didn't raise the subject again. Sarah reckoned that she sensed her determination to avoid the subject.

She did wonder if she was sterile. Twice, she had avoided pregnancy. On the first occasion, she had spent weeks in agonising suspense, waiting and praying for her period. Desperately, she had tried to find out about abortion, but there was no one to ask, no way of getting information. She did not trust their doctor, who was a friend of the family. She was determined not to have the baby– a repulsive legacy - and devised all kinds of wild schemes to get rid of it. Fortunately, the periods arrived. Nothing, thank God, came of the second encounter in Dublin either.

She made it clear from the start that she was not going to share the double bed in their room. Robert stared at her, his little hands clenching and unclenching by his side. He looked so helpless, like a child lost in a wood; she felt sorry for him.

'Is there something wrong?'

'Nothing's wrong.'

'So why not?'

'I don't want to.'

'We're supposed to be married.'

'We are married.'

'How long are you going to keep this up?'

'Don't know.'

'This is ridiculous. What will I tell them?' he said, nodding towards his parents' room.

'I'm sure you'll think of something.'

Lifting her night clothes, she left him there and went through to the bathroom. They never did share a bed.

She washed his clothes, ironed his shirts, polished his shoes, and, in the winter, when the hotel was quiet, cooked his meals. At the end of the first season she moved to an attic bedroom. She suspected that he found that a relief. Certainly, he seemed happier with the arrangement. She didn't know what his parents thought. They never spoke of it. It was a small room, but she could see the sea, and there was a painting of a sailing ship above the bed. She felt safe there, as if she was back in her own bedroom with her Daddy next door as if he was there. She used to sit on her bed and imagine that she was on his knee. She wanted to tell him, tell him everything, but there were things she couldn't say, dreadful things which would shock him. She had to hide the bottles from him under the mattress. He would have been upset if he knew. She didn't know if Robert had guessed. He never mentioned it in the early days, the days before he changed, before she felt the hidden side of his placid and submissive nature.

She liked the winters. The carpeted corridors were silent, the dining room empty.

Wandering past the closed doors and down the wide stairs, she could imagine that it was her house, her mansion. She used to sit on her stocking feet on the big, comfy sofa in the guests' lounge and read the old magazines. His parents never went in there in the winter. They had their own flat with a telephone and rarely came into the front of the hotel. They lived their own lives, so she could have had a drink in the lounge, but she never drank downstairs. She saved that luxury for her room.

It was one of those hotels that had prospered between the wars when seaside resorts swarmed with pale city-dwellers keen to escape the smoke and gloom of Belfast. The front rooms looked out over the sea and a long sandy beach. In recent years, however, it was showing signs of wear. The curtains were faded, the white paint faintly brown, the cornices dusty, the dining room chairs scuffed. It was not shabby, though, merely ageing, a little tired, past its prime.

Robert was a Scout leader, a position of which is mother approved and to which he devoted much of his time and energy. He also bought a new car– a Triumph Spitfire– and spent hours caressing its sleek body with his duster. Every spoke of the wheels was polished, every wheel arch scrubbed, every tyre blackened till it gleamed like a soldier's boot. It rarely left the garage, and when it did, it was to drive his mother to Belfast for shopping or himself to meetings of the Licensed Trade Association. Once he offered to drive Sarah to church, knowing that she had abandoned her religion years beforehand. She never set foot in his most precious possession, never contaminated the pristine interior with her presence.

When his father died, there was little fuss. After the funeral, things just carried on as before, as if he had never existed. His mother showed little grief, the odd whimper at the service and in the afternoon when the mourners met at the reception in another hotel. By the following morning, she was completely composed and back to normal, speaking cheerfully to the guests with her ritual banter. Sarah was astonished. She had hoped that she would hand over the business to Robert so that she would have more time to herself but she refused to relinquish control.

When Sarah announced that she was going to Dublin for the weekend, there was little resistance from either of them– some muttering from Robert about it being a busy weekend with guests but otherwise extraordinary acceptance. In one sense, she was distinctly aggrieved to find that she was of so little consequence, in another relieved. She knew that there was little chance of meeting Connor, but encounters with men were not the main purpose of the expedition.

Chapter 27

SPAM

Sleet built up on the windscreen as Spam drove south towards the border and flurried in the beams of the headlights. He was worried that it might turn to snow as he was returning from the Republic with his load of contraband the following night. November was not the best month for these forays into the south. It was a mistake to have taken the Anglia. The Singer Gazelle, with its twin carbs and heavy chassis would have been better but was blocked in at the back of the showroom. He plucked a cigarette from the packet on the seat beside him and was searching for his lighter when he caught up with a police car. Shit. Better slow down. Don't want to attract attention.

Just after a bend, the police car stopped, and he had to brake suddenly. There was a car across the road ahead. For a moment, he thought it must have skidded on snow, but the road was black and clear. Strange place to stop. The door of the police car opened, and the peeler stepped out, tugging on his hat. Spam thought he might turn in his direction, but he walked towards the other car, silhouetted in the beam of the headlights, just as two figures emerged from the darkness. What happened next passed so quickly. Spam was left dazed, wondering if he had imagined the incident. There was a rattle of gunfire, crashing of glass and metal, spits of flame and whine of bullets. The peeler fell, the figures ran back to the car, and it sped away into the night.

Stunned, he sat staring at the scene. The peeler lay still on the road. The windscreen of the police car was shattered. He felt like turning the car and escaping before another car appeared. With his record, it would be stupid to be found there. Yet he was not a coward. Only a coward would run away and leave the man lying there. Maybe he could be a hero and save the man's life. He opened the door and stepped out, turning up his collar as the sleet hit his cheek.

Passing the police car, he could see another officer slumped over the dashboard with blood oozing from his forehead. He didn't stop. He walked across to the figure on the ground and bent down to see if he was still alive. He was lying on his back with blood flowing from his mouth and his eyes staring blankly at the sky. They did not blink as flakes of snow settled on the surface. Spam did not need to feel for a pulse. The man was dead, the uniform on his chest shredded with bullet holes. Spam was about to close his eyes when he gasped and jerked back. He recognised the face. The policeman from his hometown had searched his room many years ago after he had chained the boy at the dance.

'Christ Jesus!' he whispered.

As peelers went, he was not a bad guy. He had come to watch him fight in the ring a couple of times and roared his support. Didn't deserve this. He felt a wave of fury rising in his chest.

'Fuckin' bastards! Fuckin' Fenian bastards!' IRA. Could only be them.

Maybe they're still near at hand. Better get to fuck out of it in case they come back.

But he couldn't leave the peeler lying in the road, so he grabbed him under the arms and hauled him onto the grass, leaving a trail of blood on the tarmac. Some fuckin' weight.

Breathless, he hurried back to the car and left the scene, deciding to drive back home to his flat in Belfast. Bad time to be on the border.

He lit a cigarette and found that the lighter shook in his hand. He could not get the picture of the peeler's face out of his head, the blood from his lips steaming in the cold air.

'Fuckin' bastards.'

There were other young men in the community centre when Spam arrived, some of whom he knew from the pub and some from their visits to the car showroom. They were standing about in small groups, clearly waiting for something to happen. Spam had shaved, pressed his trousers and shirt and worked up a deep polish on his shoes as he had learnt in the army. He wanted to show that he had been a soldier. Some of the others were in jeans, leather jackets or scruffy anoraks with hair hanging down to their shoulders. They would never make soldiers.

'What about you, Spam?' asked Freddy from his own street, 'You here for the same thing as the rest of us?'

'Probably.'

'Time to stop these bastards, eh?'

'Aye.'

The door to the back room at the end of the hall opened, and a man marched out, dressed in combat gear, a mask and a black beret.

'Fred,' he called out, 'You next.'

Fred stamped out his cigarette on the floor and slouched forward, 'See you after, Spam.'

Spam watched him join the recruiting officer and disappear into the room. He looked round the others and reckoned that he was the only one there who might make a soldier. He doubted if any of them had fired a rifle, sweated on an assault course, or suffered blisters on a route march.

When Fred came out of the room, he was smiling and holding himself more upright. 'That's me in,' he boasted as he passed, 'See you outside.'

'I'll take you next,' the sergeant said, pointing at Spam. He joined the sergeant, and they entered the back room.

There were three masked men in combat gear and berets sitting behind the table which was covered with a Union flag. On top lay a Bible and a Sterling sub-machine gun.

Spam stood at ease in front of them.

'I'm told you were in the British Army,' the mask in the middle moved its pink lips. 'I was.'

'Your number?'

'23514088.'

'A volunteer then?'

'Aye.'

'Why did you join?'

'Get to fuck out of Belfast. See the world. Learn to be a soldier.'

'Serve Queen and country.'

'No. Not really.'

'That's honest anyway. So why do you want to join us?'

'To deal with those Fenian bastards killing our side.'

'You know about weapons?'

'Course. Stens, Brens, rifles, SLR's. Got my marksman's badge.'

'Excellent. You'll be an asset. Sign here. Read it first, if you like.' He walked to the table and read the oath.

He read bits of it– 'never betray a comrade or give any information to whomsoever which could prove detrimental to my Cause... if I fail in my obligations I shall truly deserve the just deserts befalling me...'

He had visions of knee-capping or a shot in the back of the skull in a deserted quarry. 'Place your hand on the Bible and sign the oath.'

He picked up the Bible with one hand and signed the form with the other. 'When do I get armed?'

'We'll let you know soon enough. Basic training first. You should know that. Discipline. Be here Tuesday night.'

He did not tell them that he had deserted and that he made a point of avoiding British troops.

He walked out into the sunlight. 'All Taigs are targets' was scrawled on a wall across from the centre.

He was not sure that he had done the right thing in joining the UVF. They seemed such an amateur bunch. Still he would stick with it in the meantime.

He avoided Fred, headed for the car and drove back into the city. As he approached the showroom, a cavalcade of police vehicles flew past, heading in the same direction. He was worried when he saw them turn into his roadway. As he turned the corner, he saw why.

A barricade of cars, bins, shopping trolleys, doors and other items stretched across the road.

In front of it, burning tyres sent black smoke curling into the sky and a gang of dancing youths were flinging stones at the line of police, now reinforced by the arrival of the cavalcade. He was not concerned until, in the distance beyond the riot, he saw his showroom windows.

Accelerating forward, he pulled in behind the police line. A flying brick bounced off the bonnet, leaving a deep dent. He leapt out and sprinted towards the barricade, ignoring the barrage of missiles. A petrol bomb burst behind him. He caught the smell of petrol. It reminded him of Billy. He could taste it on his tongue. As he ran, he saw that the rioters in front of him were not Catholic but Protestant youths, some wearing blue Linfield shirts and carrying Union Jacks.

What the fuck are they doing? What's going on? One of them hurled a brick at him as he neared the barricade, but he dodged it and sprang onto a car bonnet. Another man flung a spade at him but missed and overbalanced. Spam kicked him in the face as he landed and ran on.

He reached the showroom to find the two large plate glass windows smashed and three of the cars missing. He turned and saw their outline in the barricade.

'Christ Almighty! Whose side are they on?'

He hurried through to the office in case they had broken in. The door was still locked, and the glass was intact. That was a relief. He had a load of cash in the cupboard and a pile of contraband fags. He let himself in, checked the cash and slipped all the notes into a plastic bag. There was no safe place for the fags, and there were too many to carry. They would have to wait. The cars were more important. Lifting the keys, he moved two of them across the broken windows to block the exit, leaving the Singer and a new Rover at the back. At least they had left the expensive models. He locked the office and was just leaving when two masked men appeared.

'This your place?'

'Aye, it's my place, and they've fuckin' wrecked it and stolen three of my cars.'

'Don't worry about it.'

'What do you mean don't worry about? Do you think I'm made of money? Insurance will never cough up.'

Spam's fists tightened, but he didn't want to get into a fight with the cash hanging beside him.

'Calm down, boy. I said don't worry. We'll see you alright. You need better insurance. Good insurance costs, though.'

'Oh, aye. Protection. Is that what you're talking about? I just joined the UVF, and I'm needing protection. Is that it?'

'UVF, eh? And who's your commander then?'

'How the fuck do I know? I just joined.'

'You'd better find out, my friend. We'll be around tomorrow. Talk business, and you'd better have the name by then. No time for guys who claim to be UDA and aren't.'

They swaggered away, and Spam noticed that one of them was armed. Just as well, he didn't tackle them.

He decided to avoid the riot and take a detour back to the community centre, heading south of the Shankill, the side streets on the other side being crowded with protesters. The streets here were empty, strangely silent. The smell of burnt timber and fabric pervaded the damp air like tear gas trapped between the rows of grim brick houses. Lintels above shattered windows were scorched black, and broken doors hung askew. An elderly man stood outside one of the doorways, a suitcase bound with a belt in his hand. His back was to the road as he faced his wife, pushing a loaded pram from the doorway. When he saw Spam, he dropped the suitcase and scuttled into the house, forcing his wife backwards. These were Catholic streets; the families burned out only a few weeks beforehand. He felt sorry for the couple. The old dear could have been his Gran.

He walked straight into the community centre, through the group of men in the hall and into the back room. For a moment, no one moved. The three behind the table stared through their masks. The one being interviewed stepped aside, raising his arm to protect his face. Only the recruiting officer sprang round and levelled a Webley at Sam's head.

'Move and you're dead meat.'

'Your mob trashed my car showroom.'

'So?'

'Cost me a fuckin' fortune. Drove cars out and stuck them in a barricade. They're wasted. What are you going to do about it?'

'Hard luck.'

'Put the gun down, Kelly,' the chairman ordered quietly, 'Hear him out. Where was this, son?'

'By the Shankill. There's some mob there. Huge. Wavin' Union Jacks, chuckin' stones, planks, petrol bombs, anything at the RUC. This is our guys taking on the RUC. Our guys are trashin' my cars. What's goin' on?'

'Calm down, son. Have you not heard?'

'What?'

'They're going to disband the Specials. Callaghan and that crowd in London. That's why folk are raging and quite right, too.'

'No need to take out on me.'

'The Taigs took it out on Isaac Andrews in the Falls, didn't they? Not much left of his showroom.'

'Prod on the Falls. What did he expect? Anyway, what's going to happen about my cars? Fucked if I'm paying protection.'

'We'll see alright. Don't worry. We'll speak to them.'

'They asked for the name of my CO. Who is it?'

'We'll speak to them. You'll meet your CO next week. You can go now. Don't ever barge in here again. Try it again and we'll fill you full of holes.'

He drove across the city to Balmoral cemetery. It was his Gran's birthday, and he always left flowers on her grave.

He had paid for the polished granite surround and the white chips that kept the grave neat and tidy. He stood for a while with the flowers in his hand and watched the reflection of the clouds floating across the gravestone. He missed her– the way she shook her head when she was pleased and the bristle on her chin when he kissed her. The kiss suddenly reminded him of Sarah, Billy's girl. Christ. Sarah. He remembered the night in the car, how she had tried to fight him off and scratched his cheek, but she had been too drunk to resist. The only one to have struggled against him. He gave her that. A trace of respect. He tried to work out what he felt about that night. A bit of a brute, ripping her clothes and forcing himself on her. He despised that, ashamed of it almost, and he felt sorry for her now. He wondered where she was now and thought he might ask around, see if he could find her. On the other hand, she might hate him. Some of them liked it rough, but she was not like that. She might even go to the peelers. He wondered if Billy knew. That was bad, doing that to Billy's girl. Disloyal. And what would his Gran think? Jesus. She would never forgive him.

He bent down and placed the flowers by the headstone. Some leaves had fallen onto the white chips, so he brushed them off and picked off a fag butt that someone had flicked there from the path.

Maybe he should look for Sarah and apologise. Gran would approve of that anyway. Liquorice comfits. That's what she liked. He should have brought a bag of them to the grave.

Chapter 28

BILLY

I stand in my room in the abbey and look out across the sound. The swell is breaking white over the rocks on the far side and the tide, surging against the gale, is whipping up a turmoil in the middle of the sound. A gull, struggling in the wind, gives in and whirls way past my window. For three days now there has been no ferry. A pity. I was looking forward to meeting the new arrival. He has been before, and the descriptions offered by the other men excited my curiosity.

A big bullock of a man, apparently with a long red beard and unkempt hair, he wears a tattered kilt and a bonnet with an eagle's feather. He is, they say, immensely strong and can haul a cart of stones as easily as a stallion. In spite of that, he is gentle and sensitive and writes poetry. He is due to stay in the room beside mine. I think the others, even Xavier, have their reservations about him, suspecting perhaps that his eccentricity is contrived, a device designed to impress. I will decide for myself when I see him.

In the meantime I will lie on my bed and pass the time reading or listening to the wireless. I had been reading a book recommended by Xavier about Toyohiko Kagawa, a Christian pacifist and labour activist who worked in the slums of Kobe, but although I admired Kagawa's extraordinary dedication, I left aside the book and am reading Christmas Humphrey's books on Zen Buddhism. The change is largely inspired by a search for healing, a lasting solution to the lingering shreds of chaos, but it is also a choice designed to impress Mark. It is a trifle disloyal to Xavier after his efforts, but there is something exciting about the esoteric. I wonder if the new man is a

Buddhist. Unlikely, I think. He comes to the island now and again and is seen in services in the abbey.

Perhaps, in preparation, I should read some poetry. What would Spam think of that?

I wonder if he is in gaol yet. He seems so far from this island, almost indistinct, a part of my life which I can recall without disturbance. The boy whom he chained may be dead by now.

I don't read newspapers or pay attention to the news, so if there had been a court case, the details would not have registered. I used to read poetry– Yeats, Flecker, Dylan, Sassoon and others– before I met Spam, and I have a soiled copy of the Penguin Book of Contemporary Verse under the bed. I will search later so that I can quote a line or two to the new man.

I have no sheets on the bed. Just a couple of rough wool blankets. I'm beginning to sleep well, and slipping into untroubled sleep is a luxury after months of torment. 'Sleep that knits up the ravelled sleave of care, the death of each day's life. Sore labour's bath, balm of hurt minds…'

He understood, all those centuries ago, the delicious descent into dreamless sleep, the drift into oblivion. I'm sure it is the hard physical labour which allows me this pleasure. That and the elemental beauty of this island.

There is a hope of healing here. Yet, having been broken, how do you learn to love again?

How do you grow again the seeds of trust, the will to give? How do you retrieve that innocence, that sense of wonder stirred by moonlit rainbows in the night or minnows in a jar?

Can you feel again the ecstasy of hands first held in love, of selfless adoration stripped of guile or artifice? It is so hard to take the first steps from the battlefield, to leave behind the torn limbs of shattered selves and rotting pools of terror and despair.

Imitating Mark, my latest hero, I have taken to wearing nothing but shorts, allowing the sun to tan my pale torso, and I'm patiently hardening my bare feet to the grass and heather of the island. This is all part of the new image, that of a man in touch with nature and the environment. Xavier, I notice, looks at it with some suspicion but says nothing. Mark smiles wryly, flattered perhaps by the imitation. I wear a shirt in the early morning when I rise at six to stoke the boilers and overalls with boots when I work in the sheep pens.

Last week, the coal and coke arrived on the island. We had to work far into the night. The small, flat-bottomed coal boat came in on the high tide and beached on the sand. As the tide ebbed, Pierre drove the Ferguson tractor and trailer onto the sand beside the boat, and the seamen on board filled one-ton steel tubs of coal in the hold, which were swung on a derrick over the side. I had to stand on the trailer, watching the heavy tubs swinging dangerously towards my head and trying to steady them as they descended. It took all my strength to tip the coal out at my feet. It landed with a roar on the deck of the trailer, and the tyres sank under the weight. I was worried that we might not be able to pull away, but Pierre sat unconcerned on the tractor, smoking a cigarette, so I carried on till the trailer was full.

The men in the hold shovelling coal had little rest as they knew the tide would turn and start to lap around the stern of the boat. It was easier for us, waiting for our loads. Other tractors came from the far side of the island to take their turn, and the work continued till the grey light of dawn. By then, the wheels of the last tractor were half submerged. Heading back to the abbey behind Pierre on the tractor, I blew the black dust out of my nose and sent a black spit into the grass.

'You look like a black and white minstrel, Billy,' Pierre shouted. 'A lot cheaper, though.'

We unloaded the trailer as the sun rose. I had a shower, washed my overalls and started work. No sleep that night.

Munro is a big man right enough but nearly as coarse as his appearance suggests.

The pale blue eyes glint with humour yet study people with intense interest, scrutinising them as if it was vital to know who they are. Many people find that unsettling. He is reading 'The Cloud of Unknowing', a medieval mystic's manuscript and comes through to my room at night to tell me about it. Last week, when I pointed out that there is a surprising similarity to Buddhist texts, he scoffed at the notion and launched into a long, erudite lecture on the differences. His knowledge of different religions was astonishing.

I have discovered one major flaw in Munro. He is writing an esoteric poem of indeterminate length, which he brings through every other night and reads to me– always starting at the beginning. He has no sense of how tedious for me this might be. I don't want to hurt his feelings by suggesting that he start where he left off the previous evening. He never asks for my opinion on the merit of his magnum opus and I never comment as the text is opaque and so complicated as to be incomprehensible. I'm not sure whether he writes as a therapy or whether he hopes to publish. I am too timid to question his motives or to seek an explanation of the verse.

It would be unfair to suggest that he is insensitive to my feelings and interests as he frequently asks me questions about my life and ambitions.

'You can't stay here forever,' he said last night, 'This is no place for a young man.'

'I like it here. I like the work and the island. It's a remarkable place and it has an atmosphere as if we were standing at the beginning of time. You can feel its age under your feet.'

'A shelter, a refuge. Cut off from reality, isolated from the forces which are shaping the world. Good for a short time, for the healing of the soul, but too long here and the light of the spirit dims, the fire smoulders and dies. Too long here, and you get like the brothers, moribund, skeletons inside their clothes, the living dead.'

'That's a bit harsh.'

'Look closer. You have emerged from the shadows. What crippled you was not a breakdown, not a psychosis. It did not need the white juice of the poppy nor the laying on of hands nor to be given a name. It was what all young men experience in one way or another– the confusion as they leave their youth and stumble into manhood, the search for who they are. You must read R.D. Laing. You have passed through the veil, killed your first lion, won your eagle's feather, survived the sweat lodge and it is time to become a warrior, time to leave the tepee. My brother has a farm, a sheep farm, and is in need of a shepherd. I will speak to him.'

'I'm not a shepherd.'

'You can learn. You have learnt a little here.'

'I have no dog.'

'Dogs can be bought. The life would suit you. You are alone much of the time, battling with the elements– blizzards in the winter, floods in the summer, gales in the spring. Caring for animals, not men. You are your own master. Long hours from spring to autumn and time to read and write in the dark months of winter.'

'It sounds idyllic. I will think about it.'

Perhaps he is right. Perhaps it is time to move, to leave the island. Yet, it is a frightening thought. I have come to depend on Mark, followed in his footsteps, shaped myself on him and his ideas, and become a disciple. To slough off that image and expose myself to a new life would be a risk. My demons could follow me, impose their will on me, torment me with terror. The darkness could return. I am afraid of that.

Chapter 29

'I've never told anyone this before...'

Normally they show a spark of interest when I say that - the vultures, the helpers, the therapists who litter my life with shattered hopes. I can play them like trout. I cast a fly on the surface of their minds and sensing their prey, they twitch their tails. They scent power like cats smell mice. They sit forward slightly or press an elegant, manicured finger into their cheeks. I can't see your response, but it doesn't matter anymore.

'I hate him, you know. If I had him here just now, I'd pull his head off in front of your eyes.

I told each of them– the counsellors that is - little bits of my life. The men feigned professional indifference, but I could see the snake uncoiling, the sulphur beginning to glow. My tales ignited the very fire from which I was trying to escape. They repeat their liturgy like priests- "How did you feel when he did that?" or "How do you feel about that now?" Can they not imagine what it feels like? Do I have to describe the terror, the appalling nausea of the descent into the pit?

'I've had a wee drink. I admit that, but it's not the drink talking, believe me.'

I know the response, what you all say to yourselves - she's a drunk, don't listen to her. But I'm not drunk, and I have to talk to someone.

'Can I be honest with you? I've never told anyone this before...'

I don't know that I can tell you everything. You'd be disgusted. Yet how can you understand unless you know how different he is from other men?

I've had men in grubby beds with creased, grey sheets submerged in a thick slick of sweat and slime. Clockwork copulation, cogs clicking unsteadily, limbs jerking like plastic crabs. In rooms tipsy with cans and rolling with bottles, I have had heavy men floating like zeppelins between my thighs, thin men squirming like lizards with flickering tongues and men whose loose flesh enveloped me like the wings of a skate. All of them were drunk. Always drunk - like myself.

I was on a train one night, a sleeper. I don't know where, and there were these men, football fans I think. All in my cabin. I was lying naked on the top bunk, and they got a razor and shaved me, and then they had me one after the other. I didn't care, only in the morning when I remembered. The shame fell like a guillotine blade sliced me in half. Jesus, I burn when I think of it.

'When you think of what, Sarah?'

'Did I say that? '

'You said you burn when you think of it.'

'Did I? I don't know. I have had sex with him. Yes. Is that terrible? With the doctor. Only when I'm drunk, though. Never, ever when I'm sober. At first, now and then, but now he hounds me around the town. Everyone knows. It's awful. I want him out of my life, but how can I do it?

He signs my benefit forms and gives me pills to get off the drink. I need him, but I want to escape. How can I? It's a nightmare. What would you?'

'You feel trapped?'

'Trapped. In a cage. In a cell with no windows.'

'Alone in the cell.'

'Oh yes. My husband tries to help, but I think he's getting tired of it all. So many times now. I leave when I'm drinking. Get a train to Belfast or Dublin and stay there till I collapse and the medics come.'

'An escape?'

'No. Running to something. What I'm leaving doesn't matter. Not part of the equation. "This'll be the last time." That's what I say to myself and I swear to God I believe it at that moment. The last time. It never is. I wish it could be.' 'Do you, Sarah? Really wish that?'

'Course I do. Just now. I want to stop, to be free. Never again the shakes in the morning, the mouth like a badger's bum, the nightmares, the look in their eyes when I come home, the puke when I swallow the first food.'

I know you don't believe me. I didn't miss the little twitch at the corner of the lip, the quiver of one eyebrow. You try to stay very still, listening, giving me your full attention, trying to share my journey, being beside me, showing unconditional empathy. I know all the terms. And there are moments when I think you understand but then you say something that shatters the illusion.

We sit opposite each other, the chairs carefully placed so that we are at a slight angle. You in your clean shirt, open at the collar, ironed slacks and suede boots, your beard neatly trimmed, and your shampooed hair gleaming like a halo in the soft light. I can smell your aftershave and deodorant. Or is it the fresh flowers on the table beside us? I sit in the armchair, my fingers trembling, running the zip of my fleece up and down by just two inches either way. The blue fleece matches my eyes– the colour of cornflowers, Daddy said.

'I miss my Dad.'

'Yes. He meant a lot to you.'

'He was everything to me. He wouldn't like me now.'

'He would say that?'

I would see it in his eyes, the pain, the disappointment. And the love. Yes, he would love me anyway, not like my mother. She shut the door in my face. Told me never to come again. The disgust in her face. You want to have seen it. And my brother. At the funeral, he turned his back on me. They all did. I fell over, and not one of them helped me up, so I crawled to a bench and sat there, watching them from a distance. Like crows round a carcass, their beaks all bent down towards the meat. When they left, I lay down on the bench and slept till it was dark. And cold. God, it was cold in the graveyard. There was this tramp…'

'You okay with the silence?'

'What?'

'Are you happy with the silence?'

I was so far away, remembering the sour smell of his overcoat, the taste of cheap wine, and the rasp of his unshaven chin. Your eyes dart to the watch on your wrist, just a flash which you try to hide. It is time to go. You probably have another client, another wrecked soul, passing the time, searching for the answer, something painless to end the guilt, the scald of self-loathing.

'See you next week, Sarah.'

Next week. Do you know how far away that is for me? You rise from the chair and look down at me. Pity. I'm sure that's pity in your eyes. If you think it's compassion and unconditional love, you deceive yourself. I know you don't want it to be pity but I can tell. I see it every day.

'Take care, Sarah.'

You touch my arm as I stand.

Next week. And tonight? What do I do about tonight?

'Thanks. I feel better.' I say that so that you like me.

'You seem very upset, Sarah.'

'I can't believe it!'

'Sit, down, Sarah. Can you tell me what has happened?'

He touches my arm, and I shiver. I don't want anyone near me. 'Spam came to the door. Horrible. Just horrible.'

'Spam?'

'I told you. He was the one.'

'I'm sorry, Sarah. You've never mentioned Spam.'

'I have. I told you all about him. A brute. A bastard.'

'Would you like to tell me? You seem very, very angry.'

'Angry? I'm fuckin' furious.'

'He came to the door.'

'I couldn't believe he had the brass neck. I was nearly sick on the spot. My whole stomach turned over.'

'He upset you so much.'

'Too right'

It comes back in my head, flashes of it. I try to blank it but it's there. I try to spew it out to find the words and vomit them onto the floor, but they're not there. It's blowing up inside me like a black bladder, bursting to get out, crushing my lungs. I can't breathe. Got to say it.

'Windscreen wipers. The car.'

There. It's out.

'Rain. Just a brute. I want to kill him. Get a knife and stick it in his guts and rip him open till he feels the pain. Rape. That's what it was. That's the word. I've said it now.'

'You were raped?'

'Yes. Spam, Billy's friend.'

'He came to the door, and you went with him?'

'What? No, no. Years ago. This was years ago.'

'You carry it with you. Kept it to yourself all these years?'

'Who could I tell? Too awful to tell anyone. Who could I trust?'

'You've carried all that pain and anger all on your own, no help from anyone? That takes a lot of strength.'

'No. Shame. Fear. Disgust. I didn't feel strong when he came to the door. I told him to fuck off– I don't swear, I hate swearing. I told him to fuck off; I never wanted to see him again. Told him I'd go the police.'

'Sounds like you were strong, telling him to fuck off.'

'I'm scared he'll come back.'

'If he does...?'

'I'll kill him. I'll get the carving knife and stick it in his guts.'

I really want to, have to. I can feel it inside, erupting, scalding. Fury as I've never felt before. I leap up and head for the door.

'Sarah.'

I hear his voice behind me, anxious, urgent. 'I will!' I yell back at him.

Chapter 30

SPAM

He felt the explosion in his feet, shaking the pavement with its force. Then he heard the thud, the breaking glass, the lumps of masonry landing. Then silence. He would remember that silence. It said more than the explosion. Then, the whimpers and the screams. The next street, maybe. He ran around as the cloud of dust rose above the chimneys.

'Christ Almighty!'

He stood, stunned by the scene of devastation.

The entire front of the building had collapsed. The first thing he saw was a body lying face down among the rubble, most of the clothing torn off by the explosion. Only one high heel and long blond hair told him that it was a woman. There was a man sitting in the road, his hands over his ears, his hair grey with dust and blood seeping between his fingers. A pram had wrapped itself neatly around a street lamp. Three men were working on top of the rubble, desperately hurling pieces aside.

'In here! In here!' one was shouting.

Spam ran across and joined them, climbing up the pile.

Rough on his fingers, unused to manual work, but he dug then into the mortar till he found the edges of the shattered lumps of masonry, some small, some too heavy to shift. He hauled wildly, tossing massive pieces back onto the road, tearing the ends of his nails and the skin off his fingers. The man beside him, still in his bus driver's uniform, swearing with every movement.

'Bastards! Fuckin' bastards!'

Spam gripped the end of a steel beam and tried to shift it, but it was stuck firmly in the rubble. At the same time, he heard a moan in the pile beneath it.

'Here! Quick! Somebody here!'

The bus driver flung a lump aside and joined him. They heaved at the beam till it moved slightly to expose a hollow in the rubble. In the gloom, they could see a hand shivering. The person was still alive. They worked frantically, tossing aside bits of masonry.

'Need to go carefully,' Spam panted, sweat dripping off his nose, 'Beam's holding up yon huge lump of stuff. Might fall on him.'

'Aye.'

They worked till they could see the face. A man about the same age as Spam with a long scar down one of his cheeks.

'My legs,' he groaned, 'My legs.'

'Hang on. We'll get you out.'

The howl of the ambulances and the police cars echoed in the street. An army truck skidded to a halt, and a squad of soldiers leapt out of the back. The sergeant shouted orders, and half of them laid down their weapons and ran to help, struggling to keep their balance on the rubble. For a moment, Spam was tempted to leave to avoid contact with the army, but his concern for himself was quickly overwhelmed by his worry for the victim below.

'Have you a torch, mate?' he asked one of the squad. 'I'll fetch one.'

When he came back, they shone the light into the hollow where the victim lay trapped, and they could see that his legs were crushed under the beam. He was bleeding from a gash on his skull.

Spam crawled under the beam and, with his back against it, tried to raise it. It didn't move. He summoned all his strength and tried again, the sharp steel edge cutting into his skin. This time, there was a slight shift.

'Give us a hand here,' he called to the squaddie with the torch.

The soldier squeezed into the space, and they pushed together. The beam lifted slightly. 'Here you,' he called to one of the other soldiers, 'Over here.'

Just a boy, Spam noted, scared too.

'When we lift, you grab yer man's hands and pull him out.'

The boy crawled in, knocking off his beret. The dragon of the Queen's regiment is on the badge.

'Right. Again, heave!'

The beam lifted, and the man screamed as he was pulled out. As he passed, Spam could see the lacerated flesh and the torn, blood-soaked trousers. He crawled out and looked at his own hands. The fingers were bleeding. He would need gloves to carry on. He hurried down the pile to ask the sergeant if there were any on the lorry.

As he reached the ambulance, he passed the victim, who was lying on a stretcher. He glanced down at him as a medic prepared a syringe.

'Thanks,' the man croaked.

Spam stopped and looked down. There was something familiar about the face but he couldn't place him.

'You'll be fine,' he said, though he reckoned the man might lose his leg.

'Thought I was goin' to die. You saved my life.'

'Don't think so.'

'I've seen you before. In the yards, maybe?'

'No. I was just passing. I live in London.'

'Oh. Never mind. Thanks again.'

They stretchered him away towards the ambulance.

Just beyond the stretcher, there was a small body under a blood-soaked sheet. A foot, no bigger than a couple of inches long, protruded from the sheet. An infant.

'Bastards!' he hissed, 'I'll get you for this. Every fuckin' one of you.'

He detested the sour smell of Guinness, which enveloped him as he opened the door of the Brown Bear on the corner of Mountjoy Street. He had been in there before but left soon after as a couple of men watched him too closely, their silent antagonism made perfectly obvious. He didn't seek trouble. However, this pub seemed the most likely place to pick up a revolver. It was shortly after the shipyard buses came up from Queen's Island, so he could barely see the bar as men shouldered each other to reach it. The air was thick with cigarette smoke, and the bar was swimming with spilled Guinness. There was little chance of reaching it without attracting attention - him in his sports jacket and flannels and the others in their working gear. He looked around for a likely contact and spotted a character on his own at the end of the bar, a small man with a child-like face. People seemed to be ignoring him, and there was something sinister in the way he stared fixedly at the gantry. Spam squeezed his way through the crowd to stand beside him.

'Another?' he nodded at the pint.

'Who the fuck are you?'

The man dropped his cigarette on the floor and stood on it. 'Nobody important.'

'Fuck off then.'

'I'm in the arms business.'

'So what? Doesn't give you the right to barge in here. Go and bother someone else.'

'Like who? Who'd be interested in the arms trade?'

'Nobody in here anyway.'

'I want to buy.'

'What? A tank? A Humbie? An atomic bomb?'

'A Webley.'

'Oh, aye. And what makes you think I'd know about that? You've some fuckin' cheek.'

'Just thought you might know.'

'Well, I don't.'

'It's for killing Taigs.'

'That'd be murder.'

'They're killing our people.'

He lit another cigarette and flicked the match at the gantry.

'Okay. Be here. After two tomorrow. Now fuck off and leave me in peace.'

I was there the next day just after dinner, and he was in the same place at the bar. He walked over to meet me.

'Come on. Upstairs. You go in front.'

There were three masked men at a table dressed in anoraks and soft hats. I heard the door shut behind me and felt the cold muzzle of a revolver in my neck.

'It's alright, Lenny. Put it down,' the mask in the middle spoke, 'You were in the British Army, brother?'

'Yes. You know that.'

'What's to say you're not still with them?'

'I deserted.'

'So we could hand you over, eh?'

'You could.'

'We'll keep that in mind. On the other hand, we could save them the trouble and execute you.'

'You could.'

'Cool customer, eh? So you want to buy a firearm?'

'A Webley.'

'Particular, are we?'

'To kill Taigs.'

'Easy to say.'

'Easy to do.'

'Okay, brother., but here's the deal. We know who you are, where you live, where your showroom is. If you go near the Brits or the police, we'll find you, and your career as an arms dealer will come to a sticky end. Lenny here is a barber by trade.'

'Fair enough.'

'Ten pounds for a Webley and bullets.'

'Jesus. Made of gold, is it?'

'We need funds.'

He places the revolver on the table with a box of ammunition.

'I'll take it.'

Spam sits by the electric fire and cleans the revolver, thinking over the encounter with Sarah.

Bloody hell. She was angry. He didn't expect that. Okay, he'd been a bit rough with her and dumped her at her house without saying goodbye, but it couldn't have been that bad. She had put up a bit of a fight, adding to the excitement, but it wasn't exactly unarmed combat.

Still, maybe he should leave her alone. She had threatened to go to the police. On the other hand, maybe it was just a bad time– one of those times women suffer from.

He opened the box of bullets, broke open the gun and fed six shining shells into the chamber. Ready to go.

Chapter 31

BILLY

A summer's dawn high in the hills with a mantle of webs glistening in the heather at my feet. Almost silence apart from the rattle of scree dislodged by the herd of hinds hurrying away on the slope below and the bleating of a lamb in the corrie. Horsehide boots gleaming black with dew. From the summit at over three thousand feet, the entire county stretches out to the horizon on all sides. 'The hill of the two winds' in Gaelic, formidable in the snows of winter with its peak capped white till the spring. A long way from the island.

The dogs waited patiently as I leaned on my crook and admired the scene. It was daylight when I left the house at four o'clock two and half hours ago, although the sun had not risen. As I climbed the steep side of the glen the black dog had hunted the sheep off the ridge down the slope towards the burn below. Tam, the other shepherd, following the burn side, had driven sheep up the hill so that we could gather the whole flock more easily as we returned from the march. I look down and can just see his dogs far below, working without commands, knowing the routine.

I had summoned the strength to leave the island in spite of Mark's attempt to undermine my determination.

'Are you sure about this? You know nothing about sheep. I hope you're not falling into a trap. Munro is a charlatan, a man infatuated with his own image, afflicted with narcissism. He will lure you into a sphere of influence and discard you as callously as he might brush off a fly.

Think carefully before you commit to this plan.'

It was the first time I had heard Mark speak ill of someone and it helped me to break free of him as a father figure. I detected a hint of jealousy. Munro was bigger, stronger and not at all interested in the impression he created. On one occasion, in his usual forgetful manner, he had left a rucksack full of heavy marble stones near the jetty, having carried this for some miles from the abandoned quarry. When Mark decided to take it to the abbey, he struggled to lift it off the ground and had to leave it, his ego visibly wounded.

Munro did not seem to care about his appearance, dressing in the same bizarre outfit at home– the frayed kilt, the feathered bonnet, the great leather belt around the house. And this was not incongruous in the circumstances as he lived in one room of a decaying mansion where he slept on the floor under a bear skin, sharing the space with several falcons. Beneath their perches, the floor was littered with bird lime and the peace of the evenings punctured with flutterings and sudden screeches. It was at first quite disturbing to sit under the baleful glare of the birds; one's every movement scrutinised by the hostile eyes, one's sight drawn to the rapacious beaks and razor-sharp talons.

His brother, who had been persuaded to employ me, was completely different– a working farmer whose household was run like any other Highland hill farming establishment. His appearance contrasted sharply with Munro's– a deer-stalker cap, blue overalls, a green PVC jacket and hill boots. When I arrived, he had made his doubts about his brother's judgement perfectly apparent, examining me as if he might study an unpleasant skin parasite. Still, his reservations did not last once he saw that I was keen to work and learn. I have been with him now for ten years.

I'm about to set off down the hill when I noticed a ewe and lamb lurking in a hollow just across the slope. Clearly, I had missed them from the ridge, so I sent the white dog out to turn them down. My best dog, she knows what to do, so I turn away and walk down through the heather. The sun is higher now and warm on my back. I know there's not much time to lose as we want to gather the sheep in before the heat of mid-day. The ewes, as yet unsheared, have heavy fleeces and will suffer if we fail to reach the farm in time.

I did not sleep well last night. A letter had arrived from Sarah. How she discovered where I live is a mystery unless my mother, keen to draw me back into her web of control, had given her the address. I think Sarah is hoping to revive our relationship. She does not say so directly, but her intentions are fairly clear. I had left all that behind– Spam, Dublin, my family and her– and it was unsettling to be reminded of it. Now I don't know what to do. I'm sorry for Sarah and would like to help, but I don't want to be sucked back into the morass from which I had escaped. I'll have to think about it.

I reach the middle of the slope, where the flock is beginning to draw together, and Tam is climbing towards us. He is still half a mile below me. The dogs turn the sheep towards the bottom of the glen, now strung out in long lines, lambs following their mothers. As we near the pine wood, I see some sheep which were missed high out near the summit. I'm tempted to ignore them and hope that I can retrieve them some other time. Yet that would mean another trip. I send the white dog out. It is a long way, and I stop to watch her as she becomes a white speck on the mountainside. There is a deep ravine with a precipice of more than a hundred feet just in front of the ewes. As the dog reaches them, they sprint towards the cliff. For a moment, I think they're going to launch themselves like lemmings over the edge, but, at the last minute, they swerve down the slope. The dog, who is racing behind them, fails to stop, and I watch helplessly as she flies over the cliff.

Stunned, I stand with my mouth open. Tam, who was watching, hurries over.

'Jesus, Billy. You'd better go up and see. I'll watch things here.'

I set off, convinced that I'd find her at the bottom of the cliff, her white coat spattered with blood. Losing a dog is worse than losing a relative. This was a working collie that I had trained as a pup, teaching her to sit beside me in the kitchen at night, watching her grow from a small white ball of fluff into a sleek, swift, intelligent partner on the hill. She was far more loyal to me than any of my own kind. She would swim spate rivers to rescue lambs; she would labour through snow drifts to find buried ewes, limp through sharp scree though her paws were raw, and leap barbed wire fences to head off wandering calves. She shared the long winter evenings with me, curled in the chair on the other side of the range. More than a companion, an indispensable part of my life.

I hurry up the hill, gasping for breath, fearing the worst. The towering cliff of the ravine, dark and sinister, slices into the green face of the hill like a wound. Surely, nothing could survive such a fall. I listen for whining, but there is only silence in the gully. I imagine her falling, turning slowly as she drops and landing with a thud which would break her back.

I hope that she died quickly, that she didn't survive for a few minutes of agony on the sharp rocks at the bottom of her fall.

I reach the ravine, and she walks out, shaking herself. There is blood on her nose but nowhere else. I cannot believe it. She wags her tail as she approaches. How is it possible? The immensity of my relief and affection erupts in a sob that shakes my whole body. I call her against me and, stroking her head, feel every muscle for injury. I sit for a while and hold her, suddenly aware that there are tears on my cheeks. I wipe them away in case Tam notices.

'That's a bloody miracle,' he says when I join him, 'A miracle, boy. Nothing less.'

'Can't believe it.'

'Look at her. Back at work as if nothing had happened.'

'Some dog.'

'Sailed through the air like Superman. Superdog, eh?'

We gather the sheep down the glen, the dogs gradually bunching them together. Once we get them into the fank we'll shed the lambs off from the ewes. There will be dust and shreds of wool swirling in the hot wind, the racket of ewes and lambs bleating for each other and the smell of sheep dung and dip. The ram lambs will be castrated with rubber rings around the cods, their ears will be cut with the mark of our farm, and their tails docked– a bloody business. The ewe lambs, too, will be marked and docked.

After that, the shearing. I'm not looking forward to that. Bent double with a beast between my knees and sweat dripping off my nose. The barren ewes and last year's ewe lambs have to be sheared this month, their fleeces peeling off like second skins. Outside the fank, there are two tall poles with a cross member from which we hang the wool bags. Higher than a man, the suspended bags have to be filled. Munro rolls the fleeces and tosses them into the bag where one of Tam's children, out of sight inside, tramps them down so that the bag is tight. As the bag fills, he emerges at the top, black with grease and feathered with wool.

Shearing is sore on the back. When I started, we clipped with hand shears, which was much easier as I could kneel now and then and straighten up. The machines, though much faster, bind the shearer's spine in one position. A day's shearing is crippling work. Yet it is satisfying, too, wielding the combs and cutters skilfully so that the trails left on the skin are the same on every sheep. That's the challenge, and having not been bred to farming, I have to be as good or better than others. I still have to prove myself. Foolish, I know, but I still respond like an idiot.

As I start on one of the ewes, opening down the brisket, I remember Sarah's letter and wonder what to do. I know that I'm going to have to sit down at night and think about it.

My stone cottage cowers in the middle of another glen, isolated and frowned on by the steep mountains on both sides. It has four rooms– a kitchen, a bedroom, a bathroom and a scullery where the milk is cooled on a stone shelf. The kitchen has a concrete floor covered with brown lino, so thin that it frayed away in places, and a fire which tries to heat the water. When I came here first, it had no electricity, and I had to cope with Tilley lamps and a torch. Now I have lights and an electric cooker. Having the lights allows me to read more in the winter– one of the few luxuries is a collection of books. Otherwise, the room is bare. Two shabby armchairs, four kitchen chairs, and a pine table so worn with scrubbing that the grain stands proud of the surface. It is all I need.

In the summer, I rarely light the fire, but tonight, I split some kindling and put a match to it, planning to bathe the dog's nose and examine her thoroughly for other wounds. I was going to dig some early potatoes from the garden, but my back's stiff from the shearing, so I've made do with some sliced bread and dripping. I've cooked some mince with onions and some tinned peas. I fetch some flaked maize for the dogs and mix it with Wilson's dog meal and hot water. I'll feed Nell in here and take her out to the kennels later.

I have lived alone for more than ten years– just me and the dogs. I take the old Land Rover and drive down to the village on a Saturday for stores, Carnation milk and The Scottish Farmer. I'm quite content, though I find myself thinking out loud at times. In the summer, I'm usually late home unless it is one of those depressing days which is wet from morning till night and I am too tired to read. I relish the winter evenings by the fire, listening to the wireless and carving tupp's horns to make cromachs.

I feed Nell and watch to see that she can eat easily. She seems to be all right, although she holds her head on one side. I sit at the table and start my own tea. Sarah's letter is lying beside my plate. I look at it as if it can speak. I can see her face as clearly as a photograph with the wind flicking that curved lock of hair over her brow. I remember the night we met at the St. Valentine's Dance. Our breaths clouded in the freezing air. I can feel her body against mine and the smooth skin of her thigh. Spam's coarse comments slice into the memory. She went out with him. How could she do that, knowing his attitude to women, his disdain for them as people? I never understood that. I did love her, though. Even now, I feel it, a yearning to hold her again, to walk beside her on the shore and feel her fingers in mine, to watch her stepping off the train. Yet, behind that, lurks the talons of the black

raptor which tore me apart, the nameless terror whose return I fear…
I know it is foolish to worry about that after all these years of freedom
from it. I must wipe it away. I lift her letter and read it.

Chapter 32

Lenny shuffled into the showroom past the workmen fitting the new windows. Spam was polishing a second-hand Ford and saw him nod at one of the men.

'What about you, Spam?'

'Lenny.'

Spam continued to polish the bonnet.

'I'll pick you up at ten.'

'What?'

The duster stopped dead, and Spam looked at him. 'What are you talking about, Lenny?'

'You said you wanted to kill Taigs. Ten o'clock tonight. Be here.' Lenny sauntered out without another word.

Spam watched him with distaste. Cocky wee bastard. He wondered if he should be trusted. Still, he'd been upstairs in the Brown Bear and under the command of the hooded men. Perhaps he was safe enough.

He didn't think much of the UVF, though. Bunch of amateurs, most of them seemed to take orders from your man in the Crumlin-Spence, their top man, in gaol, and the organisation clearly suffering from the loss. He'd met a few ex-army guys in the Force but too many idiots.

He'd decided to go ahead on his own. He knew about explosives, but not enough. One of the ex-REME men was supposed to be an expert and planned to contact him. He wanted to know how to make bombs.

He walked home that night and, after tea, changed his clothes, slipping into jeans, a navy polo-neck and a black leather jacket. He looked out his balaclava and gloves and the Webley.

Cracking it open, he loaded the chamber, sliding in six shining bullets. He remembered Kelly, the Mancunian, in the army and his clumsiness with weapons, not helped by the broken fingers which Spam had inflicted on his hand, jamming it in a lorry's tailgate on a night exercise. Poor Kelly, not quite the full shilling. Spam stuck the pistol in his belt and walked out.

Lenny was punctual, an achievement which Spam did not expect. The car pulled into the kerb, and Lenny leant over and opened the door.

'Get in.'

Spam leaned on the roof and finished his fag. He was not going to do what he was told too quickly. He threw away the butt and climbed in.

'Nice car,' he said.

'Not mine. Nicked from the Falls.'

'Clever.'

'Not just a pretty face.'

No. Fucken ugly, Spam thought.

The wet road glistened under the street lights as they headed round to Springfield Road. The streets were empty, and a low mist hung just above the rooves. As they reached the top of the road, Lenny slowed the car.

'There he is,' Lenny said, nodding towards a figure walking on the pavement.

'Who?'

'Target'

'Provo?'

'That's him.'

Spam took out his revolver, thumbed back the safety catch and cocked it. The man had his back to them and seemed to be unaware of the car. Spam wound down the window as Lenny edged in towards the pavement.

The shot echoed in the still air, and the man dropped to the ground. Lenny accelerated and raced away from the scene. He thumped the steering wheel with both hands, clearly excited.

'First class, boy. You're good,' he shouted.

'Who was he?'

'Don't know.'

'You don't know?'

'No. A Taig.'

'How do you know?'

'By the way, he walks.'

'Fuck's sake! I thought he was a Provo.'

'One of them anyway.'

'You don't know that, do you?'

'You've passed the test, boy. That's all that matters.'

Spam clicked the safety catch back and tucked the gun into his belt. He had never killed anyone before and tried to work out how he felt. It was a good shot, dead in the back of the skull, well executed, professional, but to see a living man so suddenly dead was strange. To fire into the bull of a target was one thing– and he had won his marksman's badge in the army– but to see a guy drop like that was another altogether. He had felled men with his fists, with chains, with broken bottles, but never with a bullet. Not very satisfying, really. And he wasn't even the enemy, for God's sake. Not one of the bombers. He wanted to get the Provos. He glanced at Lenny and, seeing the smirk, despised him immediately.

He was dropped at the end of Tennent Street and started to walk home, but just as he reached Riga Street, an Army Land Rover pulled up ahead of him, and a patrol climbed out of the back. He touched the gun in his belt, knowing that if he was searched, he would be in trouble. He swerved into Riga Street and hurried past the school, hoping to reach the old graveyard before the soldiers appeared in the street. He remembered that there was a tunnel there where the Farset stream came out of an archway. If he had to, he could hide the Webley somewhere there. He stood behind a cypress tree in the graveyard and waited., hoping the soldiers would pass the gate. Surely, somebody would have found the body, and there would soon be police all over the place. He could hear the squaddies in the street, their Scottish accents and their Land Rover as they approached the gate. He moved back, heading for the tunnel. He was not keen to wade into the stream and wet his shoes, but if the army entered the graveyard, he would be forced to climb into the water.

'Fuck!' he whispered as four of them came through the gate. He slid into the shallow water and waded towards the tunnel.

Just as he stooped to hide in its shadows, a figure emerged from its throat, breathless and flustered.

Spam pulled the Webley from his belt.

'Stop right there. Move or shout, and it'll be your last.' The figure froze.

'Hands on your head.'

'Don't shoot. Please, don't shoot. I didn't do it. I swear.'

'What the fuck are you doing here?'

'I didn't. Honest to God.'

'What are you talking about? What have you done?'

'You're not one of them, then?'

'Who?'

'The boys. The Ra. They say I split on them. To the Brits.'

He was a Taig then, and Spam had sworn to kill Taigs, but he couldn't squeeze the trigger without the army hearing the shot. His wet feet were freezing in the cold water.

'Are they in the tunnel? Do they know where you are?'

'No. I don't think so.'

'Come over this side where I can see you. Keep your hands on your head.'

The guy's feet splashed through the water. Spam could just see his face in the light of the distant streetlights, eyes wide with terror.

'You're not one of them, then?'

'Never mind what I am.'

Spam climbed up on the bank, keeping the gun pointed at the guy's head. The army was leaving. In a minute, he could pull the trigger. He watched as the soldiers turned up the Shankill Road. Safe now. He turned to see his target. The man was shivering, and his eyes were focused on his. Spam knew he could do it. Bam. Right between the eyes, the target would drop like a stone into the water. Yet he felt sorry for him, a man on the run, fearing for his life, a fugitive, a poor creature, staring at him from a few feet away.

'I know you. You chained my mate at a dance years ago,' the guy said. Spam's finger tightened on the trigger.

'He's dead now anyway. A bomb. Died after. In hospital.'

This guy could go to the peelers. Have him arrested. He should plug him, finish him off, shut him up for good. Yet the police wouldn't bother with a minor crime from the 50's. Would they? Far too busy trying to keep on top of the war on their streets. The guy was no threat.

He lowered the barrel, shot him in the foot so that he wouldn't follow and walked away.

He had spared him. As he left the graveyard, he reckoned that his Gran would have approved. Yes, she would have admired him for that good deed. Yet he should have put a slug in him. Maybe he was getting soft, too soft to kill the guy just because he looked him in the eye.

One thing about explosives– you didn't have to see the 'collateral damage'. That would be better. He decided to find someone to teach him how to make bombs and timers– someone really good, an expert, who really knew his stuff.

Chapter 33

Sarah woke suddenly as the shutters of a newspaper booth crashed open, the sound echoing around the empty railway station. She was lying on a wooden bench; her neck stretched and painful as she tried to raise her head. A workman in blue overalls, staggering under the weight of a bundle of newspapers, kicked open the booth door and flung down the burden with a thud. She lay still, trying to remember, but her memory spun around a kaleidoscope of scattered images that had no bearing on the immediate past. She had no idea how she came to be in the station, and that should have been terrifying, but her mind was numb, still anaesthetised. She moved her arm to discover that she was covered by an overcoat. It was not hers. She sat up to examine it. A man's navy overcoat, frayed at the cuffs and greased at the collar and smelling of decay. She struggled to remember. Nothing. She dipped her finger in the pockets, hoping to find a clue, and pulled out a spent match, the cellophane of a cigarette packet and an empty half bottle of vodka without a top. Slipping the bottle back, she tossed the coat aside and felt around the bench for her handbag, suspecting that it would not be there. It wasn't.

She looked around the station. No idea which one. There was no sign. Above her, pigeons fluttered on the iron beams supporting the glass roof. Pale morning light just managed to penetrate the grime on the panes. The station clock up there showed twenty past five. The posters on the wooden sides of the booth didn't help, although the headline read 'Troops to Coalisland Riot,' so at least she was in Ireland. Behind the booth, the white tiled walls of the Gent's toilet reflected the internal light. A poster on the wall advertised 'Scotland

For Your Holidays' and showed a diesel train passing over the Forth Bridge. Scotland, where Billy was.

She remembered his rolling walk and his James Dean frown. She thought then that she was better than him just because she went to church, had a steady job, and didn't fraternise with delinquents like Spam. My God, look at her now. What would Billy think now?

She moved her head from side to side, trying to ease the ache in her neck, and passed her fingers through her hair. What a mess and no comb! She looked down at her feet. At least she had her shoes, even if they were badly scuffed. There was a hole in the knee of her tights and she bent to see if her knee was scraped. It was dirty but not hurt. She swung round to examine the overcoat again. A man's garment for God's sake. Who gave her that? She didn't remember a man. Thinking of men, she stood and felt her hips. Her pants were still there, but that didn't mean

She gripped her fists to banish the thought and hurried to the ladies' toilets.

Locking the cubicle door, she slid down her pants to check for semen. They were clear. That was a relief. She sat on the toilet and tried again to remember. There was a bar. Not a lounge bar as it was crowded with workmen. She was the only female. Rows of Guinness on the counter, some attached to the rough hands of the men, and a smog of cigarette smoke swirling around their caps. Coarse laughter, scraping of boots on tiles, coughing and spitting phlegm from coked lungs. She was alone on a bench. Alone. She was sure of that. A few men had glanced at her and turned back to their mates. Did she look dreadful? Was she so drunk that they were repelled by her appearance?

She must have been there for some time as she remembered the bar had been almost empty when she arrived and she had ordered vodka at the counter. She must have had money then. But when was that? Yesterday, two days ago, last week? How did she get from the pub to the station? Who gave her the coat? The more she tried to recall the details, the more obscure the scene became. She tried to see herself leaving the pub, but all she could see was the empty glass of vodka on the table. The film ended there, snipped off, leaving a blank screen.

She must have had money to board the train. But had she been on a train at all? Maybe she walked to the station. She had been on a train before years ago. Jesus. Will that ever leave her? She cringed with shame just thinking about it. She remembered their laughter and the way they used her like animals and bit her lip hard till she could taste the blood, anything to block it out. Jesus, if her father could have seen her or Billy. Poor Billy and his clumsy but gentle attempts. Not like Connor. Slow and easy, stroking her skin. A beautiful boy. Long ago.

Billy had loved her. She was sure of that. She should never have cut him off. She wondered who lay with him now. He was in Scotland, they said. Maybe he had no one. Maybe they could be together again. *Don't be so stupid, Sarah. He would take one look at you and run. Wisely.* Skin and bone now, face twisted with drink, clothes filthy. God, she needed a drink, something warm and soft to soothe away the pain, something to wipe out the pictures in her head, to calm the tumult. But she had no money. It was easy, though, to seduce some guy into buying her one. So many times, so many places. Disgusting. She felt sick just thinking about it. She had to escape from the quagmire, the morass sucking her down into its slimy depths. She had to haul herself out of it.

Yet so often, she had made that pledge. Never again. Stop now. Not one more drink and, half an hour later, found herself swallowing another. This was different, though. She couldn't remember. Memory had gone, wiped away. She would have to make a real effort this time. But she needed a target, something to live for, something to strive for, and she needed help. Counsellors didn't work. She had tried that and had jigged them like puppets, convincing them that she really wanted to stop when she had no genuine intention of giving up– even deceiving herself at times.

Billy. She could write to Billy. Maybe he was free. Maybe he had no one. But Billy wouldn't want her as she was. She had to change, prove that she could win, beat the craving, retrieve her self-respect, and show him that she could take control again. That was it. Prove it to Billy. She would do it for him. She felt tears slipping down her cheeks and warmth inside as if the sun had risen in the cubicle.

She stood, hauled up her pants and tights and walked into the station. She heard someone in the booth and knocked on the door. A woman opened it and studied her suspiciously.

'What station is this?' Sarah asked. 'What?'

'What station is this?'

'Did you sleep here all night? On the bench?'

'Yes.'

'God love you; you were in some state. I saw you just before I closed. The man who helped you in– the down-and-out– old Geordie gave you his coat. Means no harm, Geordie; he's not quite right. Laid his coat over you and left.'

'That was kind of him. Is he still here?'

'Not him. He'll be away, back on the road somewhere.'

'Where is this? The name of the station.'

'Waterside. In Derry.'

'Jesus. How did I get here?'

'God knows, love. In the state you were in, I'm not surprised you've forgotten. You look as though you could do with a hair of the dog.'

'That's the last thing I need. Never again. Never.'

'They all say that.'

'I mean it this time.'

'More power to your arm, love. I'll need to get on.'

'Course. Sorry to keep you.'

Sarah walked towards the main door, searching for the public phones. Derry. How in God's name could she have landed in Derry? The bar that she could remember was in Belfast. She had no memory of a train, a bus, or a car. She found a phone box and swung open the door. One of the panes was smashed, and the floor was wet, soaking the crushed fag ends and a shred of tissue paper. She lifted the receiver and dialled O. When the operator answered, she asked for a reverse charge call to Bangor. She heard Robert answer.

'I don't know anyone in Derry.'

'Excuse me, can you tell him it's his wife, and it's urgent,' she told the operator. She heard him say,

'It's always urgent. Put her through. I'll accept the call.'

'Hello, Robert. I'm sorry. I've no change.'

'You mean you've no money.'

'I've left my purse on the train.'

'You've lost it. Why don't you just tell the truth? You've been drinking again, and you've lost your handbag.'

'Yes, that's true.'

She had to practice being honest. That was part of giving up.

'I can't believe you have the cheek to phone.'

'I need money to get home. I'm sober, Robert, and I'm going to stay that way.'

'How many times have you said that?'

'I mean it this time. I really do. I've had a real fright. I'm scared. I can't remember how I got here. It's all a blank. That's frightening. I'm going to stop. Please wire me some money. I'll go back to the flat. I won't come near the hotel. Please.'

'Okay, Sarah. I'll send twenty. Last time, though. Definitely the last time.'

'Yes, last time. I promise.'

'Main post office, Londonderry.'

She replaced the receiver. It rattled in its horns under her shaking hand. She stepped out and headed into the city to find the post office.

He was kind, Robert, and they had reached an understanding that she left the hotel when she embarked on what he called a bender. He had even bought her a small flat in town. She liked the flat, staying there at times when she wasn't drinking. In the hotel, they lived their own separate lives.

Chapter 34

Dearest Billy,

I know it will be strange to hear from me after all these years and you may fling this letter in the bin but please, please read it first. I can't tell you how terribly sad I felt when we drifted apart. I found out later that my Mum told you that I didn't want to see you anymore and that was nonsense. She was always doing things like that – trying to run my life and choosing my boy friends. Anyway she's dead now and I make my own decisions – most of them mistakes.

I expect you know that I married Robert whose parents owned the Sefton Hotel. It wasn't a great success and I'm afraid to say that I started to drink heavily. I don't blame Robert for that. He was a kind man but always a stranger to me. We couldn't have any children. Maybe things would have been better if we had. Anyway we parted company as my drinking took over my life. It was a terrible time.. I lived in all kinds of dreadful places and with people you would not want to meet. I try to forget those years but memories still haunt me. The good news is that I have not had a drink for five years and three months now and I have a small shop of my own in Bangor. I have my life back.

I don't know if you ever come back to Bangor but, if you do, I would love to see you again. Of all the people I know, you are the only person I can talk to, honestly, the only one I can trust. I desperately need to talk to sort out the mess in my head. I never stopped loving you,

Billy. I know you won't believe that but it's true. It broke my heart when we parted. Please write back. At least do that and, better still, call on me if you are over here.

All my love,

Sarah.

I will reply. Trouble is I don't know what to say. The chances of leaving the farm in the near future are slim and, if I did find an opportunity, would I want to spend the time travelling to Ireland? I read of appalling atrocities and see pictures in the paper of women with flesh lacerated by flying glass, broken bodies under blankets, burning men staggering from barricades, flaming buildings collapsing into the streets. Who would go there willingly? Yet I would like to see her, although I know that the picture I carry in my mind will bear no resemblance to the person I find. I can't imagine her helpless with drink or involved with people I 'would not want to meet'.

Perhaps the damage inflicted by those years of drinking has made her a different person, one with whom I would have nothing in common. On the other hand, the experience could have made her stronger. She needed that, something to give her the strength to be herself, to be assertive. She was always kind and thoughtful but hopelessly timid. That's how I remember her. I don't know what to do. Maybe I'll wait a few days before writing.

I sit by the fire, sharpening my lambsfoot knife. The blade slides smoothly across the carborundum stone, shaving a grey skin of oil from the surface. For the task ahead the knife has to be razor sharp.

I leans back for a moment to rest my fingers. Snow is blowing past the window, thick white flakes in the dark. The sheep at the head of the glen will be drawing together as the snow covers the ground. They will move in slowly towards the oak woods, the wet snow forming blocks of ice on their fleece-ends; some of them, unable to bear the weight, will perish in the drifts. I've done all that I can.

The light is fading. I shift my feet so that the stone lies level on my knee and once again rub the knife along the surface, following the hollow worn by the blades of my shears. I test the edge of the blade with my thumb, spit on my arm and run the blade over the skin. It shaves off the hair cleanly.

I replace the stone in its oak box, stained crimson with oil, and, snapping the knife shut, cross to the sink. I wash my hands thoroughly, removing all traces of oil, and dry them on a length of sacking behind the door. I lift a bucket from the space beneath the sink to catch the blood and leave the room.

The white dog lying under the table, suddenly alert, watches me go. As the sound of my nailed boots fades, she rises slowly and climbs into the warm chair. An ember slips in the fire and, for a moment, the room moves with shadows. The dog curls up in the chair and closes her eyes. A hen's feather blows across the bare concrete floor.

In the barn outside I light the oil lamp and hangs it on a wire hook near the door. Lifting a hemp rope, I throw it over one of the rafters and slide it from side to side to remove the dust from the beam. Removing my jacket, I roll up my shirt sleeves. Fine snow blows in over the half door and the wind blows chaff and hay seed across the cobbles. Once again I test the edge of my knife.

A small blade - no more than the length of my middle finger. Small but sweet. A tiny hole in the right place and life will just flow away. No noise, no pain, no torn flesh.

I tie a short hazel stick to one end of the rope and, lifting a shearing stool from its place behind the hay bales, place it beneath the hanging rope.

The rope reminds me of the jib sheet in sailing dinghy. Sarah holding the tiller, the breeze tossing her hair and fluttering the mainsail as we go about. She smiles as the boat swerves and the sail fills again. A long time ago. I should have written to her, replied to her letter, but something always intervened – the cow calving, the hay to turn, the lambs to sell. Just excuses. The truth is I was wary of being drawn back into the life that I had left behind, afraid of the demands she might make. Yet I feel guilty. I could have told her how I felt, explained my reservations.

That would have been honest.

I rise from the stool, shaking off the snow that gathered on my trousers and the memories that troubled me. Crossing to one of the pens, I pull out a young wedder, tie three of its legs together with a length of twine and lift it on to the stool so that it lies on its back with its head over the edge.

With the point of my knife I make a small incision in its neck. Blood streams into the bucket, steaming in the cold air. The animal barely moves, seemingly unaware of its fate. I sit beside it, holding its head so that the blood flows cleanly into the bucket.

I remember when it was born. High in the corrie on a morning hung with larks and vibrant with the drumming of snipes' wings, it had been stretched out at the mouth of an old badger hole. I had watched it grow and had searched the flocks for it at every gathering. The memories are broken by a movement beneath my arm. The beast is breathing quickly and I can feel the tension in its muscles. I speak to it. I know that it will not hear. I speak inside my head, sending the words of comfort into the darkness like young dogs into the mist, like petrels over the sea.

The wedder kicks twice, sighs, stiffens and then lies still. I touch the surface of its eye with my finger. It doesn't blink. It is dead.

I cut the twine which binds its legs and, starting at its knees, begin to skin the carcass, sliding my fist between the warm flesh and the skin. Within minutes it lies pale and naked on the smooth surface of its own hide. I remove the bag of the stomach and entrails and, pulling down the rope, fit the short hazel stick through the tendons of the back legs. I haul on the rope and raise the carcass off its skin into the air.

The task almost complete, I sever the head from the neck, cutting through between the spine bone and the skull. Then, as one unit, I pluck out the heart, lungs and wind-pipe. A perfect operation. No blood spilled and the meat not marked. I spin the carcass round, admiring my handiwork. The unblemished skin shines in the lamplight. It reminds me of the dream.

Last night it invaded my sleep, as vivid and life-like as a film. Sarah naked beneath me in the bed, thighs as smooth as silk wrapped round mine, her breath scented with passion, her lips searching mine, her hips raised from the sheets. Her body opened to me like a sea-anemone, enclosing me in velvet tendrils, bleeding me of my substance. Floating deep in a warm, sunlit sea, surrendering to its swell, swooning in ecstasy. I woke suddenly soaked in semen and sweat, trembling and breathless. I had not been assaulted by such sensations since leaving Ireland. I was horrified and shaken. I shiver just now to think of it.

I lift the lamp and the bucket of congealing blood and head back to the house. I will write to Sarah. Better still, I will go and see her.

Chapter 35

I peer in the window of her shop past hanks of wool, tubs of knitting needles, spools of thread and Aran jerseys suspended on coat hangers. Seeing her behind the counter, I'm struck by how little she has changed. Her hair, though more lifeless and grey, still has the same shape. Her face is lined, stretched over the skull like wet linen, but her eyes are still the colour of blue sky. I move aside in case she sees me and try to work out what I'm trembling.

I don't think I'm afraid or apprehensive. A little nervous perhaps but then who would not be in the circumstances? I had not seen her for twenty years. I might be overwhelmed by affection when I touch her hand or troubled by anger as I imagine her with Spam. My eyes might fill with tears of regret as I think of the wasted years or sharpen with shock as I see the devastation wrought by drink. Years ago I would have strode into the shop and flung my arms round her but I'm not that brash youth that she said she loved.

I'm tempted to walk away, to turn my back on an encounter with my past and all the pain inflicted. I don't want to be sucked back into the swamp. Yet that proves how shallow is the healing, how thin the scar tissue, and I thought the wound had vanished, firmly covered with a film of robust skin. I should not think of myself, though. I had come to see if I could help her after all. That was the purpose of the visit. Or was I deceiving myself? Did I really come to seduce her, to gratify my own desires, to exploit a vulnerable woman? That dream had sparked flames in loin which had been dormant for years. Of course that is there. It would be foolish to deny it but it isn't the most forceful reason. It really isn't.

I turn and open the door. A bell rings above my head and she looks at me, initially with a polite smile as for a new customer and then a gasp of recognition. Her hands leave the parcel she was tying and fly to her cheeks. The woman whom she was serving frowns.

‘Are you alright, love? You look as though you’ve seen a ghost.’ ‘I have. Can you excuse me for a moment?’

She steps out from behind the counter to stand awkwardly in front of me, clearly unsure as to whether she should give a hug or offer to shake my hand. To help her I take her hands in mine.

‘Hello, Sarah.’

‘Billy. Oh Billy.’

A flood of emotions, like a dam breaking, surges over me. I want to take her in my arms, protect her, look after her, make her happy but I stand still, holding her hands.

‘I’m sorry I didn’t reply to your letter. Summer’s a busy time. Just hadn’t a minute.’

‘I shouldn’t have written. I had no right to trouble you.’

‘I’m glad you did. I really am.’

‘You’re here now. That’s what matters. Listen, I must attend to this lady then I’ll shut up shop and we can go for coffee.’

She pulls away her hands and crosses to the counter. ‘I’ll wait outside.’

‘Won’t be long. Don’t run away.’

I open the door and step out into the street. The sun warms my face and glistens on the sea at the bottom of the road. I am glad that I came. Although time and her troubled life show in the creases on her face, she is still as lovely as she was when we met. What happened with Spam no longer matters. What has happened since no longer matters. I could love her anyway. I am warm with admiration for what she has achieved, taken control of her life, escaped from darkness. What strength ! 1What courage ! I will offer to take her away, rescue her from the dangers and pointless antagonisms of this province, away from the car bombs, the murders, the ceaseless tension and uncertainty.

A man hurries out of the pub next door. For a moment our eyes meet. I recognise him immediately and am about to wave when he scuttles away down a side street. It is Spam and I wonder why he ignored me. Perhaps he feels guilty. I hope he feels guilty.

At that moment, the entire front of the pub explodes towards me. There is a thunderous roar, and I am blown off my feet and into the roadway. Lances of pain slice into my face and hands. My ears burst open. I land with a thud that crushes my ribs. I bellow with agony but can't hear myself. A choking cloud of dust swirls over the street, obscuring the pub and the shop.

There is a blinding pain in my leg, and I look down to see a long shard of glass stuck in my thigh. There is blood seeping down my face. I lie stunned for a while, comforted by the realization that I'm alive, until I remember Sarah.

I try to walk but the shard of glass catches on my trousers. I roll down my sleeve, grip it tightly and haul it out. The pain makes me howl. I stumble towards the shop. The window has been blown out.

Hanks of wool, lengths of brightly coloured material, and a books of knitting patterns litter the roadway. An arm protrudes from a pile of masonry and I hurry towards it only to find that it is the plastic limb of a model. I look through window an discover that the inner wall next to the pub has collapsed and half of the first floor has fallen into the shop. I scramble in through the empty window. I call her name but I can't hear my own voice. Her customer lies crushed by fallen masonry and I climb over to find that she has been killed. I start flinging the rubble aside, hoping that Sarah is in a space beneath.

It is her hand that I find first, the hand which I had held minutes before the explosion. It is warm, but when I squeeze it, there is no response. I can't feel a pulse. I clear more rubble and find her face. Her lips are blue, and her eyes closed. I know she is dead, trapped beneath a massive block of masonry. I lean over and clear the dust from her face, using the tips of my fingers, brushing it gently as if she was still alive. Drops of blood from my head drip on to her shoulder. I'm too shocked to feel anything.

A paramedic places his hand on my shoulder and speaks urgently. I can't hear what he says but he points to the tottering beams above and to the doorway. He wants me to leave. I know it's not safe but I can't leave Sarah. I have to help them clear the masonry, see that they treat her gently, but two firemen arrive and lift me into the street.

Outside, there is pandemonium. Police vans, fire engines, and ambulances fill the roadway.

Hoses snake across the debris, rescue teams stagger through heaps of rubble, cameras flash behind the cars. A tumult of colours swirls in the dust - yellow helmets, blue lights, green uniforms, black body bags, red engines. A stream of beer flows in the gutters and the air is loaded with a smell of alcohol, smouldering timber, cordite and diesel. A soldier sits cradling an old man in one arm and holding his rifle in the other. The old man's face is white and blood oozes from his lips. One after another stretchers are carried form the pub and lifted into the ambulances.

I sit in the rubble and wait for Sarah. I should have been with her, my arms round her, protecting her from the blast. I should have borne the weight of the masonry. Now she is dead.

Suddenly, the reality of that explodes inside me. I will not see her again. Never again. A bottomless whirlpool of grief opens beneath me. My whole core plummets downward, clutching at my breath, tearing my heart, emptying my veins, leaving a vacuum of unbearable Despair. With a sob that shakes my entire body, I let go and howl.

As they carry her out on stretcher, already wrapped in black plastic, I scramble across the rubble. I reach them just as they lift her into the ambulance and see her face. I try to climb in beside her but they stop me. One of them speaks to me but I can't hear his words. I try again and he restrains me, forcing me back gently as they shut the door. I sink to my knees and weep. A workman whom I never seen before comes over and takes me in his arms. His torn jacket smells of pipe tobacco.

Spam had killed her. I had no doubt about that. I sat in my hotel window that evening, my head bandaged and my thigh aching. The room was on the second floor and had a view over the promenade to the sea. Some boats in a small harbour rocked gently in the swell, their ropes dipping and stretching. I remembered the pier in Donaghadee, the white lighthouse and the rails left by the abandoned railway. Kelly's coal boats used to tie up there, swinging their load into wagons on the pier bound for Belfast. I remembered the café where Spam and I used to steal cigarettes. I was not surprised to find that he could not resist the temptation to wade into the violence. Yet there was no excuse. What his big brother did to him was not a reason to kill innocent people. Scarred by the experience, he might be but he was old enough to make choices of his own, to be responsible for his actions. I had no sympathy for him. In fact, I despised him and resolved to see that he did not avoid justice on this occasion. He had, after all, never suffered consequences for chaining the boy at the dance. He might well avoid punishment again. He was not going to get away with it this time. I spent some time working out how I might obtain a revolver.

I returned to the pub the next morning. The entire wall had been blown out, and the second floor hung precariously above the bar. An army wagon fitted with a bulldozer blade was clearing rubble from the street. There was still a smell of alcohol and scorched timber. A man in a donkey jacket and cap was lighting a cigarette and gazing into the ruins. He looked around as I approached, noticing the bandage on my head.

'You here yesterday?' he asked.

'Yes. Terrible, isn't it?'

'Bastards.'

'Why? Why this pub?'

'Owner is a Catholic. Doesn't even live here. Nothing to do with the Provos. Barman's an Orangeman. Bet they didn't know that. Shame about the woman next door, too. Hope they get the bastards'

'Is that likely?'

'No. Police cover up for these guys. All in it together. Army, police, UVF, all the Prod paramilitaries.'

'Still, somebody should do something. Get the guys who did this.'

'You're joking.'

'If I'd a gun, I would.'

'No chance,'

'I would. Really.'

'You know who did it, don't you?' He swung round to face me. 'What makes you think that?'

'You saying you'd use a gun if you had one.'

'Well, I would.'

'You mean that ?'

'Yes.'

'You're not from here, are you?'

'I was. I live in Scotland now.'

'A Rangers man, eh?'

'No. I don't follow football, and I don't take sides in this bloody mess.'

'You said you'd use a gun. That's taking sides.'

'Only on the guy who did this. That's all.'

'Why this guy? Something personal?'

'The woman next door. She was a friend.'

'Nothing to do with the boys in the pub, then?'

'They didn't deserve it either. No one deserves it.'

'No, you're right. That's life here. Heading back to Scotland, eh?'
'Yes. Soon as I can. Want to see to your man first, though.'

'Okay. Be here at 6 pm tomorrow night. By yourself. Anyone with you, you're dead.' He walks away, pulling up the collar of his donkey jacket.

Chapter 36

This is it, his showroom.

I stand in the street, watching the rain slide down the window. My fingers are curled around the butt of the revolver in my raincoat pocket. I should feel nervous but I'm having to concentrate on planning different scenarios – if there was someone with him or if someone came in. I don't want to be caught. That would be stupid. There is no one in the street. That's good. I move closer to the glass and look through the rain, trying to see if he's among the cars. There's no one there, but there is a light in the office at the back.

I push open the door and walk in. The place smells of tyres and car polish. I can see my reflection on the wing of a Vauxhall, elongated, distorted. I expected him to emerge from the office. Perhaps he's not in. Yet the door was open. I walk towards the office. He's sitting at the desk, soldering wires. The flashes of the iron show in his eyes. I open the door with one hand, my other index finger tightening on the trigger.

'Billy Boy! What about you?'

His smile is genuine but his eyes show the truth. He is suspicious, thrown by my sudden appearance. I can see the calculations flitting through his brain. He has aged, and his head is shaved in an attempt to hide the baldness. His mouth droops at the corners, giving it a contemptuous expression.

I glance down at the soldering. Coloured wires and an alarm clock. 'Another one?' I ask.

'What do you mean?'

'Another bomb?'

A frown creases his forehead. The friendliness has melted off his face, revealing the cruel creature he has become.

'Car electrics, Billy boy. I don't do bombs.'

'You did the one in the pub in Bangor. I saw you sneak away.' 'Haven't been in Bangor for years. Better things to do.'

I take out the gun. He tries to be casual, as if a revolver pointing at him was not a threat.

'You killed Sarah. You didn't know that, did you? She had the shop next door.'

Now, he is truly alarmed.

I know it would be over in a split second that I would squeeze the trigger, and a hole would appear above the frown, and he would be dead. Instantly. I would have killed him. No more bombs from his hands. I see the fear in his eyes and his lips have opened. I hear the breath hissing through his teeth. I have never seen him afraid before. He was fearless when we were young, laughing at danger and despising fear in others. Ebullient, mischievous, daring – all the qualities I lacked. He was irresistible. My partner in crime.

He sees my hesitation.

'I was never in Bangor, Billy. I swear.'

I can see he's lying, and that hauls me back from the past.

I see Sarah's blue lips and the dust in her hair. I want revenge, and my finger squeezes the trigger. But I see her on the shore, her hair

392

tossed in the wind, her blue eyes glistening. Gentle and carefree. She would not want this. And I can't do it. I can't kill him.

I aim at his hand, pull the trigger and watch the blood explode from the shattered knuckles. He screams and bends over the wound. I turn and leave.

I will find a police station and report his presence at the pub in Bangor.

The wake streams out from the stern of the ship, churning white in the dusk. The lights of Belfast shrink into the darkness as we leave the estuary. I lean on the rail and watch the cranes of the shipyard merge with the silhouette of Cave Hill, the yard where Sarah worked, where I strutted as a youth. In leaving her, I am leaving my past buried beside her in that lifeless earth. I will not return. Like the countless emigrants sailing for the last time for lands beyond the horizon, I feel that fearful longing to remain, that suffocating grip of grief that tears the heart from the ribs. Yet to remain would mean withering, a slow stultifying degeneration. Besides, there is nothing there for me now. Sarah has gone. I returned as she requested, and I will never know where our meeting could have led or what paths we could have travelled together. If only she had asked me sooner.

Gulls glide over the wake, white wraiths in the night. I turn away towards the bow and the seas of the future.